Dancing
in the
Shadows
of the Dead

JANA MATHESON

CALLIOPE RISING PRESS

NEW YORK

DANCING IN THE SHADOWS OF THE DEAD
© 2004 Jana Matheson

Although the author has made every effort to ensure the accuracy and completeness of information contained in this book, no responsibility is assumed for errors, inaccuracies, omissions, or any inconsistency herein. Any slights of people, places, or organizations are unintentional.

Published by

Calliope Rising Press
244 Madison Avenue, No. 749
New York, N.Y.   10016
CalliopeRising@aol.com

Set in Granjon
Printed in Canada

Design: Cosi Fontutti

ISBN: 0-9743362-0-3

Library of Congress Control Number: 2003111149

*There is something beyond the grave;
death does not end all, and the pale ghost
escapes from the vanquished pyre.*

SEXTUS PROPERTIUS, 54 BC ~ AD 2

Chapter One

Newport Beach, 1993

S ome things will remain a mystery forever.

I still don't know why I chose that particular October afternoon many years ago to leave my husband Vincent.

I had finished a glass of wine and told the maple tree overshadowing my deck that if it dropped a leaf within one minute, I would divorce him the very next day. The maple had witnessed the travesty of the marriage and therefore surrendered a leaf. I was grateful.

The moment the leaf broke from the tree a great force was unleashed. That was when Andreas and I began our journey back to one another, to the year 1906 and the California coastal town of Pacific Grove.

I now know that events are never our choice alone. The Universe, both master and slave, arranges our lives so that our interests are served.

The first step toward my reunion with Andreas came at midnight of that day when I heard the clock in the hallway strike thirteen . . . .

Midnight. I drowsily awaited the striking chimes. It was a lifelong habit to count the twelve tones as if they were vital to my existence. Maybe I was grateful to have lived through to another day, appreciative of the eternal signal to begin again.

But that night, as the numbers rolled sleepily off my tongue, I heard myself whisper "thirteen." I bolted upright in bed, terrified of the error. I knew that I *had* heard precisely thirteen strikes.

Although the decision that afternoon to divorce Vincent had put me on edge, I did not suspect that it was causing me to imagine things. My Aunt Belle and I had discussed the divorce before bed. She was jubilant about my decision and her mascara-doused eyes had flickered approvingly as she congratulated me on the choice of a maple leaf. It was certainly more original than her friend Odette's tea leaves. Aunt Belle was weary of living with Vincent, whom she often enjoyed degrading with a wide variety of off-color epithets. "You are too pretty and too smart to live with him. Besides, you are thirty-seven years old," Aunt Belle had said, rolling a soggy Camel cigarette between her tongue and orange lips to annoy me as I refused to let her smoke in the house.

I sank back into the pillows. The first storm of the season that had begun that afternoon was also making me nervous. When I had gone outside to bring in Belle's cat Chester, the birds of paradise along the front drive reeled violently in circles. Crows cawed and wheeled amidst flying autumn leaves. And now, at midnight, the trees were clawing at the house like desperate strangers in need of shelter.

I got out of bed and pulled open the sheer draperies. The moonlight and wind transformed my ivory bedroom into a swaying rendition of *film noir*. No fear there, however. I was on good terms with the shadows that danced over walls and bed, and with similar things that coexist with me but cannot be touched.

The October moon was full and bright. October makes the best moons—that's what I had always told my deceased son Shea, who had seen three Octobers and agreed. "How does she get them so bright?" he once asked from his hospital bed. I told him October had a special way of polishing her moon. That she shined it in a secret hiding place so that November could not see her and copy it. Both Shea and I laughed because we knew I had lied. But don't think about Shea, I told myself. Think about leaving Vincent.

I returned to bed and wondered what mechanism could have caused the clock to slip from its seven-year routine just as I was about to slip from mine. I could not sleep and felt anxious. My friend Neil would say I was suppressing too much. But then he was a psychiatrist who was in love with me. And now that I was leaving Vincent he would expect me to marry him. Everyone, myself included, assumed that I would marry Neil if I ever got the courage to leave Vincent. "And why not?" my best friend Marla often prodded. "Neil is kind, handsome, he loves you madly-deeply and more importantly, he's rich. In fact, if he hadn't wrecked his back in that awful car accident, he'd be perfect! And Vincent," she hissed, "if you took Vincent's drunk head—which is the only way I've seen it—and hung it down the colonnade with his grotesque taxidermy collection, between the wild boar and the jackal, no one would know that it belonged to a man."

Vincent could be violent and irrational when provoked, the kind of person who overreacts to his own pain and cares nothing for another's. I didn't want to admit that I was afraid of what he would do when he received the divorce papers.

I decided that I would tell him of my decision that night at Marla's Halloween party. There would be lots of people there, including Neil. That settled, I turned on my side to face the window-framed moon.

I had pinned the fateful maple leaf in my hair before going to bed and it crackled against the sheets. At that moment I heard Vincent fumbling with keys at the front door. His Mark Cross briefcase assaulted the jamb, adding new scars. Keys jangled in the lock as the door slammed. The briefcase dropped, probably vomiting tax papers or ledgers over the marble floor. Somewhere in the windy night his poor dog Sumo howled for him.

He would walk to his bedroom drunk, as if made of wire springs, his spine curling, his knees bowing intermittently, his head protruding in front of his body as if sprung. He would stumble lamely along the colonnade beneath the steady eyes of the hunted.

With some effort I fell asleep, only to toss fitfully in a maze of perilous nightmares: Vincent hanging from a noose strung up in the maple tree, turning from man to jackal as he drew his last breath . . . Shea laughing at an October moon that had fringed mascaraed eyes and blinked knowingly, not unlike Aunt Belle . . . Neil's face looming over the sea cliffs above his stormy fortress, forcing me into a locked second story bedroom.

I was conscious though, in real time, of attempting to free myself. The struggle was exhausting and seemed endless. And then in one unexpected, jolting instant, the confusion disappeared and I awoke to a peace that was as deep and intense as the chaos that preceded it.

A fleck of gold no larger than a candle flame appeared at the foot of my bed. It rapidly expanded and its brilliant reflections swayed in the polished bedposts, silver frames, mirrors and glass of the bedroom. I began to tremble in anticipation—of what, I was not certain. The warmth of the room washed over me as the resplendent energy began to coalesce, to form itself at first into a fountain of light and then in mere seconds into the full size figure of a man. He was absolutely real and stood before me as any person in the flesh might. In that moment I realized that whoever or whatever he was, I knew him as well as I knew myself. This compelling sense of familiarity was frightening and yet I found myself moving down the bed toward him as if so much depended on our communicating. He looked at me as if he expected an answer to something vitally important. I felt responsible for the tender pain in his eyes, eyes so dramatically blue they looked painted on his face. He had blonde hair that blew in a gentle wind. So familiar . . . I could see the curve of his brow, the angle of his chin, his wide shoulders. He wore a white shirt and tan slacks, and stood before a large stone arch with green gates. I could feel his identity and my undeniable connection to him drifting into my thoughts, but before I could grasp his name I said in my voice, but with words I had not chosen, "You will hurt me again."

Our connection was severed. Like liquid, his form wavered and thinned, his body became transparent. I could see through him. At that moment the windows beyond him were admitting the sun's first rays. And in that curious mixture of night and day, the unearthly light began to pull him away. His hand reached to me as if from the grave. I knew that hand. Somewhere, sometime, I had been touched by it. I leapt to the end of the bed and knelt. I called, "It wasn't your fault. We were so young then." I didn't understand the meaning of my words though I knew without doubt that they sprang from my heart.

The light contracted rapidly. He was leaving me. My hand reached out to his. The inch that separated our fingers grew to a chasm. His mouth moved. I knew those lips. I had been kissed by them. He asked, "Angelica, where are you? Angelica, we must meet again."

"Don't leave," I shouted. "Come back!"

He disappeared into the green gates, simply vanished.

My name is not Angelica. It is Paige.

He was *real*. I couldn't doubt the energy that one life senses in another. I pulled the creamy white comforter to my chin and waited. And I thought if I remained very still he might return. At the very least, inertia and yearning fed the spell.

Angelica? I had never known an Angelica. My genealogy was earthy: Amandas, Marthas, Ethels and Melindas, names that call to mind butter churns and ox plows. Then who is Angelica? I was absolutely certain that *I* was Angelica. He had been speaking to me as I had spoken to him. Did he hear my words as well? "You will hurt me again . . . . We were so young . . . ." Pleas that ordinarily would have seemed silly were important, were essential to our relationship, whatever that was. I would have to somehow think him back into existence. *Send a message, Paige*.

The urgency to contact him swept away the tranquility of his visit. A tear trickled down my cheek as I thought of his sudden departure. I absurdly tried to sweep it back into my eye: a manifestation of denial that I first used when I was six and cracked Mother's only doll on the sidewalk. I had wanted to hold it for so long. She had handed it over to me as gently as a baby. And then, such frail pieces of pink porcelain—a nose here, a cheek there—lay before me, an impossible, horrifying puzzle. Mother had bent over and piled the fragments into her apron with a set expression that suggested a lifetime of broken pieces. I had tried to put the tears back into my eyes then too, as if effects could alter causes. I had tried to think the doll back to life just as I had tried to think my son Shea back into life, just as I was now trying to recreate the shattered ghost of the morning . . . .

My bedroom seemed unaltered by his visit. Suddenly I found

its serene order as annoying as I would have at other times been agitated by its chaos. I wanted it to be ravaged: the fresh roses, polished floors, signed prints, little oils, ornate silver-framed photographs of my past. *Explode and disappear*, I thought.

At seven-thirty my private phone rang. I fumbled for the receiver on the bedside table. It was Neil, who loved me. He was phoning from Candlesage, his estate on the bluffs above the sea.

"Paige? Are you all right?" His voice was concerned. Neil was often worried about me.

"Why do you ask?"

"Well," he murmured, his voice resuming its perfect baritone. "I saw Vincent out last night, drinking heavily of course. And then I had a bad dream. I reached for the telephone as soon as my eyes opened." He paused. "You're okay then? I've disturbed you."

"No—really. I'm still asleep, I guess," I said, trying to sound normal.

"The details of the dream are sketchy, but the feeling of doom was overwhelming. Not something a psychiatrist should reveal, I suppose," he said lightly. I could see him in his bed: tousled hair, sleepy eyes, poignantly empty space beside him. "Seeing Vincent out like that wasn't easy. It tears me apart, knowing you're married to him. You deserve so much more. But how many times have I told you that? I'm guessing that's why I had the dream. Seeing Vincent and feeling so damned morose about your marriage."

"I'm sure it is," I reassured him. But was that why he had the dream? Or had he sensed a shift in events? I had always imagined how it would be when I left Vincent. I would surprise Neil and Marla with the news. The occasion would warrant an excellent wine. Neil would provide my favorite Chardonnay—Talbott Sleepy Hollow. There would be rainbow streamers, Marla would be sure of that, and Beluga caviar on toast points while we sailed Newport Harbor in Neil's restored double-masted schooner, *Abregado*.

"Neil, I didn't sleep very well last night either. I'm glad you've called. Tell your mother that I may be a little late for her tea. I've promised Marla to meet her for brunch to discuss the Halloween party. You might say she's 'haunted' with visions of failure."

"Where are you two going to breakfast?"

"We haven't decided." I then recalled quite unexpectedly, as her face appeared mysteriously before me, that Lucetta Corneille, the proprietor of the Daisy Cotton Restaurant, was a reputed psychic. Marla had asked her about reading at her party but Lucetta said clairvoyance was not a game and that ethics prevented her from using her talent to entertain a "gathering of inebriated socialites who did not need a psychic to tell them that they already had tall, dark, handsome strangers in their lives."

"When you decide—"

"The Daisy Cotton, best omelets in Newport. I'm supposed to phone Marla this morning."

"About Marla's party tonight. Mother has set me up with a blind date, another freshly divorced niece of a friend. Sometimes I wonder if anyone she knows is still married. But I wanted you to know that this is no love match. I've never even met the woman. Becky something—Becky Chambers, I think."

"I'll look forward to meeting her," I said quickly. Normally comforting, Neil's reassurance now felt suffocating.

"Don't," he whispered.

"Well, I *will* look forward to meeting her. It is *not* fair for you to wait around for me. I'm too fond of you for that. You should be dating more. There are a million women who would commit mayhem to go out with you."

He said playfully, "Well, maybe I want mayhem with *you*.

Besides, Paige, I believe in happy endings. And that's what you and I are going to have." He was being flirtatious, but somewhere in the lilting words there was an uncompromising command. With the notable exception of the tragic Simone *event*, one could say Neil always got what he wanted.

I laughed too loudly. "I've got a busy day. Can we talk later?"

"We surely can," he replied.

"We always do," I reminded him, sounding flirtatious myself to appease him.

I hung up the receiver knowing that he would cradle the phone for some time.

The bedroom windows trembled from a thunderclap. The rain rattled as it fell and obstructed the view beyond my window.

Neil's voice had been wistful. He had caught me with my mouth down-turned and my eyes no longer on his but rather on the horizon. He had intuited something in the tone of my voice. He was trained to read between the lines, and did so assiduously. He was an expert. He would thrash about, as worried lovers will, to distract me from the nameless temptation that had overtaken me.

I nestled deeper into the bed pillows, watching the silvery raindrops slide down the windows. I was convinced that I had experienced another dimension in time but wondered if the supernatural necessarily takes precedence over the commonplace. It was not as if some creator had intervened in my life. Yet I had touched paradise, that much I knew. I had given myself away. I didn't even know the name of this ghostly man who suddenly owned me, what he was, where he came from. But I did know *him*. I would rediscover who we were. I would find the green gates. If he would not return to me, then I would leave my life to find him.

Impulsively, I threw the covers off and brought my knees to

my chest, hugging them. I felt myself slipping further into the unreality of what was yet to come. At moments I was unsure of which was the real truth—the amorphous man who seemed to have hypnotized me—or the amazing space that Neil had reserved, like real estate, for the rest of my life.

This sudden obsession was frightening.

Until this morning, there hadn't been any choices besides Vincent and Neil. Now I was beginning to wonder why I hadn't considered more options. Go to design school. Write about literature in Bath, England. Become a nature photographer. Conceive a child with a man I would not marry. Replant the rain forests. Join a Buddhist abbey. Build houses around the world with Habitat for Humanity. These options could be among the millions I would be abdicating. These and a rich life with Neil Carmichael.

As quickly as I had dreamed up these alternative lives I could hear them leaving my world as if in winged departure, off to seek and enrich those who had left doors open, fields not yet sown.

How could this man's presence at dawn, his demand that "we must meet again" be both liberating and inhibiting? It was as if the force he brought with him gave me the imagination to plan anything, but the power to do only one thing: go to him.

And it made me afraid. For if one believed that the event of the morning were real, then one had to believe in darker worlds as well, the worlds of the incubus and other nefarious creatures. Not likely, I thought, trembling. He was more like an angel, I hoped, suddenly protective of a soul I was never sure existed until now.

I stepped out of bed and reached for my white robe, which had slipped to the floor at the foot of the bed. As I touched it I noticed a smudge on the fabric: a shoe print. My heart raced. A sprig of dark green fell from it. I did not recognize the slender needles. I brought it to my face and sliced the sprig with my fingernail. The scent was sweet and familiar, yet faraway. I slipped it into the dark cavern of the robe pocket and examined the very real print. It was large and had the ragged lines of boot treads. With quivering hands I placed the imprinted robe against my cheek.

Then I heard Vincent's footsteps in the hall. He walked deliberately, his steps thudding and pausing like a stalker's. I would need to hold myself together.

I crumpled up the robe like a guilty woman and stuck it behind my back, elbows shooting out at my sides like wings. Vincent opened the door.

He stood before me with briefcase in hand like a door-to-door religion salesman, tentative yet brash, knowing he was not wanted but feeling he had some divine right to be there. I looked at him, intending to hate him, but my pity was stronger than my contempt. The light was gone from his dark eyes. Flesh camouflaged the prominent bones in his face. He was once a handsome man. Now red, broken veins singed his nose and cheeks. His mouth was twisted into a permanent scowl, reminiscent of his cold, unfeeling mother, who helped to put it there.

There was a long pause, during which we each silently strategized. It was our way. I wondered if he could see my heart beating through my gown.

"How are you?" he asked.

"Still half asleep," I lied. Of course I lied. Lies were the basis of our marriage. It was the way Vincent wanted it.

He asked, "What did *you* do last night?"

Did he really care? I wondered. Perhaps. In the manner that he cared about his Corvette, his pit bull Sumo or his female office personnel, specifically Patty, because he needed them to go on serving him.

"Not much. Belle and I had our usual chat, then went to bed early."

"Then what the hell's that?" he asked.

"What?"

"That thing in your hair."

I dropped the robe. As my hand went to my hair I touched the crisp maple leaf. "Oh, this. It was just . . . so pretty." I pulled it from my hair and felt it crackle in my closed hand. Now I could never press it into a book as I had intended. Even now, I silently chastised myself, even now after having made the decision to leave him, even now after a breath-taking visit from the spirit world, even now I still gave him the power to humiliate me. I had done the same thing with my very being that I had done with the maple leaf. Crumple it up and hide it. But no more, I thought. Today would be the end of life as both Vincent and I knew it.

"Why were you holding your robe like that?"

"Taking it to the dirty clothes hamper. What are you doing with your briefcase?"

He grinned, glad for the opportunity to insult me yet again. "Going to *work* and earning a *living*. You see, Paige, I'm not like you. I don't sit around all day."

"Yes, Vincent," I returned. "I have such a good life."

"What time is Marla's party? It *is* tonight, isn't it?"

"Yes. Eight o'clock."

"I can't make it before nine-thirty. Get my cleaning," he ordered. "By the way, was your aunt's cat out last night? Sumo was howling all night. I thought I told you to tell her to keep that cat away from him. Someday he's going to tear out its throat." He smiled and left the room feeling that he had succeeded in reinforcing what he considered my constant ineptitude.

I picked up the robe from the floor, half expecting the footprint to have vaporized with Vincent's entrance into my room. That it remained intact gave me great hope.

I opened the armoire drawer and dropped the robe into a rose-scented hatbox after withdrawing the intriguing sprig of greenery.

As usual Aunt Belle barged through the door, a tornado of dull knitting needles, Tabu cologne and barnyard clucking. "Honey, I heard what he said. He's such a piece of—I won't say it." She had two steaming cups in her hand and her knitting bag tucked under her arm. "It's so cold in here this morning I thought you might like coffee in your room." She sank into an oversized occasional chair. "What he said about Chester! Can you believe it! I wished I owned a panther. We could have Sumo burgers. But what are we going to do about all this rain? By the way, should I be packing, or trying to find boxes?" Chester, the enormous silvery Persian cat, now stole into the room and moved stealthily toward the French doors where the ghost of the morning had materialized.

"Yes," I answered. The coffee was bitter. I put it down and began rummaging through a jewelry box.

"What are you looking for?"

"My silver amulet. There." I broke the twig in two, pressing one piece of the greenery into the amulet and the other into my handbag.

"What are you doing?" she asked.

I sat on the bed facing her and asked slowly, "Do you believe in ghosts?"

Indignantly she answered, "What a question, Paige. You know that I do. Why? Did you see one? Oh, this is wonderful. On Halloween and everything."

We both looked out my window as a cloud burst overhead. A stoic crow perched on a branch of the liquidambar tree, defying the downpour.

"I've often felt Shea's presence around me and thought I heard him telling me he was all right, but I've never been certain. I think that the mind is magical and that it gives us the ability to create in fantasy what we cannot have in reality. In other words, Belle, I think that deep sorrow can manifest itself in glorious hallucinations, dreams, and sensations that transport us beyond our everyday lives."

"Well, I should hope so, dearie."

"But there's more."

"What do you mean?"

"Well, you've thought about this sort of thing more than I. But supposing you had a dream in which a man appeared, and you'd never met him before but he was very well known to you."

She nodded and tightened her lips, pretending to follow my thoughts. She reached into her cloth bag and dragged out an as yet unidentifiable knitted scrap. When she was nervous she knitted. She had never produced anything recognizable. "Well, don't stop now," she prodded. "I have a feeling we're getting to the juicy part."

"Do ghosts deliver messages to people?"

She cackled, primping her banana-yellow hair, "Why not? There are a lot of dead postmen."

"I'm serious."

"So am I!" she barked. "Anything is possible. Cyril's always nosing around in my bedroom at night. But then, we were married for forty-five years so I suppose the old codger has a right to."

"But, Belle, don't you ever think you're just imagining that? That you want Cyril back so much that you just sort of create the illusion that he's with you?"

"Of course not. But we're not talking about Cyril, are we, dearie?" She paused and looked at me knowingly. "We're talking about you, Paige. Are you going to tell me what happened or not?"

"It was last night. I heard the clock strike thirteen . . . ."

"And on Halloween to boot," she added encouragingly, trying to lure information. She retrieved Chester from the floor, stroking him affectionately.

Should I tell her? Of all the people I knew she was the one most likely to believe me. But it was discomforting to think of Aunt Belle as my only ally. Her parapsychological dealings were limited to old gypsy fortunetellers dressed in dime store satin. I decided to lie to her, as even I was not sure of the truth.

"I had a dream—or something—this morning, just before dawn. I thought a man appeared in my bedroom."

She licked her orange lips. It was her kind of conversation, the tantalizing sort that hovered on the edge of reality—precisely where her own persona resided. "Don't be so sure, dearie. A ghost, a man came to Judith in Santa Fe last year. A dead sea captain appeared in her bedroom. I don't have to tell you what he wanted—*do I*?" She smiled and raised her pencil-drawn eyebrows.

"If he appeared to Judith I know exactly what he wanted," I said, feeling that my experience with the stranger that morning was being reduced to a tawdry sideshow.

"You're such a prude," she scoffed.

"Then let me put it this way, Belle. Things like that may happen to others but not to me."

"Oh baloney. A lot of things could happen to you if you'd let them. I'll be glad when you're settled down with Neil. What a catch. Maybe then you'll get on with your life. It's been rough—

about Shea and all. So sad. But living here with that sloth of a husband."

"What makes you think I'll be 'settled in with Neil'? I never said I was going to marry Neil. I've made *no* promises."

Her fingers formed a little tent on her chest to show vexation. "Why, everyone knows you've been planning to leave Vincent for Neil."

"My intention is to leave Vincent this very day, not for anyone but myself. While I'm out today I will look for a house for us to rent on Balboa Island, or on Newport Peninsula. And then I will decide when and who, if anyone, I will marry."

She stared at me absolutely stunned. "I can't believe it." Her fringed eyes narrowed on the sleet outside. "After all Neil's done for you!"

"I didn't ask him to do anything for me! I don't want to discuss this subject again. Just pack important things and be prepared to move out today. I mean it, Belle. I won't have anyone making me feel guilty about Dr. Neil Carmichael."

She shook her head sorrowfully. "You read too many books, that's your problem. Those bookstores you used to manage before you married that ass—I mean Vincent." She begrudgingly restrained herself. "Reading, reading but what about good old doing? That's what I want to know. When you asked me to come and live with you after my Cyril died, I thought to myself, maybe I can help Paige with little Shea and out of that bad marriage with that low-down—with Vincent. Now you're finally doing it. At least you say you are."

"Please, let's just concentrate on moving, shall we?" I met her glare defiantly and regretted my confession.

"I wish your mother was alive. Sixteen is too young to lose a mother, especially you, Paige. And not having a father. You live in a dream world—the books, the fantasies. I often think that if

Cyril and I had had the money to send you to that nature college, you remember that one where they teach about trees and things, the environmental whatchamacallit institute, then this never would've happened. You'd never have met that sh—Vincent. You'd have settled down with a different sort. But then when Marla introduced you to Neil and I saw how taken he was with you—anyone could see it—I was as high as a kite. This is the man Paige's going to marry if she ever divorces that bast—Vincent, I kept telling myself. Divorce? Of course I'm happy about that! Not marry Neil? It's taken him forever to get over the Simone thing and now this! That makes me sad, darned sad and upset, and I don't care what feminists say. Some women always need men. You're one of them. Anyway, I'm sure you'll change your mind." She threw down the indescribable snarl of yarn, sublimely unaware of yet another knit failure, and sucked at her coffee.

I crossed the room to the white marble mantel where I had placed the crumbling maple leaf. I felt for the amulet around my neck. The rain had softened and over its slight tapping I could hear Chester purr. He sat smugly in Aunt Belle's lap as if allied to her cause. Both his eyes and hers watched me suspiciously as I paced the room trying to sort everything out. What actually *had* happened to me? *He was not a hallucination.* I saw him again before me, saw myself reaching toward him with such longing. Then suddenly, I knew the truth . . . I looked back at Aunt Belle and Chester and declared solemnly, "He used to be mine."

Chapter Two

*T*here was a time when I was happy.

It was a thought that came to me as I moved in a mental fog between the dry cleaners and the tailor shop to pick up my Halloween costume for Marla's party. A happy face had been drawn on a dusty car window. Upon seeing it I abruptly stopped at curbside and stared at the large beaming face. It conjured up the happy times from my past whose essence I could barely remember. I even traced the smile with my finger as if touching the glass could arouse the sensation of my former *joie de vivre*.

The memories of happiness did come with my finger stroke on the car window. Subconsciously summoned by me, I thought, in order to say goodbye as one would bid farewell to good friends before a long journey. Was I actually planning to leave my life for the world of the green gates and the man who needed me as much as I needed him?

I had been happy both as a child, before my mother died of cancer, and then more recently, several years ago when Shea was in remission, and Vincent was busy in New York. That was when my good friend Marla, who was always happy, enlisted me to co-chair the opening of the museum's new Carmichael wing. Carmichael, after Neil and his mother Maureen, known to everyone as Mo.

It was during an Indian summer that the three of us met in the museum offices to discuss the opening of the luxurious new wing that would house American Women in Art.

Marla had known Neil for some time. He was one of those local people who was perpetually the talk of the town, even before Simone Marchand died. The most eligible bachelor, the most generous patron of the arts, the most sought after tennis partner, the most . . . everything. One had to wait weeks or months for an appointment to see him professionally, no matter the psychological crisis. "Imagine all the suicides," Marla said to me on the way to his office to meet him, "while waiting for an appointment with Neil. It just proves that popularity can be a life and death thing." She winced. "Oops. I should never use the word suicide and Neil Carmichael in the same sentence lest we should raise the specter of Simone Marchand. You do remember Simone Marchand."

"How could I not? It was in the headlines every day for weeks. About two years ago, right?"

"Yes, two years ago unless you're the guy who blames himself for her death. Then it's always yesterday." She shrugged and added, "Every time I see Neil I try to figure out if he's really over it or just putting up a good front. He still has back pain from the accident. You can see the scar on his right temple and he limps a bit since he stopped using that—I must say 'stunning'—cane that belonged to his grandfather. Anyway, most of it's about Neil's mental scars. Interesting trick of nature that psychiatrists can never cure themselves."

"Or poetic justice, as the case may be," I interjected.

"Get out of my way, you tramp!" Marla yelled at an orange Mustang who had cut ahead of her on the highway. "Sorry. God that woman needs a stylist. Where was I?"

"Well, is he or isn't he over it?" I asked. "Simone Marchand committed suicide. I don't think he can blame himself for that."

"Oh, it's all one big muddled mess. There are the headlines, then there's the inside story, as always. So Simone Marchand, the one-time magazine cover girl, comes to Dr. Neil Carmichael because she's 'hearing voices from the other side.' Never mind that she doesn't tell him she's been in and out of shrink offices for five years and has stopped her medication. She was a good actress and knew by then exactly what to say and how to say it. She worked him. What else would you expect from cardboard eye candy—oh, excuse me, puhleez—a *cover girl*." Marla turned to me with an arch look as we flew through an amber traffic light. "Anyway, to abbreviate a long sordid story, Neil wants to know what these voices are saying, who they are and so forth. He thinks Simone should explore the messages, a gentle approach. He typically only medicates as a last resort. At least that was his policy back then. So she starts listening to these voices on the other side and hearing more and more. And then one night—can you even believe it was a dark and stormy one—she telephones Neil's exchange and tells the operator that the voices have ordered her to kill herself at one in the morning. And she's called to say goodbye to Neil, whom everyone thinks she's fallen in love with. She probably did it for attention."

Marla blasted her horn at a jaywalker and sped up to intimidate him. "As you know, Paige, I have no sympathy for suicidal people. I say, if you want to leave the planet, here, let me help you."

"I didn't know about the falling in love part," I commented, tightening my seat belt." Was he in love with her?"

"Surely you joke. He likes smart women who play hard to get, you know, the unattainable types. He's had only symbolic dates, I would call them, since he's recovered and been out of therapy—physical and mental. As a matter of fact, I've never thought of it before but he would just love you. Too bad about Vincent—oh, don't get me started on that."

I said, "I remember that his exchange staff hadn't been able to reach him until just before one. That's what the newspaper said."

"Right. So he finally gets the message and tears out of Candlesage during a major storm and drives fast—the police clocked him at close to ninety, which actually worked in his favor—to get to Simone in Newport before one. He might have made it if a delivery truck hadn't made that illegal left turn onto PCH in front of him. It was a gruesome scene. They had to use the 'jaws of life' to get Neil out of the car. He was unconscious for days. His head was split open, he had a concussion, a broken back and a mangled leg.

"And at precisely one o'clock, Simone Marchand did as her voices ordered. She abandoned Neil Carmichael and life as we know it with a bottle of sleeping pills. If I believed in hell, I'd hope she's there."

"Well, in my opinion," I said, trying not to sound too philosophical because philosophy annoyed Marla, "she created her own hell."

"Oh, that is good news," Marla smirked, swinging the car into the museum parking lot. "I hope so. Can you believe her parents had the nerve to sue Neil for malpractice? That trial took a hell of a lot out of Neil—he was even on meds himself for awhile—but at least he won. You should have seen him at the trial, in a wheelchair, all broken and banged up and genuinely anguished for having let Simone down. The one time when he actually cried, everyone else in the courtroom did too, even that hawk-nosed old judge who didn't have the decency to brush the dandruff off his robe. What's the world coming to when even judges don't use clothes brushes? I actually admire Neil for not settling the suit with the Marchand family out of court in order to avoid the publicity. A lot of doctors would have, you know, to hush it up."

As we parked the car in a reserved space I said, "He'll never get over it, not totally, because it's impossible. It'll just become a part of his baggage. God knows we all have it."

"Ain't that the truth," she said taking a deep breath, springing out of the car and slamming the door shut.

Neil's and my first meeting in the museum office on that balmy Saturday morning four years ago in Newport Beach transformed into something far more consequential. As it turned out, what Marla said about my being his "type" was true.

The morning was like many days or even lives that start in an ordinary manner, quiet and trivial without a conscious thought of becoming glorious. But Neil fell in love with me that day and I had the perfect time, laughed as I had not laughed in years. The magic of this shared emotional adventure created from our montage of glances, gestures and words burned brightly for years.

After a productive morning, the three of us decided to make a day of it. There was the frozen banana walk around Balboa Island in the flowered straw hats decorated with springing bumblebees and lady bugs, the stalled ferry ride to the Newport Beach peninsula, the spin on the small Ferris wheel, arms waving against the sky like tree limbs in the wind, a spontaneous flight to Catalina Island.

On the spur of the moment Neil had chartered one of the

old seaplanes. He negotiated sincerely with humor and grace, something I would see often in the future. There were no defenses against his charm. I saw no traces of the Simone Marchand tragedy, except that Neil did indeed have a slight limp, and a pale scar ran from eyebrow to hairline across his temple.

We had arrived in Avalon at dusk and after a seafood dinner decided to stay the night. At home, Aunt Belle and Shea had spent a full day at the beach with his friends and she was 'tickled to death' that I was finally doing something fun. She gave me permission.

After checking into the hotel, we spent the warm evening in a crowded harbor front bar dancing (carefully, because of Neil's back injury) to songs like "Proud Mary" and "Bad Moon Risin'." We drank tequila with beer chasers and sucked on limes. Much to my shock, as I had never been much of a drinker, I was able to outdrink them both.

Neil had made a call to Newport to have the *Abregado* brought over so that we could spend the next afternoon lazing on the deck in the harbor and take her back across the channel on Monday. Marla phoned her husband Eugene and he flew over in time for fresh cracked crab and salad on the deck of the yacht that night. A local guitarist serenaded us until three in the morning, mostly Mexican love songs. Neil looked hilarious in a borrowed sombrero. I drew him a mustache with my eyebrow pencil and he sang "La Paloma" in a never to be forgotten mixture of Spanish and French.

Then I had the idea of jumping overboard for a predawn swim. Eugene was next into the water, then Neil, and lastly Marla, who took the plunge with her olive in one hand, martini glass in the other, and Ferragamos still clinging to her feet. I then realized that Neil had jumped in to "save" me—just in case. He treaded water and asked several times, "Are you okay?" Even then he thought I needed rescuing.

The captain and crew paced the decks, fretting like chaperones and tossing life preservers. We all survived.

Life had almost never been better. And I realized that I was always happiest when I was taking chances. Danger made me feel alive.

Neil's romantic fascination with me appeared early in the weekend and did not go unnoticed by Marla, who felt proprietary for having brought us together. I was more self-conscious about the obvious—his arm around me, his hand taking mine, dancing too closely and for too long, a kiss on the forehead. Like kids on a platonic first date testing each other. It had not been easy for me to stand my ground but convention prevailed. Neil was free, a state I could only fantasize about. There was Vincent, after all, and most importantly there was Shea who was always so sick.

During the following months we three worked tirelessly on the museum opening. The situation between Neil and me developed into a synchronistic working relationship. He was impressed with my knowledge of design and my ability, he said, to get things done.

With the exception of a few innocuous slips, I managed to keep the relationship on the chaste side of romance, as outmoded and unnecessary as I often thought my position was. Our mutual sense of humor helped.

On a rainy winter night, as all the names on the social register gathered, and were looking their best and brightest, the new Carmichael wing was opened with great panache and exceptional reviews. Even I was lauded for my design contributions.

The next morning Shea was back in the hospital.

By then, of course, Neil had realized I was not in love with Vincent and that I was staying in the marriage because Shea was too fragile to go through relocating. Neil agreed with me. He was wonderful with Shea. He became a better father to Shea than Vincent had ever been.

Neil and I saw each other often in the next two years, never consummating the relationship and masquerading as merely good friends though there was always the sense that at any moment we could tumble gleefully over the precipice of conjugal love.

And then Shea died.

It was natural for Dr. Neil Carmichael, a good friend and Newport's finest, to want to take control of my psychological health. I refused. He implied that my decision not to consult with him had something to do with his failure to save Simone Marchand from suicide, something I had all but forgotten, but something he never could. He held onto the kind of anguish and guilt he counseled others to forsake.

I blamed depression for the reason I did not leave Vincent immediately. Aunt Belle helped me through it. For me, the worst part of the grieving lasted two years. Staying in the house where my son had lived, sleeping in his room, holding his toys, especially little Wazzie the threadbare mouse, and Sara the hairless lioness (we shaved her when Shea lost his own hair) was all that I had left of him.

Only recently had I begun to awake from what felt like a long sleep, to think that it was time to move on, leave Vincent, start a new life.

I couldn't have guessed the great and tragic drama that would eventually unfold.

Shaken, I walked down the street, leaving the happy face behind, leaving the joy and pain of the past four years somewhere on the sidewalk between the cleaners and the tailor's.

I retrieved my complicated Halloween costume and managed

to get it to the car in one trip. The dress was designed to depict the ascending Persephone as she restores the beauty of spring to the earth after her obligatory six months in the underworld with Hades. It was Neil's idea, and of course the symbolism was not lost on me. In suggesting Persephone, Neil had been trying to take us back to the best times: when we had first met and the months that followed. It might have worked if it hadn't been for . . .

I trembled as I drove to the Daisy Cotton restaurant, something I seemed to have been doing since the transcendent visit at dawn.

The ghost in my morning had left me emotionally strung out and reality itself seemed to have moved aside to accommodate a stirring new reality. My skin was tingling. I felt as if I had vertigo, a persistent whirling inside my head. I had become sensitized to everything from drawings on car windows, to the brighter moments of my past, to my present condition of smoke and mirrors.

And now it was time to consult Lucetta Corneille. I was at a crossroads and she would point the way.

The Daisy Cotton was perched at ocean's edge between a pier and a long sandy beach. The restaurant was named for Lucetta's great-great grandmother Daisy who had been enslaved at a cotton plantation in Georgia. Brilliant bolts of cotton and cotton plant prints decorated the crisp white walls.

I arrived at the café a few minutes late. Lucetta greeted me at the door, twirling menus in the air as if she were roping cattle. She smiled at me in recognition. "Happy Halloween! Your friend is over there at the window table." She paused and for a moment stared into my eyes. "Your eyes . . . *you're in love.* Couldn't be that fine looking shrink from down the coast, could it? Or maybe someone new . . . . But, sorry." She stopped as if she'd committed a faux pas. "Why don't you go sit yourself down and get something to eat. Go on now." She shooed me like a fly toward Marla who waved impatiently. What was Lucetta implying? Had she actually guessed? I would speak privately to her as soon as breakfast was over.

"Happy Day of the Dead, Paige, which is what I'll be if I don't make my final decorating decisions in the next hour. The florist and caterer aren't happy. Guess who's joining us for brunch?" Marla asked, managing not to take a breath.

"Neil of course." I sat across the table from her. "Your hair is . . . blonder."

"Oh God don't say that. I knew you'd forgive me for inviting Neil. It's the beginning of his month-long vacation that you've refused to take with him, but how can you when you're married. Pass the sugar. So I thought, well, at least he can begin his vacation with the love of his life. You're terrific in red and black," she said eyeing my sweater and pants.

"So was Stendahl." I knew my reply would annoy her.

"Oh please, don't go literary on me. My God, your eyes are green this morning. Eugene always says that if he could find emeralds the color of your eyes he could retire. How can I be friends with someone prettier than me? Don't answer that. Okay, here are samples of the napkins for tonight. The silver and peach combination is elegant but the purple has a lot of punch. I don't know which to choose, Paige. I'm afraid the caterers have had it with me and my pathetic Halloween party. I'm such a witch—oops, pun." She rifled through her Versace bag. "The napkins are the same color only swirled with silver. Here, look. What do you think? Paige?"

Absently, I took the napkin from her. *Why* had Lucetta asked me if I had someone new? I looked blankly at Marla's napkin.

"Peach and silver," I said indifferently.

Just as I was ready to plead a headache and excuse myself, the silver napkin in my hand began to shimmer like glittering ocean waves. As if a square piece of the sea had been placed miraculously before me. Was this a sign? I felt faint and braced myself against the table.

Leaning forward, Marla sighed, "Hello, anybody home?" She reached for my arm and then from behind me, Lucetta touched my shoulder.

"Some more coffee?" Lucetta smiled, retrieving the pitcher on the table. "It'll put your feet back on the ground . . . unless you'd rather fly off somewhere."

"Wouldn't I though," I said. "Oh yes, wouldn't I love to fly off."

"What is going on here? Are you okay, Paige?" Marla asked, stuffing her merchandise back into her bag like a rebuked vendor.

"It's stress," I said trying to calm her. "A lot of stress and I don't know where to begin."

"Well, let's begin with my party which is why we're here. It's the only party I've had all year and people are expecting something, Paige."

"It will be something," I said, aggravated that the subject of Marla's party was taking my thoughts away from my otherworldly meeting with a mystical stranger. His appearance in my room that morning had lifted me beyond the ordinary. I felt entirely different about everything. It was as if I were being called to a kind of greater understanding. What matter were cocktail parties and divorces . . . .

"Okay Paige, tell me what's wrong. I can always tell when you're stuck. What's Vincent done now? As if I can stand to hear another of his cheap melodramas."

"Something's happened to me, Marla. I don't know what.

You'll think I'm crazy."

"I already think you're crazy. Anyone living with Vincent Brighton would be driven crazy. And that also applies to your aunt."

"This morning at dawn, I saw a light in my bedroom, in front of the French doors."

"So what did Vincent do this time? Bring his girlfriend Patty home with him? I'm not surprised, Paige. That woman should be listed on that geological rating—Mohs' Scale of Hardness. Right up there with diamonds. You've never worked in an office, my dear. The deception is as high as your eyebrows. These people in offices slap on their new clothes and their designer cologne— well, cheap designers anyway—and put on their best phony behavior and then tilt their pelvises and shake their bottoms past the 'in and out' boxes as if they're all as alluring as they pretend to be. But they all know where the real truth is—at home with their families, where they don't like to be. Because you can't put over anything there, now can you? Where was I?"

"We're talking about where I am. Marla, this isn't about Vincent. Not now. I had an experience that I can't explain, and I need a psychic, someone who understands the paranormal, someone like Lucetta. Which is why I chose the Daisy Cotton for brunch today, actually."

Marla was astounded. "You're joking."

"No. I'm not. You might as well know. I'm desperate for answers. A man appeared in my bedroom this morning just before dawn. And that doesn't even begin to explain it. Since then, well, just now, the napkin—"

"Wait." She held up her hand like a crossing guard. Her red mouth curved up at the corner just as her eyebrow arched. It was her Picasso look: one side of her face an inch above the other. "Just who we need, Paige. Look, a psychiatrist has arrived and not a moment too soon. Hello, Neil. Sit down. Paige has a problem *so* fascinating that my party is slowly degenerating into the unthinkable—crepe paper and Dixie cups. I'm afraid she's not well."

Neil sat across the table from me. He leaned toward me with an intent look. "What is it?"

"Nothing," I answered, kicking Marla's leg under the table.

She ignored it and whispered. "Our Paige wants to have a psychic reading with Lucetta."

Fortunately his disgust did not show. He was one of the vintage psychiatrists, after all. There was always something inherently smug about their studied patience, though in my case I suppose he was sincerely concerned. He said to Marla, as if leading group encounter, "Go on."

Poker faced, Marla continued, "Paige says there was a man in her bedroom this morning."

"A what? I'd like to know what exactly happened," Neil said, pouring himself coffee from the thermos pot. I saw a faint tremor run from his mouth to his eye. The scar on his temple darkened. A man in my bedroom. He was jealous.

I rotated my coffee mug on the tablecloth. "I must be going crazy," I said, smiling. It was possible. They looked across the table at me, genuinely concerned. I realized that neither of them wanted the truth. They wanted to hear something that would validate their friendship with me, something to encourage our emotional dependency on one another. I couldn't blame them.

I said carefully, "I had a dream this morning, a strange one in which a man appeared." Their eyes stayed on mine. "This morning. He wanted something from me."

"What man doesn't?" Marla asked, sipping coffee.

Neil asked patiently, "What did he want, Paige?"

"I don't know." That, at least, was the truth.

"Who was he? How do you know he wanted something?" Neil probed professionally. It seemed so utterly sophomoric. They did not understand. But then, why should they? It made me feel painfully alone.

Marla smiled. "Oh come on, you two. You're both taking this too seriously. Dreams are dreams. So a man appeared. So he wanted something. It happens to me every day. Last night—much to Eugene's dismay—it was Tom Selleck."

Thank God Lucetta glided up to the table with our menus. I looked at her gratefully and she acknowledged my appreciation with an indiscernible nod. Neil and Marla were my closest friends and I could not even tell them about my leaving Vincent. I knew my "vision" would not hold up under Neil's scrutiny. He would autopsy my phantom, carve him up into logical pieces that he would prove to symbolize some neurosis or another. He was real, the man at dawn, I was certain. That would be bad enough news for Neil. If he knew how the stranger looked, if I were to describe even his eyes . . . . *The color of aquamarines, Neil. So vast, so penetrating, so unsettled, like the seas Viking ships might have sailed a thousand years ago.* I looked across at Neil who was making his breakfast selection. He disliked garish metaphors. The cultivated always do. I could say something more literary, like "He was the very image of a Bernini masterpiece." I would never speak of his eyes of freedom blue . . . his lips . . . his hands.

Neil lowered his menu and asked, "Paige, do you need something to help you sleep at night?"

"No," I shook my head. We all ordered from Lucetta. As she wheeled away, I looked at my two friends and tried to imagine what I would think if the situation were reversed.

I wanted to show Marla I cared. I asked, "What time are the musicians arriving tonight?"

She smiled, relieved, "Well, Sally Duncan said that they're

always late so I told them seven-thirty." While I watched Marla, Neil stared at me, dissatisfied. He folded his hands together and brought them to his chin. He would have been mortified to know he looked as though he might be praying. I smiled tentatively at him. He knew I was holding back.

I promised Marla that I would arrive early enough at her party to be sure the tables were appropriately ghoulish.

She chattered on endlessly about party details. I mentally withdrew and found a quieting piece of ocean beyond the white lace window curtains.

Black clouds were poised along the horizon. The sun was detained somewhere behind them. A crow swooped down from the darkened sky, circling in a gust of wind. The day had that pallor that was made for dreaming or sleeping. A boat at sea bobbed in the grey swells. It was probably a chartered fishing boat with squirming bait tanks and seasick conventioneers. How brash to be out on a day like this, I thought, when the Southern California sea was known to be so implacable. Many boats had been lost in the Catalina channel. Some believed they were cut in half by freighters or capsized by migrating whales. Our newspaper once postulated that the missing boats had been beamed up to Venus. No one in California argued.

I shivered at the thought of drowning at sea. It was the worst possible death and yet I was intrigued by it. As a child I read every article I could find on drownings, every account of the sunken Titanic, the Lusitania. I pored over survivors' accounts of pleasure craft sinkings, naval battles, submarine disappearances, and flash floods. I did not know why. Neil said that I was simply coming to terms with losses, oppression or even death.

I looked at Neil and Marla. He was feigning an interest in her vampire ice sculptures. He nodded, yawning subtly.

As I stared at the sea I tried to remember my phantom's eyes—if I could only see them again—that profound blue that shone out from them, that wild blue that refused containment.

I closed my eyes. I could remember the curve of his brow, his chin, the outstretched arm. His image was compelling. I began to feel lightheaded again, on the edge. I steadied myself against the table as I took a deep breath and counted silently. I opened my eyes but I could not stop staring at the ocean. As I looked out beyond the lone boat, pictures flashed at me, disjointed segments. At first the images began slowly, like a filmstrip on a faulty projector moving briskly, faltering, halting, and skipping forward. A sea storm. It was very dark. I could hardly see. I was cold, trembling. I was so cold. I saw a man bracing himself against the tilted mast. He fought against the wind. It howled, raged. The ocean was blue-black, the color of a hideous bruise. The film lurched forward. I had to get off the deck but I was too weak and the wind and water lashed at me. I grabbed at the boat railing frantically calling, "Andreas, help me. Andreas, come with me!" Oh God, help me. But the storm sounds were deafening. Icy seawater engulfed me. Where was he? I saw a third figure. Was there someone else on the boat? Yes . . . but who? Someone out of place, someone menacing . . . struggling with Andreas? This was not the way it was supposed to be. One of my hands was torn from the railing. I was being sucked overboard. *I was going to die alone*. I could not see Andreas. His back was toward me. Please do not let me die alone. He struggled to reach me. There was a brilliant flash of lightning that lit up the rocky coast. Then I glimpsed the shape of a whale's fluke in the craggy outcropping. It was home. I wanted to go home. Thunder rolled through the night. A wave washed over the boat. I heard him shout, "Angelica, wait for me! *Don't, don't.*" But it was too late. Seaweed slithered over my shoulders, pulling me down. I could no longer feel my body. My tenuous grip broke from the railing and I was a small child going round and round again on the carousel, reaching for the brass ring . . . .

I coughed. The lights were dim. Neil was holding my head and Marla paced the floor barefoot, having flung off her red heels during the commotion.

I was lying on a sofa in the back room of the Daisy Cotton. Pastel quilts covered the walls. Lucetta handed Neil a wet cloth and smiled knowingly at me, eyebrows raised.

Neil pressed the wet cloth to my forehead. His fingers slipped under my sleeve, feeling for my pulse. I pulled my wrist away from him. *Don't let him find out. He will take away the dream. You must find Andreas.*

"I'm fine," I said instinctively in the haughty tone that annoyed Aunt Belle. But I was not fine at all. My teeth were chattering. I was so cold. I managed to focus my eyes on Marla. "I'm sorry—your party—I've not been much help—"

"Don't, Paige," she said. "Frankly, I'm sick to death of this party."

Neil moved the cloth over my forehead. "Do you think you can sit up?" He turned to Lucetta. "Do you have a blanket on hand?" She nodded and left the room. He leaned close to me, took my face in his hands and said gently, emphatically, "We need to talk."

"No," I said, "You need to talk, not me. I have nothing to say . . . honestly, Neil."

Marla asked impatiently, "Why do I feel like I'm eavesdropping on a therapy session? We're not going to solve anything lying around this place. Paige, you need to see a real doctor—no offense Neil—and right away."

Neil said, "She's going to stay at Candlesage. She was

planning on Mo's tea anyway. But she is *not* going anywhere else but to bed. *No* parties."

Suddenly I panicked, "My bag, where is it?" I remembered the extra piece of greenery from the footprint that I had slipped into my wallet that morning.

"Here, honey," Marla said, quickly handing it to me. I pulled out the sprig, entrusting it to her. "Please take this by the florist's when you go. Ask LaVonne if she knows what it is."

Neil was annoyed. "I really think that can wait."

"No. It can't. I had planned to go and ask her myself. This will save me the trip."

"Sure, I'll take it by," Marla said frowning. "It looks like juniper or some kind of cypress. I hope you're not thinking— well, it simply wouldn't look good with pumpkins, Paige."

"Just please find out for me."

In his most fatherly manner, Neil helped me up from the sofa. "You do have a fever but you're going to be all right."

All right? It was a medical aphorism that made me want to laugh. I thought, this is not the end of anything, Neil. It's just beginning.

Marla said, "Paige, you're as white as a ghost. Apropos on Halloween. Neil, let's get her out of here and into your car." She turned to me. "Do you want him to drive you home?"

Home. Aunt Belle would be packing. The maple leaf. It was the day of my divorce, something I had wanted for years. I had always contemplated the deep joy that would come when the marriage ended. But I had plunged so quickly into this other world that it seemed my marriage to Vincent never existed. Like two segregated pieces of life held together only by a thin narrative thread. I did not want to be Paige any longer.

"I can't go home," I said truthfully. I *was* homeless now. Neil showed his approval by giving an understanding clinical nod.

Lucetta appeared at the door and handed one of her quilts to Neil. As she brushed by my shoulder she pressed a matchbook into my fingers. It was warm from her hand. "You keep that quilt as long as you want, you hear?"

Neil helped me through the door. He reached for my hand but my fingers closed upon the matchbook, making a fist beneath his caressing fingers.

The black sky allowed one ray of light to streak through. It spotlighted our departure from the restaurant. Rain was again imminent. Fisherman in blue-bottomed dories dragged the boats out of the surf and turned them belly up—like a fresh catch—in the sand by the pier.

Autumn beach strollers, sneakers dangling like puppets in hand, walked briskly toward the nearly vacant parking lot.

Neil's car was parked next to my old white Mercedes with the dented front door. Vincent had kicked it in last New Year's Eve, nearly a year after Shea's death. Later that same night, Neil and I had made love, the only time we ever had. Aunt Belle had asked me a thousand times why I did not get the car repaired. I never had an answer. Maybe I needed scars that were visible.

After Neil closed the door of his Bentley for me, I opened the Daisy Cotton matchbook. Inside, in tall, dramatic script, like the feather strokes of a bird, Lucetta had written her personal phone number.

Neil opened his door and seeing me slip the matchbook into my bag said, "I didn't know you carried matches."

"There are a lot of things you don't know about me, Neil."

Chapter Three

*A*ndreas. *That was his name.*

Neil started the engine. I closed my eyes. I needed to recreate the images of the storm, to recall details. He had called me Angelica. He told me to wait for him. His cry had been both a plea and a command. And then the name Angelica, spoken in the storm, as it had been this very morning in my room: not so much a name as it was a pledge. With his voice came the knowledge of my identity. I am Angelica. I am Paige. *I am both.*

Instantly I had been pulled into the storm and had become part of that other world. It was like a dream. But in dreams, you wake and as time passes, the day's tedious routines cause the once vital feelings and events to become shadows, recollections, devoid of immediacy. This was different because the storm had been real. The event was sharp and clear even though parts were missing. It was like viewing scattered puzzle pieces whose shapes, not unlike hazy memories, know precisely where they belong but must await your enlightenment.

Why were Angelica and Andreas on the boat that night? What could have possibly driven them out into the ferocious gale? *Where* were they? It was a rocky coast with craggy outcroppings. Who was the other person on the boat? The dark figure grappling with Andreas? Angelica knew who it was, but I did not know. An enemy, Angelica knew.

I had worn a full-length gown of Queen Anne's lace. The sharp buttons on the long sleeves had cut my wrists as I clung to the boat railing. The style seemed Victorian and hung on me in tatters, its delicate pattern defiled. I thought of giddy young wallflowers painstakingly adorned for the dances that would elude them. Had Angelica dressed for the beginning of a life that would never happen? I was tormented by the question.

The shimmer of the brass ring . . . that recollection was lucid. On that black, starless night as I approached death I had tried to seize the brass ring, just as I had as a child on the carousel. It had shone resplendently, beyond my reach, in the icy night. My last memory was the yearning to possess it at last. But it was Angelica's yearning, not Paige's.

Did Angelica die that night on the icy sea? Did Andreas die with her?

I opened my eyes as we passed through the seaside town of Laguna Beach. Neil was silent. There was no perceptible movement in the car as we passed throngs of tourists who browsed along Coast Highway in spite of the light rain. Were it not for the random blinking of Neil's eyes, we might have been a photograph floating lifelessly in a mass of colorfully dressed, chattering people.

I knew Neil's thoughts included me in passionate and eternal ways. He would view my "breakdown" (his term) as his clear right of entry into my life. He would gently play it off to his advantage. He loved me and he wanted to help me—save me if necessary—and for him, marriage was the solution. But I would never be his lover again or his wife. Not now. Not anymore. I wanted to tell him that we had no future. It was all happening too fast. Paige—Angelica—whoever I was—needed to find out her past. Find Andreas.

Could these visions be explained by reincarnation?

I agreed with many others that there exist dimensions not yet provable. I might actually have lived before as a woman named Angelica who loved a man named Andreas . . . as a woman who loves him still. It was the only explanation.

Be cautious, Paige. A jury of psychiatrists, Neil notwithstanding, would find me grossly mentally incompetent. I could see crooked fingers pointing at me, gavels pounding, coarse male voices proclaiming "insane." Much like a witch trial. They could call it any number of things: schizophrenia, wish fulfillment, delusions or whatever else might be defined in their time-honored textbooks. They would say I am simply creating what I had been denied. They might claim that reality had been too bitter for me and that loving a phantom in an ethereal world (of my creation) made it safe to love, for once. They could say that my fear of death is so great that for peace of mind I had turned to reincarnation as a means of living forever. After all, reincarnation is an enticing alternative to the traditional western religious concepts, they would say. They would prescribe drugs, of course. Anything to keep me inside their belief systems.

Neil was of the opinion that the basis for all violence is fear. I agreed. Would he also say that most mental illness is spawned by fear? Neil would say that a disastrous marriage to a maniac was causing my decline into a fantasy world. The death of my son Shea . . . .

But Neil would forgive me. He would marry me anyway. He would take very good care of me. Much better care than he took of Simone.

We left the reveling town of Laguna.

Soon we turned off the road and began the steep climb to Candlesage, past hillsides brown from lack of rain. Only a few cloudy-green clumps of sage broke the monotony. They were always there to remind visitors that after Angus and Mary Carmichael had purchased this large portion of rolling hills, they pitched tent for months in the sage and, by candlelight, had drawn up the plans for their new home.

The hillside gloom ended at two stone columns flanking massive iron gates. Arching above was the announcement "Candlesage," mostly for the benefit of those who should go no farther. Curving stone planters spilled over with a riotous selection of fall color. Needlepoint ivy crept up an elaborate intercom and camera. The gates opened to the graceful curves of Candlesage Drive, which wound through fields of vivid color. Orange trees lined the road and beyond them the meadows were spread with foliage so green and lush that one suspected it was a creation not of gardeners but of mural artists. The flowers were so perfect they defied picking.

The gardens adjacent to the main house were home to Mo Carmichael's vast collection of statuary. Aunt Belle said it looked like Forest Lawn Cemetery. The house was a Scottish shrine that Mary and Angus, Neil's grandparents, had built as a message to the world that after years of poverty in the new world, they had finally *arrived*. Like most "we've arrived" messages, it tended to scream, not whisper: a stone fortress anachronistic anywhere but on the moors of Scotland. It even had a tower.

Mac Carmichael, in deference to his mother and father's overstatement, refused to change a thing. When he died five years ago, Neil's mother Mo redecorated (more like disemboweled) the fortress in desert colors. She called it the Georgia O'Keeffe look, though it was not quite that bold or austere. The pastel tones had tamed the wild shadows in the place, had given warmth to the unforgiving stone walls and floors.

As we pulled into the circular drive Neil's hand touched my leg. "We're home," he said. "Feeling better?" His fingers gently caressed my knee.

I replied absently, "Yes."

He wrestled with a thought and said, "I think I should tell you that I phoned your house again this morning, after you'd left. Belle was busy looking for boxes."

"Go on." I said. The proverbial cat was out of the bag.

"She said that you had decided to leave Vincent." He looked directly at me, not removing his hand from my knee. "I met you for breakfast because I thought a celebration was in order."

I leaned my head back against the seat. It was raining harder now. The fountain in the center of the front lawn sprayed up against the downpour. A six-foot marble woman stood in the fountain with a basket of flowers in one hand. Her arm stretched out over the water as she sprinkled petals. On her luminous face was carved a smile whose euphoria had seemed always unattainable to me, until now . . . .

I said, "It's true. I'm leaving him today, if possible. I wanted to move out today. I didn't want to go home. At least I thought it was a possibility before I had—God, I even hate to say the word—before I fainted."

The rain slid over the statue's curling hair, down her filmy marble dress. Even in the rain she smiled.

"Paige, darling," Neil sighed, "there are often physical repercussions. You've heard it said before—and it is true. Divorce is like death. Anxiety is part and parcel even in the most civilized ones."

I nodded. What could I say? "That's why I fainted, Neil.

Why I thought I saw a man in my room this morning. You know how guilty I feel about everything. It's a big step for me, you know that. Shea—he was all I really had. He was the only . . . his memory kept me there . . . ."

She was eighteenth-century French. Her only flaw, Mo mused, was a small chip on her shoulder. I could see the triangular niche that was missing where her round marble outline curved under the clinging dress.

I said, "I have to go to Marla's party tonight so that I can tell him—tell Vincent that I'm leaving him. I don't want to tell him when we're alone."

He nodded, his eyes as intent on me as mine were on the statue. She never frowned or got old. Worry-free, luminescent white marble.

"You—" He removed his hand from my knee and with both hands clutched his steering wheel. "There's so much I want to say. Can you help me out?"

"I don't know," I turned to him, keeping my face neutral. "I was going to wait for awhile to tell you. I needed time to think. There are so many directions—"

"I was hoping there would only be one direction. Mine."

I looked back at the fountain. "I know."

"Why?" he asked.

I didn't answer.

"Why?" he repeated. "Let me tell you how I wished it had been. A phone call, a happy one from you to me, 'Neil, I'm doing it. Today. Now. Come over and get me. This is the happiest day of my life and I want you to be here with me. We have so many things to talk about.'"

"Don't," I whispered. "I know what you want." I also knew it was my chance to explain myself but I just did not have a logical excuse. I felt like a bride who has left a bereft groom at the altar.

I said in the tone of one offering a consolation prize, "Just give me time. I've taken the biggest step."

His hand touched my shoulder. "I want you to stay here."

"For awhile," I said. "You'll have to also put up with Belle and Chester."

The tension broke. Neil's face relaxed. He might have smiled if I had not looked so defeated. He said, "Stay here. I'll get you an umbrella." He opened the door and ascended the steps of the Candlesage portico. His butler Hitchins appeared at the door with the umbrella. Neil took it from him and came trotting back to the car. He opened the door for me and as I stood up our bodies touched. His free hand went around my waist. He said softly, "Anything, Paige. Just name it."

I thought ruefully of freedom but said nothing.

Neil was intuitive. He did not kiss me. He guided me from the car to the house under the black umbrella.

"Mother," he called. The long entrance hall resounded with echoes.

Hitchins took our umbrella and coats. He was a picaresque-looking butler whose skin must have had the same rufescent glow at birth. He had been with the family for thirty years. He was stocky with thinning disobedient hair. Aunt Belle said he nipped before noon and sucked in his cheeks so as not to look toady.

Mo called back from the deep triangle of some gothic corner, "Neil!"

"I've got Paige," he answered.

Prophetic . . . .

"Wonderful!" she returned. "Let's see, it's only noon." Her shoes moved silently over the floor. Cued, the ornate grandfather clock with bulging cheeks, not unlike Hitchins', chimed noon. Mo appeared around the corner, tall and still thin from years of ballet. She glided gracefully toward us. The four of us (after thirty years Hitchins had adopted family idiosyncrasies) all stared at the clock. And then, as if directed, we all turned away after the second chime.

Mo assessed my appearance, her penciled lips parting in surprise. Her prominent nose lifted ever so slightly (as if for takeoff, Marla once said). I became aware that my blouse was pulled out of my skirt, there was a coffee stain on my skirt and a run up the front of my hose. Across my face, a clump of hair dangled.

"I had an accident," I said.

Her pointed chin lowered an inch in pardon before she exclaimed, "Well then, we'll just have to fix you up. That's a nasty bruise on your forehead. Maybe an ice pack." She took me by the elbow, prepared to get on with the repairs.

Neil said, "I think Paige won't be attending the tea, mother. She's not quite up to it."

"That's true," I said.

"She'll need to rest," he said.

Mo looked disappointed. "I see." She did not like missions stolen away from her.

I offered as an apology, "It must be the flu."

"Now, Paige." Neil turned to his mother. "It's a bit more than that, mother. In fact, Paige has left Vincent."

"She has," Mo gasped.

"I have," I nodded. "It was all very sudden."

"Yes," agreed Neil. "And no. Yes and no."

A silence followed during which we all pondered the ramifications of such an event. I noticed that Hitchins was indeed sucking in his cheeks. This was accompanied by a gentle rocking on his capped heels. As a child he had been a Vaudevillian star.

"*Do* be still, Hitchins," Mo chided.

"Madam," he murmured waggishly, departing the entrance

hall backwards, shoes tapping, his tubular eyebrows rising to mid-forehead.

I decided to satisfy Mo's curiosity. I explained, "Vincent doesn't know, not yet. I have to see a lawyer. This week sometime . . . ."

She nodded, "I see."

Neil's mouth moved nervously. It only happened in his mother's presence. "Well," he said to me, "we'd better find a room for you." I followed Neil toward the stairs.

Mo said, "Indeed," with a peculiar twist of her vocal chords, as if the word would help her to digest Neil's new state of affairs. Except for her son's complete emotional and physical healing over Simone, I suspected that I was the only thing Neil wanted in his life that his mother could not give. She presumed, quite erroneously, that he had just acquired me. She wasn't sure what to feel.

I said, "Maybe we can talk later, after your tea. I don't want to keep you any longer."

Mo's cook Helga, whose body was notably similar in shape to her famous breakfast biscuits, appeared at the doorway. "The piroshki are in," she said in her thick German accent.

"Thank you, Helga," said Mo, turning back to me. "You're welcome to stay as long as you like, Paige, as I'm sure Neil has told you."

"Thank you," I said, feeling the words were inadequate. Her facial features, which in certain conversations sharpened awesomely, remained smooth and relaxed.

Mo said to Neil, "Take her to Glynis' old room, the Ed Hopper room." Then for the first time since my arrival, she smiled at me. "It is by far the warmest room in the house and some say it has the best view. I'm coming, Helga," she said as her cook turned away. "Oh, and tell Hitchins to put out the tiny ashtrays stacked in the Welsh cupboard." She looked at me and took my arm, "Don't hesitate if you need anything. I'll send someone up with something—tea, sandwiches? Now, go on Neil, take her up to bed."

More prophesy?

I could feel her eyes watching me as we walked toward the elaborate staircase. She was an attractive woman of sixty-five, thin, unblemished, emblematic of how natural plastic surgery can look when executed by an artist. Her hair was an unfortunate color of beige but the style was not dated. She wore it pulled straight back from her face in a tight knot, which gave her the look of an eccentric, one who would boldly plunge into any new experience. But it was not true. Her style was guarded. Her conservatism prevented her from being really interesting. She lived in a world where identities were primarily determined by owning and consuming.

Neil took my elbow as we ascended the stairs.

In each of Mo's upstairs rooms hung a painting of substantial value. I wondered if she had avoided choosing the Paul Klee room for me that day because she knew about last New Year's Eve. It had been in the Paul Klee room that Neil and I had finally made love.

We were silent as we approached the door to my room. He opened it for me. I was sure he was recalling that night nearly a year before in the room next door. His hand paused on the bronze doorknob before letting me enter the room.

Neil took his hand from the knob. It was a pivotal moment. I entered the room alone. "Thank you," I nodded as if he were a bellboy.

"You're welcome," he answered as if I were a patron.

The door closed between us.

Now I could finally think freely of Andreas. Would he be

able to find me at Candlesage? "Spirits" don't have anything quite so ridiculous as logistic problems, do they?

But as I sank into the bed, eyes closed, I could not think of Andreas. Unbidden, unwelcome, thoughts of Neil and last New Year's Eve passed through the cloud of fatigue settling over me.

Chapter Four

Mo had an Andrew Wyeth room and a Jasper Johns room, but it was appropriate our lovemaking last year had occurred in the Paul Klee room. The rendezvous was unplanned, a scribble of hopeful spontaneity.

That New Year's Eve party was, stylistically, the grandest. But then everyone always agreed that Mo's parties were unsurpassed.

Vincent and I had arrived late. He had been drinking heavily before he got home—an office party—which is why I had driven us to the party in my old car. As we curved up the dimly lit hill toward Candlesage, I regretted our coming. Vincent was frenetic, hostile, and loud. He told me that I looked like a whore in my red dress. He made sure that his words were coherent. I wanted to strike him because he was stealing from me again. Like all alcoholics, he was a self-obsessed thief. Stealing, always stealing. And tonight it was New Year's Eve. That was the booty, what he would take from me tonight. I thought of pushing him out of the car, letting his body roll back down to Coast Highway. After all, there were gutters down along the road to break the fall.

But instead of striking him, I said, "Maybe we should go back home." To what? I thought. To the alcoholic nightmare?

Vincent grumbled something profane as he groped for the cigarette lighter. There would be ash burns spattered down the front of his white shirt.

I had worn the backless red wool jersey dress for Neil. I would flirt with him, of course I would. The more I could make Neil want me, the more I felt wanted in every way. It was a connection, a lifeline to something beyond my life with Vincent. The flirtation, which had grown more serious as time went on, gave me a way of coping with a marriage I did not know how to end. Neil's and my interest in one another was like having a delicacy one does not eat. The combination of desire and restraint became a diversion which helped me survive after Shea's death.

Neil did not consider himself used any more than I did. I always suspected that wanting me excited him more than having me. Our desire for each other had intensified with our first *real* kiss just a month before that New Year's Eve. It happened under the pier at the beach after a late birthday dinner given by his sister Glynis. The kiss ended the midnight stroll down the moon swept beach. The feverish embrace had come to a halt when we were called back to the house for the cutting of the cake. We had been too breathless to help blow out the pink candles. Neil had lost his grandfather's pipe in the sand.

I avoided Vincent most of New Year's Eve. I noticed guests propping him up as his legs gave way, as his elbows slid off tabletops. Ladies in glitter forgave him for spills; gentlemen in satin lapels patted his back like empathetic reunited fraternity brothers. It was New Year's Eve, after all. Give the fellow another drink.

At midnight, I found myself alone by the enormous Christmas tree in the entrance hall. Crystal stars the size of my hand, papier-mâché angels and mauve bows all glittered with gold dust amid garlands of silver and gold. I could see my reflection in a silver globe. I had always trusted my reflection more than I had myself. That representation of me in the globe, imprinted by the miracle of physics, absent a capricious heart. Uncomplicated. Undisturbed.

As expected, "Auld Lang Syne" whined out through the bagpipes, one of Mo's traditions. Voices in various stages of gaiety now became solemn to accompany the piper as New Year's Eve came to a close in the stone and glass fortress.

"Happy New Year," he whispered.

I turned around. "Happy New Year, Neil."

We kissed, his arms around me, then mine around him.

Had we fallen to the floor at that moment to make love it would have been wondrous, I am sure. But instead, the drunken Vincent pulled Neil harshly away from me.

His words were slurred but discernible. "Get your fucking hands off my wife, Doc Carmichael."

Unruffled but reluctant, Neil stepped back. He ran his hand through his hair for composure. He conceded to moral and legal dictates. Vincent was my husband. It was New Year's Eve and surely I was to kiss the man I married. I did very lightly on the cheek. But Vincent wanted to put on a show. He tried to press me to him. He had a sour, poisoned smell. I broke away. He snarled at me, his eyes unable to focus.

I whispered, "Let's go home."

Vincent turned to Neil. "You're a bastard, you know that?" He laughed. He swayed a foot in every direction. He was going to fall. His dark eyes rolled as his mouth sagged open. His hand reached out to a tree branch and groped in the gold-frosted needles until it closed upon a large crystal angel with a gold lyre against her breast. He crushed it into a handful of bloody shards.

"Not the tree," I cried, as it swayed from its base . . . not this too. The moments I had spent alone with the tree had become a keepsake memory, something beautiful and optimistic, a physical exposition of what I once hoped my life would be—flawless and certain.

The tree trembled, its ornaments jiggling on the full green boughs. Neil steadied Vincent, grabbing his elbow, but Vincent's other arm came at me. The bloody hand clutched at my neck. I grabbed his wrist and pushed it away but not before the wet, sticky finger marks were left on my neck. Glass splinters stung my skin. Vincent fell against the tree, his legs coming out from under him. Neil saw my neck. Perhaps the vision of Vincent's blood streaked across my neck would become one of Neil's collection of symbols, a fixed moment in time that would leave him changed, as the tree on New Year's Eve had been mine.

"Let's get that cleaned off," he said to me.

Vincent was off the floor. He clawed his way up the wall until he was standing precariously. "Where are the car keys?" he managed to ask, his lips slouching into his chin. "Cause I'm gonna get laid, but not by you." He grinned.

"I don't know where the keys are," I lied.

"Here," Neil said to Vincent, "Why not let me fix your hand for you and we'll call a cab." He shouted to Hitchins in the living room and then turned back, "Wait a few minutes, Vincent."

But Vincent bolted toward the massive door and threw it open. We ran after him. Cold wind whipped around my skirt.

"Vincent, you can't drive," I said, but he plunged into the night shouting at the valet. Before Neil could stop him the valet had sprinted off to get the car.

"I think it would be a mistake, my man." Neil clutched

Vincent's shoulder, whipping out a handkerchief to wrap Vincent's bleeding hand.

To a distant onlooker, they might have been good friends in their tuxedos, one touching the other's shoulder on a chill evening before a Scottish mansion. At the very least they resembled a Chivas Regal holiday magazine advertisement. Until Vincent jerked his shoulder away and swung at Neil shouting, "I'm not your man."

The valet drove up with my car. Neil reached out and said, "I'll take those." The valet handed over the keys. Neil said, "And don't let anyone else drive who's had too much."

Vincent lunged toward Neil for the keys but the valet held him back. "Jesus, he's big," the valet said. "The agency didn't say you wanted a bouncer."

"All the same," Neil replied. "Can you hold him?"

Vincent was engaged in a full struggle. "Lemme go, you punk," he mumbled kicking a dent in my car.

Somehow Vincent was poured into a cab. I heard him give the reluctant cabby Patty's address. How I pitied her.

We bolted the door behind us. It helped. Neil touched a finger to my chin and looked at my neck. "Let's take care of this. Here, the powder room's down the hall. I think there's a pair of tweezers in the drawer."

A tiny light cast shadows on the swirling pastel wallpaper. He flipped on the overhead lights and turned on the gold plated faucet. The sink was hand painted to match the wallpaper. Neil picked up a piece of antique Irish linen embroidered with blue bells. He dampened it and laid it across my neck. There were bloodstains on the linen as he lowered it into the faucet to rinse it. But his hands were beautiful.

"How are you otherwise?" he asked getting the tweezers from the drawer.

When I was sure the blood was gone from my neck I looked at my reflection in the mirror. There she was, Paige Osborne Brighton, student body choice for the one most likely to succeed . . . nearly twenty years ago. I never thought to ask them what I would succeed at and when it would happen. *She* was the one chosen, not the failed person who lived under the flowing chestnut hair, full lips on white skin, long slender body and green eyes. The frightened *me* looked out from those eyes.

Neil's reflection pulled glass shards from her neck with tweezers. He whispered faintly, "Stay the night."

It was *her* he wanted to have sex with. I answered. "Yes, I will." Was it a game? Maybe by dividing myself up I thought I could handle intimacy, somehow send my body ahead of me like an army, while the real me crouched somewhere inside. We left the bathroom.

The party wasn't over. Neil had gone off toward the kitchen, no doubt to tell Marla of my ordeal. Mo had scheduled crepes for midnight. As I made my way toward the ballroom, I saw three cooks dressed in tartan kilts and argyle socks juggling flaming copper pans over an oak banquet table. Someone who was trying to sound like Ann Murray sang my favorite song, "Snowbird."

"Paige!" Marla cried, plucking at my arm. Her platinum hair flew in every direction.

"Thank God Vincent's gone. Maybe now you can have some fun. Lohman Griggs was asking about you, wanted to know who you were. You've heard of Lohman? The soon-to-be-famous artist who's already been shown at the Norton Simon? Well, Eugene told him your name and he says he's going to look you up. He likes married women. Oh, don't look at me like that, Paige. Look at Neil over there showing them how to flip crepes. My God he's so in love with you he makes Tristan look like a nematode. You better not break his heart because, my dear, there's not a woman here that wouldn't jump into his arms if given half a chance. But for some strange reason—I don't mean that the way it sounds—he's obsessed with you. I don't see how you can be so damned afraid of Vincent with someone like Neil at your beck and call. He's as close to a knight in shining armor as any of us will ever get, except maybe for his guilt over that psychotic cover girl Simone Marchand. I sure as hell hope he's *really* over that and not just pretending to be."

"Marla, I'm not afraid of Vincent. I am afraid of doing the wrong thing. That's what governs my life, my sense of morality. It's an insidious virtue. Every moment, every word, trying to decide what's moral, what's the best thing for everyone."

Marla turned her empty glass upside down and held it out until a waiter appeared with a refill. "Who's to say what's wrong? *You*. That's who."

"But what *is* wrong?" I asked.

"I don't know and I don't care. My feet are killing me. You always complicate things, Paige. Do whatever you want. I am never buying this brand of shoes again!"

"That's what I plan on doing tonight Marla, exactly what I want. I'm going to bed with Neil."

"Oh my God, how fabulous, how ecstatic! Wait till I tell Eugene! Eugene!"

At three-thirty Neil and I said good night to Mo and several friends who were sprawled over pale turquoise sofas before a sparkling fire. No one thought to wonder that I was leaving. Hands were flying, voices clucking. They had Jackson Pollock on the block and everyone wanted the final word.

We strolled languidly hand in hand up the staircase, pausing once among the shadows to kiss.

The Paul Klee room was cool and dark. The moon had only one edge left and it gave what light it could through windows facing the sea. I walked to the window instead of the bed. I could still say no, refuse the endless implications: unfaithful, extramarital, forsaking all others. I could wait until I left Vincent. But even as I thought it, my fingers went behind my back to the button that held my dress together at the waist. How fortuitous, a dress that slid off with one touch. It came undone. I held it to my breasts, not letting it fall.

Neil's lips were on the back of my neck. I turned to him. I wanted him because he wanted me, and Neil knew how to want a woman.

He kissed my hair, my lips, my neck, my shoulders, whispering repeatedly, "Paige."

His fingertips moved up the skin of my back around to where my hands held the dress. He took my hands in his. The dress fell silently to my hips, stopped for an instant, then collapsed to the floor. Softly we fell back onto the bed. His kiss was warm and slow. So were his fingers as they traced a line from my knee to my chin. I reached down to remove my slip. He murmured, "No. Let me do it. Let me do the rest."

And he did.

The next morning I slipped out of bed before him, showered and dressed and had coffee on the garden terrace before he woke. I was happy for Neil. I liked to see dreams come true. But I felt uncomfortable when I considered my new status: I was actually someone's lover. It might have been a tantalizing adventure for someone else. But for me this affair was simply another emotional millstone. I didn't know why.

The sunlight was brilliant but the stone lay cold under the January chill.

Mo had left for a New Year's Day football brunch. Hitchins and Helga had set out an elaborate breakfast that I had not touched.

I thought about the night before, the scene with Vincent and then Neil's touch. It was all too confusing—violence and then such sensual safety. Was I afraid of a good man? Someone I could trust? I convinced myself that it had not been a mistake. I also knew Neil would want to talk about my leaving Vincent. He would *analyze* my situation. He would act like someone from the fifties. He would think we were engaged or something.

I decided to leave and avoid any conversation. I was headed for the entrance hall, keys in hand, when I saw him on the stairs, hair tousled, a knee-length robe of navy blue quickly thrown on.

"I have to go," I said.

He walked silently toward me, took my arm and dragged me back out onto the terrace.

"Sit down," he said, pulling out a curved white chair.

After I did as directed, he poured himself a cup of coffee. I watched the steam curl past his chest, past the stubble on his chin, past the scar on his temple. He looked good in the morning. But that was not the point.

"Why aren't we in bed?" he asked.

"I have to go, Neil," I said.

"To where?" he asked sipping coffee with the insouciance of someone discussing a travel itinerary.

"I have to go," I said.

"Go to where and with whom? Vincent? How naive of you. With *Vincent?*" he spat the word. He paused and snapped his fingers, which brought Hitchins hobbling forward from a corner that was very much within earshot of our conversation.

"Champagne, Hitchins. Mrs. Brighton and I have something to celebrate. It's New Year's Day." Hitchins nodded and disappeared.

Neil said, "Then answer me *why.*"

"We had sex. It was wonderful, Neil. I'm not sorry, but—

but it doesn't necessarily mean it will happen again. I don't know if it changes anything for me."

Hitchins arrived with a silver champagne bucket and two Baccarat glasses. Neil dismissed him, popped open the bottle and poured. His fingers looked so tan for winter.

"To us," he said, drinking, watching while I did. "And to your metamorphosis which is bound to come. After you've made yourself sufficiently miserable with Vincent, when you are sufficiently fed up with your pain, sadness and futility, anger and—what else? Fear, of course. When you are sufficiently exhausted from living with an alcoholic who is incapable of loving anything but his bottle. When you weary of being victimized by a sociopathic womanizing heel who thinks that none of life's rules apply to him. When you get sick of playing his mommy, sick of trying to save a man who is unsavable. When you are sufficiently disgusted with your low, and I do mean *low* opinion of yourself because anyone with any self-esteem at all would have gotten the hell out of that marriage a long time ago." He winced. I could tell from the way he was braced that his back hurt him.

"Stop this, Neil."

"Know anything about shrimps, Paige? When they are hatched, some swim off to become shrimp, like those over there," he pointed to a platter of prawns. "And some don't. Guess what they become? They become *barnacles*, Paige. They attach themselves to the closest rock, build a shell and live forever with a tiny window to the world.

"I see hundreds of women like you every year. Maybe thousands. If it weren't for women like you, *Paige*, half the goddamn psychiatrists in the country would be out of work—at least all rich ones would."

I stood up.

He stood up with me. "You're too smart not to change."

"Don't ever talk like this to me again," I said, leaving the terrace.

As I passed the grandfather clock, I heard Neil's champagne glass shatter against the garden wall.

I avoided seeing him for a month or two in spite of the fact that I missed him terribly. Especially at night when I thought of his beautiful hands playing over my body. It was I who had phoned him for lunch on Valentine's Day. We resumed a warm, but sexless relationship.

Chapter Five

That was ten months before. Mo's tea had brought me back to Candlesage. I sat by the window in a pastel armchair and watched the rain. I had wrapped Lucetta's quilt around me.

The view from my room encompassed the brown hills, the vast Pacific, the rooftops of Laguna Beach and the quiet triangle of garden that contained the marble woman.

The downpour had transformed her pool into a cauldron. She smiled her perfect smile, scattered her petals from her outstretched hand. Around her, dark green hedges formed a rectangular maze. In the rain, the flowers were shades darker. The russet stone of Candlesage was darker too. A silent crow flew from one statue to another before swerving to miss the formidable walls of Candlesage.

I saw movement in the shrubbery. Bits and pieces of color appeared and reappeared. Children were causing the flashes of movement. They were skipping near a low brick wall. It was raining but the children's clothes appeared to be dry. What were they doing in the garden at Candlesage? The little girl's hair was blue-black. It swam freely over her white print dress and over the butterfly bow of her starched white pinafore. The boy's hair was the color of straw. He wore short pants and a white shirt with long sleeves. They looked as if they were from a different age. The girl tossed a small daisy at the boy and ran behind the marble woman, peeking out from behind the low wall of her pool. The boy found her, took her hand and led her to the cauldron. He pointed to the water and spoke to her. She leaned forward and peered into the pool.

I murmured to an empty room, "She'll fall in and catch cold . . . poor things. Someone should find their mother." I pressed my hands against the window glass.

I began to worry. They hadn't left the pool. It was pouring rain, yet they were dressed for Victorian-age sunshine. The little girl's hair was dry, but surely it was an optical illusion.

There was a knock at my door. It was Hitchins with a terrycloth robe and a tray of sandwiches and tea.

Relieved, I said quickly, "Thank goodness, Hitchins. There are children in the garden—the little girl and boy. It's raining harder."

He set the tray on a table and blankly looked at me. "Mrs. Brighton?"

"The children," I pointed toward the window. "They're playing outside in this dreadful weather—dressed like summer. Their mother should be told. Come here and look," I said, drawing him to the window. "Down there, near the statue in the maze."

But they were gone. Hitchins and I looked at each other. "She must have called them in to the party," I said absently.

"Yes, of course," Hitchins nodded, rocking on his heels.

"Thank you for the tray," I said, dismissing him.

He sucked in his cheeks and departed.

I swallowed the aspirin that had been placed on the tray and then pressed my fingers to my temples. My head throbbed with pain. Steam curled up from the Spode teapot on the gallery tray. It smelled of cinnamon. I poured myself a cup, took off my clothes and slipped into the thick white robe that Mo provided. It was cold in the room in spite of the soft, luxurious upholstery and the dark wainscoting. The fireplace was clean and there was no wood in the bin nearby. I tried not to think of the children in the rain. All children reminded me of Shea. Those children are not your responsibility, I told myself. But still, I crossed to the window and looked down on the maze. I saw a flash of the girl's blue-black hair flutter near a hedge. Where had she gone? *Behind a stone arch with green gates.* The same green gates that Andreas had appeared in front of this morning in my bedroom. Where was this place? Then I heard giggling, faintly at first, then louder. The girl's laughter and then the boy's. It became intertwined, reverberating loudly.

"Angelica," the little boy called.

"Andreas, I'm over here," she replied merrily.

I dropped the white cup. Tea splattered over the pale rose-dappled carpet. The cup bounced to the wall and quartered itself into neat pieces. I quickly locked the shutters over the windows. Something had to be done. Lucetta, I thought. I would call Lucetta . . . she could help me.

I fell across the bed, reached for the phone and dialed the number on the matchbook. It was the restaurant. "Lucetta, please."

"She's in the kitchen," the man sighed.

"It's important—very important."

"It always is," he said. "I'll get her." I listened to chattering voices, clanking dishes while I waited.

"This is Lucetta."

"Lucetta, this is Paige Brighton. I was in your restaurant this morning and I—"

"Yes, Paige, how are you feeling?"

I said, "I have your quilt . . . I need to return it, but the truth is, I need to talk to someone." I looked toward the window. "I don't know what's happening to me. Lucetta, I don't think I'm crazy but I'm thinking maybe I might talk with you. If you could—" I paused. "Nothing this strange has ever happened to me. I'm in Laguna Beach. I'd be willing to pay . . . ."

She laughed. "We'll worry about that later. I live in Newport but I'd be more than happy to come down to Laguna. Depending on traffic, I could make it by around three."

I gave her directions. As I hung up the receiver, the telephone rang. Hitchins knocked at the door. I answered it.

"That would be Mrs. Fishbein on the telephone for you, Mrs. Brighton. We took the liberty of giving her your private number." An armload of wood rested cumbersomely against his black coat. "Dr. Carmichael asked that I make a fire in your room."

"I'd like to take this call now. Will you come back in a few minutes?"

He put the wood down. "I've spoken to Dr. Carmichael about the—the children." His eyes expanded dramatically.

And now Neil would be up to inquire. There were no children at Candlesage. *But there were children in the shadow world behind the green gates.* The phone stopped ringing. Marla had given up. Hitchins' eyes rotated to the window and then dropped to the floor, noticing the stained carpet and broken cup.

"I can't imagine how I dropped my tea," I offered. "I'm afraid it's an awful mess."

He nodded. "I'll send up Lulu."

The phone began ringing again. "Thank you, Hitchins."

Appropriately dismissed, he pivoted on this capped heels and left the room quickly.

I grabbed the phone, "Marla."

"I've been worried sick about you. How are you?"

I relaxed against the pillow taking a deep breath. "Not well, I'm afraid."

"Does anyone know what's wrong? You really gave me a scare when your face hit the table."

"Is that what I did?"

"You mean you don't know?" She puffed on a cigarette.

"Are you smoking?"

"Sorry. I'll snuff it out right now. I promise. I haven't had one for a week but today my nerves are raw."

"What did I do at breakfast?" I asked.

"Well, Neil and I were talking and you weren't doing much of anything, just gazing out the window like you often do. I tried to get your attention but Neil shushed me up. You were really pale. Then Neil asked if you were okay. You began hyperventilating or something. We couldn't make out what you were saying. You were crying or shouting but it was all muddled. Then you keeled smack over. Not an attractive fall, Paige. You were almost convulsing. It sure as hell scared us. But how are you now? What does Neil say? If you don't talk to him about this then you'd better talk to someone. It could be diabetes, or a stroke, God forbid, epilepsy and who knows what all . . . and another reason I phoned was that you seemed in a hurry about that twig you gave me. I took it to LaVonne and she says it's from a Monterey Cypress tree. There aren't any here. Where did you get it? She says they grow mostly up the coast toward Big Sur and Monterey. You know—up north." I heard her inhaling smoke.

Up north. Then that's where I can find Andreas.

"Paige? I said, where did you get it anyway?"

I answered weakly, "Believe me, it's a long story. Someday I'll tell you."

"I wish I could talk more but this is the worst damn day of my life. I've got to schlep home and assault the party planners. Now, try to make it tonight if you can. Anything else I can do?"

"No thanks, Marla. I'll see you tonight early. There are some things I have to talk over with Vincent. He's meeting me at your place later."

"*Hasta luego*," she said. "Call me if you need anything."

As I showered I thought of every possible way a twig of Monterey Cypress could have appeared in my bedroom. If Andreas were a "ghost," how could he have left something tangible in my room?

There was something else about his visit that puzzled me. The man in the sea storm, Andreas, felt different from the man who appeared in my bedroom and yet I knew they were one and the same. And the little Andreas playing in the garden maze near the marble woman, that Andreas evoked still another emotion.

As I had watched little Angelica darting in and out of the dark shrubbery surrounding the phantom green gates I became a little child again. I, too, had adored the little Andreas with the golden hair. For an instant, I felt what she was feeling. Had I gone even farther back than the sea storm? Each Andreas was a part of me, from whichever life those aspects of him were emerging. How many Angelicas were there?

The warm shower water was not helping. I decided to shampoo my hair and try to relieve the throbbing pain from the knot on my forehead.

When I finished, I wrapped a towel around my head, slipped back into my robe and went to the phone to dial Aunt Belle.

Someone knocked at the door. It was Lulu with a small bucket of cleaning solution, towels and brushes. She nodded, her bright eyes searching the floor. "Not a problem. I know exactly how to deal with tea."

"Thank you," I said meekly. "Over there, by the window and against the wall. I hope the stain hasn't set."

She hurried across the carpet, her long black braid swinging heavily down her back. It was a thick, glossy plait that probably had not been cut in her life. She kneeled, her white embroidered blouse brushing the rose carpet. Her short legs folded up under her, disappearing. As she scrubbed back and forth, her braid swung spasmodically, its tail end teasing the edge of a scarlet rose entwined in the carpet pattern. Hypnotically, it swung over the sea of roses.

My flesh began to tingle; it was a prickly feeling that began in my chest and spread over my shoulders. My head was bursting with pain. My vision began to blur. *She was no longer Lulu.* I stumbled against a table. She looked up at me. Her face was ashen, bloated. Her eyes bulged from her face. Her throat was slit; dark red blood gushed from her alabaster skin. Her tongue thrust out; her eyes rolled back into her head until they were white, bloodless spheres. *She was dead.* Someone had killed her.

I backed away from her and ran to the door. Before I could get away, I collided with someone. *Andreas.* My arms fell over his shoulders, my face into his soft sweater.

But it was not Andreas. I asked deliriously, "Why are you here? *He* was with me, not you . . . not you." My fingers pulled at his sweater. He led me to the bed and I sank into the down comforter.

It was Neil.

Chapter Six

In a matter of moments, the lines of the room had come into focus and my thoughts were coherent. Neil was seated on the bed next to me, a steely look in his eyes. He was being paternal again, mistaking my revelation for weakness. I could see what he was thinking: nervous breakdown. If I were to argue with him that would cinch his theory. People often defend themselves against the truth. I told myself not to be defensive, to take the path of least resistance.

"I'm sorry," I smiled.

That seemed to be what he needed. He returned the smile slowly, ready to get on with the "session."

"How do you feel?" He took my hand and held it between his fingers.

"Better," I said. Why can't you love him the way he wants you to? I asked myself. In so many ways he was the perfect man for me.

"Good. Paige—why did you faint?"

"Because I was frightened." I answered honestly. "I saw something."

"What did you see?"

"I thought I saw—" Was it safe to tell the truth here? Would he think me as crazy as Simone? "A dead Chinese man." I paused. "Lulu changed all of a sudden. One minute she was normal and the next I thought she was a man with a—someone had cut his throat." I had seen it happen before. It was too familiar. I had seen a Chinese man die in that other life. My fingers began to crease the pillow case hem. I expected to see the petals in the print bleed. I pulled my hands away and sat up. "I'll apologize to Lulu."

"We need to talk about Shea, Paige." He looked gentle yet resolved.

Please . . . not Shea, I thought.

"Tell me about his death. You were alone with him when he died?"

I could see where he was taking this. "I was always alone with Shea. That's what happens when you have a child whose death is predicted at birth. No one can live through the pain but his mother."

"You were alone with him in the hospital?"

The words carried a note of demand, less sympathetic than the concerned look on his face. "Yes. I was alone with him. The doctors had just told me that he would live a few more days at most, perhaps only hours. He was in pain. I went in to see him and minutes later he stopped breathing . . . he died." I didn't take my eyes off Neil's. I met them square on. Don't you dare, I thought. This isn't your business. Shea and I belonged to no one but each other.

My antagonism must have shown. He changed his strategy. "What made you decide to leave Vincent today?"

"The maple tree, the one over the deck. I asked for a sign. It dropped a leaf. Is that crazy enough for you? I bet you just adore how very insane that sounds—leaving my fate to a deciduous tree in fall."

"I've heard crazier. What do *you* think, Paige?"

"That something is happening to me, that I'm hallucinating. Probably because I'm afraid of—"

"Of what?"

"Of Vincent," I lied. "But maybe it isn't Vincent. I'm not sure of anything, Neil, not any more. It could have been some other unresolved issue in my life. Like not crying when I was three years old and my father put on his buffalo plaid coat and smashed brown hat, and soft-shoed out the door of my life. He was going to the liquor store. He said he'd get me a Coke—and he never came back. I didn't repress it, though. I did not shove it back into my unconscious so that I could hallucinate about it someday, like now. I never cried because his presence in my life didn't matter. I missed the smashed brown hat more than I did him. I used it for dress-up games."

"I see," was all he said. That was the problem with knowing a psychiatrist in professional mode. They never let on what they're thinking. Neil, sans the doctorate, would have been honest, would have come right out and told me I was crazy.

"You may not have missed your father. But you did miss your mother."

"Yes. That was later, though. I had a close relationship with her. Then she died."

"How'd she die, Paige?"

"For God's sake, Neil, you know how she died. Why are you asking me?" I was angry.

He said, "*You* told me she had cancer. Your *aunt* said she killed herself."

"Both," I said, indulging him. "I was sixteen years old and I was at school reading in an essay competition. A neighbor phoned the school and I went home. I got there at the same time the police and ambulance did. While they were carrying out her body, the phone rang. It was the school congratulating me for having won the contest. My mother's limp arms dangled off the stretcher as they carried her out the door. At that very moment the English teacher on the phone had told me I could be another Katherine Anne Porter. I decided never to read Porter's books. I still haven't. I don't want to know what I missed. I mourned losing my mother. But trust me that I didn't keep it inside waiting for it to reappear today."

Neil waited for me to finish my justification.

I said, "My mother had terminal cancer. She didn't want chemotherapy or surgery. Maybe Belle would say she killed herself. She was a proud woman who wanted to die in her own way. Maybe it was her Indian blood. She was part Cherokee. Her great-grandmother walked the Trail of Tears. But you know all of this, Neil. What are you fishing for?"

He was looking for an obvious reason for my "mental collapse." Maybe he thought my troubles were the result of a culmination of all of the above. He was very disturbed by my actions. There was a slight wince in his grey eyes that always appeared when he was dissatisfied.

"I've called Belle," he said. "I explained everything. I told her that the two of you would be staying at Candlesage. I've already sent the gardener over with the truck. They should be returning shortly."

Neil's hands had enclosed mine. I traced the vein on the back of his hand with my finger. It ran almost to his watchband. "I've always loved your hands," I said. But I thought of the hand in my bedroom that morning, Andreas' hand, reaching toward me, urging me to leave my bed and follow him. Then I raised my hand and touched the scar on his face. "I'm so sorry, Neil."

"Paige," Neil said. His voice had the inflection of a lover's. Andreas had not called me Paige. But he would. And Vincent . . . Vincent had called me a great many things . . . .

I said, "It's probably about leaving Vincent. One holiday season I dreamed that his mother Dorothy gave me a twinkling Advent calendar decorated with exquisite holiday scenes. You know, the little numbered doors leading to Christmas. In the dream, Shea and I opened the little doors one by one expecting to see the usual red and green surprises. But there weren't any sugarplums or Stars of David. Behind every flap was Vincent's drunken head wreathed in holly . . . grinning."

Neil's hand tightened on mine. "That's over now. You are free to remarry. Have other children."

"When Shea died, I didn't have anyone to love. People go mad from not loving more often than not being loved." Neil's hand loosened. My words had hurt him. He was thinking, *Why didn't you give your love to me. I was there waiting for you.*

I quickly added, "But that's behind me too. Right now I have to think of Marla's party, and what I'm going to say to Vincent."

"Phone him."

"I need to do it in person. What can happen at a party?"

"Promise me something, then," he said, "When you get ready to tell him, let me know. I want to be within view. He's capable of anything. What happens when you turn on him? There will be nothing intelligent or predictable about your divorce from him. And frankly, in your state of mind—"

"I won't drive. I'll take a cab."

"I don't have a good feeling about this."

"Don't tell me you believe in intuition?"

"Of course I do. We can't explain everything." He stood up, reluctant to leave.

I did love him in a way. But I thought it was a kind of love that existed for itself. A physical relationship as such was not required. I could love him from a distance, and wanted to. But . . . wasn't that what I'd always done?

"My Halloween costume is in the car."

"I'll have the costume brought up." He started to leave.

As his hand touched the knob, I said, " Lucetta, you know, from the restaurant, will be coming by to pick up her quilt. I'd like to see her before she goes."

He wanted to protest, but nodded silently as he closed the door behind him.

I sat up in bed taking the towel from my damp hair. Under the window, across the large garden-colored room, the tea stain was gone from the carpet. Its print was slightly marred by Lulu's brisk scrubbing. The Ionian clock, which ruled the mantel, ticked softly upon curved gold legs. The dark day, raining still, loomed beyond the shutters at the leaded windows. And below me in the bold and beautiful fortress I could hear occasional laughter as the ladies had tea.

I was intrigued by the vision of the Chinese man. I felt instinctively that it had been a replay, an incident that we— Angelica and Andreas—had experienced together at another time. Somehow I knew I had turned away and expected to be comforted by Andreas just as I had been once before. And I felt calm, as if I were coming to terms with this mystifying situation. It was more seductive than eerie.

I closed my eyes, hoping to sleep, but instead drifted in and out of consciousness. One moment I was in a dreamy, golden state, and in the next I was aware of the room around me. I dreamed I was in school. I had liked to play chess, but in this particular fantasy game my moves were careless: white queen trapped pitifully in king's castle one, adjacent to two black pawns.

A black castle and bishop blocked them. All I had left was a knight alone and he could not save me. The queen's timing had been off, her movements thoughtless and naive. "Shah mat, Shah mat"—chess' antiquated cry of defeat—echoed repeatedly through the dream in a loud, crushing voice. When the end came, when the pawn closed in, the vast board slanted across my field of vision. I watched terrified as the stunned white queen rolled over and over—eyes wild, mouth gaping, octagonal crown clacking past the black and white squares and into the wooden box. It was a desecration. The proud lady would share a common grave with the two pawns who had ruined her life.

Chapter Seven

*L*ife can't be measured by what happens in the end but by the process and by intention," Lucetta pronounced in a rich contralto, her hands forming a slow, careful circle in the air.

The afternoon was cold and dark. We had turned on the bedside lamps. Lucetta's hands made shadows on the walls and an echo sprung from the ancient bell-like tone in her deep rhythmic voice. "Even measurement," she continued, caressing the African amber beads around her neck like a rosary, "is ludicrous. Life isn't linear, Paige. There is only the eternal and measureless."

It was not the answer to the question that I had asked as we greeted each other warmly at the door. After Hitchins had shown her in, she tossed her shawl onto a striped silk chair by the hearth and sat down. I asked simply, "What do you think is wrong with me?" When she answered so enigmatically, I felt stupid and uninformed, while she, draped in a flowing caftan, was statuesque and as adept as Athena herself.

She flashed a smile.

"I don't know what you're talking about," I said sitting in the matching chair opposite her.

Her grin widened. "You know very well what I am talking about, Paige Brighton. You understand perfectly, or we wouldn't be here together, you and I. Nothing in this universe is accidental."

She breathed deeply, her hands tracing the air around me. "Can you feel it? The silence that makes us one? Can you feel the energy? Yours, mine, theirs . . . ."

"Whose?" I asked, swallowing hard.

"Those who might be sharing this space with us." Her lips curved knowingly, the beautiful skin of her face glistened in the lamplight.

"Maybe that's where we should start," I said tentatively. "I just need information—or maybe understanding is a better word."

She nodded approvingly. "You see, Paige, you already know the difference. Information? I don't think so." Her voice deepened. "Oh yes, I know, I know," she closed her eyes and spoke beatifically. "Information might be necessary to get us through our everyday lives but understanding is the quintessential—"

I interrupted, "Lucetta, please, I don't want a magic show. I'm scared. And I know that if I listen to you much longer I'll be terrified because I don't know enough not to be. I don't know what's going to happen to me if I don't get some answers."

She smiled, "To you, your problem is more important than the reason you have one. Tell me about it," she said, leaning back into her chair.

"Until this morning I've never really had any, I don't like the word 'occult' but I guess it applies, I've never had any occult experiences. But this morning at dawn a figure appeared in my bedroom from nowhere in a cloud of light, in front of green gates. That's all I saw. He called me by the name 'Angelica.' It isn't my name and yet—somehow I know that, well, it *is* my name . . . or once was. He held out his arm to me and wanted me to go with him. I spoke to him. I said something like, 'We were both young.' I don't know why I said it. I haven't been the same since. It was frightening and calming all at once, and I choked or something and made him leave. I think I said, 'You'll hurt me again.'" I shrugged. "He disappeared, just vanished. When he left I felt like my insides were being torn from me. I don't like this feeling that I'm not in control. And then, at breakfast this morning, when you helped me, I had been staring out to sea when suddenly I was out there, in a boat, in a storm. I was a young woman and I was dying. He was with me. I called him Andreas."

I explained the dream. I told her about the children that I saw in the garden by the marble woman and I told her about the murdered Chinese man. By the time I had finished my voice had dropped to a whisper. Lucetta's eyes widened and narrowed as I spoke but other than that she had been perfectly still. Now she leaned forward intently as I took the amulet from around my neck and handed it to her.

"If it weren't for this, the cypress needles in this amulet, I would really think I am crazy. Andreas left a footprint on my robe. These needles were imbedded in it."

Her fingers enclosed the silver-chased amulet. She dangled it from its heavy chain. Pendulum-like, it swung in the dim room, snapping up what little light there was. With a long scarlet nail, she flipped open the catch. She let it swing until it stopped of its own accord. She gathered it in the palm of her hand and returned it to me, pressing my hand upon it.

With a long, audible sigh, all the breath leaving her body, she said, "You've crossed over, honey."

I drew back, completely ignorant of what she meant.

"Don't be afraid, Paige. Be careful."

"Crossed over?" I asked.

"Another life. It happens spontaneously, randomly sometimes." Her face, her body relaxed as if she had solved yet another of many psychic misadventures.

"How? Why?" I asked.

Lucetta shrugged, resuming a soft-shouldered posture in the chair. The amber beads wove through her fingers like a snake. The silver pyramids dangling from her ears rotated slowly.

I crossed the room to the window and looked out, wondering why people always went to windows when they were troubled. "The children in the garden," I said, "were Angelica and Andreas. The woman on the boat *was* Angelica as a young woman and the murdered Chinese man was something I experienced with Andreas during that life."

"The memories don't always come in logical order. You often remember karmic experiences or occurrences that happened *then* but influence something that is happening *now*. Those experiences might be revealed in dreams, or expressed in your preferences, in likes and dislikes, strengths and weaknesses. Sometimes the memories come when we're off guard, or begin to clarify our lives. They're more likely when we happen to be suffering."

"Suffering . . . ." I almost brought up Vincent but instead said, "This morning when Andreas came to me, I got the feeling that he wasn't just a memory. I felt like he was alive now, in this life. It was a different sensation from the other . . . visions. Does that make any sense?"

She smiled, "As much sense as anything has to. Several things could be happening," she offered, raising a long regal finger.

It had begun to rain again. I looked out the window and thought of the children in the garden, innocent, faithful. I had to know what happened to Angelica and Andreas as they grew older.

She said, "He could be from your other life, this man at dawn. He could be from a third, a totally different life, one about which you know nothing. Or, Paige, it could simply be a thought formation. That is, an image with no reality, or rather no identity. An entity created by someone's imagination. The mind is creative. It can create out of nothing. If you think a thought long enough, or, in this case, if you think an image long enough, it can develop—like a drawing can develop or a sculpture, or a melody can develop. It is real but it has no life. It is our sixth sense working."

"That's ridiculous. It may be true but that is not what's happening here. I know it. I can feel it. *He is real*."

Her eyes widened. "Explore, Paige. Learn. Trust me. A thought formation," she emphasized, "may float around until it is drawn to the energy that attracts it. Like a magnet. Andreas could be your own creation, your own thought formation or whatever. Maybe he's someone else's and you've drawn him to you for who knows what reason. A lonely woman might attract an Adonis thought formation, like a religious person might attract a saint. A thought formation doesn't have to make sense. Your imagination will fuel it." She closed her eyes again. When she opened them they appeared brighter.

She shrugged. "Well, maybe he is real. He could be from a former life. Maybe he's come to you from a life you haven't yet lived, come back from the future."

I asked desperately, "How do I know?"

She didn't answer. She was perfectly still, her hands intertwined in her lap.

I returned to the chair and leaned toward her. "You're *not* finished, Lucetta!"

"Listen, Paige, you've got work to do. You must let go of this Andreas if all he's doing is causing you problems."

I snapped, "I have never let go of Andreas and I never will." What was I saying? I spoke the words before I thought them out. Was it true that I had never released him? Lucetta stared at me. Neil had tried to take Andreas from me and now Lucetta was telling me to let him go. I stood up.

"Sit down," she said.

Commanded, I folded my legs under me and sank to the floor.

"Listen to me," she ordered, her eyes shifting momentarily toward the windows pelted by rain. "We are all of us energy. Know this. Our energy relates to other energy, and because it's all coming from the same source, all energy responds to all energy. We're here to learn, Paige. We live, and we learn. Each time the lessons are different. Everyone has something different to learn and sometimes to teach. We are spirits who incarnate in groups. And people who are together for a lot of lifetimes are what we call soul mates. We do our 'work,' that is, we learn our lessons from our soul mates. Then there are twin souls . . . ." She paused and looked at me sympathetically. "Twin souls are the same soul—divided. It's the most powerful connection in the universe." Her eyebrows drew together, causing her eyes to change shape. "They've got strong bonds, and are drawn together, their energy merging explosively."

Lucetta's palms were rubbing against her knees. Was *she* nervous?

She continued, "However, if your lesson, Paige, is to learn how to be unattached, selfless, or something like that, you mustn't get sidetracked."

"But it's like we're pulled toward each other, as though we cannot help ourselves," I tried to explain.

She whispered not to me but to the room, "Then maybe, and baby, it's a *big* maybe—maybe you and Andreas were born together at the creation, lights in the darkness, morning stars, two halves of the same whole, one male, one female, separated and now drawn to each other . . . beyond your power to resist . . . ." Her voice had fallen into a hypnotic rhythm.

"Yes," I said emphatically. "That's what it's like. I feel that we made a pact. We are souls who agreed to meet in another life, this life." I stood up and returned to the window. I knew the answer and she knew that I knew. "Andreas and I made a pact and it's now fulfilling itself. We're drawing closer to one another. I know it. I can feel it." I broke away from the window and hurried to her side. "Oh Lucetta, I know that it's true."

"Then you *will* find each other in this life, not as apparitions, but as Paige and—whoever he now is. A florist, a banker, a cabby . . . who knows? And you will have each other *or else*." She stood up rather ceremoniously, putting her beads in order.

"You're not leaving are you?" I asked. "I need to find him."

"Paige, you need to search on your own. There are a lot of paths to the truth. Choose the one that'll work for you. Meditate. Clarify. Let go. Only you can do it, not me. And if Andreas is your twin soul, believe me, you *will* come together in good time."

"But how?" I begged. "How can I call him back to me? I need to know when we lived before and where. *When I find him in this life, will he know me?* Will he remember our past life together? Will he feel what I feel?"

"Maybe yes, maybe no. He will feel something: deja vu, a touch of yearning, a chill up the spine. Who knows what form the awareness will take? Whether he recognizes you as his twin soul or soul mate depends on his intention, what the two of you agreed to on the other side for your personal growth this time around. If the man who appeared to you this morning is alive right now, like you he should be aware of you to the same degree that you're aware of him. He could be searching for you just like you're searching for him." She chuckled and shook her head. "But then he might just be a lil' ole thought formation. You never know." She picked up her shawl and threw it over her shoulders. "Paige," she said, "sometimes this kind of regression gets dangerous. It has become my personal policy never, never to return to a former life. I think we have to deal with the life we have now, keep in the present moment. After all, that *is* why we're here and why we don't remember everything from our former lives. It would be too confusing, as you can see."

She beamed like a teacher who has been on the path herself and knows too well the delights and dangers. "If you wander too far or too deep, you won't be coming back. People have died for less, Paige Brighton."

I handed her the quilt.

Chapter Eight

Aunt Belle arrived. Battered boxes, clanking trunks and bulging suitcases thudded along the corridors and staircases of Candlesage with the subtlety of a freight train. She even whistled like a churlish old engine.

"Sound like the old 5:04?" she asked, her head popping through the door, followed by suitcases exploding into the room, shattering my reverie.

She looked appreciatively at the fire in the hearth. "It's freezing on the stairs," she said. Stepping over her cases, she plopped down in the chair Lucetta had recently occupied. "I have to tell you, sweetie, how happy I am that you're here with Neil." She looked toward the entrance to the room and winked. "Well, here he is! Just look at that handsome devil."

I turned toward the door expecting to see Neil, but instead found handsome Chester sprinting in, head low and stretched toward Aunt Belle. Chester mewed like a cheap squeak toy and pounced on Aunt Belle's lap, kneading her thigh with his curved claws.

"Neil took care of everything," she said, her hands comforting the haughty feline. "I'm supposed to stay in the Paul something room. And who the hell is this Ed Hopper guy, anyway?" she said, not looking in the direction of his painting. "Isn't he that guy that rode around the country on motorcycles with Peter Fonda?" She groped around in her purse for one of her unfiltered Camels and furrowed her brow. "No, that wasn't him. Damn, can't recall . . . ." She finally found a cigarette stub and stuck it to the inside of her lower lip. It dangled and bobbed as she spoke. "I've got it!" She was triumphant. "Ed was Hedda Hopper's son, that guy on Perry Mason! Wow, I didn't know that Mo knew him, and I sure as hell didn't know he could paint." She lit the cigarette butt and marveled at the work of art across the room. Seeing my expression, she stole a quick puff before snuffing it out in a thimble.

I heard the welcome noise of her luggage being installed in the Paul Klee room next door.

"You know, Paige, I almost left Vincent a note on the chalkboard in the kitchen. But I honestly couldn't think of a polite way of saying goodbye to that worthless son-of-a-rhymes-with-itch. So do you know what I did? I took that damned chalkboard and stuffed it into my purse. I figured there weren't gonna be any more messages on it. Not ever again." She sighed happily.

Toward the end, that chalkboard was all that Vincent and I had: mundane scribbles on department store slate, a thousand messages, nearly all that passed between us lay turned to white dust in the slot beneath.

"Have you heard the news?" she asked.

"What news, and by the way, Aunt Belle, please don't smoke at Candlesage."

"The gardener Aurelio told me on the way over," she said, putting the cigarette to her mouth for affect.

"Told you what?" I asked.

"Well, you know that—" she leaned closer to me, her voice dropping to a whisper. It always did that when she thought she was saying something important. "You know that Neil is in the top ten in California . . . money."

"That isn't news," I said. "You know how I hate to talk about people's money."

"Just lemme finish," she snapped. "Well, Odette—you know my friend Odette—she reads all those magazines, like *Fortune,* and all. She said this morning there was an article on Neil, about how he was contributing a lot of money to some East Coast senator's campaign fund. Now let me remember his name—"

Wouldn't she ever just go into her own room? I said dryly, "You know I'm apolitical."

"I know, I know. You got that way when you managed that bookstore. I can't remember his name just now—Nolt? No, that's not it. Dolt? Ha! That's funny—Dolt. Can you imagine anyone voting for a Dolt? On second thought . . . his name is Long-one— no wait—Langston. Yes, that's it. Langston Something-olt. Anyway, Aurelio said that this Langston Something-olt is coming here to Candlesage next week. He'll be staying the weekend. They think he'll be nominated for vice president. That's what Neil hopes at least, in the next election. You know, I've always had a thing for politicians. That LBJ used to send me through the roof. Something about that Texas accent. So gritty . . . so . . . ." She caught her breath and looked at me. "Isn't that exciting?"

"Not particularly, since we aren't going to be here then."

"What do you mean 'not gonna be here'? We're leaving? We won't be meeting the Senator?"

"Aunt Belle, we need to get settled in our own place. Staying on at Candlesage won't help."

"Oh come on, Paige, Odette says that he's gonna win the

nomination because he's so tall and so blonde and has these hypnotic blue eyes. And you know, Paige, Odette is usually right."

I stood up. "I think I'll try to do something with my hair. I have to leave for Marla's party in an hour and a half. Is that my makeup?" I picked up the bag off the floor. "Why don't you and Chester go get settled in your room?"

She looked crestfallen as she shuffled for the door, grumbling under her breath. "His eyes are bluer than Paul Newman's," she mumbled. "That's what *People* magazine says."

"I'm sure they are," I said, rummaging through my overnight bag for a brush and hair spray, deliberately not looking at my aunt. I felt suffocated by the small talk.

Finally she moved to the hall with Chester in her arms, who was gloating over what he thought was my loss and his win. "By the way," Aunt Belle said over her shoulder, "Did you ever figure out who you *saw* this morning? You know, the ghost?"

"No," I said, exasperated.

"I worried about it all day, Paige. I thought that maybe Vincent was playing some gruesome trick on you. I mean it *is* Halloween. After the sock incident last year I wouldn't put anything past that moldering bast—you remember. Insulting you by throwing his unmatched socks around the room in front of everyone like, as Marla said, a dethroned sock designer king . . . . Well, gotta go."

I relaxed when I heard her door shut. I put another log on the fire. From the window, the ocean looked like crumpled steel. In the sky, here and there, blue chips flecked behind the black clouds. The storm was breaking up just in time for sunset. I was happy for the children who would be trick-or-treating that night.

I opened the boxes and peeled the plastic cocoons from the hangers with my costume, and tried to enter into the festive spirit.

I dreaded the party. I dreaded the costume, even though it

hadn't seemed like a bad idea six weeks ago, when summer was still in the air, and I needed to recreate myself into something fantastically romantic in order to stave off the reality of my dissolving marriage.

But I had to go. I had to get it over with Vincent.

The dress was fussy. The white silk was scattered with green silk leaves that swirled up from the hem in circles, drawing itself up to my shoulders in a boa. The tufts of green silk were dotted with spring wildflowers of Aunt Belle's choosing: tulips, daisies, poppies and violets. A cluster of morning glories and sweet william with yard-long ribbons was made for my hair, which I had dutifully piled high on my head, as the costumer had insisted at the last fitting. There were matching shoes, which looked ridiculous in size nine-and-a-half. The dress, once worn in an opera, had been altered to our specifications. I had no one to blame but myself, I thought, wincing at my reflection in the mirror. But the longer I stared the more I liked the image. I looked like a young person who still believed in magic. The dress had the power to edit reality, if any dress could: Romance in the face of devastation.

And then I thought of Angelica dying in her tattered white gown.

Aunt Belle whirled into the room, declaring "You look like you haven't a problem in the world."

"Don't believe it," I groused.

"You look too beautiful to be troubled, that's the problem with pretty girls. No one takes them seriously."

I accepted the matching cape from her outstretched arms. "Let's go downstairs."

I might have known Neil would dress as Robin Hood. He stood with his mother in the library, leaning against the hearth.

Mo exclaimed, "Why, Paige, how enchanting."

"Thank you," I answered, feeling my lips tighten. They were not aware that before long, I would make a stealthy exit from their lives. The double masquerade made it worse. The sweeter I looked, the more deceptive I felt. I steadied myself and said in a silvery voice, "Neil couldn't have chosen a better costume for himself."

"It was sister Glynis' idea," he shrugged. "Archie wore it last year."

"But the crossbow is real," Mo put in. "It belonged to some forebear or another, I don't remember who. Now, let's have a little glass of wine before you two are off. And Neil, see what we can do about another log on the hearth." But as he poured the wine, Mo grabbed an ornate poker herself, jabbing at the crumbling wood. It metamorphosed into hissing orange ash.

I was aware of Aunt Belle coming into the room behind me, and of Mo saying something about Senator Langston Holt. My head began to pound. The books on the library wall—there were thousands—began to swirl as if in a vortex. My heart raced and my vision blurred. Tossing something into the fire . . . yes, she was. She turned around and sneered at me, her face white against a black brocade gown, her pale eyes mocking me triumphantly. No. I could not let her burn the letter. "Don't, Isabel!" I cried out. I stumbled toward her, upsetting a table and lamp. I grabbed her thin wrist. It twisted easily but still she laughed at me, her high-pitched giggle filling the black crepe-shrouded parlor. "The letter," I said, "give it to me, Isabel, or I swear I'll kill you!" I twisted her arm behind her back. She tried to wrench free. I pried her hand open but it was empty.

The room was hazy. Once again it was Neil's arms that caught me as I collapsed into a chair.

"Paige, stop it," he said, "Get hold of yourself."

I could barely discern the sound of his words. I said, "I don't know why—I'm so sorry. I couldn't let Isabel burn the letter. I—I did it to save Andreas."

Neil said nothing, just stared at me. I was hearing voices and it alarmed him. Could he understand what I said? Then I heard Mo's voice.

"My God Neil, she attacked me."

I saw her hunched over by the mantel, Aunt Belle and Hitchins helping her into a chair.

I dropped my face into my hands. They were cold and numb. "Oh God Mo, I'm sorry. I don't know what happened—nothing's clear to me right now. I thought—I thought you were someone else."

Aunt Belle handed Mo her wine. She gulped it down, then stood slowly and said, "I think I need to get this wrist on ice." Hitchins helped her to the door. She turned back toward us, face rigid, and said in a scathing tone, "This will never happen again."

When they had all left (Aunt Belle salvaging the lamp and table on the way out) I managed to say, "I know what you're thinking, Neil."

"Don't be ridiculous." He knelt next to me, needing to compose himself as well. "The issue is, what are *you* thinking?"

"Will your mother ever forgive me?" I asked, my hands trembling.

"Of course," he said, trying to be casual. "Mother doesn't hold grudges and she needs her dramas as much as anyone. It will provide her endless fascinating phone chats."

I thought of how happy Mo would be when I left Candlesage. But my appalling behavior had in no way diminished Neil's fervor. On the contrary, the incident had given his grey eyes a bright sheen. Under the dark green cap, his skin was flushed. Did he think I was another Simone? Was he gathering clues? And . . . could he be onto something?

"I can't explain what happened."

He nodded, saying tenderly, "I know."

"I think that once tonight is over and once I've told Vincent, things will be easier." I stood up, nervously straightening Persephone's dress.

He rose. "I'll send Belle over in a cab with you—along for the ride, so to speak. You shouldn't be alone. You might—" he didn't finish his thought.

Might what? I thought. Kill myself? He called a cab from the phone on the library desk, exchanging his crossbow for a telephone receiver. He fit the Robin Hood persona so well I wondered if he were not his incarnation. Giving, always giving. He did not make any inquiries about this latest "hallucination." Hadn't he heard me say Andreas' name? Surely he must have wondered.

He hung up the receiver and crossed the room to me, taking my shoulders in his hands. "Somewhere within you there is a Persephone. I've seen her." His hands slipped behind my back. His warm lips touched my cheek, then my mouth.

I found myself kissing Neil.

And Neil did know how to kiss.

Chapter Nine

Obviously I had no integrity. Why else would I have lapsed into kissing Neil in the library? I was simply allowing him to do it, I decided. My response had simply been a kindness.

Aunt Belle, hunched in the corner of the cab with Chester in her lap, chided, "Stop pulling at the flowers on your dress."

"I didn't know I was," I said absently. We were halfway to Marla's and Aunt Belle had not spoken a word about my attack on Mo. She was afraid to ask. For whatever reason it had occurred, it threatened her security. The wrinkles in her brow which had earlier that day shot off in hopeful new directions sank back into their furrows as she glowered at me.

"I'm sorry about what happened," I offered. "I can't explain it. I just want you to know that I'm not crazy."

A "humph" boiled up from her and she turned away to gaze out at the black night.

I had no clue what I had done. As Mo had stood at the

fireplace she had become someone else, someone named Isabel. In an instant one reality had become another. Angelica—for that is who I had become—had to prevent Isabel from destroying the letter because of Andreas. I had to save Andreas from something.

Aunt Belle growled, "You're going to have that dress in shreds if you don't stop clawing at those flowers. Honestly, you're worse than Chester."

I retorted, "That cat has gotten so fat! Why don't you try fixing him for a change instead of me."

Chester opened his eyes. Food was at stake.

She asked, "What are you going to say to that bast—to Vincent?"

"I don't know."

"Is he wearing a costume?" she asked. "He need only go as himself to spook everyone."

"I don't know what he planned. I never asked." I folded my hands in my lap and let my thumbnails dig into the flesh of my palms.

Yellow headlight beams, flashing signals and shop windows competed for attention along the dark road. The cabby was chewing gum. The meter clicked rhythmically through our silence. Outside I saw a cluster of trick-or-treaters dashing up a tiny porch to a front door.

When we pulled up to Marla's house, Aunt Belle relented and gave me a mournful smile, signaling that she forgave me but would not pander to any more mysterious demonstrations. Both she and Neil, it appeared, understood that they would not know everything for awhile. I leaned to kiss her pancaked cheek, patted Chester and climbed out of the cab. "See you later, Belle."

At first glance, as I stood in the drive, the stars seemed brighter than usual, chunks of glitz strewn against the heavens. I might have found the moon if Marla had not come dashing out of her house, down the long driveway, shouting, "Thank God you've come early. How are you?"

I answered, "Under the circumstances, remarkable." Marla was dressed as a black-sequined cat. The body sock, skin tight, made her lithesome body look dipped in oil. Cat ears sparkled above her platinum hair, blowing seductively in the light autumn wind. "I'll give Chester your number," I mumbled, straightening her ears.

"And look at you!" She touched my arm and turned me around. "You must be a princess."

"It's that bad, huh?"

"*Bad*? It's divine. You don't look a day over twenty-nine."

"Do you need me to help?" I asked.

She grabbed my hand and led me up to the house. The front facade was a long curve of travertine marble that shot up in front of the house's lower roofline. A glass door in the center led to a garden entrance filled with orchids. The house had appeared in *Architectural Digest* the year before. Marla was reluctant to change even one silk pillow that was not displayed in the double spread of her living room. White over-stuffed furniture, fields of reflective surfaces, dimly lit alcoves and towering green-black plants existed serenely in the enormous room against the lush sound of a waterfall. The passage to the master suite was a glass bridge over a pool in which playful Koi darted back and forth. Harbor lights twinkled beyond the large windows and the scent of the ocean found a way through the wall of doors that opened to it.

Halloween stuffed, dangled and draped itself in every niche, from every overhead fixture and on all surfaces.

"I want you to be my taster," she said, weaving me through a group of servers. "Eugene likes the quiche. I say it stinks. And those canapés outside on the terrace are going to sog out on me,

I just know it. Sometimes I hate living on the bay. Oh, I'm so damned selfish. I want to know if you've recovered."

I took a piece of quiche from her. "I've made a decision, finally. I'm telling Vincent I want a divorce—tonight."

She grabbed my chiffon sleeve with her black claw-like nails. Her eyes bulged out. "Oh my God, you're kidding. You're joking."

"No," I said, tasting the quiche. "Eugene is right. The quiche is wonderful."

"*Here?* At my party? There won't be a scene I hope. On second thought that might be interesting." Her claws released my arm and she embraced me saying, "Oh Paige, I'm so proud of you. We'll make it a star-studded scene. We'll all throw him into that vat of dry ice. It'll be great fun." She released me. "He will make trouble you know," she said, eyebrow and lip raising toward one of her spangled black ears. "Eugene won't believe it! Eugene! Eugene!" She dragged me toward her husband. "Honey, guess what is happening tonight!"

Eugene called back, "I *should* know. I *am* paying for it."

"Not the party, dummy! It's Paige. She's asking Vincent for a divorce—"

I corrected her. "*Telling* Vincent."

Eugene emerged from the hallway, a very slick red devil with a stiff tail, which was lit on the end. It was definitely him.

"Good God," he exclaimed to me. "Venus? Aphrodite? The Love of My Life?"

Marla sighed, "Oh stop it Eugene. Paige is asking Vincent for a divorce tonight. Right here."

"Christ," he said, "I hope there's no bloodshed. I only carry a four million dollar liability. He's such a greedy son-of-a-bitch, he'll sue me for at least nine."

Eugene's hair was slick and black and looked more sculpted

than usual. His eyes were beetleish and the skin around them openly confessed of a million scotch-and-waters. He was soft and sweet, the way those men are when they are rich and they like you. Dangling in his hands was a red devil headpiece. He leaned toward me and planted a kiss on my cheek. "You can handle it, angel eyes. I always told Marla that you had more guts than either she or Neil suspected."

Marla looked at me slyly. "And this news certainly explains your little fainting spell this morning." She clapped her hands together. "Well now, this calls for champagne." She called to the bartender, "Douglas!" Then to me, "What did Neil say? I'll bet you had to nail his shoes to the floor."

Eugene added, "Among other things."

Marla snapped, "Oh shut up, Eugene! We haven't got much time to talk. Now, Paige, you'll stay in our guesthouse until you've found one, won't she, Eugene? And Eugene will have our man Wally—it is Wally Ramsey now, isn't it?—handle everything, won't you, Eugene?"

I said, "I'm staying at Neil's. I promised."

Marla bit her lip in ecstasy. "Even more cause for celebration. Oh Paige, I'm so happy for you two."

Eugene's eyes traveled up and down the white dress as if reading a road map. "He's a lucky guy."

"Please don't misunderstand," I said peevishly. "I'm really not sure about what's going to happen next. I know that everyone thinks . . . ." I wanted to scream, *will everyone quit planning for me! I know who I want.* It was like loving the hero in a book. You cannot prove that he's real but you know him so well and wish it so ardently that he must be. "I know that Neil and I have given the impression . . . ." I said to Marla and Eugene as they finished their champagne and waited receptively for something consequential to pass my lips. "Not to worry," I said. The

Fishbeins emoted a simultaneous sigh.

Marla asked, "Do you know when Vincent will be here?"

Eugene said, "I hope he doesn't show up soused. If he is, you better wait until morning. Vincent doesn't like to lose."

"No. I have to do it tonight. It's important to me."

"She's right," Marla said to Eugene, holding her empty glass upside down at arm's length. She was handed another.

The doorbell rang. In mock exasperation, Marla threw her hands in the air. "I don't know why it is you don't have a crisis when I have the time for one." As she walked toward the door she asked, "What is Vincent wearing—no, don't tell me. He's coming as Bambi." She swung open the door for an unlikely pair of guests: Marie Antoinette and a man in a gigantic bucket labeled "Sheep Dip."

The shredded melodies of the combo warming up could be heard throughout the house. As I drifted out onto the terrace to check the table they began to play "Green Dolphin Street."

I leaned on the railing hoping to witness the reflective shimmer of moonlight on the dark bay. But the only lights emanating from the other side of the water, gold and bright, looked as if they had dripped into the sea. Lustrous streaks quivered on the water's surface. I could see people moving in front of their windows on the other side. Black silhouettes and gold light, as vivid as a monarch butterfly's wing.

I felt dead and cold inside. It was what I used to feel when I thought of Shea, what I felt as recently as this morning when Angelica's hand had slipped from the boat railing, when Mo— *Isabel*—had tried to destroy the letter. Perhaps I doubted that I would be able to find Andreas, for since his parting this morning I had had the sensation of being locked in a crypt without even a hint of how to escape.

Maybe that's why I had kissed Neil. I needed to furnish the

emptiness with something warm and safe.

Neil's blind date was an attractive freckled woman my age who was dressed as a French maid. I had the fleeting thought that Neil might marry her after I had gone from his life. He found me behind a palm tree and said, "Remember your promise. The minute Vincent arrives, find me—*then* tell him."

But I did not.

My husband arrived at a little after nine. He crept up behind me and startled me as I stood on the terrace. He was a hangman, a medieval executioner. And he was drunk.

"What're you doing out here?"

"Stargazing. Vincent, we have to talk. I have some very important things to tell you."

"Not now," he said. "I have to get another drink." He pulled off his black hood. His face and neck were flushed, his forehead was sweaty. His eyes had that drunk, unoccupied look that still had the power to make my heart freeze.

"It can't wait," I said. "Let's go into Marla's bedroom to talk. There won't be anyone in there."

We passed over the glass bridge into the massive suite of rooms. The round bed on an elevated platform dominated the room. Puffy white silk furniture piped with black was accented by pieces in lipstick red. It was as Marlaesque as anything gets.

We faced each other in the middle of the room. Perhaps he sensed what I was going to say. His mouth was open, his stance—hands on hips, feet spread apart—was the aggressive body language that at one time would have shut me up.

"Well, what is it?" he asked.

"I want a divorce." My lips quivered. Every muscle in my body tensed. But I had actually said it.

He smirked and swayed. "What the hell does that mean?"

"I don't want to be married to you anymore. There's nothing

left for either of us. You know it as well as I, Vincent. I have tried everything that I know of, before and since Shea's death. It's not good for either of us . . . this relationship."

"Shea—he should have never been born," he stammered.

"Please let's not. Shea is not the issue. I've had some things moved out of the house. I won't be returning. I'm contacting a lawyer Monday morning. And I would—I just hope more than anything that we can end it amicably."

"You're not walking out on me."

"I left the house this morning. I'll never go back."

"What do you have, Paige? Some boyfriend?"

"No, Vincent. I don't conduct my life the way you do."

"You think you can just take a hike? Just like that? Well, you have the wrong guy. A boyfriend? Is it Neil, Paige? You're not going to cost me one dime. I'll see you starve in the streets and if that doesn't work, I know people. They owe me favors. I could have you taken care of, Paige, you know that, don't you? You know what I'm saying. You're not worth a damn anyway. Everyone knows you couldn't even have a normal kid."

He began to walk toward me. I thought he would hit me and so I prepared myself for the strike. It was a small price to pay for freedom. But instead, he grabbed my wrist and twisted my arm until I heard myself scream. He forced me down onto the bed, bent my arm behind me, ripping the delicate sleeve from the beautiful Persephone. The pain was excruciating. He muffled my cries by placing his fleshy mouth upon mine. I tried to get out from under him but the sharp pain in my shoulder shot through me. I thought I would vomit. He was panting. Sweat from his forehead trickled over my cheek. I felt his other black-gloved hand reach for the top of the dress, ripping it open down the front. "Get off of me, Vincent!" I yelled. He bit me. He reached for my hair and jerked it. I could hear it pulling out of my scalp. I involuntarily cried out but I could not tell if my voice was making noise. The last thing I remember was his hand ripping at my skirt and his bloated, grinning face.

In an instant I found myself in a different world.

. . . Spots of brilliant gold and periwinkle dappled against a soft green landscape. And above the green was a bar of wild blue sky. My canary yellow dress swished across the meadow as I danced under the shade of my parasol. I tossed it into the air. It stayed stretched taut then landed gently near a clump of wild lupine. I ran through sprinkles of golden poppies to retrieve it.

Nearby live oaks grew with thick limbs twisted and bent. In one of the oaks, Andreas sat staring toward the sky, his long muscular legs propped on a limb. He wore a straw boater tilted back from his profile, a profile that looked perfectly carved against the massive tree.

He called to me, "Angelica, we have to get back."

"Only a moment more," I said skipping farther away. "There are a million monarchs in the meadow today," I said. "Look, Andreas, can you see them all?" The gold and black flecks fluttered against the sky like tattered paper. As I approached a shoulder-high manzanita bush, the branches trembled and the butterflies gaily floated into the air.

"We'll be late," he said, holding up his hands but not moving otherwise. "If you're late to the Chautauqua again, I'll never hear the end of it from your Aunt Marion."

"Who cares? I'm seventeen and you are twenty-one. And besides, they think I'm with Diana. I lied to them."

"But they'll be waiting all the same," he said, dropping from the tree limb, brushing off his breeches. "And you should not lie, Angelica."

"Do I ever do what Aunt Marion says?"

"Almost never."

"Then I shall not today either." I kneeled behind the manzanita bush. "You'll have to find me!" I called.

He was poised on the tree limb, hands on hips, silhouette merged into the dark twists of the oaks. "And if I do?"

I stood up. "I'm over here. And I won't leave this field until you kiss me." I hoped I looked as beautiful as I felt. I had tied a yellow satin ribbon into my waist-length black hair that morning before Andreas had picked me up in Knute's carriage. I had tied the knot loosely because I planned for it to fall into the grass. I wanted my hair to be undone because that is the way Andreas liked it. He never touched me when my hair was loose because he said he was not sure if he would be able to stop. And, for the first time, now he would not stop.

He walked toward me. It was a distinctive swagger that identified him throughout our seaside town. A mile away people could tell it was Andreas. "Like he owns the walkways," Uncle Robin always said grudgingly.

As he came closer I pretended I was a statue.

His blonde hair was the color of straw, his skin brown from working in his mother's garden and his eyes the same blue that is found at the heart of a flame.

I waited breathlessly as I watched him approach, my heart beating three times for every long stride he took. Why was he walking so slowly? Did he know too? We were always reading each other's thoughts. It frightened Aunt Marion because, she said, God-fearing people were not given that gift.

My legs weakened. A wisp of hair freed itself of the yellow ribbon. It blew across my eyelashes.

He was so close to me now that the sky and the field had disappeared. He stooped to pick up my parasol.

"You dropped it," he said.

"Leave it," I whispered.

The parasol dropped from his hand. He lifted the straw boater off his head and flung it into the air. We watched it until it was gone from our view, had incorporated itself into the warm spring landscape. I pulled the yellow ribbon from my hair.

He turned to me, taking my hand in his. He kissed it. He spoke, reciting Shelley,

"The fountains of our deepest life, shall be
Confused in Passion's golden purity,
As mountain-springs under the morning sun.
We shall become the same, we shall be one
Spirit within two frames, oh! wherefore two?
One passion in twin-hearts, which grows and grew
Till like two meteors of expanding flame
Those spheres instinct with it become the same . . .
But its reward is in the world divine
Which, if not here, it builds beyond the grave."

His fingers touched the buttons of my yellow dress. Soon the dress slipped easily from my shoulders and lay spread in the tender, sunstruck grass like another person.

Our kiss was long and slow and deep. And I felt our bodies being freed from years of imprisonment, as if my heart had broken open at last.

. . . Which, if not here, it builds beyond the grave . . . .

Chapter Ten

*N*ot him.

Was I speaking or thinking the words? I whimpered, "Oh God, my arm."

"It's okay, darling," Marla said. "Your arm is going to be fine."

Was it foggy in the room? "It hurts. What happened to me? Where's Andreas?"

"Vincent tried to rape you, that's what happened. But you're all right. You're just fine, Paige."

My eyes opened. "Where are we?"

"In the guest cottage," Marla said. "We moved you in here. Hush now." She leaned from her chair and took my hand.

"We're here at the party . . . ."

"Yes, the damn party's still raging on. It's such a success that nobody's leaving. Neil and Eugene strong-armed Vincent into the front drive and are waiting quietly, *I hope*, for the police. You're going to have to press charges. But we'll worry about that tomorrow."

"I told Vincent, didn't I? Yes. He threw me on the bed, now I remember. He tore up Persephone's dress. But where is *he*?"

"Going to jail, I pray to God."

"Not him, not Vincent. Andreas, where is he?"

She said, "Did I invite an Andreas? I wouldn't put it past me. Last year I invited well-dressed, nameless people I met on the street. Paige, as soon as Neil comes back he's going to give you something for the pain. Thank God he hasn't forgotten what he learned as an intern. How do you feel?"

I looked up at her. Her sparkling cat ears had slid to the left side of her head. The only color on her lips was the pencil line that framed them. "I feel like I've been brought back from the grave." I tried to sit up but a jolt of pain seared down my arm and across my back. I fell against the pillow.

Marla ripped off her ears and threw them on the floor. "It breaks my heart! I hope to hell he gets five to ten on the hard rock pile. But you can just bet he won't. There're too many men on the bench."

I closed my eyes. "I was dreaming . . . but no, Marla, it wasn't a dream, you've got to believe me. It was real." Waking up toward the end of the twentieth century seemed absolutely incongruous. I wanted to go back. "I can't remember being brought in here," I said to Marla.

"Of course not! Let me tell you what happened. About thirty minutes ago, Neil found me and asked if I'd seen you. I hadn't. He said that he'd seen Vincent come in but that he couldn't find him either. He was afraid that you'd gone off with him. I told him that you wouldn't be that stupid but he said you would be—sorry. So we started to look for you. We ran into my bedroom and there you were. Your dress was torn to ribbons, Vincent had your arm bent back behind you and was— well, it's a damn good thing I don't keep a loaded gun in the house or I would have shot off his—"

She took a deep breath and put her hand gently on my arm, "You're lucky you passed out on him. There's one *little point* worth gloating over—he was too drunk to do anything, but then, what else is new? Anyway, Neil was right behind me, grabbed Vincent and threw him on the floor. Neil actually kicked him in the face, genteel Neil brutalizing the beast. I covered you and ran to get Eugene. Then Neil checked your pulse and examined your eyes. He thinks a muscle could be torn in your arm but he'll have to have an MRI done."

She paused and leaned closely to me. "Paige. Are you alive? Can you hear me?"

"Yes," I murmured, opening my eyes. "Of course I'm alive."

She continued. "Vincent was out cold on the floor for a few moments and in comes Eugene, sees what's gone on and *he* kicks Vincent in the ribs, and says 'I've always wanted to do that.' Then Eugene called the police from the bedroom phone. He told him that a drunk husband had battered his wife and to send up a car, no sirens please, that they'd be waiting in the drive. Eugene knows all the cops around here. He actually tied Vincent's hands together with the belt from my Dior robe! It doesn't look like I'll ever get it back. Not that I care about that, it's just the idea of having that wonderful champagne-colored silk sash wrapped around the sweaty paws of that animal—not animal, they're too kind . . . creature. My robe sash going to jail with Vincent Brighton. It makes me ill. And imagine Eugene actually tying someone up. Anyway, my party's such a damn success that nobody's the wiser. What did they care if a stiff little devil was kicking a hangman out the door of the Fishbeins' under the watchful eye of Robin Hood? Makes me wonder what kind of people I know, to tell you the truth."

She shook her head from side to side and took my hand in

hers. "You're the most challenging friend I've ever had, Paige Brighton! Just please don't be a life-long project! I don't know how many times I can save you from yourself."

I asked, "Did I say anything while I was unconscious?"

She shook her head again. Marla looked old and wilted. "Just mumbling incoherently. When I covered you with this blanket, you smiled, which I thought was sort of strange. And another thing. Just a couple of minutes before you came back from the dead your eyes opened and stared a hole through the ceiling. It scared the hell out of me. You actually looked dead. But you also looked young, you know, like dead people do, like all the worry had gone out of your face. You know I don't know a thing about pulses, except that we're all supposed to have one. I decided to check yours because I felt I had to do something. Your heart was racing. I thought maybe you were having a heart attack. What's wrong?"

"Just my shoulder. I won't try to move it." As I spoke, she watched the door nervously. Marla Fishbein was ill suited for the role of Florence Nightingale. She was terrified of tragedy. To her problems were parasitical in nature. One was never challenged by a problem, one was devoured by it. Real problems, when they belonged to others, were to be avoided; when they were Marla's, they were to be ignored or indulged, depending on the circumstances. I knew she would babble mindlessly until Neil returned.

There was pain in my arm and my shoulder. My eye felt swollen. The sensations gripped me at intervals as if something raw were being pulled through me. But the loss of that spring day in the field with Andreas made Vincent's attack insignificant. If I could just get *that* back, that moment—that feeling.

Marla said, "You're not crying, are you?"

"No." I swallowed the tears. I hoped Neil would come back and give me something for sleep. Yes, even drugs, if they would return me to that perfect meadow.

Marla's guesthouse was a quaint counterpoint to everything else in her life. It was warm and woody and filled with fairy tale antiques. The bed I lay in was hand painted turn-of-the-century Swiss. I had helped her choose it a couple of years ago. There were Shaker chairs around an early American oak table and white embroidered curtains trimmed in handmade antique lace. Danish tiles depicting the stories of Hans Christian Anderson bordered the hearth opening. Tin toys of every style and shape paraded along the fireplace mantle and over the shelves framing it. She had given the room everything she would have given a child, if she had decided to have one.

The cottage door opened. Neil, still decked out as Robin Hood, carried his briefcase in his hand.

Marla jumped up, sighed deeply and grabbed her cat ears off the floor. "Her shoulder's killing her," she said.

Neil sat on the edge of the bed saying to Marla, "You'd better go back in. We don't want anyone coming out here looking for you."

She nodded and was nearly successful at trying to look reluctant.

When she had gone he relaxed and looked at me, scolding me with his eyes. Hadn't he told me not to be alone with Vincent? Hadn't he been right again?

I said, "You can say it. You can say 'I told you so.'"

"I will not. I think you learned the lesson. Right now," he said, opening his briefcase, "I have to ask you a few questions. You have bites on you. Are your tetanus shots current?"

It did not seem right that I should be embarrassed about what was *done to me*. They say victims always feel guilty. Duly humiliated, I told him that my tetanus shots were up to date. It was a lie.

"How bad is your shoulder? Can you move it?"

"Not really. It hurts when I try."

Neil was so clinical that he could have been a stranger in service in the emergency ward of the hospital. But I sensed that once outside the door of the guest cottage under the curved lantern from the Cotswolds, Robin Hood, the doctor, would crumble.

"You also have a black eye, you know."

"Marla spared me that detail." What difference did it make now? Andreas was the one person I cared about seeing and he would not see me, not as Paige Brighton, anyway. But as Angelica . . . .

Neil took my hand in his, the same hand Marla had held. "I don't see any point in moving you right now. I think you should spend the night here. I've phoned Belle at Candlesage and she's coming over to be with you. In the morning we'll take you over to Dr. Davis' office and have your arm checked. In the meantime, I've called a lawyer. I honestly don't think they can hold Vincent even if you press charges. But we can get a restraining order, I can hire a bodyguard and maybe there'll be a hearing. We'll have to just wait and see. Right now, I'll give you something for the pain, and something to help you sleep." He produced the pills and got the water from the kitchen. After I had taken them he said quietly, "You need to rest, Paige, for longer than you'll probably want to. After Senator Holt's visit I was thinking that we could go over to the cottage in Scotland for a month or two, just you and I. You've never been there but it's the most perfect place on earth. You don't have to answer now, just think about it."

I closed my eyes whispering, "I will."

Chapter Eleven

Pacific Grove, 1906

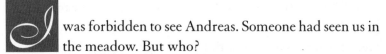 was forbidden to see Andreas. Someone had seen us in the meadow. But who?

Someone could have been in the field that day flying a kite. Some child may have been gathering wild flowers to press in her book, or a young boy exploring with a butterfly net.

Then I remembered that the Ladies Ornithological Society had their outings on Thursday afternoons. Colonel Roberson and Mr. Rollo Beck would march into the fields followed by a group of dour matrons in their picnic clothes, equipped with long black binoculars searching for goldfinches and vagrant warblers. My body went rigid at the thought of the Ladies Ornithological Society focusing en masse upon Andreas and myself in the grass near the manzanita bush. I will be the scandal of Pacific Grove!

But the birdwatchers could not have seen us clearly and reported their "sighting." Otherwise Uncle Robin would have done a great deal more than just forbid my seeing Andreas. He would surely send me away if he knew I had had the kind of carnal relations to which Aunt Marion often alluded.

Outside the gulls were screeching. I went to my third-story bedroom window, opened the sash and searched the dark, brooding bay that lapped the shores in front of our home. For as long as I could remember I had looked out at the bay, waiting for it to deliver the answers to the questions I asked. Surely, I thought, I was the bay's most patient supplicant. Why had Uncle Robin forbidden me to see Andreas? How would I meet him today as promised? Lie to them?

I slammed down the sash and drew the curtains closed. The cream and violet flowered wallpaper became cheerless in the shadows. The fringes on the table scarves flapped as I gave the velvet drapery a final jerk.

I fell onto the bed. Three whole days. I buried my face in a pillow. It was a lifetime! And I have not seen my dearest since he slipped the yellow dress back onto my shoulders so gently, not since he carried me to the big black oak tree, sat me on a crooked limb, got on his hands and knees and pledged with his hand over his heart to love me forever, to love me beyond time itself. Not since he slipped his grandfather's ring from his finger onto mine, and announced his intentions to a party of wild purple irises who nodded their assent. I had not seen him since he walked me to the front of my house and escorted me up the steps to the broad porch.

He had kissed my gloved hand at the door. I could swear his lips burned through the white glove and onto my flesh. I was so certain that I could not wait to tear the glove off so that I might see the shape of his lips branded forever on my hand.

Three long days. And yesterday . . . the scene in the morning room when Uncle Robin called me in and suggested that I should not see Andreas before he returned to Harvard. But he won't be returning to Harvard until early autumn, I told Uncle Robin, and Uncle Robin said that perhaps I should end my association with him altogether. I had stamped my foot, actually bruising it through my cloth slippers. His suggestions quickly became hissed commands. His brown eyes had squinted to the size of peas, the sharp brown mustache above his round mouth twittered.

I ran out of the morning room convulsed in tears. It was the first time I had ever hated my uncle. He had, after all, taken me in when my mother and father died in the terrible fire fourteen years ago. I had been just two years old when it happened. Before the ashes had cooled, Aunt Marion, my mother's sister, had come by train to San Francisco to fetch me from Cousin Dixie. I was so frightened, yet she never comforted me. How I will always remember Aunt Marion never touching me unless she had to. Then I had been embraced by a young boy six years old who was named Andreas, with a mother named Signe and a father named Knute. He picked me up and hugged me so thoroughly that everyone laughed. At that moment he became my protector. Forever.

What was I to do about the promise Andreas and I had made to meet in the butterfly trees in the woods outside of town? Aunt Marion was watching the doors in the house like a sentinel while Uncle Robin, one of our town's two doctors, scraped back his receding brown hair and tiptoed with his black bag down the steps toward his office. I would have to get a message to Andreas soon. I would meet him tonight while the house was asleep. Perhaps Theda would carry a message for me. She often went into town in the afternoons for Aunt Marion.

I rustled myself off the bed and tugged the tapestry bell pull. I paced the floor until a quiet knock sounded at the door. But it was not Theda. It was my little cousin Phoebe whose face displayed a piqued anxiousness as she guarded something behind her back. Her head nodded forward and released bright red pigtails that swung over her shoulders like tether ropes. Phoebe was eight years old, the same age I had been when she was miraculously born to Uncle Robin and Aunt Marion. I had hugged and held her a great deal when she was younger because I so needed to give what I had not had. Her feet turned inward and she rotated the tip of one shoe indicating that she had something important to say.

"What is it, dear Phoebe?"

"Virgie Orwell—" she bit her lip with the one remaining front tooth. "Oh, this news will not sit well with you, dearest Angelica."

"Oh, do tell me," I stammered, my agitation reawakened by her long pause. Her nose was wrinkled, her forehead made furrows on her freckled skin. She was a theatrical little pixie. I knew that she spoke the truth.

"What is it, Phoebe?" If it had to do with the Orwells, it was bad news. There was nothing good about Virgie, Luther or Isabel. More gently I asked, "Did Virgie do something? Here, come into my room." I drew her in and closed the door.

She burst out, "Oh Angelica! Virgie gave me this!" From behind her pink dress she thrust out Andreas' straw boater. "Virgie said somebody found it three days ago in the high field, someone who was there."

"Who?" I asked, taking the hat, which I had not seen since Andreas pulled it from his golden hair and tossed it against the sky. My hand went to the lace at my throat.

Phoebe stammered, "Virgie said to give it to you. Then he said to tell you that someone you know had followed you up there. Virgie said to tell you that somebody knows." She gulped as she watched me sink into the fireside chair. "This is a bad portent, isn't it, Angelica? Has Virgie done something dreadful?

Is this why Papa forbade you to see Andreas?"

"I was in the field with Andreas and he—he—kissed me."

"Does Papa know?" Phoebe asked timidly, her pale skin flushing.

"I think Uncle Robin must have heard rumors. I don't know. Oh God, I don't know. But he knows that I'm in love with Andreas and he knows that Andreas and I want to be married. But everyone's always understood that."

She brought her pink hands together at her chin. "Oh, isn't it wonderful. I'll be an auntie or something." But suddenly her bright smile faded and she got that far away, much older look in her eyes, the frozen stare that signaled insight. She believed that angels spoke to her.

"What is it, Phoebe?"

She shook it away with a slight shudder. "Mama and Papa wouldn't understand about the kissing. They're too old. Why, I'll bet they have never even kissed."

"But of course they have, silly, or you would not have been born." I took the hat from her and slipped it under the bed. "This is our hiding place, Phoebe. Theda has just done the room and so she won't be cleaning for a few days. Now, come here and sit down while I write a message to Andreas. I must tell him about the hat, mustn't I?"

"Of course," she nodded eagerly while I sat at the French secretary by the window. "I'll take a message to Andreas." She sprang from the chair, and running to the bed, leaped into it. The feather bedding all but swallowed her. "This is such fun, isn't it, to be in love?" she stated dreamily into the flower-sprinkled wall. "I wonder who *I'll* marry."

I laid down my pen, turning to her. "Love has no right to be as confusing as it is. Conventions enslave us on the one hand and passion on the other. I must be a fool."

"Not you! You are no one's fool."

"I shall address that comment and then I *must* finish this letter. School, Phoebe, has taught me almost nothing, nor have my aunt and uncle. There," I pointed out the window, plunging my arm into the bracing sea air. "Those gulls cry like something born of my soul, I've been living with them so long. In the few times I left this town as a child I was frightened by the silence of other places. Where were the gulls? Had they died? I have learned more by watching them, by observing the birds and the whales in the bay and the wildlife in the sea, forests and ponds than in all the answers I've got from mankind or in all the books that I've read. If you want to be wise you must think yourself back to nature. You must watch the birds and stare at the big open places, like the bay or the meadows or the mountaintops down the coast—and the sky. That's what I've done. That is where you will find volumes of unprinted words that come from nature, which is, after all, the mother and father of us all. It makes sense, doesn't it? Doesn't it?"

"Yes! And I do! I do just as you say. That is why you and Andreas and his Cousin Diana are the most gifted people I know!"

I sighed and shook my head. Phoebe would jump from Kissing Rock into the sea if I asked her to.

My dearest Andreas,

We cannot meet this afternoon for Uncle Robin forbids it. He says that I am not to see you privately again. Therefore, meet me at midnight instead, at the butterfly trees, for we need to make plans. I am also deeply concerned about another matter. Apparently Virgie Orwell was in the field that afternoon and has delivered your hat by way of Cousin Phoebe with an abhorrent message that indicates he may have been privy to more than just a sailing hat. I miss you terribly and

*ask that you speak to Uncle Robin immediately as regards
our future. I cannot bear to think of life without you.*

*Your dearest love,
Angelica*

I sealed the letter with a drop of wax and sprinkled it with perfume. Phoebe waited impatiently on the bed for the letter. "Phoebe, come here," I said.

She marched forward, soldier to centurion.

I placed the large white envelope in her small pink hand. "This, Phoebe, is my heart," I announced somberly. "I have entrusted it to you. If you should lose this, then I shall perish."

Her eyes shone. "Oh Angelica, how beautiful."

"If you deliver it safely to Andreas then you will have delivered my heart to the one I love. And we shall live happily ever after. Raise your right hand."

"I swear I will deliver it."

"Thank you, little Mercury." I bent down and took her shoulders in my hands. "He will be at the Sparring Construction office on Lighthouse." I paused, brushing a strand of orange hair off her forehead. "You know, Phoebe, you are going to be a wise and great beauty with a special gift for seeing into life." I took her into my arms. She returned the hug.

"And what of your life?" Phoebe asked thoughtfully.

"I shall marry Andreas. He is all that I have ever wanted, all that I shall ever want. We will grow old and die together. That is what I want but you—" she looked at me wistfully as I spoke "—you will accomplish important things. You were made for the world. I was made for Andreas."

"Yes, Angelica, I do believe you are." She walked toward the door.

"Phoebe," I called after her, "you have my heart!"

Her high-pitched hummingbird voice became leaden. "Oh yes, Angelica. I know, I know."

When she had gone, I succumbed to my terror. I felt like a rag doll whose stuffing had been picked away bit by bit. The Orwells! Why were such people born? Their subversive evil was a grand argument against the existence of God. For when hadn't the Orwells plotted to undermine my life? Could I recall a time in my youth when I was not threatened by some unctuous black deed of theirs? The devil could only say which was the worst— the pale, whining, thin-lipped Isabel who had always wanted Andreas; or Luther, scrubby and big and fat, who used to follow me home from school and grab me off the paths and pull me into the bushes, who leered from street corners, schoolroom desks and church pews? Or little Virgil who, under their tutelage, promised to be the greatest scalawag of all of them?

Oh no, I would not let them do this to me. You are not a rag doll, Angelica. Get up, get out of the chair. You are young and you are strong and you will have what you want. Let the Orwells be the ones to perish!

Chapter Twelve

When Aunt Marion's hand timidly knocked at my door I knew that I would have to talk my way out of appearing at the dinner table. It was twilight. Fog had descended, evincing, as always, its domination over the peninsula. But where was Phoebe at this hour? Surely she had run the errand, returned and simply neglected to report back to me. We had not planned a later meeting.

"Oh my dear, my dear," Aunt Marion gushed, sweeping into my room as if she were made not of flesh under the taffeta, but of more taffeta. She closed the window I had just opened and drew the draperies over it. She lit the lamps, flitting from one to the other like a shiny green moth. And she was wearing that strange Oriental belt that one of her friends had purchased in the Chinese village. It was quite a departure from her normally predictable retiring clothing. She wore it like a souvenir of something that never happened. Red dragons spit fire over her round abdomen. No wonder she had intestinal difficulties. Oh, but do be fair, Angelica, I told myself. She is as fascinating as her life has allowed her to be.

Wringing her hands, she said, "I'm dreadfully sorry about yesterday. I know you've had a case of nerves from it. Haven't you, my dear?"

"I wish it weren't so, that it could be written off that easily."

"Come dear, come and sit down and let me brush your hair."

I sat on the dressing table bench. Was she actually going to tell me what had happened that had caused Uncle Robin to become so changed?

We faced the mirror, her image speaking to mine. As she stroked my hair with the silver brush from Cousin Dixie in San Francisco, I examined her familiar face. The skin never moved, only the lips had motion when she spoke and her eyes skittered around in their sockets as if being chased. At times a hint of red struggled to shine out from the flat brown of her hair. But the red would always disappear before I had the chance to validate it.

She began, "You mustn't blame Uncle Robin, dear." Then drawing the silver brush from my scalp to my waist she added sweetly, "He only wants what's best for you."

"Andreas is the best thing for me."

"I believed you would marry him. Yes, the thought even crossed my mind the day you met him, after you had come to live with us. He was only six years old. You were two. You met at his birthday party, down at their home, Green Gates. It was Theda who carried you through the stone arch. Andreas fell and skinned his knee as he came running to see the little angel, Angelica, who had been saved from the fire her parents had burned in. Perhaps he was so taken with you because his mother Signe read him fairy tales. To him you were magical, a little fairy graced by God."

"I'm afraid Andreas would take exception to the allegory."

"He thought you belonged to *him*. That's how possessive he became. We began a routine of having our Saturday dinners at Green Gates because his father Knute was designing this house for us, and there were always so many details to discuss. But as time went on and the house was finished, we continued those Saturday dinners. Signe often remarked at how changed Andreas was when he was with you, Angelica. Normally, he was like any other boy his age. He stole his share of candies from the jars at Tuttle's and liked to frog watch at the pond by the dunes. But he was different with you. He watched over you as if he had been appointed your guardian. He followed you about the gardens at Green Gates, helped you when you had fallen, brushed your clothing of soil, retrieved flowers when they fell from your hair—you were always tucking them in there just a little too loosely, my dear. And once, I remember, he washed tears from your face with water from the birdbath. For weeks I thought you might contract some dreadful disease. Uncle Robin, as you know, says one can never be too careful.

"Green Gates, Green Gates. It's not that it is such a grand place. But it was secluded and quiet back then and one could hear only the surf pounding at Moss Beach in the wintertime. Oh, but you know Angelica!

"Signe has always been a wonderful cook and gardener. On those Saturdays we sat on the flagstones under the oaks at her Swedish outdoor table and sipped tea while you and Andreas whiled away the afternoon playing hide and seek all along the stone walls of the garden. The thorns of those exquisite rose bushes tore many a sleeve, many a scratch was doctored.

"I do miss the Green Gates of the old days. The Sparrings have led a quiet life since Andreas left for the university three years ago." Her hand stopped. She laid down the silver brush, taking care to place it exactly where she had found it. Her eyes then searched the room almost as if she were looking for somewhere to hide.

"Green Gates is my memory too, you know," I said as I stood up from the bench and crossed the room to the hearth. With my back turned I said, "Andreas and I have always planned on marriage. Even you and Uncle Robin understood that. What could have possibly happened to change it?"

"There are stories, unsavory stories."

Turning swiftly I asked, "What stories? There are always stories about people like Andreas and like his cousin Diana. Men are jealous of Andreas and women want him."

"My dear!" The handkerchief came out of her Chinese sash and flew up to her nose like a bird.

I continued. "Yes, men are jealous of him and women want him. He seems to generate a passionate response in everyone. And what do people do with this passion that he makes in them? They weave stories with it, the human mind being what it is. Everyone, Aunt Marion, wants a piece of Andreas. It is the same with his cousin Diana. Men fall into an absurd stupor when they see her. You've witnessed this. Those two are revered on the one hand and despised on the other. You say you've heard stories. Well, surely you have! How can you not have?"

"My dear, my dear, I know what you say is true," she cried unexpectedly into the white linen. Tears filled her eyes, yet no sign of sorrow showed on her soft skin, not one line deepened in her face. "Your uncle has heard stories in the past. We *do* know people in Boston, you know. Your uncle's second cousin, William Weaver. Your uncle has magnanimously ignored the stories as rumor. And then there have been times when Andreas is home from school that he has gone into Monterey to . . . *Alvarado Street*. People have reported to your uncle that they have seen him *gambling.*" She choked on the word.

"Twice!" I heard myself shouting at her. "He has gone to Alvarado Street twice and gambled. He told me about it. Once to deliver papers from Sparring Construction to some man from Salinas and the second time he went to help a friend out of trouble and yes, he threw the dice!"

"My dear niece, if that were all."

"There's more? Then let's hear it now." My toe began tapping against the rug, my arms crossed over my chest. There was nothing she could say, that anyone could ever say, that would change my love for Andreas. Gambling indeed! And what did they propose he was up to at Harvard? *Drinking*! Dear God. In Pacific Grove *everything* is forbidden. No spirits. No dancing. No kissing. For years the shades were required by law to stay open at night so that the constable could peer through the windows to be sure that nothing immoral was transpiring. There is even a fence around the town to keep out undesirables! As if everyone outside the Grove were corrupt and everyone inside uncommonly virtuous. Ha! I remember all of us having to sit in absolute silence on Sunday afternoons in horridly uncomfortable chairs in observation of the Sabbath. What Andreas said of the Grove was true. The Pagrovians couldn't find hell and so they invented it!

Calmly I prodded, "You say there's more, so what is there?"

"Three days ago . . ." she began, her white handkerchief pecking at her nose, "when you went to the beach with Diana, you know, the day you missed the Chautauqua because you'd gotten your new yellow dress soiled? Well, Claudia Orwell and her family were picnicking in the high field and Mr. Orwell, being the birdwatcher he is, saw a straw hat go flying. He pursued its point of origination, a manzanita bush. He saw a . . . oh dear Lord, where are my smelling salts? I feel as though I may faint.

He saw a pair of men's trousers coming from round the bush and heard Andreas' voice saying words that you, Angelica are too young to hear, that your Uncle Robin spared me but that indicated that Andreas Sparring had fallen from God's grace. He had chosen another young lady—woman—to marry."

My throat constricted. I murmured, "I see."

She sank into the bed, handkerchief hovering about her eyes. "So you see my dear, it is impossible for you to marry Andreas or for him to marry you. Mr. Orwell had no idea, of course, who the young lady was. One can only assume that she was from some *other* place. Mr. Orwell packed up his family with great speed and they rushed home to pray."

I thought: I'll bet they did. Isabel prayed it would someday be herself behind the bush, Luther prayed that he would find an opportunity to blackmail Andreas, and Virgie prayed that he could force Phoebe into subservience by possession of the hat which he had most likely stolen from his father, the dubious Mr. Phineas Orwell, who had plucked it from the field. My God. Mr. Orwell surely prayed to bear witness once again for a closer look at the "activity" in the brush nearby, and Mrs. Claudia Orwell, the grand swine, prayed that someday Mr. Orwell would whisper those exact words to her. If she only knew what they meant!

"I need to be alone," I said to my aunt, who nodded understandingly and was relieved to depart.

Chapter Thirteen

had the velvet drapery drawn open to permit the moonlight into my room, but beyond the glass panes a dense fog pressed in giving the night a funereal atmosphere. It was just past eleven, and the fog had hung on since afternoon. I felt it had no right to invade the picturesque evenings the Grove had been having lately. But more, I felt discovered, as if God had known my plan to meet Andreas and thought better of the idea. Fog frightened me.

But I had written to Andreas that I would meet him, and fog or no, and Orwells or no, I'd do just that. I lingered at bedside for a moment in order to manufacture the courage that was not answering my summons.

I slipped into a woolen blouse and serge skirt and laced my boots. I threw a black cape over my shoulders and tiptoed down the long maple staircase.

Where was Phoebe? I cursed the fog as I made my way to the front porch. She hadn't come home at all. She'd been invited to dinner at little Victoria Derrough's house and had been asked to stay the night. I had to presume that the message had been delivered to Andreas, or I felt sure she would have tried to get word to me. And if she hadn't? Then I would have lost an hour of sleep and been forced to learn to brave the night fog alone, something I had always promised myself I would do when I had grown up. And hadn't I grown up? Hadn't our moments in the meadow demonstrated that?

The arched door creaked open to reveal a mist so thick that it eclipsed the very darkness of night. Well, at least no one would see me. It was against the law to be out past ten o'clock at night and I did not want to have to answer to the constable. I could not make out the familiar white wicker settee that I knew to be some distance from where I stood on the porch. The stillness was maddening. I strained to hear the surf crashing against the rocks of the bay. But there was not even the meekest gurgle of sea foam upon sand. The wind had been forced into retreat. And it seemed that all other elements of the night, animals grubbing in bushes, owls calling forlornly, a horse's whinny, a bat's flapping wings, had been struck dumb by the pervasive grey mantle of fog.

I closed the door behind me and told myself to think of the warm arms that would encircle me at my destination.

I stumbled into the settee. Its weathered weaving looked skeletal. Bracing myself, I stood tall and walked to the steps as if I had a book on my head. I gripped the railing. I walked several steps from the house, then turned quickly back toward it. I could not see it. Those soft, soft jaws of the mist had devoured it.

I resisted the desire to turn back, for though I had been to the butterfly trees nearly every week of my life, I'd never been at night. Not like this. Would I even be able to find them in the dense woods?

I walked onward and when my shoulders began to droop I marched instead. I liked the sound of my boots striking the earthen path for it was all I had, save my thoughts. The image of Andreas' face brought comfort and beckoned me forth.

The fog lifted slightly and I could discern the shape of a clump of pine trees that were familiar to me. I took a deep breath and pressed on, a solitary figure in black moving further into the fog, using my mind like a compass, counting my steps from the pines for fear that I would miss the woods entirely and end up on someone's doorstep or become lost and wandering until dawn.

I came to what I knew was a crossroads but could see nothing. I halted my crunching steps. The boots were silent. My heart lurched in my chest. I covered it with my fist and tapped against my breastbone. If I was to keep walking straight and my bearings were correct I knew that I would hit a white picket fence. I began to hurry with my arms stretched before me so as not to run headlong into a tree. And when the ground turned smooth and level I knew that I must surely be near Edith Banbury's house. There! Her white fence loomed out of the fog just a few feet in front of me. I laughed with relief. A row of petunia heads sagged through the delicate fencing. For a moment I clutched a picket. I felt as though I were home free from a game of tag. My house was still a good deal closer than the butterfly trees. I could turn around . . . but Andreas! I had to tell him about the hat and that the Orwells had found us out. I had to tell him that he and I would have to make a confession. And then, yes, everyone in town would see to it that we were married. My fingers dropped from Mrs. Banbury's fence. Encouraged by the fact that I would be married within the month, I strode forth.

Mrs. Andreas Sparring, I thought dreamily. He had once told me, "There is a God, Angelica, which lives between the lines in the Bible. This God knows we are bound to one another. It isn't mentioned in any sermon I've ever heard, that garbled balderdash. No, it sleeps silently among the words waiting to be awakened by the truth. It seldom hears it though. It hears the truth in people like us, Angelica. Can't you see it? I used to think that I was the only one who thought this way and that they were evil thoughts, but I've studied enough theology and philosophy at school to tell you that a great many people agree. What a discovery! Others think as I do, as we do. You and I need to leave. We need to live in a place where ideas are exchanged, where thinking on our own is encouraged. Not here. This isn't the place for us anymore. When we get married, we'll go away to somewhere like New York or London or Paris. My French is improving, *ma chere*." He had given me a copy of *Emerson's Essays* then, which I kept hidden at the bottom of a bandbox.

The path was rough with roots and as I walked I saw only an occasional low slung tree branch. They were black scraggles that looked more like thin cracks in the indomitable grey night than the leafless limbs of growing things.

I knew that I was not far from the iron gates of the Orwell mansion. The fog spared me its tall white walls and gabled roofline, which to me had always loomed up from the earth like the planes of Pandora's Box, containing the depraved Orwells. Once I had chased Isabel home and she had scrambled through the front door like a devoured rodent. Why was I chasing her? She had been eight years old and had been hiding in a berry bush waiting to ambush Andreas. She was nearly as old and nearly as tall as he was. But I was with Andreas and when she tried to grab him and kiss him, I shoved her down and she skinned her knee. She was dressed in pink. She always wore pink, and it was always the same shade, like something one might find in a bottle at Tuttle's drugstore. Andreas was angry that I had not let him defend himself but he helped me chase her home.

Later Isabel had gone screaming to Uncle Robin's office on Lighthouse declaring that Andreas had forcibly kissed her and had thrown her down onto a tree stump which was infested with ravenous termites. She kept screaming that the termites were feasting on her abrasion and crawling into her body. No amount of alcohol on the wound would appease her so they had sent for Andreas at Green Gates to receive his testimonial. Andreas told the truth but they believed Isabel. She'd won over him many times, but he always said to me that she was too insignificant to bother about.

Like a grotesque effigy, Isabel Orwell hung in my life. Everyone knew Isabel was the one who started the rumor about Diana Sparring having committed the unspeakable with Royal Shaw. Diana was far too beautiful for Isabel to endure. She was also far too kind to be discredited by a rumor. When that failed Isabel and Luther had drowned Diana's cat named Knickers. All the children knew that Isabel had told Luther to snatch the cat away from Edith Banbury's butter churn where it sat under the tree in spring. The Orwells had killed Diana Sparring's cat but no one's parents took a position on it. Andreas said it was not just because they did not have proof. He had said, "People who live in grand houses, and moralize at the Woman's Christian Temperance Union and wear hats the size of turkey platters to church on Sundays, are not punished because people feel they would lose more than they gained by prosecution and besides nobody wanted to be bothered until it happened to them." Cruelty to animals, Andreas said, is just as immoral as cruelty to people.

Luther never pestered Andreas the way he pestered me. But as we grew older, I knew Luther was constantly watching. In town, he could usually be seen hanging on the barber pole, his huge bulk looking like a canker against the red, white and blue pole. His face was pink and swollen. His hands were round and soft and pocked with dimples. His eyes were flat and shallow like disks. But they were always watching me above a pouting sullen mouth. At my birthday party three years ago, he had tossed a dead squirrel into the ice cream bucket, then run away. He hadn't been invited. Neither had Isabel. Instead of pitying the poor squirrel or pitying me, Aunt Marion had chosen to pity Luther. Such is justice, Andreas had said.

Bony tree branches that walled and canopied the dirt paths signaled the edge of the woods. Thickets abounded in the woods and were veined with thorny scrub and poison oak. Elk and black-tailed deer roamed freely and occasionally a mountain lion prowled for dinner. But not tonight, not in the fog, I prayed.

Strange configurations loomed here and there. I began to walk faster through the dense woods. I stopped. Had I heard something? I listened closely. Surely I was very near our meeting place. I heard a scraping noise. I stopped and drew my cape closely about my shoulders. "Who's there?" I asked softly. "Andreas, is it you?" There was a mad scramble in the bushes. I stifled a cry. Gold eyes glared at me through the fog. I gasped, stepped back and I fell against a twisted cypress trunk.

It was a raccoon. He scurried past me and vanished into a clump of scrub oak. As I caught my breath and struggled up, I had visions of the Lost Maiden appearing to me. She was a popular legend in the Grove, said to roam these very woods. Once a year, if one listened carefully, one could hear hooves thundering through the woods . . . a man riding a wild black horse, searching for his lost maiden, gone long ago. The maiden, it is said, sees her love but he does not see her. She rushes after him and calls his name forlornly but he rides too quickly and the wind and sea drown her voice. In the woods you can hear her plaintive voice. And for the first time, I believed the legend, for had not I, myself, just called out Andreas' name, and was not I just as lost as she?

If I could only find the century-old cypress carved with our initials, I would know exactly how many steps from there to the butterfly trees. If I were to shout, Andreas would hear me but so might someone else, as unlikely as it seemed. What a fool I had been not to ask him to meet me at the thicket across from Kissing Rock.

Moments later, I stumbled into the cypress tree. I reached down its trunk and felt the scars of our initials. My fingers traced the A's carved by Andreas on a brilliant day when he was twelve and I was eight.

We were sitting at the base of the tree, sharing a bright red apple. We had been running through the woods and had flopped down at the tree like boneless creatures, tired and thirsty. Andreas took off his hat and a great red apple tumbled out of it to the ground. We shared it greedily, one slice for him and one for me, and then buried the seeds where we sat. I asked him if an apple tree would grow there. Then Andreas had the idea to carve our initials in the tree. He thought it might inspire the seedlings. They would grow because we loved them and wanted them to grow.

"Can love make an apple tree grow?" I'd asked him.

"A certain kind of love can make an apple tree grow," he'd answered. "Can make anything live."

"Live forever?"

"Everything lives forever. Most people don't know that. I think other things are alive right now in the woods but we just can't see them, not with our eyes as such."

"What things?"

He had shrugged, wiping his blade on his pant leg and etching at the tree.

"But what things are here right now that we can't see?"

"Maybe there is another world, other people, but we cannot see them."

"Can they see us?"

"No . . . well, I don't know, maybe sometimes. Maybe sometimes we can see them. Didn't you ever think you saw something, Angelica, that nobody else has seen? Well, maybe you did see something. And maybe other creatures give us ideas. Maybe we get ideas from them."

"Are they ghosts? Like the Lost Maiden?"

"Maybe. Maybe they are dead people or maybe they are people living in another world in the same place. And maybe they are both."

"And what about heaven?"

"Well, people go somewhere when they die, but who says it's up in the sky? Maybe it's not just another place but another time. Heaven could be anywhere. Just because you haven't got a body doesn't mean much. It's probably more fun without a body. Then you travel around and never get tired."

"Are you going to travel far away?"

"Not without you."

"But what if I die?" I had asked.

"Then I'll die with you."

I had closed my eyes against the brilliance of that day. While he carved our initials, I gently patted the earth over the apple core praying for the tender seeds that slept in their grave.

Chapter Fourteen

I heard a sudden noise in the black forest. A broken branch? A chill swept over me. I was cold. "Andreas, is that you?" I called, hoping I was near our meeting place.

I tripped on an outcropping of pine roots, which tugged at my cape. I cried out and then something banged savagely in the leaves overhead. It was an owl ferociously departing the woods, breaking free of the darkness. I heaved a great sigh when I heard it cry long and low as it soared above the fog-drenched trees. I tried to get my balance but fell on a bed of pine needles. Courage, Angelica, I told myself. You vowed you would overcome the night fog and you are. Think of this adventure as an experiment. Don't hide from your fear by thinking of how you will view it tomorrow. Don't push it away. That is what you have always done when you have been afraid. You have sacrificed the moment of fear for a comfortable time that does not yet exist. Only facing it will make you braver.

The palm of my hand stung from a scrape. I stood up trying to assess my exact position in the clearing. Andreas could not be far now. "I'm here," I said hopefully.

And then I saw him; a moving, clouded form fifteen feet away. "Oh Andreas," I sighed clutching the ties of my cape which swung over my heart. I pulled off my hood. "I've been so frightened. I know it's childish but you know how I am about the fog—"

He lunged at me, seizing my shoulders. A large pink head floated atop pitch-black clothing. I cried out, "Oh God no, not you!"

It was Luther.

His gloved hand covered my mouth and he wrenched me around so that he was behind me. He lunged forward and we both fell into the soggy pine needles. He pinned down my arm and twisted me until I faced him, the weight of his body smashing mine into the earth. I fought him and over the sound of crushing pine needles, he whimpered breathlessly, "I saw you with him in the field. I saw what you did." His wet mouth left cold saliva over my lips and cheeks. With his tongue he tried to pry open my mouth. I bit his lip, my teeth tearing at the flesh. He howled and began to rip at my clothing. "It's always been him," he whined, his soft pink hands clawing at my blouse collar, his breath against my neck as I struggled to free myself. When I felt his gloved hand at the hem of my skirt pulling it up past my knees, I found the strength to push forward, to sit up and wrench one arm free. I almost knocked him over when he let go of my bare thigh and shoved me hard onto the ground. A ripping pain shot through my head as I hit. He had thrown me onto a large granite rock. For a moment my senses blurred and yellow lights danced before my eyes. He said, "I've seen you with your clothes off. I saw what he did to you and I'm going to do it too. Just wait, you'll like me better than him. I always knew I was going to get you. I always knew."

I told myself not to move. Instinctively it seemed the thing to do. I let my body go limp. Warm blood oozed from the gash in my head.

I must have lain like a dead woman staring into the surreal night, because he began to shake me. "Angelica! Angelica! Wake up." Luther slapped my face and then looked at his hand, which was warm with my blood. "What's the matter with you? Answer me . . . ." The predatory tone had gone and now he whined, "You're not dead . . . you're not dead." But he thought that I was. Buckling his pants before he had managed to accomplish the rape, he screamed, "I didn't mean to kill you! No, I didn't mean to do it–it was Satan . . . Satan did it. He has killed you because you are a bad woman!" Holding onto his pants, he stumbled from the clearing and ran from his own shrieking demons.

I pulled my petticoats and skirt down over my legs. I tried to sit up. A grinding pain made me dizzy. I felt faint, as if I were being pulled from consciousness, beckoned by the tranquility that lay beyond. To forget, oh to forget Luther Orwell's imploring hands on my body, his soft, dripping mouth. But at least he had not finished what he'd started. I clutched at my stomach and became nauseous.

My clothes were torn and I had twisted an ankle during the fall. The bleeding on my head had slowed. The hair over it had formed a large, sticky clot. I got on my knees and crawled to the cypress tree, clawing my way up its trunk, past our initials, until I was able to stand against it.

I thought of the human sacrifices I'd read of, such undeserved cruelty meted out by the most morally repugnant men of status. Did Luther's sight of me in the field with Andreas have the power to transform my lovely dreams, cause the coagulation of everything good flowing in my life? Had I exchanged one life for another, had one event triggered an onslaught of other, unbearable events? Yes, what Andreas said is true. Life is a hallway of ever-forming rooms. One's conduct in the present room determines the nature of those that follow, for good or ill or both.

Andreas had always said he would protect me. When he was ten years old and I was six we had climbed an oak on the back of the property at Green Gates. We were called for lunch. Andreas had dropped to the ground but I had been afraid to jump. "Jump," he told me. "You won't get hurt."

"Why won't I?"

"Because I'm here."

"But you're not always here."

"Even if you can't see me, I'll be there so you won't get hurt. My feelings will save you. Feelings can go anywhere. I'll send them to you."

"But you could lose me," I had said, "You might *someday*."

"I'll always find you again." He had held his arms out. "There isn't anywhere in the universe you'll be that I cannot find you. A thousand years ago or a thousand years from now. Even a million because time is not for me. Not me. And you could find me too, if you wanted. Now jump. Momma has made pancakes for us."

"Oh . . . I know where the universe is. That's where the moon lives." And I jumped without hurting myself.

My hand formed a fist and I slammed it into the tree. It was either that or give in to the tears that were pressing beneath my eyes. I slammed my fist into the tree again. Possibly Andreas' feelings *had* saved me from Luther's ultimate intention, had prevented Luther's body from entering me. But it was more likely my own cunning, *mine*, not Andreas'. Why had he always pretended that he could protect me? How could I have believed him? Did it matter? Had he always told me that because he wanted to give me courage? Or maybe it was to take my own away? Had I been gullible? Had I been foolish to trust him? After all, where was he now? Perhaps I had never heard him correctly. Perhaps my own need for his protection had transposed itself upon the meaning of his words.

He had not received my letter. He couldn't have. Phoebe had either not delivered it or Luther, Isabel or Virgie had intercepted it. Perhaps she had left it somewhere for Andreas and thought that he would find it. Luther sometimes did odd jobs for the Grove tradesmen. Maybe he had gone into Sparring Construction and seen it.

I hid my face in the tree trunk. The unpitying fog was cold and thick in the ravine, its droplets were larger now, engorged and falling like rain.

I threw the cape off my shoulders. It was far too heavy with water to wear back home. It slouched against the damp orange pine needles like a spectral scar on the earth.

I set out in the direction of home, favoring my swollen ankle. Maybe I'd be fortunate enough to find a sturdy walking stick. I staggered through the brush and found the footpath. My torn blouse was damp through to my skin. I rubbed my shoulders vigorously for warmth. I ached everywhere. After several minutes I came upon a fallen log and stopped to rest. I thought I saw gold eyes in the brush and in the trees. I thought I saw pink nail-bitten hands like Luther's and swollen orb-like faces.

As I sat on the log, I felt my resolve giving way. Life was a trick. That was it. I had been suddenly placed in a dark hallucinatory world in which situations swayed deliriously beyond my control. The past hour was like no hour I had lived before. Pastel, demure, reasonable: that was the world from which I had been plucked. And now I had been tossed by some demigod into a different world of bold, black, choking uncertainties. I could not adjust to the deviation.

And now I heard my name being called. Luther Orwell had driven me mad.

"Angelica . . . ."

It was Phoebe's voice.

"Angelica! Is that you?"

"Phoebe?"

Gold lantern light emerged from the dark. It swayed at the end of her sleeve, clutched by a tiny white glove.

Her quick steps told me that she was as grateful for my presence as I was for hers.

She sat on the log. One hand urgently pressed mine and the other lifted the light to my face. A little gasp escaped from her throat.

"Don't look at me," I said. I took the lantern and set it down. "I'll be fine. It's just the frightful cold."

The small white gloves covered her face and she sobbed between tight little breaths. "I lost the letter. I don't know what happened to it. I went into the milliner's for Theda, and Isabel was in the store and she saw me try to hide the letter from her. I stuck it into my belt. She bumped into me when she left and I didn't notice until I got to the construction company that it was gone. I was ashamed to tell you. I wasn't going to come tonight into the woods because then you would know that I had read the letter. I tried to find Andreas to tell him what was in the letter but he was out riding Candide on Moss Beach and Knute said he wouldn't be back until dark." She wiped her nose with her gloved fingers. "I couldn't sleep from worrying about what I had done, so at midnight I stole home and snatched the lantern off the porch." Fresh new tears poured from her blue eyes. "And now that I've found you, I can tell that something dreadful has happened. Your clothes are torn and there is blood on your face. Something terrible has happened and it is my fault . . . all my fault." She refused the comfort of my arms and wept loudly when I tried to wipe away her tears.

"Nothing is your fault, Phoebe. Somehow Luther got the letter and he was waiting for me. He—tore my clothes."

She stammered, "He—he tried to kiss you, didn't he?"

"Yes. Come now. Let's go home." I took her hand. The lantern light smacked against the fog and it turned a pale warm grey. Phoebe and I, clutching each other, struggled home in the warm glow of the lantern.

Chapter Fifteen

Our walk home expunged my feelings of panic. Worse things than this happen to people, I told myself. And yet I craved warmth and sleep in the way that a fugitive does, desperately, but with little hope that rest would ever again be the same. There was a new place in me, initiated by fear, that would be ever watchful. Is this what it means to grow old? To fear? To be wary rather than trusting? I had seen old and young alike with sunken hollow faces. Had people like the Orwells sucked trust out of them? Had their souls withered under cruelty?

"Did you say something, Angelica?" Phoebe whispered.

We stopped at the front steps, quietly putting out the lantern. "Shhhh, Phoebe. We must be very, very quiet. This is like the end of a game, Phoebe. We're almost home free. Now we have to be very careful not to wake anyone. Here. Hang the lantern at the back porch. I'll wait right here for you." She disappeared around the corner of the house. I leaned into the railing post and breathed deeply closing my eyes.

Someone touched my shoulder. My nerves froze. I whirled around. It was Andreas. He held a finger to his lips and pulled me to him.

He whispered. "I waited for you this afternoon. When you didn't come and I didn't hear from you, I worried. I was unable to sleep and so I thought I'd come and throw pebbles at your window." His hands discovered the tears in my blouse and moved gradually up my neck to the bloody clot on my head. "Angelica, what has happened to you?"

"It's over," I said, hoping my words would assure him that whatever had happened had not changed me. If I were to tell Andreas, then it might also change him. Our life would not be the same. "Everything will be fine." I said unconvincingly.

"Angelica . . . ." he whispered, pulling me to him. "My Angelica. It was Luther, wasn't it?"

"It was Luther," I said, unable to contain myself. "I sent a note with Phoebe but it must have been intercepted. It had a message for you to meet me at midnight. But Luther was there instead."

It was best that I could not see Andreas' eyes. I knew they would fill with tears and fire. His mouth would twist bitterly. His arms tensed across my back.

I pushed him away from me, saying, "I'm glad you're here now. I was wondering how I would get up the stairs. I've twisted my ankle. I'm so afraid we'll wake someone." My attempt at smiling failed and I said in an uneven voice, "I don't like the look on your face, Andreas. He did not—he tried to take me by force, but he didn't succeed." I wiped my face with my sleeve. "We watched too many possums. I played dead after he threw me on the rock, and he thought I was dead. But don't look at me like that. It's a hateful look. We can't hate Luther so much that it changes us. And it will, it will if you hate him too much. It was Isabel who took the letter from Phoebe. She probably put him up to it. Oh Andreas, there's so much more to tell—but here's Phoebe. She brought a lantern to me in the forest."

"Angelica?" Phoebe whispered through the dark.

"It's Andreas. He's here. He's going to help me up the stairs," I said.

"But how did he know to come?" she asked quietly.

He said, touching her crown of red hair, "The same way you knew to take her the lantern. Come open the door, Phoebe, and I'll carry your cousin up. You go to your room. I'll see to Angelica."

The stairs gave out a few more groans than usual as he carried me upstairs to my room. My aunt and uncle's room was on the opposite side of the house, although Aunt Marion had taken to sleeping in one of the guestrooms at the top of the landing.

I had left the door to my room ajar. Andreas nodded goodnight to Phoebe and nudged open the door. A Tiffany glass lamp glowed at bedside. He put me on the bed, covered me with a bed throw and crossed the room to the fire. He placed two logs into the hot orange ash and rolled them with the heel of his boot. He slipped out of his coat and turned toward me. The thin white fabric of his shirt clung to his shoulders, his muscular chest. He always looked different than the other young men in Pacific Grove, as if his ship had just docked and would be sailing soon . . . as if no place could hold him.

"I was just thinking that you look like a mysterious sailor," I said.

"And you look like Dumas' Lady of the Camellias. Your skin is so white and your eyes are so tragic . . . Let me help you take your boots off. This will be uncomfortable, Angelica. Which one is injured?"

137.

He removed the right boot first and then very carefully unlaced the left, his long agile fingers moving slowly, his eyes returning again and again to mine.

When the laces were undone he gripped the heel of the boot and began to slide it off. I bit my lip as the blood rushed to my swollen ankle. It gave several urgent throbs before subsiding into a dull ache.

He sat on the bed and removed my stockings. Then, with one finger he stroked my foot from bottom to top.

"I'll get hot water," he said. "Don't fret. I won't awake anyone."

I fell asleep for a few minutes and woke up as he was unbuttoning my blouse. He slipped it off of me, tossed it on the floor and went to my dressing table. He picked up Cousin Dixie's silver brush, propped me up on pillows and took down my hair carefully, spreading it over my shoulders. He drew the brush gently through my hair. He dipped a cloth into the warm water and dabbed it against the open skin on my scalp. His hands loosened my camisole, slipped it over my neck and slid over my bare breasts to the waistband of my skirt. He unfastened it and taking hold of my petticoats moved them to my feet. There was a bruise on my stomach from Luther's belt buckle. Andreas lowered his face and kissed it. He kissed the wound on my head. He kissed the scratches on my hands and arms. Again he dampened the cloth and washed my face slowly, and then my neck, my arms and my breasts.

He began to unbutton his shirt. I pulled it back over his shoulders and down behind him. His back muscles tightened and he reminded me of the figurines in Aunt Marion's forbidden Italian Art Treasures pictorial in the downstairs library.

He turned quickly toward me, and laying me down on the bed, his hands grasping mine above my head, his eyes inches above me, he said, "Angelica, would you forgive me anything . . . anything at all?"

We had spent our lives vowing allegiance to each other. But why pledge forgiveness? At that moment we borrowed gold from the lamplight and it appeared to dance between his eyes and mine.

"Anything," I nodded.

I closed my eyes as his lips met mine, as his fingers traveled over my skin.

"No," he said, "Don't close your eyes. I want to be able to see what is in them, see the pain disappear. I want to watch you forget him."

I woke at dawn. The window toward the sea was open. Andreas was gone. The fog had withdrawn from the Grove and crouched over the bay.

But what had he said about forgiveness? He had said it again while we talked afterwards by the fire. He said things like "love makes such fools of us before she makes us wiser." When I asked him what he meant he turned from me. I told him about my uncle's suspicions. His response was to carry me to bed and cover me. Then he had left me, had swung from the window to the oak tree to Candide tethered below. Something important was left unfinished between us, something he needed to confess. I lay in bed feeling pallid and incomplete, like a colorless, half-sketched portrait whose maker had abandoned her. I used to be confident.

There was a knock at my door. At this hour? I quickly grabbed the pillow on which Andreas had lain and plumped it up against the tall burlwood headboard. I straightened the bed on his side and shoved the bowl of water under the bed.

I walked to the door. "Who is it?" Then seeing my soiled clothes in a heap at the foot of the bed, I stuffed them in the wood box and covered them with logs.

"Angelica, my dearest, I must speak to you at once." Aunt Marion's fingers twisted at the knob.

I unlatched the door. She entered the room oblivious to anything in it. "I have dreadful news." Her frail white hands wrung ceaselessly against her grey alpaca robe. I had never thought of it before, but it matched the fog.

"What is it?"

She bit her pale lip to stop it twitching, then sat down on the chair by the fire. "Oh Angelica, I love you so!" Out came the handkerchief. Strange how I never saw it before it materialized in her churning hands. "I wish I had been a better mother for you. I wish now, my dear, that I knew how to tell you this. It's terrible news. I don't know how to make things easier for people. I have never been what one could call a comforting person."

"What news?"

Her fingers formed a hard knot over the tear stained linen. "Uncle Robin got a telephone call two hours ago from Mr. Tuttle. It was an extreme emergency . . . ." She halted, stared at me, her eyes filling like pools.

"Please go on."

"Mr. Tuttle had been awakened by the Orwells. Isabel had heard something in the house at about four, I think that's what he said. A loud noise. She went upstairs to investigate and saw— *Luther was dead.*"

I caught the arm of the chair. "How?"

"A gun. Phineas' gun."

"I see. Luther and I weren't friends, though, you know that. You have no reason to worry about me, Aunt Marion—"

"Someone killed him." She was as horrified by her words as I was. She turned her face away from me and dropped her chin. "Someone shot him."

"Who?"

140.

She began to pluck at the handkerchief like Theda plucked at dead chickens for Sunday dinner. "Isabel saw someone leap from the window."

"Yes . . . ." I said, straightening my spine, drawing in my breath.

"Oh why couldn't Uncle Robin have told you? Men are that way, Angelica. They take the best for themselves and leave the rest to us!" Without a pause she rasped, "Andreas. Yes, Andreas. Angelica! Please don't look like that my dear, you look . . . you look deathly pale. Both Isabel and Virgil say that they saw Andreas leap from the third story chapel window and then onto Candide. He rode into the pines to the east of the house. Who could ever have believed?"

"Oh Aunt Marion, he couldn't kill anything." I got up from the chair and crossed to the window, trying vainly to conceal my fear.

"The constable is looking for him as we speak."

"Aunt Marion, the fog was so thick last night that it could have been *anyone* leaping from the window. No one could have been identified, not accurately." What could I do to help Andreas? I asked myself, searching the bay outside to avoid my aunt's agitated presence. "Does Uncle Robin know what time Luther died?"

"He can't be sure but he thinks about two this morning."

"Two? But they didn't see Andreas jump from the window until four?" I turned to her.

"Robin could be wrong," Aunt Marion suggested meekly, "but the constable thinks he must have killed him at two or so and gone back to retrieve something, maybe evidence. Why else would Andreas be at the Orwells' in the middle of the night? What business could he have had with any of them?"

I wanted to shout, "He was here with me at two o'clock, in this very bed!" Calmly I said, "Luther Orwell is a person whom many would wish dead. Don't pretend, Aunt Marion, that he will be missed by anyone other than his family. He is also the kind of person who *would* take his own life. He was a coward of the worst kind, a bigoted, self-righteous, self-important coward. I, for one, am glad he is dead. Yes, I am. I am glad."

"Angelica! Luther had been praying under a crucifix, the candles were still burning. That is what the constable said. Luther had slumped onto—he was face down on the floor. The bullet was in his chest. He had fallen onto the family Bible. Uncle Robin said it was soaked with blood." She coughed into the handkerchief as if she would be sick. "He was a troubled child but he was God-fearing."

I wanted to shout but thought better of it. I needed to stay in control. "He had good reason to fear God. No amount of Bible reading or Sunday school or beatings or subterfuge could have made him different. In fact, I strongly suspect that those are the very things that made him what he was. The Orwells never spared the rod. And Pacific Grove's pristine little Orwell family are as cruel as people can get. I don't understand how the constable can take their word against Andreas'. Surely he won't."

Aunt Marion looked forlornly out the window. "I don't like growing old. Things are changing too quickly."

How much should I confess? That I had gone to meet Andreas at midnight under the butterfly trees and had instead been attacked by Luther Orwell who tried to rape me? Should I tell them that Andreas was worried and had come to my house at one in the morning and had been with me in my room until well past two, the very hour Luther's blood was obliterating a century of graven names in the Orwell family Bible?

No, I couldn't confess. My words would prove that Andreas had a motive for killing Luther: to avenge his attack on me. It was probable that Luther had killed himself and was dead when

Andreas later went to the Orwell mansion. But would Andreas tell the authorities why he had gone there? Would he allow me to be his alibi? Why not? To save my reputation? What difference would it make now?

The door opened. Uncle Robin, disheveled in his blue robe, entered the room. He looked ancient. The skin on his face had sagged into jowls. Three strands of hair fell over his forehead. They were almost all that he had.

"I would wish you a good morning, Angelica, but by now you know what a folly that would be." He glanced around the room, both hands kneading within his square robe pockets. "I have received another call. They found Andreas. Candide was tethered in the trees by Moss Beach. He was lying against a sand dune with a Henry David Thoreau book propped open across his chest! He has been taken into custody for questioning. Isabel, the poor girl, has been asked to bear witness." He turned to me and after a long pause said, "We know this is very hard on you, Angelica, but you must bear up."

He reached out for Aunt Marion's hand. She grabbed it as if it were a lifeline. They departed my room, her lids dropping over her tumultuous eyes and his free hand swatting at his three hairs.

At the lock of the door latch, I stumbled to the water closet and vomited.

Chapter Sixteen

The next day I was forbidden to leave the house, lest I should go to see Andreas. I was trapped in an unfolding nightmare, knowing nothing of his fate.

As the afternoon wore on, the clicking of the mantel clock from the parlor below became loud and distorted. The thudding of my heart as I paced the room beat sharply in my ears, undermining my rationality. It was as if my very own heart were conspiring against me. What did I fear? Loss of love? Loss of time?

Phoebe was in her room sobbing but she would not let me comfort her. It was all her fault, she wailed through the door. The droning was intermittently smothered as she lowered her face into the thick rose-emblazoned chintz coverlet on her bed, the cabbage roses whose peach-colored edges were the delicate color of her freckles. "Go away," she cried. "I should have told you about my dream. I dreamed that Luther would die. I knew it, Angelica, but I'm afraid to tell people about my dreams because they will think I'm a witch and they burn witches." And on and on, she wept above my protests until in my own fantastic state of mind, I imagined the curling stalks of the print roses she watered with her tears growing up out of the bed and ending sorrowfully in twisted knots against the ceiling, their fragile neck stems bent in the direction of extrication. God, I needed to be free.

Uncle Robin had gone to his office to confer on the condition of Luther's body.

I heard Theda's heavy knock at the door. I bid her to enter the room. In her big rough hands she carried hot chocolate and pie. Setting them down, she turned her face to me and said what was permissible, "There, there, Miss." Her wiry eyebrows rumpled across her forehead. "If there's anything I can do . . . anything . . . ."

I nodded, unable to speak for fear of bursting into tears at her ever-present kindness. I suspected that Theda's pitiful dented brow and her pocked face were beautiful to no one but me. To me, Theda was a vital sanctuary in my house, more a place than a person.

She brought me the hot chocolate, timidly holding it out. "Don't let it get cold, now," she said.

I took it from her and thought I felt better merely for the kindness. Over the years, I had spared Aunt Marion my troubles and had instead taken them to Theda. She heard me without speaking and left me feeling healed. But just now I could say nothing. I closed my eyes. She touched my shoulder and left the room.

Aunt Marion had been "under obligation" to call upon Andreas' parents, Signe and Knute Sparring, in order to lend support in this "very dark hour." She had departed the house at one o'clock, giving me a prolonged, vexed expression, one that proposed the idea that her burden was the heavier one; that she had knowledge of another's grief was more grievous to her than anyone else's adversity. To me it was further proof that her concern for others had something to do with self-protection. Her kindnesses were fortification not for others but for her own preciousness. She was a selfish woman and had paid for it in many lonely ways. It would have been easier to send over one of Theda's pies. That's what Aunt Marion usually offered in the way of succor to our fellow Grovians: one munificent, pious pie created with true love by Theda's gnarled hands.

I awaited her return with any kind of news. Upon receiving it, I planned to spring forth from the house and go to Andreas. From there we could leave Pacific Grove for San Francisco. I looked older than my seventeen years, everyone said so. Someone would marry us, for a price.

The noise of the doorbell tingling at three o'clock was a welcome one. From the top of the staircase I saw Aunt Marion's profile in the oval glass of the doorframe as she fumbled with a package. Such a cameo of propriety. She came through the door as smooth and cold as a river stone; not a wisp of hair had freed itself from her hat, not a surreptitious facial line fouled her full, white face. She had not gone to see the Sparrings; she had lacked the courage to risk her precious self on them. Having failed them, she dug even deeper into herself until no sign of life showed at all. I had seen this before. The worse the problem, the more becalmed she was.

In an affected manner, she plucked at the gloved fingers like they were grapes and laid the pair on the hall tree tidily. With prim ceremony, she unpinned her hat, then looked up the staircase at me. Our eyes locked. Her shoulders slumped slightly.

"Angelica, let us sit in the parlor, shall we?"

To Aunt Marion, the parlor could fix anything. She offered it for all manner of ailments, like the British offer tea.

146.

"Certainly, Aunt Marion," I said, slowly descending the staircase.

Through the bay window a ray of sunlight struck Aunt Marion's prized Indian rug. The tables, chairs, sofas hunched around it as if waiting for a show. Aunt Marion caressed a bouquet of wild flowers that nodded tiredly from a trumpet-shaped extravaganza on a pedestal table. The colors of the flowers reminded me of the colors that had danced in the light around Andreas and me as we lay in the field that day. Pure gold. Periwinkle blue. Butter yellow. And green. Vast, endless, pure green.

Bluntly she announced, "I have seen Andreas."

She moved from the vase to a Tiffany lamp, tilted it slightly and whispered, "the dust . . . I'll have to speak to Theda." She moved to the mantel and ran her finger along it. "That's better," she nodded. Then, shifting her eyes to the somber portrait above the fireplace, she said, "Grandfather Emmett was a handsome man, was he not? A general, you know. Of course you know. When your portrait is done, Angelica, I thought we could hang it here, next to his. When you were a child he frightened you, this picture did. But not so anymore. You are a brave woman. Strange how I can use the word 'brave' when I have no idea what it means. But then my father, General Emmett, didn't believe that women should be brave. Maybe it frightened him. Yes, it must have frightened him.

"He doted on me, Angelica. He treated me as a banker treats an investment because mother died and I was something left in his care like stock . . . or property . . . things that needed nothing save protection. One does not talk to an acre of land, at least in my world one does not. One does not embrace one's stock certificates, but one watches out for them. My father watched out for me. That is what men do best. They protect us from enemies. But should the enemies penetrate our doors, we find we've been given nothing with which to protect ourselves. At least it was true for me. I was not allowed to play outside in winter. I had few friends. Your mother, my sister Beatrice, was much older. She'd already gone off to boarding school. A governess was engaged but my father selected the books and lessons from which she should teach. Mythology was banned. Nursery rhymes were unthinkable. Poetry would lead to wanton thinking.

"My rooms were scrubbed diligently every third day. There was no dirt. We were very clean people. I do not ever remember touching soil. When I used the chamber pot, Nancy was instructed to have me lift my hands over my head, close my eyes and let her see to the unfortunate task.

"This spring, just two weeks ago, I saw Phoebe in the garden, barefoot. I watched her shamelessly wriggling her toes in the mud. She sat in it and pinched the dirt with her fingers, enjoying herself. I was so mortified when she smiled that I found my vocal chords paralyzed. I could not reprimand her . . . but then have I ever? You are brave, Angelica, and my Phoebe is brave because I am incapable of courageousness. I am a coward and my cowardice has made the two of you courageous, if not brash.

"I don't know what it feels like to walk in a garden barefooted and I am afraid to try."

I said, "I'm sorry."

She walked about the room. Her hand twitched the red tassel hanging from the bookcase key. "These are your Uncle Robin's books. I've never read them. I'm afraid to." She looked directly at me, her eyes, fabulous in their stillness, penetrated me as never before. "What if I were to read one and it were to change my mind? What if I were to discover another way to live? No. I have my platitudes. Like patriarchs, they guard the borders of my life, they are the bulwarks of my failed existence, memorized sayings that keep me from exploration, from discovery. When in a quandary, I recite them. I say, 'never lend money to a relative' or 'turn the other cheek' or 'cleanliness is next to Godliness' and others that stand right here at the front of my brain ready to sanctify my action, or lack thereof. I know nothing else. I fear I am nothing else." Her eyes filled with tears. She drew out her handkerchief and twisted it unmercifully. "I want you to have Andreas! He is everything I turned away from. Don't you see? And you are everything I never was." She spoke quickly, her handkerchief working on the new gush of tears. I had never seen my aunt cry anything but parsimonious tears. Now she truly wept and I loved her for the first time.

"It's not your uncle's fault. He is a good man but our arrangement from the onset precluded intimacy. He is not unlike me that way. We are not bad people, Angelica, we are merely empty—not like you, or Andreas or Phoebe who are ransacking life like giddy pirates, yes, like brave, brave pirates. We, your uncle and I, are spectators. We keep our distance. We live by passing judgement. Our righteousness provides us an imitation of life.

"Andreas . . ." she choked, sinking into her favorite indigo blue velvet chair. "I knew a man like Andreas . . . and do you know who he was, Angelica?"

"No."

"Your father, Angelica . . . Angelo, my sister's husband. In my life, he was the only forbidden thing that I allowed myself to claim. Imagine it, Angelica, if you can. Your dear Aunt Marion has a past. Well, not so much a past as an afternoon.

"Yes. Merely one afternoon long ago.

"It was because of my sister's sizable estate that he was allowed to become the actor, the poet, and the dreamer. It was on a hot September day in the garden at Green Gates that he was all three for my benefit. Knute and Signe accompanied Uncle Robin and my sister Beatrice, your mother, to Moss Beach. It was a very long time ago . . . you were being carried by your mother and Andreas was barely four years old. I stayed behind to put Andreas down for a nap but he fell asleep beneath my parasol.

"Yes, Angelo was a wonderful actor. I thought he was asleep near the red camellia bushes but as I passed by him he grabbed my ankle and pulled me down onto the grass. He laughed at me as I tried to pull away. His mouth covered my cries." She gasped and quickly put her hand over her mouth. "It has been seventeen years and I can still feel his lips pressing upon mine . . . seventeen years . . . and his hands moving over . . . .

"My little afternoon. How I treasure it because it crushed the order imposed by an authoritarian father, by an enslaving society. It is the only time I have taken a chance. But you see it was Angelo who gave it to me. He was the brave one, not I. Oh, how I enjoyed the death of convention, as shameful as it was." She moved from the center of the room to view the bay through the window. She stroked the leaf of an aspidistra growing near the chair she sat upon. Her head fell back and her eyes closed, a posture of abandon so uncharacteristic that I was taken aback. "I saw Andreas in town today. He was handcuffed to a pole for fresh air and he was sitting on the ground reading from Whitman's *Leaves of Grass*. Yes, he had been arrested. Isabel swore on the Bible before a town gathering that she had seen Andreas leap from the third story chapel window last night."

"No . . . ."

Her eyes opened and gazed dreamily at the high ceiling. "It was you, was it not, Angelica? It was you in the field with Andreas that day? Not someone from the other side of the fence, but you . . . ."

"Yes," I said. "It was I."

150.

"You are so like your father," she said into the heavy air about us. "The night he died in the fire, I awoke with a burning fever . . . ashes. The lips that took mine, the man who was braver than I had melted into ashes."

I knelt at the edge of her chair. She looked at me blankly. I said, "I wanted him to kiss me, Aunt Marion. I called him over to me. When Andreas walks toward me it's like there's no one else in the world; he doesn't move toward me unless he means every step. As he walked toward me I could feel my heart ignite. It took me over, I lost myself as you did, Aunt Marion . . . I forgot who I was. I was no longer contained. That's what love does. It sheds itself like the butterfly in its chrysalis. Love flies forth to form creations incomprehensible to those who cannot feel. But you, Aunt Marion, have felt that . . . and so you understand why I have to go to Andreas."

She breathed deeply, her eyes catching the branch of the red rhododendron beyond the window glass. I stood up and looked down upon her pale face; her rouged cheeks were splattered with tear stains. Her guarded, missionary look had been replaced by the yielding face of a lover. She said nothing as I left the room. I looked back over my shoulder to see the shadow of the rhododendron branch dancing over her bosom and upon the hand that lay over it, collapsed.

Chapter Seventeen

This was my world.

I surveyed it from the steep porch steps of our tall house on the knoll as if I were leaving it forever.

In a matter of days I had learned that things are seldom as they seem. The awareness had been long in coming.

This *was* my world. Nothing between our home and the Monterey Bay but the Southern Pacific Railway train that daily chugged past the harsh rocks of Lover's Point jutting out to sea. And just over there, a hundred yards away, the Japanese Tea Garden with upturned roof corners looked as if the wind were sucking in its middle, its fragile paper lanterns tossing from curved eves. The gulls dotted along the roof edge waited attentively for afternoon tea guests to leave cookie crumbs or cake lumps.

How placid the bay was today. The rickety pier scored the ocean like a spine, the boats bobbed like cradles. How beguiling to the naïve. This bay rolled out over the earth claiming hundreds of unwary ships, boats who had sailed on her, throwing them upon the rocks, suffocating them in its unmeasured depths, splintering their hulls, more vicious than the pirates that once plundered down the coast near Big Sur.

Things are seldom what they seem.

I gripped the porch railing. Our house was one of architectural importance. Every window view facing north and west was half filled with the water of Monterey Bay and half with the sky. When I had come to live with my aunt and uncle, I had been placed in that upstairs room facing the bay. And day after day and year after year that massive body of blue-grey water quivered, stormed and wept and then lay like something murdered at the shore. It had all the characteristics of a madwoman. The gulls sparked up and back and down and around, keeping alive on scraps and fresh air. Shrieking, always shrieking as if God owed them something more.

This was the world Andreas and I had shared. The stately, stiff, angular houses on the coast, damp closets with more mold than sachet, fires in the hearth in summer when the sun refused to shine for weeks, the hot grey steam of the Southern Pacific, the call of the pigtailed Chinese. They left before dawn each morning, those elegant, black-haired men in triangular hats. They left for the horizon of the bay in boats that curved like swans' necks. The black bay sparkled with pine wood fires that glowed from their yawls to attract squid. For years I woke myself early and marveled at the bay, lit like fireflies with sparkling pinewood baskets. Until I was seven years old I thought that that was where the stars went at dawn, into the sea out there to await their resurrection at the beckoning of the moon. It was not true.

Then there was Chinatown. Down the tracks past Hopkins Marine Station, past the rank smelling squid fields where the little gentlemen dried their catch.

I saw a man die in Chinatown.

Andreas was not to blame for my witnessing the murder. I had begged him to take me there, to see the legendary bogeyman Old Lee. I wanted to see up close those star-filled little boats that floated across my dark blue window at dawn, which were, Andreas informed me, not filled with stars at all but with a mixture of abalone, squid, rock fish, cod, halibut, yellowtail, mackerel, sardines and shellfish, all of those smelly things I had seen drying in their vast fields, that I had seen piled into wagons and shipped north to San Francisco or to China.

We could not sneak down to Chinatown in daylight so we went under cover of dark. We crept along the railway tracks with a moon sliver at our backs and wisps of cold fog growing thicker. Andreas held a lantern he had taken from his carriage house. It was less than a mile and soon we could smell the fish and see the unpainted clapboard shanties on skinny stilts in rows that wound along paths and narrow roadways. Colorful paper lanterns glowed from shops. Scaffolding was hung with drying fish and tinseled banners. Chinese characters flashed incomprehensibly before our vision. Andreas had been to Chinatown many times but never at night. He led me down a path with borders colored by garments hung from makeshift clotheslines, and then onto a walkway dimly lit by lanterns. Shops burgeoned with tiny shells, abalone, sea cradles, shark's teeth, pearly rice-shaped shells, wax flowers, sea urchins, paper ornaments, firecrackers and opium for ten cents a vial.

The people spoke rapidly in their foreign tongue. Thin, wiry music played over the sounds of drums and the smell of mutton wafted through the streets. Andreas bought me a yellow paper fan and a worn silk purse from an old toothless woman whose kind eyes looked like stitches in her face, whose mouth was as slight as a needle and whose feet were cruelly bound stumps.

We then passed a shanty where Andreas said the opium smokers slept. It was next to a curious smoke-filled house from which the clatter of voices rang out. The men inside were arguing. We heard the sound of crashing furniture.

"Dominoes," Andreas whispered, drawing me behind the corner of the shack. We peered into the smoke, our hands gripping at the doorjamb.

"You mean they're gambling?" I asked.

"Look," he said. "A knife."

"Don't look," I said tugging at his sleeve.

A handsome young Chinese man leapt from the floor. He held a black dagger in front of his face. He scowled bitterly at the old white-bearded man across from him as their angry words tangled in the smoky air. All others stood away, lining up against the walls as still as posts.

The old man drew a blade from the band of his black trousers. His eyes tightened, his wrinkled lips turned down at the edges. He screamed and leapt forward, his feet shooting toward the young man's torso and slamming him to the floor. Before he could get up, the old man had jumped across the small room, grabbed the young man's pigtail and thrust his head back, slitting open his throat with a short twist of his wrist.

But the cold black eyes would not close.

Blood spurted from the youth's neck onto the old man's beard. Then the old attacker dropped the knife and fell back. He buried his face in his hands and wailed as if it had all been a mistake. The others in the room ran to the young man and hovered about him. Through their scrambling legs we saw the face of the dead man looking at us, his eyes wider in death than in life, his tongue thrust forward above a river of blood.

We ran past the crowds, down the curved trail of shanties and beyond the colored lights into a dense pocket of fog that gathered against the craggy shore of the bay. From Chinatown along the Southern Pacific tracks we heard the distant wailing of the shocked villagers. The movement of the ocean just yards from where we crouched made its own noise, a low, foaming hum that in minutes slowed our heartbeats.

When I had caught my breath I said, "I do not want to talk about the Chinese man, ever. I do not want to talk about how he died or what we saw. Not even when we are sad. Not even if someone else dies or if someone asks us if we know anything about death. Not then either. Not when we are old, never."

Andreas nodded at me as we leaned back against the rock and stared up through the fog, grateful to see nothing.

This is my *world* and that is how I learned that the walls of our worlds are as thin as paper, that security is an illusion and that things are seldom what they seem. Even presidents die for less than the Chinese men do.

President McKinley was shot to death six weeks after we children of Pacific Grove sang to him on the steps of the octagonal museum building on Central Avenue, sang in our crisp white dresses and trousers and white caps; chorused out "Columbia, the Gem of the Ocean." Dressed in white, we had carried roses and strewn them in the path of the presidential party.

Six weeks later we were dressed in black. The town was draped in crepe. McKinley had been shot and killed.

That is why as I stood on the steps of Aunt Marion's dignified house, looking out to sea, hat pinned firmly on my head, gloved hands clutching the railing, light spring coat buttoned to my chin, why I was afraid to take the first step, afraid to walk three blocks into town, to enter the jail house, to confront Andreas. Aunt Marion's treasured indiscretion sixteen years ago under the blush of the camellia bushes had been seething all those years beneath the implacable posturing.

Things are seldom what they seem.

Chapter Eighteen

*I*t was never necessary to see Diana, Andreas' cousin, to know that she was near. Men loitering on Lighthouse Avenue grew grimly silent when she passed as if reminded of something they had lost. Boys elbowed each other's ribs, laughed and drew their caps off their heads to cover flushed faces. Little girls danced behind her skirts for was she not as kind and beautiful as the fairy tale princess that mama read to them about? The pinched faces of women who never sat without their ankles touching grew so narrow that their nostrils all but disappeared. High school girls whose large lustrous eyes followed her admiringly down the street often ran home and sat at their mirrors and tried to imagine what magical application—a new hairstyle, rouge, lace collar—could transform them into Diana Sparring. And then in a rag doll heave, they would throw themselves on their vanities, upsetting every little promising potion, and weep because whatever it was Diana had, it did not come from Mr. Holman's store, or from a jar or a catalogue.

She walked briskly down Lighthouse Avenue toward me, her eyes downcast, deep in thought. Her skirts—they were a soft pearl blue—did not flow as usual but rustled in rhythm with the hard steps she took. She was so given over to her thoughts that she passed me by.

"Diana!" I cried.

Two ladies on the corner, Mrs. Mathews and Mrs. Hansen, turned their backs to me. Somehow I had been implicated in the town scandal.

Diana turned at the waist, her skirts forming a circular swish against her legs. "Oh Angelica!" She opened her arms and embraced me. "I've just talked to him."

"Andreas?" I asked.

"Come with me to the Japanese Tea Garden. I'm to meet David there but we have time for tea before he arrives."

She took my gloved hand in hers and we walked with our hats toward the sun, down the street and over the wooden walk bordered with swaying paper lanterns. We were seated at a table under a glass wind chime. She removed her gloves and lowered the brim of her wide hat against the sunlight. I fidgeted restlessly waiting for her to tell me what she knew.

She announced, "He is being sullen. He's simply lying on his cot reciting Whitman. It is not exactly what one would wish for. As I left him he said, 'Whoever you are holding me now in hand, without one thing all will be useless. I give you fair warning before you attempt me further. I am not what you supposed but far different.' We should be grateful. I think that it was not anything too suggestive."

"It suggests a great deal to me. But how's he faring? Is he well?"

"He will not answer the charges."

"He hasn't claimed his innocence?" I asked.

Her mouth tightened and small dimples appeared in her cheeks. "Little Dre?" she asked, using his nickname, "Knowing him as we do we should have expected this behavior. That he *is* innocent will be reason enough for him not to prove otherwise. My thought is that he wants the town to pursue his guilt in vain. He thinks it will teach them a lesson. Oh Angelica, don't look so disappointed. He has always professed to believe more in the laws of nature than the laws of man. This gives him a chance to prove it. It's a game. When he is finally called to a hearing I've no doubt he'll present a brilliant case in his defense. It will take a great deal of talent but it is that same talent that will someday make him a fine lawyer."

"I fear it's more than that, Diana."

"Do you?" she asked, tilting her head slightly. "Perhaps winning his case is not enough. Perhaps he is merely testing his wings. He will prove himself innocent while at the same time proving the town guilty. So while it may appear that he is hanging himself by his refusal to speak, he is, in fact, hanging this very town: our prejudices and our limited vision and our blind trust of symbols, of people like the Orwells. Dre will let them bury themselves."

"I could do it for him," I said. "I could prove him innocent and put an end to his ridiculous game," I said, suddenly angry.

"How do you mean?" Diana asked. She looked at me, awaiting my answer, and I saw the odd light playing in her almost violet eyes. When I was younger I thought that if I looked deeply enough into someone's eyes, I could see their heart. I was ten years old when Royal Shaw broke Diana's heart, when he hopped the Southern Pacific with his counterfeit promises stuffed into a valise too small to hold them. She ran after the train. She ran and ran, waving her arms until she fell limply on the hot tracks in the mists of steam and smoke. She would never know that I had seen her that day. I was sure that Diana's broken heart was behind her eyes because they became tender after that, as if the light that shone from them had forever shattered.

"I was with Andreas last night when Luther was supposedly murdered. I'm not sure I want to explain," I said, raising my eyes defiantly.

The colorfully costumed waiter appeared and took our order of black tea and cakes. Diana set her little embroidered handbag, a gift from Signe, on the table. She raised her chin and said, "If you were with him you must tell me, Angelica. It's apparent that Andreas doesn't plan to tell anyone where he was. They have asked him and he has denied them an answer. When it comes to you, Angelica, Dre is capable of any degree of self-sacrifice."

I hesitated, "It was rather compromising."

"I see."

"It all began in the high field three days ago. I thought everyone would be at the Chautauqua and we were . . . kissing but I am afraid it was more than that and when Andreas sailed his hat across the field the Orwells saw it. And they saw Andreas. Then somehow Virgie Orwell got hold of Andreas' hat and gave it to Phoebe with a message that 'he knew.' The Orwells recognized Andreas but didn't know whom he was with. Of course, they were very quick to impart their information. And when Uncle Robin heard the news, he forbade me to see Andreas and so I sent a note telling him to meet me at the butterfly trees at midnight, that is, last night. And while Phoebe was at the milliner's, Isabel absconded with my letter, unbeknownst to poor Phoebe. It is my guess that Isabel then passed the missive on to Luther and it was he who met me instead of Andreas and tried to—it was terrifying."

"Did he?" she murmured, her eyes dropping from mine to the small glass vase of curling orange nasturtiums.

"No. No, he did not. But I led him to think I was dead and so he ran off wildly through the pines crying about the devil and God's forgiveness. Soon Phoebe found me. And we returned home. Andreas was there. Andreas stayed with me in my room until nearly four in the morning. I find it difficult to believe he went to the Orwells but if he did I know why."

Diana sighed, the brim of her hat tilting toward me. "Andreas' horse has a missing shoe. The prints outside of the Orwell house match those of Candide. So it must be true that Andreas went there but why Isabel insists on making such a spectacle of herself by testifying in public is incomprehensible. Her brother dead . . . ."

"Just because Andreas went there does not mean he killed him," I remarked weakly, thinking . . . things are seldom what they seem.

The waiter brought our tea and cakes.

An ache grew slowly in my chest and I clutched at my throat. Not Andreas. He could *not* have murdered Luther. Why, just hours before Luther died the shadows cast by the fire in my room had played over the curves of our bodies as we planned for our future. Murderers don't plan for futures, do they? We had formed our future, had taken that vast, unused expanse of time and space before us and given it form and color . . . *elan vital*. Late at night, in the shadows of my room, we married, moved to Boston, had children and went to places like Zanzibar and Samoa. We'd even grown old and died last night as the embers in the hearth hissed and crackled. So real was the game of our future that as I tossed his ashes over the sea, I wept. He became silent as I told him that I would depart the earth in a flaming ship as his Viking ancestors had. On a ship with a dragon's head. Then he had said, "Death will not separate us."

Diana's white hand fell upon mine. "He's protecting you,

that's why he hasn't defended himself."

"I wonder if that's all of it," I said shoving the cake aside. "At any rate I haven't the letter asking him to meet me. It could have been evidence of some kind though. Phoebe, I know, would testify about last night if asked to."

Diana's lips parted before she began tentatively. "Andreas knows how it will be for you if the truth of your—*intimacy* becomes known. And you know how it will be for him if the town believes that he went to Luther Orwell's to avenge the attack on you. No, perhaps Dre's right in waiting until he's spoken to a lawyer. His parents have retained a man from San Francisco who should be arriving on tonight's train."

My hands enclosed the teacup. "Did you hear Isabel's account of the story?"

Diana nodded, a strawberry blonde curl unwinding on her cheek. "I spoke briefly with the constable. The gun that killed Luther was on the floor next to him. It was kept in the Orwell's chapel, for what reason, no one is certain. The constable isn't quite sure of anything yet. He says that Luther could've retrieved the gun when he heard Andreas scaling the wall, thinking, naturally, that he was a burglar. Andreas could've overtaken him. The constable admitted that it could've been an accident. What puzzles him the most is the motive and the unlikelihood of Andreas Sparring killing anyone. Still, the constable said, Isabel had seen him and the hoof prints in the mud below verified his presence."

"Luther killed himself," I said vehemently.

She said, "I've thought so myself. But why does Isabel insist on implicating Andreas?"

I avoided the question. I pictured the coral-colored, obese Luther Orwell in the black suit that was too small for him and made him look like a storybook pig. I had no compassion for him and it frightened me. For who knows what kind of man Luther might have been if circumstances had been different, if his parents had not been such an insult to the God they professed to worship: praying on Sunday, preying on Monday.

Finally I said, "We've known Luther all of his life. He has committed the most unspeakable acts and following these vile incidents he atoned for them in the most perverted ways, as if the sinning and the atonement became a ritual. And if that didn't work, then his mother Claudia was always manipulating ways to have him forgiven. Their desire for perfectionism created the opposite. Luther was a monster. It was Andreas' opinion that Luther behaved badly because he actually found pleasure in atonement. I am quite sure that Luther killed himself because he thought that he had killed me. Perhaps even as he attacked me he was not without guilt and the fear of his God's wrath. Who knows what dark workings go on in a mind such as his? And yes," I admitted, "it looks as though Andreas did go to see Luther last night to have words with him regarding the attack. That is simply all that happened. The rest is merely speculation until Andreas decides to enlighten the constable."

Diana spread her hands on the table and let them lay still, as if displaying something precious brought out from underneath glass. "I know that Andreas is innocent but he's also brash and the people of this town have been too quick to judge him. In a way it's as if they want to believe he did it."

"It's true," I said, thinking of how Diana had not escaped the same prejudices. Had she lived two hundred years before, someone would have found a good reason for having her burned at the stake. I shuddered as I thought of Diana's mind, body and soul transcending the fire to heaven on a winding ribbon of smoke, all that reverential beauty misconstrued as weaponry in a woman who hadn't the least idea how to be wicked.

She withdrew her hands from the tablecloth quickly as if she suddenly knew their value, folded them in her lap and said, "The question now is: Why would Isabel deliberately indict Andreas?"

With more rancor than I intended I answered, "Because she cannot have him . . . and she never will."

"Angelica," she said softly, leaning forward, "do you know of any cause Isabel would have for blackmailing Dre? Please, please don't be so shocked. I'm not saying that she has but . . . ."

"One cannot blackmail another without cause!" Then lowering my voice I said, "She's always tried to control him."

"Yes. That is why I have suggested blackmail." She paused. "I don't know." Then continued. "Even if Andreas were trying to protect your reputation through silence, I find it hard to believe he wouldn't have said something to me about last night, about his being with you. As regards you, he has always been frank with me. Our family has no secrets."

Damn Isabel, I thought as I looked out across the bay. Sinuous fog moved over the dark blue water. Soon it would encroach upon the tea garden, choke out the sun and cast a brooding shadow over everything. I looked at the wind chime as it announced a breeze, then back to Diana. "Andreas has never been one to let others solve his problems for him and for that reason I think you're right. He's not keeping silent for my sake. He believes too much in our pure intentions to worry much about dispersions being cast. There's another reason, too. It could be that while he didn't kill Luther, he in some way caused his death. How do we know he didn't tell Luther that night that I was truly dead? Perhaps Luther's suicide was prompted by something Andreas said. Or it could be true that Isabel is using this tragedy as leverage against him. And yes, it is possible that Isabel knows something that you, Diana, and I know nothing of." I could not stop the tears as I recalled Andreas' words begging for forgiveness. As I drew out my handkerchief I mumbled, "I'm afraid that he has betrayed me."

"Angelica, listen to me. It's senseless to worry until you have spoken to him. My dear, we must make a plan. First you must speak to Andreas and if you aren't satisfied, you must speak to Isabel herself."

"I can't," I sobbed.

"You might have to."

"Never. I could never ask her for anything." I smothered my protest in the handkerchief and wondered if I looked like Aunt Marion, wondered if I was being transformed into the woman I swore I would never become. I would not let Andreas fade into an old story as her Angelo had.

"Not even to save him?" she asked, her soft eyebrows rising in astonishment.

"Surely he couldn't have given that kind of power to Isabel Orwell," I choked out.

She sighed and her beautiful face became the consummate mask of tragedy, so authentic that it did not look real. "Dre is not perfect."

"No," I nodded. "Dre is not perfect. But there was a time when he was. Yesterday he was perfect and all the yesterdays before."

Chapter Nineteen

The steel bars clanked behind me, sending a shiver up my spine. It was dark and dank in the jail cell, save a high window opposite the iron cot. Andreas did not turn from the window when I entered and kept his closed book in hand. It was Emerson's *Oversoul*.

Standing stiffly, the bars pressing into my back I cleared my throat. "Andreas."

Quickly he looked at me, putting the book aside. "Angelica!" he smiled, springing up from the cot. The day's growth of beard made his face look older and his worn, wrinkled clothes only served to increase the despairing nature of his appearance. But his manner was too casual. He acted as though I were making a social call. Facing me, hands on hips, he said, "Mother and Father are posting bail. I should be out within the hour."

"That says a great deal of nothing." My feet felt rooted to the stone floor. "What happened?" What was he thinking as he looked at me? His eyes, normally a stunning blue, had clouded over. Maybe I was right after all. Maybe a broken heart crystallizes somewhere in one's eyes, for Andreas' had changed. I was afraid to look too closely for fear that my own prominence had been vanquished in some internal conflict about which I knew nothing.

He took a step toward me, stopped and said sadly, "I'll never forget you last night."

"Nor will I forget you. I don't feel the need to commit it so heartily to memory, however, since there are to be a lifetime of nights like that." But my words rang cold. Even I did not believe them.

His dark lashes flickered. He turned sideways, stretching his neck. He reached for the bars of the high window and said, "Do you remember the time . . . ."

"Yes."

"Yes, you would remember the time," he sighed.

"On the rocks by the sea near Point Piños four years ago. The lighthouse beacon shone out across the sea. It was nearly dusk and the day was dark . . . like this one." I paused as he took a step toward me. "There was a fishing boat still at sea and we huddled in the shelter of the high dunes waiting for the lighthouse to call it home. It was the night before you left for college, for Boston."

He continued the narrative, "And then the man came, the stranger from down the coast, came out of the fog toward us. He looked like a rabid dog. Remember his eyes? And his beard was full of sand. When he stumbled drunkenly I went to help him up. And then he grabbed at my collar and threw me down against the dune and lunged at you. He fell on you . . . ."

"You were going to kill him, Andreas. You pulled him off me and tossed him against the dune and beat his head into the sand. Blood trickled from his mouth. I begged you not to kill him. I pulled you off of him and told you that he wasn't worth the price you would have to pay for the murder. And you stopped. *But you would have stopped anyway*, Andreas. We have the same conscience. It's just that mine spoke sooner that time."

He turned back to the window and slammed his fist against the stone wall. "I might have killed Luther if he hadn't already been dead. He didn't deserve the power though, the notoriety that comes from being murdered or from committing suicide. He deserved to drown in a damned mudflat, not with an antique pearl-handled pistol at his heart. No, not like that. I always thought 'now there's a fellow who will choke to death on a chocolate-covered bon bon.' But there he was in a stained glass chapel. The wretched gold candles were even burning at half-mast. It was theater at its best. And when I saw him sprawled across the floor it wasn't pity that I felt but contempt and disgust that he achieved in death what he was denied in life—sheer poetry, rich, tragic poetry." A faint smile played over his lips. He ran his fingers through his hair and sighed "Isabel."

Biting my lip I waited for him to continue.

Finally he said, "Isabel threw open the door just as I had rolled his body over to reveal the gunshot wound and the Bible that this town has sought to immortalize in embellished gossip. What could have completed the scene better than the thin-lipped, newtish sister-of-the-victim who played it with all the fury of a dishonored ingenue? Isabel, who, when she sprang forth upon this earth, was born without a heart or a soul. I looked at her through the gold of the chapel and thought that she was deader than her brother. My God, Angelica, she didn't even look at him when I told her he was dead. She stepped over him and came to me. We . . . exchanged words and then I left. I leapt from the window and rode down to the beach, toward the sunrise."

"Then tell them," I whispered. "Tell them that he killed himself."

He left the window and came to me. His hand stroked my hair and slid down my back. "Oh, to touch you, Angelica," he said, fighting the impulse to draw me to him.

Ignoring his hands, I said, "What words did you have with Isabel? Why was she provoked into incriminating you? For the love of God, Andreas tell me."

His hand withdrew from my back and his eyes stared into mine.

"I must know," I said.

He shrugged and pulled his eyes from mine. "Isabel, Isabel, Isabel. We had the usual words. It's always the same with her, isn't it? How, I have wondered, could nature have allowed her to happen? Surely her ancestors died out with all those cold-blooded monsters that used to roam the earth." He circled the room and leaned against the damp wall.

When I did not speak he sighed loudly and folded his hands across his chest. Though the Orwells had always evoked venomous thoughts in him I had never heard Andreas speak with less conviction of his loathing. His words were weak and empty. They did not ring with his usual assurance.

"Tell me the truth, Andreas." He refused to speak. I walked to him and pulled his fists from his side. His arms swung down heavily and he made no effort to refold them. I felt stranded in a strange new world.

I repeated, "Tell me."

"No," he said.

I raised my hand and brought it against his face. I slapped him a second time and a third and then a cry broke from my throat and I shouted, *"What have you done?"*

He took my wrist and leaned me against the wall, pressing his body to mine. He pulled me to him and held me so tightly I could not breathe. "I can't answer you, Angelica, because I don't know what to say."

He allowed me to pull away. I turned sharply from him and backed up to the door.

"Angelica . . . you must believe me. I want to tell you the truth."

I rattled the cell door, unable to turn and face him.

The constable unlocked the door, let me out and closed it behind me.

Chapter Twenty

Bewildered by his rejection, I started toward the woods. I could not go home. Aunt Marion would put me through an unmerciful interrogation and what would I say to her? That Andreas had abandoned me after all these years? That I had in some way been betrayed? That my mind was desperately grasping for an answer while willfully avoiding one? I was physically ill as if I had been kicked in the stomach. In my chest, throat and eyes a pressure swelled that called to mind those horrible waves of ocean that grow as tall as walls and then pause in a climactic crest before explosion.

I found myself on the trodden path to Green Gates. It was unlikely that I would meet anyone going this way.

Green Gates was nestled in a forest of pines with only the tall rolling dunes separating it from the sea. It was like a painting on an English country postcard. Its two-story Tudor architecture blended comfortably in the wild habitat.

The old rock wall that Knute Sparring and my Uncle Robin had once built in the fashion of the old country, without mortar (but with a great deal of Swedish bread and sardines) had not yet fallen away as Signe feared. The rock walls and columns had twelve green gates, the color of the pines, surrounding the property. When Signe's roses were not in bloom, she opened the gates and let the deer graze. Creeping nasturtiums and needlepoint ivy clung to the stone, twisted up the dark green pickets, and veiled the large stone arch whose green gates I now creaked open.

The smokeless ivy-shrouded chimneys told me Signe and Knute were not home.

On the left side of the flagstone path, near the garden birdbath, a large buck raised his antlered head, and still chewing, gazed at me as if I were expected. For a moment I thought how comforting it would be to throw myself against his chest and weep my troubles to those large eyes whose depth and character suggested an unattainable wisdom.

The buck's head dropped back to the earth, sweetly unaware of the homage, and I took the flagstone path around the side of the house and into the garden at the back.

It was close to dusk. I was comforted somewhat by the mist and other familiar things: the ornate gazebo whose plans came all the way from London, the ancient wicker rocking chair whose paint was pock-marked from the weather, the tiny guest cottage with the clipped roof, the apple trees Andreas and I planted from seeds ten years ago.

As I sat the familiar chair creaked and groaned. I rocked back and forth, my head pressed against the back so that my tears would slide down my temples and into my hair.

Was this garden truly the place in which I had played out the happiest times in my life? My connection to this garden had diminished. The past echoed without the passion that made it memorable.

How did I know that Andreas' mother Signe would never again bake cookies for me? She used to serve them on a big, bright yellow platter. Andreas and I would sit in the garden and eat until only the platter was left and then if there were any crumbs we would hide behind the cedar tree and lick them off until we could see our reflections in the deep yellow glaze.

I knew as well that his father Knute and Uncle Robin would no longer sit next to the woodpile with their legs crossed, backs hunched and smiles curved, glowing like quarter moons, while they laughed about piling stones on the Sabbath declaring that they *were* praying, yes, praying that the wall would hold, then slapping their knees while Andreas and I flitted about the fountain insensitive to the future. Signe planted purple iris bulbs one Sunday and in the spring they trumpeted their colors like nothing else in the garden at Green Gates; like little kings and queens. They were gone too, for one had to discount their wild purple cousins who were planted by wind and tended by rain.

The tree limbs were too high to climb now. I no longer knew the names of the squirrels that skittered up and down the long tree trunks that once looked to me like pathways to the sky.

The fog became thicker as I sat in the rocker. Droplets of moisture had formed on the gazebo and in its diamond-shaped latticework; they dripped and spread from one white diamond to another. Finches in the trees above twittered and dipped in the air, rousing the tree leaves. One scrub jay perched on the railing of the gazebo and squawked at me.

I told it, "Years ago your ugly old grandfather robbed every blackbird nest at Green Gates."

Again it squawked, straining its neck toward me, its beady black eyes looking, Andreas once said, like watermelon seeds. It took off, flapped in a great circle then landed even closer on a lantern post and skulked at me. Its beak opened and closed several times, its neck feathers rippled.

"Go away. I haven't anything to give you," I said.

But instead of leaving it chirped in a loud shrill tone and dove at me. I ducked quickly and wondered if I were near her nest but remembered that scrub jays roost higher than the smaller birds that were more apt to attack people on foot.

I stood up and prepared to leave when the jay appeared again in the grey sky. It flew from one tree to another then charged head on. I lowered my face, drew my arms over my head and cried, "Go away!" I could feel its blue wings scuffing against my hat. It retreated. Pausing before I straightened up, I thought I'd hurry for the back gate, the one that led through the forest and over the dunes to the lighthouse. I moved past the guesthouse and over the path to the barn whose hayloft door creaked in a light, cold wind. The bird had gone from sight; the loft door was still.

I leaned against a pine trunk and closed my eyes. But the bird screamed in the air near me and attacked again, its claws and beak tearing at my hat. I dropped into the soggy orange pine needles and lay still for a moment taking great gulps of air into my lungs. A crooked pine branch lay within a few inches of my reach. I clutched at it and rose, brandishing the knotted wood. This time when it came at me, I was ready. I struck at it, holding the branch like a baseball bat. I missed but it came at me again and this time I made my mark. The bird backed off, seemed to fly backward into the heavy mist, its wings spread, its cold black eyes challenging mine with a vacuous glint that I had seen before.

I stumbled toward the back gate, pausing beneath an oak tree. Evil women in fairy stories, witches like Isabel, always had wicked birds such as this one, their familiars.

Tears formed in my eyes and a great wave of pain surged up into my chest, but I could not hold back the memory, the knowledge that was summoned: Isabel had gone to Boston just three months ago to see cousins. She paraded down Lighthouse Avenue in her new wardrobe after her return home. She strutted as if she were owed something. What had fortified her sense of entitlement?

What was it about Andreas that had changed? When he returned for his holiday, hadn't he been melancholy? He had a new way of reciting poets and philosophers that I attributed to a class he was taking at school. Now that I thought about it, the quotations always followed my questions and were clearly being used by him to discourage answers. I felt uneasy. *But why?* And when he hopped off the train this time he didn't shout as he had unfailingly in the past, "Will you marry me?" I had dismissed it as newly acquired self-consciousness. Odd that he should become reserved about marriage when our ages now made it a very real possibility. And yet he never gave me doubt of his love.

Just as I was about to swing open the back gate I heard footsteps on the path near the rose garden. Andreas walked slowly toward me. I cannot say why his presence did not surprise me, unless it was because this magical garden had a way of replacing lost things.

"I was released pending a hearing," he said as he stopped under the blossom-heavy branch of an apple tree. He leaned against its trunk, pushing his shoulder blades into it, then lowering his eyes to mine he said, "I hoped you would be here. I kept telling myself, if she's there then I know everything will be all right."

"That's the way it once was. Every little tiff brought us back here to Green Gates, to make up."

"And now?" he asked. "What does it do now? This garden?"

"It tells me to find the truth," I said, hardening my words.

"The truth . . . ." he mused, resuming his walk toward me through the growing mist, "is that we are bound together no matter our faults or errors." He touched my face with his finger and let it slide down my cheek, my chin to my collar. "I'm sorry you've been crying."

I said, taking his hand away, "Sorrow is something neither of us needs more of."

His hands reached out and without warning he pulled me to him, our bodies colliding first into each other and then into the oak tree trunk. Before his mouth covered mine, I said, "Please don't," which did not stop him. The tone of my protest sounded like Aunt Marion's and I wondered how her voice had appeared in my throat.

There was no salvation for the misgivings that had come into our relationship, but we took each other under the oak tree at Green Gates that day at twilight as if there were.

Chapter Twenty-One

*W*ith a dress in my hands I paused over the tapestry suitcase on the bed. Andreas had said to pack only a few things, just enough for a few days in the City, enough to get us through a wedding ceremony and a trip both ways. I held the soft ashes-of-roses dress up to the lamp, scrutinizing it. Then, folding it rapidly, I thought it did not make a difference what I wore. I tossed it into the bag.

"It's a very pretty dress on you," Phoebe said, her lips quivering. "I always thought I'd be at your wedding."

"Please don't be sad, Phoebe. I promise to be at *your* wedding."

Andreas and I had agreed that legal or not, our marriage and "consummation" would render my Uncle Robin defenseless. It would be the one time, Andreas had said, that he would be grateful for conventions. For Uncle Robin and Aunt Marion would be forced to sanction the marriage. Then we would leave for Boston together. He would assume the position of law clerk to a legal firm that had invited him to join them as he finished his last year of school.

The swiftness of our plans dazed me. I had confided in no one except Phoebe whose help I had enlisted. She stood despondently with her back pressed against the door and acted as my guard should anyone knock. Tears now glistened in her eyes, making them look like tiny stars across the room.

Her mouth puckered, "It isn't just that I'll miss you."

I turned to her, "But I will miss you, Phoebe. And you will come next summer to stay with us. I feel sure that by then everyone will have come to terms with the matter. Oh, you'll see that all will be well."

She slowly shook her head, her eyes shining. "I feel—terrible. I feel like there's a beast in me but it is not a beast . . . it's a feeling . . . like the feeling you get when you dread doing something that you must do. It's that same feeling, only before . . . like you know beforehand that something horrible is going to happen . . . ." Her voice broke and the starry tears ran down her freckled cheeks.

"Someone's coming." I said. I grabbed the valise and shoved it under the bed. Phoebe leapt from the door and onto the bed, propping her elbows out. I rushed to my vanity and grasped Cousin Dixie's silver brush.

Aunt Marion opened the door. "Angelica, I have a message for you." She held a crisp white envelope. "It was delivered by Claudia's house woman." She brought it to me and laying it on the vanity, she paused, looking at my face in the mirror. The expression begged my forgiveness. Was she then sorry she had confided in me that afternoon? No. For square on the bone of her cheek there lingered the spot of flushed pink skin that had appeared with the memory of her secret afternoon.

"Thank you," I said. "I would prefer to read it in private."

She nodded at me, looked at Phoebe and left the room without questioning the letter's contents.

As the door closed I tore open the letter. It was from Isabel. She had written in a very forced hand, "Come to the small parlor by way of the garden at eleven o'clock tonight or I will testify against Andreas at the hearing. Isabel."

Her signature looked like something scratched out in stone by a lonely, crazed prisoner.

I tore it in half, making sure that her name was in two pieces before I hurled them both into the fireplace.

"It's Isabel," I said to Phoebe. "She says if I do not come to her tonight she will testify against Andreas." I pulled the case out from under the bed and stuffed some underthings into it. Phoebe resumed her guard position at the door.

"I will not leave you to explain things to your mother and father. I will write them a letter which you can give them tomorrow."

She nodded, her head drooping forward.

"With posture like that you cannot see the sky," I said.

She asked, "Where are you to meet Andreas?"

Knowing Phoebe wouldn't betray me I said, "At the fence, near the gate, on the Monterey side. There's a clump of oak trees. We are to meet at eleven-thirty. No one will be there at that time. We'll go on horseback to Monterey. From there we'll hire a team. We won't arrive in San Francisco until tomorrow sometime and as soon as we find rooms, we'll be married." She was uneasy and so I added, "Oh Phoebe, I am not running from something—at least I keep telling myself that—I am running *to* something. One can have *new* truths, can't one? Bright new truths that grow up out of the withered old ones? It must be so . . . ." I pushed a pair of slippers into the valise and fastened it.

Phoebe came up from behind me and tapped my shoulder.

As I turned to her she threw herself into my arms and begged, "Don't go to Isabel!" She looked up at me with those ageless eyes.

I took her head in my hands. "I must," I said, my own thoughts of dread left unspoken. But a gnawing curiosity beset my dread. I had to see Isabel and hear what she had to say.

"No," she wailed. "Go meet Andreas and get married and go to Boston and never, never come back to Pacific Grove. Please, please, please."

I stroked Phoebe's hair and said nervously, "I have no fear of Isabel."

She cried softly into my blouse. "Please—I will do anything you ask if you do not see her. Anything, Angelica."

"All right, Phoebe. I promise." I could not see how a little lie would hurt anything.

She looked at me with weary eyes, her fragile shoulders shivering with anxiety.

The Orwells were in mourning but their large, twisted mansion looked no more funereal than usual. I stood in the dark before it, watching the fog play around its chimneys. It was tall and its cupola stabbed at the sky. Bats flapped between house and trees like dismembered pieces of night.

I tucked my traveling case into a clump of scrub oak and started around the back of the house. It was difficult to see the winding brick path in the fog, but a border of shrunken golden poppies marked my way. I paused at the small parlor door that opened to a courtyard. The door was thick, but I could sense Isabel through the wood. I hesitated before knocking . . . if I stepped over the threshold it would be too late. If she were to kill something within me that night I was not wholly sure that I would recover. Love can endure tempests but not so trust.

I knocked.

The door opened quickly. She knew that I would come and pounced at the knob like a spider on a fly. But her smile was slow and sweet. "I'm so glad you have come, Angelica. It's such a chilly night. I have tea for us and berry tarts."

"I'm not hungry."

"Oh," she responded. "Mother baked them yesterday before—they were to go to the church bake sale. She makes the best tarts. Do have one, Angelica. Well then, if I cannot coax you then do let me take your coat. Oh, it's so soiled and yet it looks positively new. Isn't it wonderful that you've finally gotten a new coat."

"You'll not need to take it, Isabel. I won't be here long."

"Perhaps not," she agreed lightly, circling the settee that faced the fireplace. "But at least sit down, Angelica."

"No, thank you, I'll stand."

The pause that followed was designed to give her time to enjoy the seduction. The purple vein that striped her broad white forehead to her temple seemed to wriggle in response to an internal pleasure. Hard and thin, her fingers ran back and forth over the welting at the crest of the brocade sofa, plucking at it here and there as if her claws would benefit from the fussy movement. And as if she had rehearsed it, the orange glow from the hearth flames shot from her eyes as we stared at each other.

She plucked a berry tart from the table and in it went with one snap of her crooked, receding teeth. She chewed it slowly, dabbing her fingers on her mother's fine linen napkins. Her collapsed teeth turned violet. She grinned at me absurdly.

"Oh Angelica, I don't know how to say it. We've been such good friends all these years." She sucked at her purple teeth, then brought her thin lower lip over them in an attempt to pout. As bizarre as the thought was, I imagined it was possible that she *did* think we were friends. She had no criteria for friendship save her own distorted conception of it, an Orwell mutation that poorly mimicked the real thing. Then, walking her fingers forward and quickly pulling them away she sighed, "I will miss Luther terribly. We were very close."

"My condolences," I uttered. "Luther was many things to many people. What do you suppose it was that led him to take his life?"

She tilted her head and leaned toward me like a hound that has caught a scent. "Do you think so? That is quite interesting. I cannot possibly tell you the grief I felt when I confronted Andreas in the chapel last night . . . deep grief."

"Poor dear," I said looking at the ceiling then towards the door.

"Yes," she lowered her pointed chin. "To see one's own flesh and blood dead and gone forever. And to suspect that one's very good friend is responsible . . . ."

"Of whom do you speak?"

She jumped toward me, "I know you were with Luther last night."

"But of course you knew, Isabel. You sent him to the butterfly trees knowing I would be there. Did you tell him to attack me or is it something he plotted on his own?"

She straightened her back, "Angelica, you are not being civil."

"There was nothing civil about last night. Your brother tried to rape me. *Your* darling Luther."

"I am in mourning," she professed, curling her hand into a white fist. "How dare you speak ill of the dead."

"My dear Isabel, in life Luther was so ill that one can hardly now speak of anything else."

"You lured him there."

"I will not listen to this," I said. "It has been a long day for me as well." I moved toward the door. "My aunt and uncle extend their sympathies. They will, of course, attend the funeral."

She made a move toward the door, wedging herself between me and the exit. And then she drew the letter from her skirt pocket and waved it in my face with a defiance in her eyes that almost blistered me. I reached for the letter I had written to Andreas requesting he meet me at the butterfly trees. She ducked and bolted toward the hearth. Before I could prevent it she had torn the letter in half and had hurled it into the flames. Our eyes locked. If I had only had the letter to show to the constable . . . but instead my words to Andreas shriveled into black ashes.

"As far as I am concerned, Angelica," she said, her eyes returning to the ashes, "as far as I am concerned you and Andreas are responsible for my brother's death. Last night is rather a blur to me and so today I was unable to tell the constable what I really saw. But you see suddenly—suddenly I recall—" she looked at me "—that I saw Andreas kill Luther."

"You lie!" I cried. My hand rose from my side and found her face with such force that the sound appeared to crack open the room. She lunged at me but then withdrew like a predator that recoils slowly and with great poise plots a new attack.

The vein on her forehead bulged, her face was a deep rose and her eyelids dropped nearly closed as she said, almost singing, "I also have another story. This one will interest you a great deal more. You've been such a dear friend that I've been reluctant to tell you. I was not sure how you would take the loss."

"I have ten minutes. Long enough for you to be sufficiently hideous. You've done it in far shorter periods of time." I thrust my hands into my coat pockets as I did not trust how I would use them.

She positioned herself before the fire, her fingertips playing at her lips.

"I loved Boston," she began, her eyes narrowing. "I often told mother it was the perfect place for me. So genteel, you know? No, of course, *you* don't know Angelica. But trust me when I tell you that it is a city of ladies and gentlemen. Mother often said that the people of Boston would truly appreciate me but then she has always believed that I have been wasted on this uncivilized area of California. Dear God, Angelica, one cannot even find an enlightened dressmaker south of San Francisco. One has to be content with Chinese squid fields, church socials and monarch butterflies. So, as you know, mother sent me to Boston every other year to make up for this town's shortcomings. When your Uncle Robin first told me that Andreas would be attending Harvard I was overjoyed. Why?" She leered at me, her mouth puckering under fully blown nostrils. "Because I am often lonely in Boston . . . and because I love Andreas. Yes. I love him, Angelica. Love him . . . ." She stroked her cheek with the back of her hand. "Every night of my life I have lain in bed and wondered how on earth I could make him mine . . . *mine*. Perhaps I am speaking to someone who knows precisely how I feel. Perhaps you, Angelica, have wondered yourself how you could make Andreas yours."

"I haven't concerned myself with the thought, Isabel, for he already *is* mine."

She threw back her head and laughed savagely and I thought how much her neck looked like chicken flesh. Then in an affected little moment she recomposed herself and said coyly, "Forgive me. It struck me as humorous in light of the present circumstances. Oh, but then you do not know about the present circumstances. I don't suppose Andreas would tell you, now would he?"

Her lips parted as she gaped at me through rows of purple teeth. She drew in a deep, audible breath. Her fingers spread out over her collarbone, circling round and round her brooch. They stopped. She said, "Like you, I've always held him here, in my heart, even though mother and father expected more for me, a better match, if you will. It is not that Andreas lacks money but, well, *breeding*. Mother thought a young Bostonian would be more in keeping with our family lineage, but then mother's heart has never gone wild in her chest like mine has . . . like maybe yours has, Angelica. You remember when Andreas helped run the line to town, how he jumped in the ditch and tore off his shirt and grabbed an axe and began splitting up the road? I watched him for hours from behind a stack of barrels. And I asked myself, what would it be like to have those arms around me? What would that feel like, Isabel, I asked myself. You see I had to know. Don't you see that, Angelica?"

"I've heard enough," I said thinking that my voice would be commanding but it sounded ineffectual. I turned toward the door.

"But I've just begun. You mustn't leave now, Angelica. You are so important to the story; you give it that element of tragedy. Every ripple in his back, in his arms, in his face—seething in the hot ditch as he swung his axe up and down, tearing at the tangled roots in the road, crushing the granite rock. Everywhere I have gone I have looked and I have never seen any man like him.

"So there I was, Angelica, in Boston with my very proper Bostonian cousins for three months. But cousins or not, it can get very lonely in a strange town. Have you ever been in a strange town? No, of course not, so you do not know how your imagination can get the best of you, how you can positively explode from loneliness. My cousins left for a long weekend holiday and I begged off on account of nerves, and there I was with four long days ahead of me. And that's when I thought of Andreas—right in that very town! And I thought it just the most wonderful thing because you see my Uncle Kenneth is a lawyer of some reputation and I knew that Andreas and Uncle Kenneth would get along swimmingly. So it occurred to me to invite Andreas for a visit before Uncle Kenneth returned from the country house so we could discuss the numerous advantages of knowing someone like Uncle Kenneth, and at the same time, I would not be lonely anymore. It's lovely when both parties can benefit. But it is a shame that Andreas misunderstood me. *He* thought I said that Uncle Kenneth was there at the house and that they were giving some kind of party. I honestly cannot imagine how he got the story so utterly confused . . . .

"It was as hot as Hades that night, unusual heat for that time of year. It was far too insufferable to work and so I gave Aunt and Uncle's servants the evening off. It was the kind of heat, Angelica, that positively burns one's skin, suffocates one's breath. To put it simply, I just could not get dressed. You know how tender my skin is and I'm prone to heat rash. All I could manage was a light gown. Andreas swore that I said eight o'clock when in fact I said nine, which is why I was forced to answer the door in such a state of undress. We were both rather shocked and so I poured Dre a sherry and went upstairs to dress. A little while later he came upstairs looking for me, explaining that he thought there was to be a party. Well, it was embarrassing, terribly, terribly embarrassing because I had taken all my clothes off and had fallen asleep upstairs on my bed and there he was at the door of my dark room looking in toward the bed. I apologized, of course, but he thought I said I was sick and had asked him to come to the bed and help me . . . so he did. And there I was on the bed naked as the day I was born.

"Oh, Angelica, if what you say is true about my brother Luther then you know yourself what it is like to be taken advantage of. He fell over me and I reached my arms around his neck thinking, naturally that he was helping me off the bed. But then, well, he had had quite a lot of sherry to drink and he . . .

Angelica . . . he had his way with me! Do you know what it's like, Angelica, to have—"

"Shut up!" I sprang at her, wrenched her shoulders and threw her backwards over the settee. I jumped on top of her and slid my hands around her corrugated white throat. I would crush it. Squeeze the life from it. I watched as her color became darker, as her eyes widened and bulged like a fish's, as her tongue hung through the stained teeth. The sounds in her throat creaked and gurgled. I heard a word form. In a burst of strength her hands tightened on my wrists and jerking me to the floor she gasped, "Baby . . . you are killing his baby . . . ."

My hands fell from her and I stood up and backed away. She was on all fours in front of the fire, her brownish hair had come loose and hung like tentacles down her face. But she laughed, her nostrils dilating, her lungs heaving in and out for air. She raised herself to her knees and grabbed her belly in her hands. "Here is the proof, Angelica. In here. And when a man of virtue—and we both know how virtuous Andreas is—when a man of virtue fathers a child there is one thing to do—one thing or go to jail for Luther's death."

I found the doorknob behind my back.

"Luther's death. And you'll be the godmother!"

I opened the door.

"And if it's a daughter, we'll name her Angelica. Our little *angel* made from a heavenly night . . . *a heavenly night*! You thought you had him! Yes, I'll name her Angelica and I'll show to her the same kindness you have shown me. Andreas' child!"

As I closed the door behind me I could hear her cackling at the fire and, for a moment, thought I heard the fire cackling back.

Chapter Twenty-Two

I found my valise near the scrub oak and walked blindly, stumbling in darkness down the side streets to the edge of town. Not a light shone anywhere and but for the sound of singing insects, all I heard was noise under my skin, tearing through my body. A bird of prey, talons on the mark ripping away at my heart. My heart felt fragmented and beat against the wall of my chest as if to recompose itself.

I was thinking of Diana and the shattered light in her eyes after Royal Shaw had left town that morning years ago. She had never spoken about it and now I knew why. There are no words to mend betrayal, spoken or not. You can cram your head with prayers and excuses and pledges and platitudes but they merely shriek around inside of your brain like warriors who have not been told the way into battle. Words cannot stop you from loving just as betrayal cannot, but, oh God, how you want to stop loving.

Tears spurted from my eyes and rained over my cheeks and down my neck. I could not walk and so moved off the road and into a fallow field, a perfect brown square struck with moonlight. My legs gave way. I fell to my knees and lay down flat against the earth, smothering my face into the rich brown soil. I pressed my face against the earth. I dug with my hands until I had created a hole deep enough to cover my face. I wept into it, into the dark, damp ground. I rolled onto my back and, sobbing, stared at the moon whose perfect edges appeared to be melting beyond my tears. Stop staring at me, I told the moon. I grabbed a fistful of earth and flung it toward the moon. "Stop staring at me! You are a liar!"

Andreas was waiting for me.

I stumbled to my feet, picked up my valise and, looking back at the field could see the impression in the earth where I had lain, the earthen bowl that held my tears. I needed to commit it to memory. I wanted to remember this night in a field that was as dark and barren as my future.

I could see him now beyond the clump of trees on the other side of the fence, his back toward me, hands on hips, facing east. Andreas . . . always Andreas.

I sat on a boulder and stared at him thinking about what almost was, thinking of the man I used to know and watching the stranger in the shadows pacing as if his life depended on my arrival. His eyes were now on the ground, his fingers combing through his thick golden hair. Even in the dense night the moon had found his hair and illumined it. I thought of him as a deposed God, an Olympian traitor whose invincible power had, in a mere moment, been revoked. He had erred and that error would ignite the anguish that stirred in him. I could do nothing to help him. He would guess that I had gone to Isabel and learned of the child, not meeting him as promised.

But could I separate his pain from mine?

He never looked more alone to me than he did that night, pacing, waiting for a woman who would not come. How long had we both been hanging on to a fragile thread when we once had woven an entire kingdom out of hope? A kingdom we ruled. It began and ended at Green Gates.

Andreas paced faster now, his boots kicking up the dusty earth. He sat on a large boulder, covered his face with his hands then spread them over his knees and stretched his back straight. He looked into the sky. Or at the moon? His strong profile looked perfectly chiseled as if born of the rock on which he rested.

There would be no marriage. No Boston, no Samoa or Zanzibar. There would never again be a night like last night or an afternoon like today in the garden at Green Gates. Like children's tales, they had retired to memory. And the far off places would remain simply names printed in small black letters in the atlas in someone's library, as insignificant as the poetry that we had made from our life together, scenes inscribed on fading tablets.

He turned toward me and searched the darkness. But I was well hidden. He took several steps in my direction. His eyes glittered. They had those tones of sympathetic light that moved and changed and bespoke sorrow at other times. For whom was he sorry now?

He turned from me and walked toward the fence built by townspeople to keep out the undesirables. The brooding face became a vengeful one. His hands fell upon the wooden gate boards and he pulled at them with all his strength. He began kicking, his hard boots smashed into the gate hinges until they collapsed. He ripped the gates from the posts and cast them aside, pulling a loose board off. With the board he hammered at the fence. One after another the boards were ripped from their foundation. Nails screeched as their holds were broken, lumber groaned as it was thrown into a ragged heap. His hands were bleeding now, sweat soaked his white shirt, which he tore off his body and flung onto the stack. The pillage continued until there was a twenty-foot section uprooted and lying in a pile like war dead.

Andreas staggered to his suitcase, chest heaving, blood from his hands running to his elbows. He reached into his valise and pulled out matches and paper. He crumpled the paper, lit it with a match and threw it on the pile. Thick blue smoke soon blocked my view of him. Then flames the color of ocean sunsets burst from the woodpile. I could feel the warmth from where I sat fifty feet away. Andreas stood back from the flames, the skin on his arms and chest was red and gold. Nothing, not even my presence, could tear his eyes from the fire.

I stood up and started home.

The burning fence made me love him more.

Chapter Twenty-Three

Newport Beach
Marla's Guesthouse
The Day After Halloween

*A*unt Belle's profile was the first thing I saw as I awoke just before sunrise. She was slumped forward sound asleep in an occasional chair that had been drawn to my bedside. In her lap was a knitted yarn something that vaguely resembled a muffin tin. Her pink fingers were splayed over it, the needles still puncturing the lump.

It was nearly light out, and chilly in Marla's guesthouse. Cool blue light pressed through the sheer curtains.

Andreas, I was going to cross the fence. I wanted to go with you—I swear it. It was Isabel who deserved punishment, not you . . . never you.

I was trying to think through what seemed like an impenetrable dream-like haze, only I knew I was not waking from a mere dream. Angelica's and Andreas' past was something I had lived and I was still living now. Yet I had been asleep in this very bed since Neil had given me a pill and whispered that he loved me. Were the past and present both happening at once?

If so, I could not yet grasp time without borders. I now understood that there was no death, but was there truly an Andreas? Where is he now, in this life? Should I return to him in the other? There was only one answer available to me: Lucetta. She would know. I checked my watch. The Daisy Cotton restaurant would be opening at seven o'clock.

Aunt Belle stirred in her chair as I drew the covers back. I did not recognize the shimmering peach-colored gown I wore. It was undoubtedly something from Marla's guest closet as she kept an extensive wardrobe of castoffs for sudden overnight guests.

I tried to sit up. Pain shot from my shoulder through my body as if to remind me of Vincent's attack last night, not at all unlike Luther's assault in the forest near the butterfly trees. One incident was no more real than the other and yet I moved my ankle to see if it was still swollen from my fall in the forest. I could feel nothing and thought it odd that the vital pictures in my mind and the warm, electric emotions from that other life survived into this one while physical pain did not . . . at least, not that I knew of.

I stood up, favoring the aching shoulder, and limped toward the bathroom, past Marla's collection of wind-up toys and whimsical clocks. When I reached the bathroom, I saw the bizarre figures reflected in the large oval mirror over the vanity.

An ugly bruise smeared over one brow was beginning to seep beneath my eye. My skin was paler than usual and felt dry. I took a drink from the faucet and splashed water over my face as I turned on the shower spigot. The air in the bathroom became warm and moist and the mirror, beaded with steam, began to drip pure silver streaks.

As I opened the glass shower enclosure I head a noise, a tiny rattling that came from behind me and grew in intensity. The rattling was joined by a metallic clanking. It became louder and then in severe contrast, music began. First a lullaby, then a nursery rhyme, and then a show tune. The toys had begun to move. The music boxes tolled and warbled their melodies and they tangled in the air. An old tin monkey in a red suit spasmodically lifted his red cap and circled the planked floor of the main room on a unicycle. He was chased by a grinning clown in a fire engine who squirted water from his hose. Three ballerinas toe-danced in pristine pink tutus on the flowered circles atop their boxes. A yellow and black harlequin stretched on bars did flip jacks, his wooden legs clacking rhythmically against the mantle. Euphoric puppets jangled on twine, bouncing against each other, a prince and a princess locked necks, their heads banged together and their mute mouths opened and closed over toothless gapes.

I leaned against the doorway jamb wondering if it were not some kind of hideous trick of Vincent's. Who would do this to me? And then, as the toys jittered on the shelves and floor, a blue white light filled the room, swirling into the bathroom mist. The toys spun faster, the room was windy, the hems of the curtains jerked in the air. Aunt Belle, slumped in her rocker, was still but for a few strands of hair that lifted and lowered like something at sea.

I squinted against the bright light, then used my hand as a shade over my eyes. My feeling of terror subsided as it was replaced with one of expectancy. White lights . . . and now the flame which manifested at the foot of my bed that dawn, sparkled in the middle of the hand-hooked rug. The toys wound down and were silent, their cacophony dispelled by the ethereal light whose arrival they had announced.

It was deadly silent.

The flame billowed out and disappeared.

It was Andreas, the same Andreas who had appeared to me at dawn, not the one of Angelica's time, but the Andreas of today, of this present life. He was taller than Angelica's Andreas and his hair was darker. He was older, in his forties, I thought. His features were strong. But the eyes—there was nothing different about the eyes, the eternally immutable feature.

He wore a white shirt that rippled in the tumult of air as he stood silently before me. But he was not real. I could see through him. Was he merely an image? Had he projected himself to me? He had never been born, this man, he had never died. And as I watched him watching me, I felt for the first time my own immortality. Mortality of the world is a lie. Life is a cosmic impression, we are impressed forever and though our bodies and our lives change and even our places in the universe, death is not possible, it is contrary to cosmic law. How did I know this? Because I knew what he knew as he stood before me, his understanding immersed me and in that moment I was free. My heart felt uncontained, as if it had already left the tall, pale, frozen shell of a woman in the peach colored nightgown. I had moved out of my own body through a place between my shoulder blades, a glowing shadow connected by only a thread, and towards his outstretched hand. We touched. I turned around and there stood Paige Brighton asleep against the door, poor Paige Brighton, limited, puzzled, tormented by a life of lessons she still had to learn.

And here was I, the impression, the soul energy that was reality, the unchained, free entity that had chosen to be Paige Brighton on earth for awhile.

Together we were bathed in white light that then united us and buoyed us up, up through shimmering iridescent channels of liquid light. Pink, blue, gold, white, sparkling, resplendent. And as we joined one another, two halves of

the same whole, we were consumed. Not two people but
morning stars, born at the creation together, and again
together at last.

They were shaking me. Two of them.

"Paige, Paige dearie, wake up! What on earth . . . ." It was Aunt Belle's husky voice. I could feel her cold soft fingers on my arm. "Sweetheart, get up off the floor. You'll catch your death."

"Let me go."

Then it was Neil's steadfast voice saying, "Wake up, Paige. Now, now, over to the bed. You've fainted."

I opened my eyes to see the last emancipated sparkles of a dream. "Don't!" I cried bursting into tears. "Let me go. I want to go to him." I shoved Neil and when my defenses proved futile and he lured me back into the bed I began sobbing. Something had torn one perfect half of my body from the other. Though my vision was blurred with tears I glimpsed the toy clown and he was grinning wickedly toward the bed . . . such pleasure, he seemed to say to me, such infinite, soul rattling pleasure, something *real* people never attain.

"I don't want those toys in here," I said to Aunt Belle. "I don't want to see them."

She scooped them up and tossed them into the firewood basket. "In they go, look dear. Nasty little things. They really, really are."

Neil pulled the covers to my chin and tucked and re-tucked the quilt as if it gave him great pleasure to secure me like cargo bound for a tempestuous voyage.

He said, "You passed out, Paige? Or did you slip on the way to the bathroom? You were unconscious on the floor."

I thought: Unconscious? My God, Neil, you do not know what real consciousness is. To be conscious of everything, to deny nothing, to be as open as space, unshackled, to swim in the ethers: to *be*, Neil—I know what it is like to be conscious. It is only in *this* body, *this life* that I have been unconscious. You men of mind and medicine have so much backwards. *You* tell *me* to wake up? I am awake for the first time in my life. It is *you* who need to wake up, *you* who are unconscious.

He gently suggested, "You were dreaming, I think. Would you like to talk about it?"

"Let me sleep, Neil. I need to sleep."

"Do you need something to help you?" he asked stroking my hair from my forehead.

"No." I closed my eyes.

Andreas . . . I called. We did not speak words, our thoughts exchanged. We were in a milky white chamber with walls of light that waved like water.

He turned from me.

Don't leave.

It is too soon, he replied.

But there is no time.

There is in the physical. I should not have come to you. They woke you while you were out of your body. You could have died.

I want to leave.

It is not time. We have work left to do, he said.

Then let's do it together. Here or there or then . . . back then . . . .

Whether we experience each other in this life or not, our union cannot end. It is not always possible or for the best to have what we want, he said. We must learn to want what we need—the experiences which are offered to us. There are mistakes to be corrected, pardons to be asked. This time our work is with others. It is with them that the lessons will be learned. In a spark of infinity we will be together. When physical death reclaims us we will once again have the choice of rebirth.

I approached him. The closer I got the more intense the light became until I was burning. We merged and were absorbed into one another, two ethereal figures swirling inward, inward, like angels compelled into heaven.

Chapter Twenty-Four

When I came to, it was into Neil's face that I looked. Old, red, wrinkled eyes against white hospital walls. I had lain comatose for two days in earthly time, while I transcended to a supernatural union with Andreas in spirit time. Aunt Belle said that while I had not opened my eyes, Neil had not closed his. He had endured the solemn and sleepless nights at my bedside.

After I regained consciousness both Neil and the medical specialists (whose pencils were still poised in the air over a diagnosis) had decided to release me to Neil and Aunt Belle's custody. I had been driven to Candlesage in an almost morbid silence. I refused to talk to anyone. Aunt Belle, in the back seat beside me, afraid to speak, chewed an unlit cigarette and Neil, who was convinced that Vincent's attack had caused my mental trauma, honored the silence like a devotee.

Aunt Belle had insisted on stopping at a market on the way home, and while she shopped and Neil stretched his legs outside of the car, I opened the California map tucked in the door's side pouch. I traced my finger up the California coastline until it stopped at Monterey and there beside it, a smaller black dot above Pebble Beach, was the name Pacific Grove. I guessed it to be about 350 miles from Laguna Beach. I could drive it easily in a day and soon I would make the journey.

Neil turned to look at me as he got back into the car. My silence made his condition worse but I could not speak to him, not yet, for I knew he would leap upon the first word out of my mouth and the arduous monologue would begin . . . all about how he cared for me, loved me, loved me. God. I never knew if he was trying to save me or Simone Marchand.

But it was with Andreas I needed to communicate. I had concentrated for hours on his face hoping that, like radar, he would receive my message. But I was a novice at such transmissions and I hadn't the least idea how to psychically summon someone. Why hadn't Andreas returned to me . . . the Andreas in the dream or the Andreas at dawn? Why hadn't I returned to my former life? One could not will it, that much I had learned. But what could one do? Had I angered him? Made some immutable mistake? Insulted God? Broken the rules? Was I not worthy of moving forward toward the truth? Was I destined for punishment? Had I no friends to help me through this? Lucetta. Soon I would contact Lucetta.

Aunt Belle began to babble to Hitchins the moment we set foot on the grounds of Candlesage. The hubbub was over the Senator Langston Holt visit. My installation in the quiet of my room did not protect me from learning the details: in three days the Senator was flying in from Central California, where he had taken residence while studying the impact of offshore oil drilling at the Monterey Bay Aquarium. Neil was sending his jet to pick him up at the Monterey airport. Aunt Belle droned to me at odd times about the Senator's philosophy. He was, among other things, an environmentalist, a consumer advocate, a human rights "activist" in his younger days at college, and his name was being bantered around as the likely vice-presidential pick in the next election. Soon my lack of response silenced her. She began limiting her conversation to celebrity gossip, the need for eating plenty of red meat and yarn-fuzz density.

So for two days, I sat on the lawns near the marble woman, dumb and as deaf as I could be. Aunt Belle, Lulu and Helga hovered about me with fresh squeezed juice, classical music, newly cut flowers, robes and what were intended to be purple yarn slippers. Once when Neil came down to sit with me he lifted my hands to his lips, kissed them and then placed them back into my lap like dead things. He smiled because if he had not he might have cried. Mo ignored me so well that one could barely tell that my presence was annoying to her. If I could have turned to stone during the Senator's visit, I would have. Such an apt addition to her statuary collection.

It was the night of Senator Holt's arrival that my desire to return to the mist-filled days of Pacific Grove manifested itself. I had not gone down to meet the Senator and my presence at dinner, in the state I was in, would have been at the very least embarrassing. I was left alone.

When I slept that night I dreamed . . . . I had worn a pearl blue nightgown to bed, the satiny kind that women in the forties always wore and that Aunt Belle had purchased at a vintage clothing store in town. The night moon shone through the silvery windows. A pair of wall sconces on either side of the fireplace were dimly lit and smeared fan-shaped light from their etched crystal bowls to the high ceilings. Before I fell asleep I remember thinking how the light outside and in the room had managed to create an iridescent shade of blue in my nightgown as if I were the room's light source, a glowing body beneath a membranous blue shade.

I dreamed that I emerged from the bed, floated up from the covers effortlessly. I stood next to my body which lay on the bed twisted toward the window, toward the night moon. I leaned over and stroked my own arm as if to assure myself that I was freed of an earthly body. Free. *I was free.* The sensation was reminiscent of youthful innocence, soft and unfettered.

The window was open and on the sill a large crow hunched in the chill night wind. Her blue black feathers stiffened and rippled down her body. She entranced me as her eyes caught the lamplight and reflected it back into the shadowed room. And then came a great, euphonious call, a cawing from her throat and flapping of her wings. She had put me at the ready. I wanted to follow her. I lifted off the earth at the very moment that she, too, deserted her perch for the freedom of flight. She led me, soaring ever higher over cities, black mountains and shimmering seas.

In no time I saw the deep curve of Monterey Bay and I rejoiced at the sight of the fog patches, the treacherous rocks that guarded the Central California coastline. The deep green waters stirred restlessly, home to a million precious creatures.

She took me to the coast, flying over a forest of age-worn cypress trees with deer unmoved by our presence, before passing over the familiar Moss Beach, across the shrunken sand dunes and into a familiar garden.

Green Gates. Like old arms, it embraced my spirit. The gazebo had gone to near ruin, its fragile white sticks slouching toward earth from solitary nails. But the rock walls were still sturdy and gave themselves over to orange nasturtiums, climbing pink roses, ivy and scented geraniums. Brick walkways still wound about rose bushes, and apple trees nearing the end of autumn were laden with overripe fruit, some of which had fallen to earth.

The tall Sparring house Green Gates, once home to Knute, Signe and Andreas, brooded in the dark. An entire neighborhood had sprung up around it. A small light emanating from the guest cottage behind caught my attention.

We descended to a spot behind the gazebo, and with expectancy I watched the cottage door until it swung open, revealing an old woman who hobbled into the moonlit night. She was wrapped in a long red robe and walked uncertainly with the help of a warped wooden cane. In her other hand she bore a flashlight and on her arm a basket swayed as she drew near the small apple orchard. She meant to pick the apples, midnight or not. Her body was as bent and twisted as the wind-sculpted cypresses, but all the same, she moved through the garden with spunk, prattling on about the condition of the bricks and the dim beam of the light from her flashlight.

"I wait to pick the apples so he can have fresh pie and he takes off on a trip," she complained to the dark garden, "But I said I'd bake an apple pie and apple pie it will be. I'll eat it myself. Now, if the jays or the worms haven't taken the best of them."

She fumbled in the orchard, her aged hands squeezing and thumping the fruit, picking one here and one there. "Ah, there's a beauty!" she exclaimed. "I've been watching you grow. Your life as an apple is about to end, and your life as a pie is about to begin. Is that why you fall so willingly into my hands? Eh? This will be the best damn pie any ninety-five-year-old woman's ever made. But I have an advantage," she tittered. "How many ninety-five-year-olds are still baking? Not many. No, not many."

A gentle breeze blew through the trees, and for a moment the fog parted and the moonlight found a path to the garden at Green Gates.

Abruptly she turned toward me and said, "Who's that?"

I was careful not to move, to startle her. "Who's that I say?" She then clutched her throat and with a faint gasp said, *"It's you."* I could not see tears but her voice cracked and shook as if with joy.

She stepped toward me, peering. I moved behind a pine. Her crooked stick poked at the earth ahead of her, the basket of soft green apples swayed on her dark red sleeve. As she tried to place my presence near the gazebo, the white beam from her flashlight tunneled through the dark. She stopped, lowered the flashlight and said to herself while peering blankly in my direction, "My imagination . . . my old age. That's what Denholm always told me. All those years of marriage and he never once saw what I saw. Because he didn't want to, that's what I told him. But I could have sworn I saw Angelica just now. I could have sworn it was her."

I moved as she turned away. She twitched her head around. Her hair was dyed a brilliant flame color . . . so very like the color of . . . .

"It is me," I said timidly. "It is your Angelica."

"Just an old lady imagining things . . . I remember when I *could* talk to spirits but that's when he and Angelica were here." A dreamy spell settled over her and she paused, looked up into the tangle of pines overhead and spoke to the darkness, "For years after she died, for thirty years at least, she came here to the garden. She was wearing the very dress she went to sea in—her mother's wedding dress. For awhile she stopped paying visits and then the next time I saw her in the gazebo he was here too, dancing with her. They would laugh and dance and call to each other. 'Andreas,' 'Angelica.' Oh yes, I watched them many a night. Happy creatures of light and mist darting here and there like children—as if they had never died at all. Right here in the apple orchard at Green Gates I watched them." Her voice choked and she coughed. She craned her neck to the sky. "I've never stopped missing you, Angelica." She lowered her head and secured the apple basket, letting the cane drop. She turned off the flashlight and whispered, "It's so quiet here . . . I can hear the stars burning."

She creaked open the dark iron gate that led to her front door. In moments the inside lights sparked off. I stood in the garden alone and awestruck, for I knew that she was *Phoebe*, my young cousin who was now grown old and bent with age. Tears sprang to my eyes. I yearned to take her into my arms . . . but I was no longer Angelica. I was *Paige*. Would she understand that?

What had I hoped to see this night in Pacific Grove at Green Gates? My past? Had I hoped to encounter Andreas? He would have been long dead, just as Angelica would have been . . . I was confused . . . I could not remember our ghostly dances in the garden that must have occurred between that life and this one.

The crow appeared, circling the apple trees. I knew it was time to leave. We ascended through the thin fog over the pine trees. Soon we were moving over the bay along the California coastline, south to Laguna Beach and up into the hills. I was in my room at Candlesage and I saw myself against the bed, my body twisted toward the window. The crow sprang from the window ledge and vanished quietly into the night.

How long had I been out of my body? I climbed into bed. I climbed into myself.

Chapter Twenty-Five

Candlesage

My spirits rose with the sun that morning and for reasons I could not explain, my apathy was replaced with an immense drive to make something happen. For all of my life, circumstances had led me. But after the ethereal visit to Green Gates, I was infused with determination to chart my own course.

Despite my sore shoulder, I decided to go riding, though I had not ridden in years.

I rummaged through my things and found a pair of jeans and plaid shirt and jacket in place of riding clothes, which were not packed in the move to Candlesage.

The air was brisk and the colors of dawn swept inward from the earth's edge, blanketing even Candlesage. A euphoric pink hue stretched west away from the rising sun.

The groom was having breakfast but had a horse saddled for me in minutes. She was a spirited strawberry roan with a white star and a daring flash in her dark eyes. She was ready.

Once out of the stables I ran with her at full gallop away from the house, away from the sun, toward the deep purple hills that marked the northern border of Candlesage.

The air was cool. The horse's quick hooves flew through the tree shadows that lay out long and tall against the earth. We galloped on through the tangy scents of orange groves, over the broken fencing that once surrounded a herd of Holsteins. The meadows had turned green from last week's rain and they now waited to drink the sunlight as they had drunk in the dew of the night.

I let the horse forget me. She ran as if she had waited an eternity for this kind of speed, for this freedom. She ran as if she had no earthy destination but that she ran against time, through time, beyond time. She was the perfect thoroughbred.

Nothing mattered to the horse or to me but to leave it all behind. So we galloped like a centaur, wasting no time. We could not feel anything pulling us back—the restraints engraved in lifetimes of discipline were run out of existence, crushed by hoof beats at dawn. It was insanity and I laughed, as she must have too, at the beauty of mindlessness.

The clouds of pale brown dust might have been the only evidence of us, we moved so swiftly down the hills. I hoped that if a lost hiker had looked in our direction she would have seen only a funnel of silken earth churning itself. The horse and I had created in our frenzy a private destination and a route that the physical world would never detect.

It was the feeling of the sublime nothingness-that-was-everything. It was a place in mind that knew nothing of choices, explanations, and submissions to the workaday world, the eleven o'clock news, crime and famine, a starving earth with its starving peoples, rich and poor alike starving for so much, food the least among them. We left it behind.

In the pounding, there was purification, and in the speed there was the absence of thought and knowledge. The song of the Universe is not sung with knowledge but with a melody that springs forth from the heart unrehearsed. We had our song. And we sang.

Then I saw him. On the crest of a hill that lay in the shadows of the purple mountains. He stood beneath a black oak tree whose ragged limbs curled up from the earth. His horse was tethered to a nearby tree and he stood, one hand shading his eyes as he looked toward us, his back to the fresh morning sun. Was *he* a part of this escape? And then my heart stopped so suddenly that it beat with a profound ache. The horse sensed the intrusion and tried to run faster, beyond him, far beyond him as if she would pass into oblivion in the breast of the purple hills.

We drew closer. I slowed our pace. My face and eyes stung from the wind and from my hair that had blown free. My lips were dry. My throat, parched. My horse reared and snorted.

Was it he? Or was it a mirage?

I dismounted and left the horse unreined. The man was a hundred yards from me . . . and yet I knew. I took a step. My feet were heavy, my legs almost numb. The horse whinnied, her hoof stroked the earth. The man's body turned slightly and now his eyes, which had also witnessed the birth of this day, looked directly at me. I imagined that I saw the same pool of light that I had seen last week in my bedroom at dawn. But this light was a mirage. The sun had tossed me an optical illusion and the thin, watery veneer vanished.

But he was real. And the unexplainable sense of identification was real. It was Andreas. Here at Candlesage. Not a ghost or a spirit or an image from my past life. And he could not take his eyes from mine.

And the feeling that began in my heart like the sunrise that day spread deeply and thoroughly. And I gave myself over to our timeless covenant. We had, at last, found each other in this life.

I walked toward him as tired as one is on the last mile of a long journey. The horse followed behind me. Our steps were slow.

But Andreas did not walk toward me. Apprehensively, he looked away and then mounted his own horse. He was still some distance from us. The moment before he turned to ride off I heard him say, I thought I heard him breathe, "Angelica."

The vision of his retreat was blocked by the straw-colored dust from his horse's hooves. I was stunned. He had seen me. He had acknowledged me. He had left me and ridden toward Candlesage.

But why? He had come to me last week at dawn and had said, "Angelica, we must meet again." He had held out his hand to me. But he was also the same man who had, just a few days ago, appeared to me in Marla's guest cottage, in that dream place, and had said we must *wait*. I turned and hid my face in the horse's mane. I mounted the horse and we returned to the stables slowly, disconsolately. Before dismounting I held her neck in my arms and whispered, because I thought she might understand, whispered, "I want to be loved again by the man who says Angelica the way that he does."

Senator Langston Holt. By the time I reached the hallway to my room I was running. I scooped up the newspaper outside my door and hurried into the room, pressing my back against the door as I closed it. I tore the wrappings from the newspaper and frantically scanned the pages for any mention of his visit. On the first page of the second section I found his picture, smiling and waving upon his arrival at John Wayne

Airport. *It was Andreas*. Neil stood a foot behind him, his eyes nonchalantly on the camera.

Langston Holt was Andreas. My Andreas.

I threw the newspaper on the floor, wishing it were brittle enough to break. *But he is mine. He is my dream.* He doesn't belong to the world, to politics or to *Neil,* who was reputed to be his most generous financial supporter. *He was mine.* I fell to the floor and knelt among the crumpled papers until I found his picture again. I smoothed out the wrinkles across the picture and, suddenly sobbing, asked, "Why have you bothered to come back if you won't let me have you? Why have you done this to me?" I brought the paper to my face and buried my tears in it as I saw, in the dark depths of my closed eyes, saw him mount his horse and turn away from me toward Candlesage.

Someone knocked at my door.

Quickly I gathered up the paper and stuffed it into the fireplace. Wiping my nose on my sleeve I went to the door.

It was Neil. He was not surprised to see me up, dressed and a great deal more alive than I had been.

"Langston said he thought he had run into you while out riding at sunrise. I told him he must have been mistaken but it looks like I was the one in error." He walked into the room, put his hand on my arm and said, "I'm so glad you've rejoined us. You're feeling better, then?"

I nodded. "It was an impulse—the riding. I woke up this morning feeling like I had to do something. I knew everyone would be asleep."

Neil closed the door behind me. "Not quite everyone. Langston is an early riser. Did you talk at all?"

"No," I said pulling my robe from a hook in the bathroom.

"Oh," mused Neil. "He seemed taken aback by the whole episode, as if something about it bothered him."

Was he fishing for information? I wondered.

He went on as I took my hair from my ponytail and brushed it vigorously. "You know, Paige, last night after he arrived, we were having brandy in the library and he saw your picture on my desk. You know, the snapshot Glynis took last year at the beach party? He looked as if he'd seen a ghost. I explained to him that you were my fiancée. He said he thought you were someone he had once met . . . but realized he was mistaken." He paused. "Have you two ever met?"

"Langston Holt? No, never," I managed to say. Then, "Fiancée? Neil—"

"Funny the two of you didn't finish your ride together."

I came out from behind the bathroom door. "Yes, it is strange. We saw each other from a distance, near the hills. I suppose politics has something to do with it. A senator can't be too careful, can he?"

He smiled. "I hope this means that you'll be joining us for dinner later tonight."

Could I do it? Could I sit at a table with Andreas while sixteen other people talked about the ills of the world and its political prescriptions? *Oh God, how I despised politics.* I did not even know what state Langston Holt represented but I was too embarrassed to tell Neil.

He said, "Mo was hoping for an even number."

I thought, that fits. "You know me and politics, Neil. I'm as apolitical as anyone can be these days. I've heard the name Langston Holt, but I know nothing about the guy. I'm afraid I would embarrass you and Mo. And politicians—"

"But he's not just any politician," Neil said enthusiastically. "That's why I'm supporting him. You wouldn't really expect me to get behind anyone who is merely a political machine, do you? Unfortunately, like all good men in government, it'll be the thing that kills him, his lack of political savagery. But, Paige, he is the *only* person in government in this country who makes me feel there might be hope for the country—for the world. You'll have to meet him, talk to him to know what a truly remarkable guy he is. I'll bet, just bet, he'll win you over *and* he won't care if he does."

"I certainly believe that," I said.

"Then I'll tell Mo to put another place on." He crossed the room to the door. I followed behind him.

As he was about to leave he turned to me and said, "There's newsprint on your face."

Chapter Twenty-Six

he phone rang five times. At last Lucetta's heartening voice answered.

"It's me, Lucetta. Paige Brighton."

"Well hello to you, Paige Brighton. I'm sorry I haven't kept in better touch, I've been visiting family in Savannah, but I *have* been thinking about you."

"It's no wonder," I said. "You're the only person I know who would believe the things that have happened to me in the last few days."

"Good things?" she asked.

"Some. What you said was true, I mean, about leaving one's body and not being able to get back . . . about Andreas and I coming together in this life. Lucetta, it's happened. And I must talk to someone to help me sort this out. Would you be willing to meet again? Here, at Candlesage?"

She laughed. "I wouldn't miss it."

"This afternoon?" I asked, knowing that I could not face

Langston Holt at dinner without a plan of action, without at least attempting to understand the dynamics of our meeting.

"What time?" she asked.

"Two o'clock?"

"Wonderful things have always happened to me at two o'clock. I was hoping you'd choose it . . . but then, of course you would." She chuckled.

"When I hear you laugh like that I'm jealous. I want to be that happy, Lucetta, happy the way you are."

"Oh Paige, really, girl. I don't know if it's happiness, do you? For sure? It's probably more like acceptance and attitude, don't you think? But let's discuss it at *two o'clock*. Make a fire and I'll bring the incense." She hung up.

"Goodbye," I said to the dial tone.

I held onto the telephone waiting for more of her words, thinking illogically that the receiver might have magical properties since it carried her voice.

A senator. Damn him.

Wanting as little interference from the household as possible, I waited for Lucetta in the entrance hall at the front door. I could not be sure if Hitchins would let her in. The Senator's presence had given everyone in the house a smug new idea about how things should be run. You would have thought they had never before entertained dignitaries. But Lucetta's unannounced arrival would throw them into a quandary. In Orange County, a Georgian psychic in the hands of two amateur inquisitors like Hitchins and Aunt Belle would find herself detained in the kitchen musing over chitlins while Hitchins and Belle waited for word from a higher authority.

Neil's ancestral watchdog, the grandfather clock, chimed twice down the long hallway, just as Mo Carmichael swung around the corner and, on a sharp intake of breath, declared, "Paige! You're up and about, how nice."

"Thank you," I said, then wished the tone of my voice had been softer. I tugged at the sleeve of my white silk shirt nervously. Her momentary pause seemed long and weighted.

"Neil says you'll be having dinner with us tonight, but that's not why I'm here. It's the security guard. He says there's a woman in a purple Volvo down at the gate who says she has an appointment to see you—at two o'clock. He is awaiting word from me."

I nodded. "Yes. She's—a counselor, my friend. Her name is Lucetta—"

She sighed, raised her shoulders to her ears and remarked, "Yes. I know of her. We have to check on everyone. Senator Holt's life was threatened two months ago and since then security has been tightened. We cannot be too careful. I'll phone down, then, and have the guards open the gate." She turned to go, then remembered something. "Oh, yes, we *are* dressing for dinner tonight. Eight o'clock. And by the way, your aunt's cat is loose somewhere down here and has gotten into the plants. If you see him . . . it would be appreciated."

"Certainly," I said, "I'm sorry." I could not detect any chastisement in the smooth arch of her eyebrows, no ignoble trace of annoyance that she had been saddled with an idiosyncratic old woman, her mentally unstable niece and a cat named Chester who rooted as well as any peccary. It was a tribute to the graciousness of the upper class.

When she had left, I felt it my duty to peer into the adjoining rooms to look for Chester whose felonious nature I had endured for years. He never came when I called and never would, I was quite sure. But still I called, "Chester, kitty, kitty" into every open door along the hall, feeling enormously indignant that I was being detained by a cat while I stood on the threshold of cataclysmic psychic discoveries. Lucetta would have something to say about this, something about humility or something about the tiniest incidences sometimes embodying the most prodigious lessons. God is in the details. There is a reason for everything, a plan beyond every experience. Even Chester.

I saw Chester on the other side of the library, digging his claws greedily into an exquisite maidenhair fern which I knew had never borne a brown or wilted leaf. The doorbell chimed and Hitchins appeared to answer it. Lucetta stood on the threshold in a red silk sari. I looked back at Chester and the dangerously tilting plant stand. I had two seconds to catch it. I dashed out of the entrance hall and across the library to grab the plant stand and snare the ubiquitous cat. Lucetta, sensing something, followed me down the hall and into the library. In the opposite corner, Senator Langston Holt abruptly hung up the telephone and ran to help. Lucetta nearly collided with him. I snatched Chester from the plant while Langston Holt grabbed the pedestal to steady it. He leaned across me—it was almost an embrace. Chester clawed at my silk shirt and yowled, sprang into the air and out the door. We stood together, he and I, just inches apart and breathing laboriously.

Suddenly, the outlines of the room altered and everything but Andreas vanished. Nothing between us had changed, all that had shifted were the circumstances of our temporal situation. What could we do? What was our choice at that moment while the heat between us obliterated reason? *We are not who we once were,* I told myself above the ringing in my ears. *Oh God, if only we were.* It was only for a moment that we were lost in one another and then his eyes pulled away from mine as he remembered the room in which we stood and the people as motionless as the furniture while they watched us. Hitchins rocked on his heels next to Lucetta and behind her Mo and Neil had arrived in time to see us disentangle ourselves.

Lucetta cried out, "Now that's what I call a cat!" allowing all of us to smile and recover our composure. My hands were shaking so badly I plunged them into the deep pockets of my slacks.

"Has everyone met?" Mo queried melodically.

A round of awkward introductions followed. I introduced Lucetta after they introduced Langston Holt. He didn't smile and neither did I.

The two men, dressed in tennis whites, left for the courts. It was Neil who turned to look at me during a brief pause in the doorway, Neil who smiled reassuringly. And then when we heard the last clack of Mo's slingback heels in the hallway, we closed the door.

I collapsed into the fireside chair and tried to collect myself. Lucetta went to the brandy decanter and poured us drinks. "Here you go, honey, take a deep breath." I nodded and took the drink, sipping.

What could Andreas and I have done? What had been our choice at that moment when more language passed between our eyes than would ever pass our lips? Conventions had to be honored. We had planned our lives that way . . . . And yet, I wondered, did he forgive me for leaving him at the burning fence in Pacific Grove in 1906? Did I leave him *forever* that night? What happened to us after that parting?

Lucetta swallowed some brandy and planted her glass firmly on Mo's cherry wood library table. At last she said, "I saw it. Have no doubts, Paige Brighton. That man is, indeed, your twin soul."

Chapter Twenty-Seven

*T*he day had turned cloudy and the fire from the hearth warmed the library, washing the walls of books in gold. There were thousands lined up in rows from floor to ceiling but I suspected that not one of them could explain what had recently happened to me.

"Now listen good," Lucetta said, drawing her chair closer to mine. "See how your skin looks near this fire: it's warm and glowing . . . alive, not washed-out and pale." When I did not respond she stood before the fireplace whose mantel was higher than her shoulders, and raised her hands upward. "I could see it, Paige, between the two of you. He is here and you're confused because now that you've found each other you don't know what to do." She bit her lower lip, but her eyes revealed a smile. A very deep "mmm, mmm," emanated from her throat. Then her eyes grew wide and her tone became grave. "And do you know why you're confused, Paige? You're confused because this is not some afternoon soap opera *love affair*. You are trying to make sense of something beyond the language of mere emotion. This is an *affair of the ethers*, this is *eternity*." She leaned toward me and whispered conspiratorially, her eyebrows raised, "This is so blissfully rare, Paige. There are so few of us who recognize . . . who consciously reunite in life, aware of such transcendent togetherness. You and he . . . separate halves of the same soul, man and woman." The reverie died on her lips and her manner became stern and professorial. When she raised a hand in the air a silver bangle slid from her wrist to her elbow. She pointed at me. "In a lot of ways, you would both be better off if you didn't know. The responsibility is overwhelming."

I asked, "Not know? What do you mean 'not know'?"

With her other hand she slid the bangle back to her wrist and twisted it. "This simultaneous regression that the two of you are having, your other life as Andreas and—"

"Angelica," I told her.

"Angelica. Through regressions you've discovered your former life and through telepathic projections, you have found each other in this life. If you hadn't had these you would've met by chance, perhaps on some rainy day in a midtown coffee shop. You would have become immediately, strongly attracted to each other. Perhaps you would've had a wistful love affair—perhaps not. But you would always remember the man in the coffee shop, or the library or the theater. You wouldn't forget him or he you. You would've gone your separate ways, marveling at life's mysteries. But you would not have known what you know. And it may be better that others, who must be satisfied with unexplainable yearnings, a hint of deja vu, have been spared the knowledge that you and Andreas have and the specific pictures of one another. It can do nothing I now see but disrupt lives."

"Don't say that," I protested, not caring, momentarily, whose life I disrupted. What did it matter as long as we had each other?

She went on, the red silk sari reflecting the gold fire, her words forming slowly. "If you had never sent out that call, you wouldn't have gained this burning awareness. But now there are conditions. This knowledge that you both have, you and Andreas, or shall I say you, Paige, and Senator Langston Holt, will restrict you more than it will liberate you. You have a past together, and a past beyond that past, just as you have a future together in another life, and a future beyond a future. But what good is it to know this? The two of you are already confused. I suspect that both of you are wondering if you should dare acknowledge one another. You are afraid but it can be a good thing, for it will make you both cautious. You must be cautious, Paige. I suggest you meditate. It will help you sort it all out."

I stood up and joined Lucetta at the hearth. "I want to tell you everything that's happened so you'll understand why I must have him . . . . We are so close . . . inseparable. And it's not as if I have intentionally beckoned him to me, that I have manipulated our meeting. My God, Lucetta, you cannot know how shocked I was when I saw him this morning, at dawn, while I was out riding. That's not to say that I haven't wanted him to come to me, or to go to him, for there is nothing I have wanted more but I haven't hurt anyone—"

"Not yet."

"Last week, while I was at my friend Marla's Halloween party, in fact the day I was in your restaurant, I told my husband that I wanted a divorce. I was in Marla's bedroom alone with Vincent and he attacked me, and I passed out. But while I was unconscious, I returned to Pacific Grove, the town Andreas and I lived in at the turn of the century. The town still exists. It's on the Monterey Peninsula south of San Francisco."

"I know it well," she nodded. "Just north of Carmel."

"We were young in that life. We had known each other

practically all our lives and were very much in love. It's a long story . . . ."

I told her what had occurred during my return to Pacific Grove, leaving nothing out. I explained that when I woke in Marla's guesthouse Andreas had appeared to me. I told Lucetta what Aunt Belle had told me, that my heart had stopped beating for at least a minute while I was in the hospital. I finished by describing my "out of body" experience that morning, my astral flight to Pacific Grove and to my cousin Phoebe who was still alive, now a woman past ninety and living at Green Gates.

When I finished, Lucetta breathed deeply and exhaled slowly. Her lids hung over her eyes, giving her a sleepy look.

Receiving no response, I added, "I seem to have no control over what happens and when it happens. I didn't plan to—what do you call it—leave my body this morning. It was an exhilarating experience, but eerie. What I've learned in one week is monumental. And I have not willed any of it. My only desire was to find Andreas and now . . . ." I turned toward the fire. Was what Lucetta said true? Would Andreas and I be frightened into returning to our own lives alone? Was reunification impossible? The thought sickened me.

"Desire is the curse of humanity, Paige, for it usually converts to avarice," Lucetta announced, her heavy eyelids opening wide. "It is powerful, for any thought held for long enough imprints itself on the universal mind and becomes reality, whether it's good for you or not. You've heard the saying—be careful of what you pray for, you may get it."

"Yes, of course I've heard it. But I am willing to risk everything, Lucetta. I didn't intentionally make any of this happen."

"You say you didn't will any of this but that, my dear, is absurd . . . for conscious or unconscious, we are all the authors of our own lives. Each day we take a blank sheet and inscribe existence. We are the true masters of our fate, with help from the Creator who knows, after all, what is best. But petty desires too often usurp our wisdom. Like children, we would choose nothing but thrills for gratification. That is what greed does to us. It turns us into a parody of true life, a shallow, grotesque assemblage of skin, bones and cravings."

"That's quite an accusation," I interrupted defensively.

She pointed toward the window. "That is what you see out there, in this world, Paige, an assemblage of skin, bone and cravings. Everyone wants more. And where does more get us? Our minds and bodies and the very earth are diseased from all forms of the media, governments and false prophets. Oh there are plenty of them, all right. They instruct us to desire . . . desire . . . ." She shook her head and thrust her bracelets to her elbows as if ready to dig into something.

What I hoped would be spoken softly came out of my throat in a cry, "I want to be free. I want Andreas away from all of this. I want to be with him again. Somehow, with all I've gone through, I feel wiser. I know I could do it right. I would make it right."

She gently asked, "Have you heard anything I've said?"

"Yes! Damn it, yes I have." I glared at her. Did she know *everything*? Swallowing the brandy, I stated carefully, "Before Andreas appeared in my room that morning, I was half a woman. Nothing was happening inside of me after Shea's death. I was like one of those ridiculous gourds that people are always thumping on to hear what hollowness sounds like.

"There's enough spoken and written about bad marriages and I have nothing new to add. I often wished there were something unique about the 'badness' of my marriage. Vincent wanted to hurt me and I didn't think I deserved anything better. Neil helped me to see that much. He was right. But then I had dreams. I didn't know what I needed or wanted but sometimes in the late afternoon, or just before sunset, I'd go into my bedroom and lie down on my bed and in a half-sleep state, I would dream that I was happy, and I would pretend to be someone else, living somewhere else. The emptiness would disappear and my heart would feel complete. But the dreaming would sometimes hurt more than the emptiness because there was always the hope, but never the reality of deliverance." I paused. "Having nothing in here," I said, touching my heart, "made me long for that twin soul."

I sat down in the chair and wished that my glass were not empty. I waited patiently for Lucetta's next auspicious pearl of wisdom. The glow from the fire moved through the room and spread itself over the rich patina of the furniture. A portrait of Neil hung on the southern wall. He had tried so hard to fill the emptiness for me. He was a man who knew how to love, in his way. Surely he had given me more than I credited him with. Was the emptiness my own doing? I got up and refilled my glass. Neil was out on the courts playing tennis with *Andreas*. I took a sip and watched Lucetta, who looked as though she had hypnotized herself.

She said, "A longing . . . of something nameless and formless . . . an intense yearning to fill one's life. This is how he found you, Paige Brighton."

"Andreas?"

"Your twin soul, Andreas, was summoned to the rescue. The second half of the circle. Somewhere in the ethers your energies locked and you appeared to each other. You needed assistance. He came."

I stumbled over my words, "You mean, I called him? He 'heard' my dreams? He sensed something? And that's why he came that first morning—because of my need for something more? But then—how does he know who I *am*? How did Langston Holt recognize the picture of me over there, on the desk, last evening when he arrived? And this morning, when we were out riding? How did he know that I, Paige Brighton, am Angelica?"

Lucetta got a sly look in her eyes, "And what makes you think that you did not appear to him?"

"Me?"

"Suppose in your longing, you projected yourself, your image," she offered, shrugging.

"But I don't know how to do that. Like a film projector or something? Until last week I did not know such a thing was even possible. Me? Project myself?"

She explained, "We are so used to trying that we think nothing can be accomplished simply by being. The most important events in the universe occur when we are not *trying*—the very word implies stress—but rather when we are doing and being. Perhaps your ignorance of the process is what allowed it to happen . . . yes . . . suppose on those quiet afternoons as you lay in your room, your desire for something nameless with which to fill your heart projected itself out as astral energy. Whose would have been most likely to receive the image you were projecting? Someone on the same wavelength, so to speak? What soul would be the one most likely to respond to your grave unhappiness? Your twin soul, that's who. And let us suppose that he too longed for something nameless, formless . . . for his unidentifiable second half and projected himself into your room that very morning. Yes, that is what happened, there's no doubt in my mind. How can you be sure, Paige, that he *knows* he has projected himself to you—"

"But he said, 'Angelica, where are you? Angelica, we must meet again,'" I reminded her.

"Yes, yes," Lucetta said. "But he could have been anywhere that dawn saying to himself, 'Angelica we must meet again.'"

"Then he saw my image as I saw his. And neither of us knew . . . ."

She smiled, her white teeth gleaming, her eyes bright, "Imagine the surprise when he saw your picture last night!"

Grudgingly I said, "He couldn't have been any more surprised than when I saw him this morning."

"Perhaps he knew you but was afraid you didn't know him! A senator taking his benefactor's fiancée in his arms and carrying her off into the sunrise! It's a Hollywood idea, to be sure, and a stupid one."

"And I'm a fool to wish that he had."

"Yes," she agreed, "you are, for can you imagine if *you* had not recognized him? It makes for a bizarre plot."

"But we *have* recognized each other . . . ."

"And so the old song goes, 'the smile you are smiling you were smiling then, but I can't remember where or when . . . .' It does not have to be deja vu in the reincarnated sense. We meet each other in dreams. There is so little we know about our non-physical selves, how our energy draws us toward one another. The five senses are absolutely unaware and then—bam!—you meet like you and Andreas have, and it's so intense that it feels fatal—that you want to die for it. And if you're not careful—"

I sighed deeply, intentionally trying to silence her, got out of the chair and walked toward my picture on the desk. Neil had had it framed in burlwood. It was not a bad picture but the smile was not real. I seemed to be looking out of the picture toward this very day. I appeared to be smiling for the benefit of the musings of my future self. With a loud crackle, the fire beckoned me back to the hearth.

Lucetta and I stood silently for a meditative moment and

then she said, "In a situation like yours, it's difficult to behave responsibly."

"And thank heaven I don't have any responsibilities in my life right now," I sighed.

"Oh please," she murmured softly shaking her head, "You have a husband. You have a lover. Should I go on?"

Shocked, I turned toward her. "Vincent! What has Vincent to do with responsibility?"

She rocked back and forth on her hand-painted leather sandals. Their rhythmic squeak grated on me. She straightened up, squaring her shoulders. In a low, melodious tone she said, "Some would say you have karma to work out with him. Perhaps the pain of your marriage to him was a debt, that you injured him in another life and must now atone for it, that you must now assist him with his spiritual evolution."

And give up Andreas? I choked out the words, "No. Oh my God—Vincent? . . . No. *No.*"

She shrugged her shoulders. "Well, ultimately one must determine one's own life. That is the nature of soul evolution. We can't allow some other person or some religion or institution to choose our path for us. But you must ask yourself, what motivates *me?* What is my intention? Is it pleasure or is it Truth? What is the driving force behind my actions?"

I moved away from her. "I don't understand you, Lucetta, and I don't have any answers. I don't know what motivates me. I only know what I want. What I must have."

"And what of Andreas, of Senator Holt?" She was indignant. "In each life the lesson is different. While you might be all for this passionate reunion, he may have a different idea in mind. Have you thought of his feelings?"

"Of course I have," I said emphatically. "He came to me and he said 'We must meet again.' He's here isn't he? Here at

Candlesage just—just several hundred yards from here." The thought caused a wave of faintness. *Here. He's here.* I reminded myself. "For what other purpose would he be here?"

"And yet you told me that when the two of you met in 'the other world,' in the dream in Marla's guest cottage, that he said something about waiting, that the time was not right . . . ."

"He said something about waiting." I made the words sound inconsequential but Lucetta took in their importance. "I want him."

"And what of Vincent and Dr. Carmichael?"

"What of them? Vincent is inhuman, a man without a shred of integrity, of decency. He is to be pitied, I suppose, but not by me, not any more. And Neil?" This was a more difficult question. My eyes found the portrait, the soft curve of his mouth, the thoughtful gleam of his eyes that watched me from the canvas. It had been painted before Simone died. His arms were folded across his chest, one set of fingers showed on his cashmere arm. He looked like an advertisement for some English country aftershave, as if his life would always be perfect. "Neil has been a very good friend to me—well, more than a friend I suppose. But I haven't promised him anything. It would've been simpler—well, none of that matters now. I've made my decision, Lucetta."

Lucetta straightened her spine and took in a deep breath. Her hands reached behind her back, she clasped them and looked toward the ceiling. Then releasing the posture she looked at me warmly and said, "Then choose *your way*, Paige—and endure the consequences."

Chapter Twenty-Eight

*N*eil's lips brushed the back of my neck as he finished clasping the ruby and pearl necklace. I was not a gracious recipient. I felt at once unworthy and suspicious, and though it hung against my skin below my collarbone I gasped for a moment, as if I were being strangled.

"What's the matter?" He turned my face away from the mirror and toward him.

"I—I couldn't breathe for a moment."

"Maybe I should have waited to give this to you. It's just that I have been waiting so long—since last Christmas. I knew you wouldn't accept it then. I was hoping that now that you've left Vincent . . . ."

I had wanted to look *simply* dressed for the dinner party, a black dress on which *imagination* might hang. The stunning jewelry was a power piece. I thought of myself descending the incredible Candlesage staircase in this necklace.

"I can't do this," I said. "It just—it isn't what I want, Neil."

He returned quickly, "I'm not fool enough to ask you if you'd rather have emeralds."

I managed to smile. "I'll wear it—just tonight."

His fingers dug into my arms as he began to kiss me and thought better of it. He smiled assuredly, not letting this temporary setback discourage him. "You don't need jewelry, Paige, not with eyes like yours. That's why I didn't get emeralds, as a matter of fact. They're no match."

As absurd as his declaration was, I supposed he believed it. We walked out onto the landing together and down the staircase. The guests were assembled at the bottom.

When he steadied my elbow halfway down the stairs I impulsively said, not stopping my steps, "I am going to hurt you, Neil."

He said, "You already have and you may again. But ultimately I'll win. Paige, someday we'll be married for better or worse. Because I love you and in every picture of my future I see your face."

A quiver ran through me. The only way he could win is if Langston failed, if *Andreas*—

Aunt Belle whistled up the staircase with a noise that only a gaudy tropical bird could make. It was the necklace.

"Holy smokes, honey, what a set o' rocks," she guffawed.

Langston Holt turned away from a group of men in tuxedos and looked up the staircase. My foot missed a step and I slipped. And from the moment Langston Holt's startling blue eyes met mine, I was stunned nearly insensible, as if I'd been injected with a drug.

Mo's capacious drawing room was lit only with candles, hundreds of them. The profusion of flowers sucking bottled water from priceless vases bespoke of ravaged English cutting gardens. It was a perfect, perfumed November evening in which even the stars outside the expansive French doors were drawn to the occasion and blinked winsomely from the terrace toward the flickering candles and faceted jewels.

My necklace was the color of blood. Congressman Harry Yamaguchi's eyes stared at it in amazement. Anyone who wore a necklace like that must have done something important to get it. As he began to lean closer Neil appeared, introducing me as his fiancée—which was news to me—and thereby assuaging the Congressman's curiosity. More introductions followed but before I could meet everyone I found myself withdrawing to the side of the room, until I stood apart from them, hearing their noises but not their words, feeling for sure that if I were to reach out with my hand I would touch a movie screen and cause the room and its occupants to ripple before my eyes.

He would not look at me.

"Fiancée!" Marla squealed from behind me. She popped a prawn into her mouth and washed it down with a vodka martini. "Did I hear that right? You've finally agreed?"

"No, I haven't agreed. Neil didn't tell me you were coming," I said.

"Hey, don't sound so disappointed," Marla smiled. "If the donation's big enough, it will get you in anywhere. That's something you'll learn when you've been married to Neil for awhile. Langston Holt has everything but big bucks. With Neil's influence, Eugene and I are convinced he can do anything. God, he's even better looking in person than he is on TV, Langston Holt, I mean. Don't you think so? Come on, Paige, what's the matter? You look utterly tragic. Do you need another drink? Or maybe some jewelry polish?"

"I don't need anything."

"Have you heard from Vincent?" she asked. "You know he was released on bail. I don't suppose Neil's spoken to you about it. He said he didn't think you were up to discussing restraining orders and court hearings and he doesn't trust Vincent any more now than he did before he was thrown in jail. In fact, Neil's afraid it will provoke him into doing something equally as stupid. All those security guards out there," she gestured toward the terrace, "are as much for your benefit as for the Senator's but Neil didn't want you to know it. So why my big mouth?" she asked, emptying her glass and holding it out at arm's length for another. "Because I don't think you're nearly as fragile as Neil does and I think you should get the ball rolling toward the divorce courts." When I did not answer she put her arm around my shoulder and said affectionately, "I want my old friend back. Just imagine life without Vincent."

I smiled at her because I felt I owed it to her but thought that she would never get her old friend back. I was different. I was no longer the Paige she knew. I was also Angelica. The awareness of my past life had altered my identity. I was not in love with Neil Carmichael. I was in love with Langston Holt. And that alone redirected the pattern of my life.

"Do you believe what Justine Doyle is wearing," Marla hissed in my ear. "I haven't seen orange that bright since 1971. She looks like Cinderella's coach. And God, it's funny, isn't it? Her husband has that little, whiskery look, like one of the little mice that drives *it* to the ball. Oh, come on, *laugh* Paige. I *am* funny. You've got the world by the tail, not to mention Neil. Look, he's staring at you."

With a smooth gesture, Neil raised his glass toward us and smiled. He leaned against the fireplace mantel, his elbow resting on it in a gesture of determined nonchalance.

"Here," Marla said maternally, "let me get you another drink. I'll be right back so perk up, will you?"

When I had been with Vincent parties were a way of making

me forget who I was. They were the glittering lies that kept me believing I could be happy. Strange, it was like adorning a shroud with jewels. Nothing had been able to change our grim marriage. But this party at Neil's was not a lie, it was the truth. I was as remote from the others as were the stars peering in from their drift in the heavens. I knew Andreas but not Langston Holt. I knew Neil Carmichael but did not know why he insisted upon loving me and what he really wanted. I thought I knew Marla and Eugene but they did not know me. And the others . . . we really didn't much care about one another. I didn't know what we were doing here together.

I felt pinned to the wall, incapable of pulling myself away from the elaborate oriental chest that served as my backdrop. Marla winked at me when she returned and shoved a glass of wine into my hand before saying, as she departed, "We're right in the middle of acid rain. And here I thought it was a new form of skin peel!" She giggled and returned to Congressman Yamaguchi's jovial group. Several people made the effort to include me in conversation and then disappeared, relieved, it would seem, that they had failed.

One look, I thought, *just one look*, one small sign of recognition. *Anything* Andreas.

After an interminable time, although it was barely an hour, dinner was served. Langston Holt escorted Mo to the table and because of my inability to pry myself off the wall Neil and I ended the parade into the dining room. We paused at the door as the others were being seated. Neil pulled me back into the hallway and said, "I think it was a bad idea to have you down to dinner tonight. It's too soon after . . . ." He was going to say "Vincent's attack" or "your hospital visit" but his voice trailed off as he looked deeply into my eyes. "Do you want to go up to your room?"

"I'm fine. I'll eat then go to bed."

Gently he raised his hand to stroke my cheek but it was intercepted deftly by my own.

He said, "I'd give anything to touch you right now."

"I know," I said quietly, entering the dining room and finding my place to Neil's right, which surprised me. With a stricken look he seated me. Marla and Eugene were placed somewhere in the middle of the elaborately laid table. Langston Holt was seated to Mo's right. And when I looked through the chorus of blazing candles I caught glimpses of him in the shadows between the trembling flames.

I ordered a drink from Hitchins—a vintage Chardonnay. My fourth one. Neil whispered, "Wine is being poured, Paige." But I had him bring it anyway.

Fortunately, Congressman Yamaguchi and his wife supplied Neil with endless conversation and he did such a superb job of responding to them that only I could tell he was preoccupied. For awhile I followed their words and then the words, like the candles, began to blur as I watched Langston Holt talk with Mo while she stroked the stem of her wineglass. And then it happened. Through the fluid glow of candlelight rising from the table he looked at me; not a glance but with deliberation in the way that only Andreas could. *His eyes had not changed* and when they struck mine they lingered there, shutting out all else. I wanted to talk about the burning fence. I wanted to tell him that I would not leave him. *I wanted to talk about us.*

Dinner passed without another look from him. I gave up watching, hoping, and when I mentally turned away from him isolation gripped me. His attention was my survival. It was pathetic, I knew, to subject one's very being to the whim of another. This acknowledgment brought me back to Neil who, as he stared portentously at me, could have been thinking the same thing of me that I was of Andreas. What irony. For the first time I wondered if Neil had been in that former life with Andreas and me. What about the others at the table?

My attention snapped back with the rattle of china and chair legs. Mo had risen and was leading the party back to the drawing room.

The candles had softened in the room. The guests formed into three small huddles. Hitchins appeared with chocolate-dipped strawberries, moving from group to group. Someone from the caterers was offering cappuccino. Langston Holt took nothing.

I sat near Marla who talked enough for both of us. While she held everyone's attention I thought, could it be possible that he would leave tomorrow morning without an acknowledgement? Would this be the extent of our expression in this life . . . a chance meeting during the formation of a political campaign? That I would be left with contemplating only the past?

As the guests began to leave, I slipped out of the terrace doors and into the cool night air. November nights always smelled spicy to me. The fragrance of brittle autumn leaves and roses, the last of the season, traveled through the air from the garden walls. Pear trees plucked of their fruit dropped leaves one by one. But it was to the marble woman that I walked, through the arbor, down the stone steps and across the icy green lawns.

I sat shivering for awhile on a wrought iron bench staring out across the statuary garden and thinking, without revelation, that I fit in better out here where everything communicated in stone. Nothing happened the way I had hoped for. I had failed. I was numbed by his lack of an acknowledgement.

I heard cars whirling down the circular drive, away from the glow of Candlesage mountain. A distant voice called goodnight. Like crickets, other voices chirped.

The necklace felt as if it were growing colder, heavier. I ran my fingers over the smooth rubies, the perfectly matched pearls.

There was nothing sharp enough on the necklace to tear flesh and yet it had the definite feel of a weapon.

I walked into the statuary garden. The moon shone beyond a cloud, giving the sky foamy effulgence. In the distance the purple hills lay shrouded in black. Each piece of garden art was the object of a spotlight creating dark and lonely paths between them. I strolled between the statues and touched their marble skin, which was no colder than mine, their marble chests no less empty, and their marble lips just as still.

This was the first time I'd seen her at night. She stood as if lit from within. Her outstretched arm flowed away from her body toward the basket of petals, toward the bubbling blue-black water that was the color of Angelica's hair. Light flooded her skin. She looked carved of opal.

I slipped off my shoes and stepped into the pool and walked through the water to her feet. I was immersed to my knees, my long black dress dragged behind me. I knew the water must be cold—it was November. I climbed up and stood on the pedestal with her. I could just reach her neck. I reached beneath my hair and unclasped the necklace and placed it around her throat. And the way the moon and clouds were playing in the sky, I thought I detected a glimmer in her eye. I stepped back down into the water and looked up. Perfect . . . it was perfect on her. The necklace would never be more beautiful than it was at that moment when the spotlight catapulted off the rubies, when the pearls lay against her skin as if born of it.

And that is how he found me.

Chapter Twenty-Nine

I turned abruptly in the water. We stared at each other as either friends or enemies might, sensing the power of the rendezvous, speechless because there was too much to say. Were we recapturing each other in those silent moments? His blue eyes carved away on my heart and with a desperate move, I lifted my skirt to my knees and stepped out of the pool, wringing out the bottom. I was afraid to speak and so I wrenched at the fabric until my hands ached.

"Can I help you?" he asked.

"Help me . . . you surely know the answer to that."

Tenderly he said, "You look like you're having . . . you have a problem."

I paused before speaking, hoping he would say or do something more. And then, "I do have a problem, Senator. But there aren't any political solutions for this problem, I'm sorry to say." My heart was breaking. "It also has nothing to do with garden pools and soaked dresses. Except one dress . . . a long time ago. A wedding dress in a storm on the sea."

He leaned over, found my shoes and said softly, "Maybe you should put these back on." How like Andreas. He touched my ankles, helping me guide the black heels onto my feet. I leaned into his shoulder. Had I felt his fingers pause for a moment against my skin? I recalled a time when Andreas slipped Angelica's boots off her feet . . . in another world . . . another time. My God, what were we waiting for?

I asked, "Did you follow me out here?"

"Yes."

"Hoping for . . . ."

He repeated, "Hoping for . . . ."

"I knew a man once . . . how like him you are." I took the plunge. "He was everything to me. It was a lifetime ago."

He exhaled sharply, his chest slightly caving as if his heart had been touched. "And I knew a woman. She had black hair and eyes that could see forever."

"His name was—well, you know his name."

"And her name . . . surely you've heard me say it."

I felt his hands on my shoulders, "She looks better in the necklace than you did." He smiled consolingly, as if he had a reason to pity me.

"I feel the same way," I said of the necklace. I would not let him make me look away. I kept my eyes on his. His hand left my shoulder and traveled up to my chin and through my hair to the back of my head. With his fingers spread in my hair, he pulled me close to him. My head fell onto his shoulder where, just a moment before, the moon had shone. But the embrace had the tender quality of parting lovers, not of lovers beginning a life together. We were not celebrating anything. I felt as if we were confirming a tragedy, like friends who meet at a funeral. Or was I imagining this failure?

I opened my eyes, searching for the moon whose glow had been smudged away by a puff of silver cloud. I said, "All of my life, even when I was a child, I felt like there was something missing in me." I found my eyes closing involuntarily against the sky. "Whatever it was, as the years passed, it did not appear. The more I searched the emptier I felt.

"This summer I went to the beach at sunset and thought about the last few years of my life. It *was* a cemetery. Deaths, endings, dashed hopes, broken promises. I thought, well, maybe that's just the way life is for everyone, and that my problem was that I wanted what was impossible, that I was pathological or idealistic or just a self-pitying fool.

"And then I knew what was missing—the recollection of you, my journey with you. It wasn't a 'piece' that was missing. I'd misplaced myself, my other self. I'd just been wandering around trance-like, waiting for this reunion. And then when you appeared to me at dawn, it happened, life happened. You were the missing self."

His arms dropped away from me and he stepped back, breaking contact. He circled around me to the edge of the dark bubbling pool. I turned but his back was to me.

"Andreas," I whispered.

He turned slowly around, moving closer as he heard his name.

"You can't . . . you can't do this now that we've found each other," I said.

He was momentarily disarmed. Then, taking a deep breath and, plunging both hands in his pockets, he began to talk and pace, looking up, looking down as if he must keep busy, as if his life depended on what he would say.

"I went back to Green Gates," he said, stopping suddenly, staring into my eyes. "I went . . . home . . . ."

I nodded. The moon had moved over my shoulder.

"What do you remember . . . about us . . . back then?"

He sighed heavily, stopped pacing and said, "Everything."

We were momentarily silent. I knew we were recalling those long ago days in unison.

"About leaving you at the town fence . . . ." I stammered. "I didn't mean it—I was hurt, you know—"

He nodded. "I know. It's hard for me to think . . . that I could have done that to you. Isabel, I mean—in retrospect—"

"I know."

"It's there," he said. "Green Gates. I found it two months ago. I'd been having dreams about it for the past year, dreams about a place near the sea, near the Pacific Ocean. I thought I was crazy and then when I came out here to California, to the Monterey Peninsula for the environmental symposium and was looking for a house to rent for a month, it was there—Green Gates. To be honest, it scared the hell out of me."

I nodded, trying to keep my composure. *Keep your hands still. Don't reach out. He doesn't want you to touch him, not yet.*

"And you," he inquired softly, "How much do you remember?"

"Where it began and ended."

Quickly he said, "Phoebe is still living. At Green Gates. It seems that she bought it from my parents—that is, Signe and Knute—before they died. There's so much that's happened, things that no one in their right mind would believe unless it happened to them personally, as it has to me." He paused looking up at the starry sky then back to my face, into my eyes. He went on reflectively, "When I got to Green Gates, when I walked through the house, into the garden—I was in shock. I knew I had been there before but I kept telling myself that it reminded me of a place from my childhood, or maybe a picture I'd seen.

That's the only way I could explain it. And then when I'd been there a few days, I had a dream. It was a cold evening, heavy mist, and the foghorn was blowing all night. I had a dream about a man named Andreas who once lived in the town of Pacific Grove and a woman named . . . ."

He took my hand in his and looked down at it as if to prove to himself that I was actually there.

"Please, go on," I said, feeling his hand enclose mine warmly, firmly, as if he might never let it go. "At first I thought maybe the house was haunted. This Andreas was trying to tell me something. But then the second dream came and I realized that I was, in fact, Andreas. I was living the dreams, or rather, had lived *that* life. Those dreams were a reality as true and distinct as this one. Of course I thought I was going crazy—but only for awhile. The woman who rented me the place, whom I later learned was little red-haired Phoebe, watched me carefully and it seems she knew all along who I was. She let me discover it for myself. After I'd been there a couple of weeks, she brought in a portrait and hung it in the entrance hall. It was your portrait, or rather my lover's portrait. You—she—looked back out at me from the canvas as if she were still alive. And then it occurred to me. *She was alive.* Like me, she was out there somewhere, remembering just as I was. And you were remembering . . . ."

"Yes," I answered.

"I wanted to find her, find you, but I did not even know how to begin. My enthusiasm became an obsession. I stood in front of the portrait, sometimes for hours, thinking, even speaking to her, to you. Then one morning when I was up at daybreak, because I couldn't sleep, I went down and looked at the portrait and instead of her face, I saw another, a different face, but the same woman. I knew then that the face I saw was the woman she had become in this life and that it was *you*. She had become you. I couldn't breathe. I went outside and leaned against the green gates under the stone arch. I saw a vision of you. You were frightened, it seemed. I reached out to you to tell you that we must communicate, that we needed to find each other but you—you were upset and were afraid that I would hurt you again. And then you disappeared, just vanished. But I remembered your face."

Reaching out with his other hand, he stroked my cheek, my neck with his fingertips. "I remembered your face as well as I remembered hers." Then he slowly pulled his hand away and looked up at the sky, then away into the dark shadows of the statuary garden. "Finally Phoebe and I talked. We stayed up the whole night by the fire talking about my life back then, and about finding the green-eyed woman who was probably as mystified as I was but who, Phoebe was sure, would know who I was, who I am. She said to me, 'Langston, trust the universe. If you trust the universe, she will tell you her secret.' She has."

"Your eyes haven't changed," I said, wondering why he had taken his hands away. It had felt so right.

"Nor have yours, but for the color .... When I saw your picture last night in the library I thought it was another vision, that my mind had replaced the photograph in the frame with my own fantasy. It was the woman I had seen while I stood under the Monterey Cypress at the stone arch with the green gates, and her name, Neil said, was Paige Brighton."

"Andreas," I murmured, reaching toward him.

He looked at my outstretched hand as if he were afraid to touch it again, then said softly, "How could I have betrayed you? I asked myself that as I stared at your picture, as Neil said that you're his fiancée. His inflection told me that the commitment was sealed. It was strange, the way he said it, as if he knew—but then I was staring at the picture speechless, my breath knocked out of me. It was an awkward moment."

"And this morning," I said, "near the purple hills. You knew it was me and yet—"

"If you had come any closer I would have forgotten myself entirely, lost control, not just of the moment but of my life."

I understood. He did not want me enough to lose control. *He did not want me.*

"Paige, for God's sake, don't look at me that way. I have— we have commitments."

"Don't speak for me," I said despondently. "I have no commitments. If I did, I would break them." It would take willpower I didn't possess to keep from begging him to love me again, as Paige.

Turning away, he said quietly, "The hurt I caused you then was immeasurable. You were so young and you trusted me. More than that even, you gave your life to me. Please try to understand I don't want to hurt you again. After that first morning when I said 'We must meet again,' there was another dream. Do you remember the other dream?"

"We met on the other side," I said. "I was in Marla's guesthouse. It was during her party—I fainted in the bathroom and left my body. You came to me."

"It was not a flashback," he added, "nor a dream, not really. It was something else, I don't know exactly what—Phoebe calls it astral energy or a meeting of higher selves or something lofty sounding. It was in that state of mind that I realized, as Phoebe had taught me, that there are things such as commitments of the soul. We have that commitment." He came to me and taking my shoulders in his hands said, "—not this time. It can't work."

But his words lacked conviction. His eyes closed, and I could feel, though we were not touching, his breathing, the sound of his heart.

I stepped back, pulling his hands from my shoulders.

243.

"What do I want?" he asked looking at the sky, a question directed more toward the moon than me, "I want to take your hand this very moment and before that cloud passes the face of the moon, I want to be gone from here and away somewhere where we can live the way we need to . . . ." He looked back at me. "But I can't."

The finality of his words shocked me. Desperately I said, "It's Neil's money, isn't it! It's your damn political career. I can't believe this is happening when we know what we know. We aren't just two people—we're two people who *remember*. Oh God, Andreas, you are right. Why are you hurting me again? Why did you come out here by the pool? Why did you acknowledge me at all? What is the point of us remembering, reliving, going back, finding each other? We've been blessed with this gift— this knowledge. It's so rare . . . and we are just two ordinary people in spite of it all. Is that what we are? Nothing special?" I looked into the macabre green-black maze of shrubbery. The garden was brightened with marble faces and limbs that slashed the night with white. But I was gratified to see that he, too, was suffering. He wanted me. He was the quintessential man in need. Even his fists were clenched as if he might just as soon destroy the object of his desire as have her. In that way he was very like Andreas had been back then. But was I any different than Angelica? Had Lucetta been right when she said that human beings were nothing but skin, bones and cravings?

He said, "I can't." It was final. Cold. Hard. Devastatingly final.

I closed my eyes against the dark night, and the spontaneous picture of a garden, soft and pastel like a Monet, sprang into view. Andreas was leading me through the soft blush of color and I had the thought that someday maybe someone would take a picture of our souls and see Giverny. Was this a vision of heaven, of what would come? We had to be more than skin and bones and cravings. I opened my eyes. Oh yes, he wanted to touch me.

I said "I could die and be done with it because I think that I could not live with the longing. But I am too smart for that now. I'd wake up in a different body and remember you, and want you all over again. That's the hell of knowing the truth about life and death. One can't hide behind illusions. One cannot depend solely on heaven-after-life." I turned away from him. "There was a heaven, Andreas. It was with you in the field that day when we were children. As we grew up. It was the quality of your voice, it was how you said things, how you did them. It was how you led me through the green gates and picked foxtails from my socks, it was how you took a flower from the garden. It was the shape you saw in the clouds that I could never see. It was the way you thought about life. How much you loved animals, nature. And when I saw you this morning at the purple hills, that was heaven too but this, this, Andreas, is hell. This is what hell is, isn't it? Standing this close, just an arm's length away from everything you have ever wanted in life and knowing that if you reach forward your flesh will shrivel. Hell is wanting to die but knowing it won't make a difference."

"There will be other times," he said.

"When? Two hundred years from now?" After pausing, I turned to him, resigned. "Just once before you go . . . call me Angelica."

"Your name," he said in a whisper. ". . . *Angelica.*"

Then he turned from me, from the garden, from the blackness in which the statues and I posed indignantly. The moon was blank-faced and the stars withdrew behind a cloud that came from nowhere.

Chapter Thirty

he full-length zipper on my black dress slid down with a touch. With my free hand, I tapped on Neil's bedroom door. As I leaned into the doorjamb waiting for Neil to answer, the back of the dress peeled open from my shoulders to my waist. The air in the hallway was cool against my skin.

I did not expect to see Langston Holt entering the corridor in muffled conversation with his aide, but there he was, in the dim light at half past midnight. He caught sight of me, half-clad, slouching, as if I had nothing better to do than haunt hallways. He came to a dead standstill as his eyes fell on my loose dress. Embarrassed, his aide hurried down the hall to his own room, leaving the two of us alone in the shadows. Neither of us spoke. After resignation there is never anything left to say. We were common after all.

Neil unbolted his door and it opened slowly. He hadn't been asleep though his thick, grey-streaked hair was tousled, and his grey eyes peered dreamily toward me.

"Do you still want to touch me?" I asked.

His hand reached around me and stoked my bare back. Neil could not see Langston but I could. As Neil's arm enclosed my waist and pulled me into his room, I looked back to Langston and felt an adolescent thrill of victory: I had managed to enrage him.

I pretended Neil was Andreas, was Langston Holt as my mouth and my hands moved over his body and I let his do the same.

I was asleep at dawn when, after sounds from the hallway, Neil returned to bed to say that the Senator had received a message and was leaving Candlesage that very hour. His luggage was already outside on the drive and the car was waiting.

As Neil lay back down upon the bed, I heard the roar of the car engine. I heard the engine noise grow fainter and fainter and when I could hear it no longer, when I was sure it was not coming back, I put my arms around Neil's neck and accepted his warm mouth.

Every night for nearly two weeks we did the same. After dinner we retired upstairs and undressed each other and came together, sensuous and bizarre. "Let's make love," he'd whisper. I made a mental compromise by thinking of it as creating passion, for how can one *make* love. It makes itself, doesn't it? And what could it possibly have to do with what our bodies did to each other?

Mo bit her nails to the quick. Aunt Belle unraveled a "new" pair of turquoise yarn bunny slippers as she paced incessantly with Chester sprinting beside her, pawing at the loose strings. Did the all-night charades mean that we would be married?

"When are you going to court anyway?" Aunt Belle asked impatiently one afternoon. "You can't be married to two people at the same time."

"I'm not married to anyone, not really," I smiled sanguinely. "I'm meeting my lawyer next week and I'll go to court when she tells me to."

Aunt Belle huffed, "You're not acting normal." Her chin tilted in the direction of Neil's bedroom.

"On the contrary," I retorted. "Based on everything I have seen in this world, I am behaving quite normally, very normally."

"It's not normal for you." She pointed at me when I turned away and whispered to Chester who looked eager to support any accusation. "Boy, Chessie, she's really losin' it—a few sequins short of a Wayne Newton jumpsuit, if you know what I mean."

I couldn't help but ponder which was more disquieting—Aunt Belle's analogies or her knitting attempts.

Two events occurred that brought our brief sexual adventure to a sudden cold end.

Early one evening as I was showering in Neil's room I heard the shatter of glass. Neil was arguing, shouting at someone. I turned off the water, grabbed a towel as quickly as I could and opened the door. Vincent had bolted through the window and at that very moment was lunging at Neil, who stood on the other side of the rumpled bed. Vincent's eyes were afire, his jaw hung open, teeth bared. He was drunk but not enough that he did not have the strength to leap onto and over the bed to Neil, who had pushed a discreet button on his night table to summon the guards posted downstairs in the statuary garden. I closed the door, thinking that my presence would provoke him further. After a moment, I threw on my robe and entered the room with a heavy wooden mirror—the only weapon I could find in the dressing area. Neil's guards were at the door and Vincent, who was by then brandishing a gun, ran to the window and disappeared into the night.

"Will they catch him? Will they find him?" I asked,

bewildered by the shattered glass, by the tension in the air, and by the fear on Neil's face, which I had never seen before.

He composed himself immediately. "He may do a lot of crazy things before he's caught but I will guarantee you that it will never be to you or me or ever again on my property."

I slept in my own room that night, rousing myself at the sound of every creaking board, of every rustle coming from outside my window. Rats in the ivy? Bats swooping and flapping between garden and house? Vincent knotting ropes for entrance through my window? Had he wanted to hurt Neil or me or both of us? The answer was obvious. Anger made Vincent feel powerful and he was forever looking for something to provoke it, a course for his anger, a target, anything to justify hate, any action to feed the rage.

Aunt Belle and I had planned a shopping trip to South Coast Plaza the next morning—I had to get away from Candlesage. Neil saw no reason why if accompanied by a guard and driver we could not carry on as planned. But the morning mail changed everything.

Aunt Belle said over the breakfast table, "Oh, by the way, you got a letter. Here, it's in my pocket. Hitchins asked me to give it to you. Now where is it?"

She laid it next to a crystal vase of late summer flowers. The parchment was the color of butter. Who . . . ?

"Well, aren't you going to open it? I thought maybe it was from cousin Naomi because she's the only one who knows you're here but that isn't her letter B. Her B's are as lumpy as my backside. No, that's a man's handwriting and look, turn it over, it's got personal marked on the back . . . *oh la la*." The black rings around her eyes broadened as she gave me a suspicious look. She picked up her coffee cup and gave a big slurp as the steaming liquid was sucked through pursed, orange lips. "Don't mind the little scratch on the front of the envelope. I'm afraid Chester had a little claw on it. Couldn't be helped."

The script was bold and neat with large capitals and loops. The dot of the i was directly over it—the first thing I looked for when someone wrote my name. This man was not a dreamer. A handwriting analyst would say he was strong and exact and knew what he wanted when he saw it.

I reached past the summer flowers to the envelope and slid it over into my lap and took a bite of toast.

Aunt Belle sighed and rolled her eyes, "Aren't you goin' to open it? Don't mind me. I'll just look out at the garden. Did you ever in your life see windows that tall? What, what did you say? I thought I heard you say something, Paige. I thought you said, 'I can't.'"

"I said no such thing. Please stop talking to me."

She scoffed and fed Chester a piece of ham.

I used my butter knife to slice open the letter. Before I unfolded the thick sheet of paper I took a deep breath. I thought of all the silly rhymes and games I played as a girl: he loves me, he loves me not; A, B, C, D, twist the apple stem and when it breaks you'll know who loves you. We have such simple ways of determining our fate. Apples, tea leaves, jump ropes.

The letter said, "Tantalus: In Greek mythology, a king, son of Zeus, whose punishment in the lower world was eternal hunger and thirst; he was doomed to stand in water that always receded when he tried to drink it and under branches of fruit he could never reach. I want you. Please come back to Green Gates. A." He had written the address.

My suitcases sat neatly at my feet as I waited for Neil in the entrance hall near the "General," who chimed two-thirty. At last Neil walked through the door, humming Vivaldi. I stood up, moved my traveling case aside and tightened my grip on my handbag. I said, "I couldn't leave without—without saying good-bye." I was shocked by the cold, unfeeling tone of my voice.

He looked at me quizzically as if he had misunderstood. As he absorbed the news, he became as still as the life-size bronze that stood behind him in the shadows.

"I've decided to take off for awhile. Neil, I've asked Aurelio to get my car out. He says it's just fine for driving."

He looked at the luggage then back to my face, and as he did so his shoulders slumped slightly. "You're leaving?" He was alarmed and dismayed at once.

Quickly I added, "It was unexpected or I would have said something sooner. I know what you think—"

"No, you don't know what I think. Well, maybe, yes. Maybe I did think that you being here two weeks in bed with me meant something," he said accusingly.

"It's not that it didn't mean anything. It's just that it's over. Neil, I didn't plan it this way." I said apologetically. He walked toward me—I thought maybe to say goodbye, but he was quickly past my shoulder and at the luggage. He bent over, picked up the wardrobe that sat behind me and flung it against the wall. He kicked another piece, lifted it from the cold floor and hurled it toward the door. The zipper split on impact and its contents spewed into the room.

Stunned, I said, "You don't understand. It's not the way you think, Neil." My voice was soft and I forced it to become stronger as I finished the sentence. Stand firm, I told myself. It was frightening to see him being physically forceful.

"I don't want to understand why you are doing this. I am tired of trying to understand." His bravado ebbed but his face was flushed. He came toward me, took hold of my wrist and said quietly, "I can't let you go anywhere, Paige. You're not yourself."

"Let go of me." I tried to pull away from his grip but it was as if we were locked together. I whispered, "Friends don't do this."

"Trust me, Paige. I'm the best friend you've ever had." He released my wrist, letting his fingers linger against my arm, unsure when he would be allowed to touch me again. "I'm not trying to control you. I'm protecting you. There's a difference. And I think you're not fit to travel alone, that's all."

I left his side and walked to my luggage. Making an attempt to stuff a shoe back into the broken suitcase, I said, "That's ridiculous. I'm perfectly capable of traveling alone." My God, Neil, I wanted to shout, I've even traveled into another life alone, something you certainly wouldn't have the courage or imagination to do.

I was astonished to see my white robe with the boot tread peeking out of my split luggage. And there on the cold floor next to it, having fallen out during Neil's outburst, was the disintegrating maple leaf that had changed my life. I knelt on the floor and reverently tucked the fragments back into my case as if they were devotional relics in danger of exploitation.

Neil took my arm and helped me off the floor. "Lulu will take care of that." I could tell he regretted losing his usually cool demeanor. To him, this uncontrolled outburst was a personal loss. I suspected he kept track of these rare tantrums as some measure of his own sanity.

And then, as if preparing for a private conversation, he closed the double doors that led to the parlor and those that led to the library. "Let's sit down. I have something to tell you."

I did as he asked, sitting stiffly on the bench, watching him circle the room before seating himself next to me. His eyes were a shimmering grey. I folded my arms over my chest. I would appease him and then I would leave. Forever. I was crushed to think that our friendship would end but I could see no way around his unshakable position. Our lives had changed.

"I need to say this, Paige because I care about you. I love you. And when I say I love you, I mean it. Sometimes I think you believe it's not possible." He sighed, finding it difficult to continue. "You need to hear what I have to say, whether you want to or not."

He took my shoulders in his hands as if to brace me. He looked steadily, benevolently, into my eyes as he spoke. "*Andreas does not exist.*" His words were cruelly invasive and echoed darkly though the cold entrance hall.

Did he actually say it or was I imagining the words? I put my hands over my ears and tried to hear a tune. Something big, loud. Beethoven's Ode to Joy. Tchaikovsky's First in B Flat Minor . . . Chopin's Polonaise . . . .

"This romantic delusion of yours . . . he's a fabrication, Paige. You have fantasized this man you call Andreas. This other life. You—"

I sprang from the bench, flinging his hands from my shoulders. "Who do you think you are, Neil? Do you think you have the right or the power to crawl into my brain—my heart— and challenge the things I love? Who are you?" I shouted hysterically. My hands trembled. "Don't come near me!" I turned away from him and leaned into the dark wainscoting. There was nowhere else to hide. Why had I agreed to stay at Candlesage? Neil always made it his business to know everything about me but this time he had gone too far.

"This Andreas fantasy, these voices you hear—this could become dangerous." He was so close that I could feel his warm breath on my neck.

My heart was pounding. I spun around and shouted, "*I am not Simone Marchand!* I am not crazy, Neil! You don't have to save me. I am not your patient and I am not going to die! Because—because for the first time in years I have something to live for."

He maintained his cool professional attitude and gently commanded, "Stop this, Paige." He paused, knowing his words must be perfect. "I don't have the right to do anything, it's true. But I do have the duty to tell you, to warn you. You think I would hurt you—the woman I love—intentionally? This will only get worse, this delusion. You need help with this. If not me as your friend, then someone else—professionally, if you will." He touched my shoulder.

"Don't touch me," I said quietly, willing myself into a semblance of calm.

He let his hand drop away.

"You need to let me go, Neil, and let me live my life in my own way."

He replied simply, "I can't."

I collapsed onto the bench. "You want to put me out there," I gestured toward the statuary garden, "with your cold imitations of life who stand around being perfect for your benefit. Or place me neatly in your Simone disaster category where you can nullify her death through saving me. I don't know what Simone saw or heard, whether she was crazy or not. But I know about me. I've been there. I've seen for myself. I know the truth now. And nothing you do or say will change my mind."

He sat down upon the bench, running his fingers through his beautiful hair and looked crestfallen, as if he regretted the tension between us. "Imagination is more powerful than you realize."

I said, "Well, we agree on that."

"Practically every day since you left Vincent: at Marla's house, in the hospital, here at Candlesage and even in your dreams as you slept next to me in bed . . . I've heard you whispering his name," he winced at having to divulge the insult, "talking about him and Langston and some place called Green Gates. The entire staff has been concerned. Hitchins inadvertently overheard your meeting with Lucetta in the library."

"Well, you must've been really desperate to have the whole household collude with you."

"Paige . . . I believe that you believe in him, that you are convinced that he did appear in your room at dawn that morning." Cautiously he continued, "It would be easy, in your state of mind, to fantasize that this—this Andreas person is Langston Holt. We could spend days if not years trying to sort out the reasons . . . your mother, your father, Shea's death, or life with Vincent. It's possible all these aspects come into play. And there could be other factors . . . brain chemicals and so on. Paige, Langston Holt is not Andreas, your imagined Lothario."

"Are you finished?" I asked rhetorically. I knew the real truth about what had happened to me and that was enough. It wasn't important that Neil believe me.

"And nothing could be more disastrous for you and embarrassing for me than for you to follow this daydream to Pacific Grove hoping, vainly, for an acknowledgement from him. So far his bid for the vice-presidency is free of scandal." He waited for a response.

Neil wouldn't believe me if I told him that his "Senator" had validated the dream. He might believe the note from Langston Holt if I were to show it to him. But then again, Langston hadn't signed his name to the letter, just the initial "A." Neil would suspect me of sending the note to myself, of course. Anyway, why should I share the secret with Neil? Why should I jeopardize Langston's political career? No. Let Neil think that Andreas is a fictitious love. He could even think me insane for all I cared.

I stood up and looked down at him. "My plans are to spend a few days in Santa Barbara alone. After this, I don't feel much like leaving today. I'll go tomorrow first thing but I want to be left alone until I do. And as far as your 'insights' and 'suspicions' about my sanity, Neil—you'll have to deal with them yourself."

I left my luggage where it lay, glancing toward it only once before I ascended the staircase to my room. Maybe Neil was capable of behaving aggressively after all. Maybe tomorrow at this time it would be me lying against the front door, seams split open, heart exposed and beating ecstatically for something that lay beyond his vision.

When I arrived at my room, I took a pill and fell asleep.

Chapter Thirty-One

Pacific Grove, 1906

or three weeks Andreas persistently called at our front door in Pacific Grove. And after each inquiry, someone in the household had closed the door gently, apologetically against him, as I wished. Then like rhythm in a pattern, the knock and door closure was followed by the soft pelting of gravel crackling against my bedroom window. Unlike the years before, I did not dash to the window in anticipation. Instead I would cross my room to the farthest wall, and to strengthen my resolve would place my hands over my face until the pelting stopped. I would return slowly to the window when I could be sure that his back was turned, that he had mounted his horse and was traveling away from me. And when I saw him do that—ride away from me through the pines, never quickly— I tried to memorize his departure so that I would not die when he left me for the final time.

I did not trust myself with him. We hadn't spoken since the night he burned the fence. Isabel had changed her story of

Luther's death in favor of Andreas. Luther had killed himself, Isabel proclaimed. The proclamation would have been inspired by one thing only: Andreas' oath to marry her. Isabel had captured the man she had wanted all her life. Andreas was guilty of betraying me. But I wanted to remember him the way he used to be. I could not abide a cursory parlor chat, a passionless farewell.

Then he sent Diana. I could tell that Phoebe hoped that his beautiful emissary would create some sort of miracle for her cousin Angelica. Phoebe's nights had also been sleepless. The circles under her powder blue eyes grew darker. She was having terrifying visions. She kept vigil outside my door when she was not tripping on my skirts like an irksome shadow.

Diana's petticoat rustled and she smelled of rose water. She wore a skirt and blouse that I myself had ordered from San Francisco. She was radiant and perfect in the ensemble. I knew that I would never wear mine now that I had seen her in the same outfit.

As Phoebe solemnly closed the door behind her, Diana embraced me and took off her gloves.

She smiled, "I don't know who looks worse—Dre or you, Angelica." Her cheeks dimpled like a porcelain doll. "Andreas asked me to speak to you since you won't see him."

"I gathered that. But we needn't spend time thinking things can be the same between him and me." I felt a constriction in my throat. "Things will never again be the same. This has changed everything for me. I have renegotiated my very position in the world."

"No, they cannot be the same . . . ." she said, lowering her square chin, seating herself in the chair by the fire.

The curtain at the window billowed into the room then snapped back to the sill and was sucked against the seascape outside.

She said, "I know about Isabel."

"What about her?"

"I know about Dre's 'encounter' with her. I know he regrets it. I could go on and on about the agony he's in—but you know. He lost his mind. There is no other explanation for his behavior in Boston. It's possible, isn't it, Angelica, for someone to be insane for a moment or a day? He knows that you have spoken to Isabel and he knows that that is why you did not meet him at the fence the night you were to leave for the city. You should know, too, that the constable suspects that our Dre burned down the fence but he hasn't any evidence. I think the Pagrovians were getting a little tired of that fence anyway."

"I saw him tear down the fence, I saw him burn the boards. I'll leave it to God to decide if it was the act of a hero or a coward."

She was silent for a moment. "I also know that Isabel is expecting a baby. He does not want to marry her. He feels nothing for her but contempt and yet there is the child."

"Yes, the child," I said, thinking, Oh, God, Diana, were I to tell you my secret, you would fall from your chair. For once you would look like something other than a goddess in repose.

"He has asked me to give you this." She produced a letter from her small bag and extended it toward me. When I did not take it, she rose from her chair and crossed to the secretary and propped it up against a perfume bottle on a white lace doily.

She collected her gloves and said, "Tomorrow is the Ring Day Festival. Davey and I would like you to go with us. Angelica, you need to get out into the air. Do think about it, won't you?" I nodded. Satisfied, she turned toward the door then hesitated, her hand gripping the knob tightly, her fathomless eyes peering blankly beyond me, and whispered painfully, "I too was once betrayed." Not offering any other admissions, she swung quickly out the door, leaving the room bathed in the sweet smell of rose water.

Quickly I grabbed the crisp white envelope and took it to the fire. I held it over the glowing ashes until the muscles in my arm ached, until my fingers, which crackled the immaculate paper, grew just as white. What was there left for us to say to one another? My arm retreated from the fire. I held the warm white letter to my breast. Would its contents alter my life? What if I were never to read it? Vehemently, I tore it open. "Tomorrow after the Ring Festival, in the garden at Green Gates, we will decide, Angelica, on our beginning or our end. Love, A." I sat on the bed and clutched my stomach and promised myself I would not tell him the secret. An unexpected tear, like the mist that gathers on petals, slid down my cheek.

The acrid smell of the Chinese squid fields permeated the air. Children, wide-eyed, ran as if parentless through the throngs of people who gathered in the field with giddy anticipation. In the center of the field, an enormous pole was erected after having been festooned with masses of red and green firecrackers. The parade began. Hundreds of Chinese men of the Tong Organization, from all over California, dressed in their best blue uniforms, donned grey and red buttons on their circular caps, buttons that signified their rank, and marched to the cacophonous Chinese music into the center of the field. They were prepared to fight each other for the gold ring, for the captor of the gold ring would be the undisputed ruler for a year.

Phoebe's hand tightened in mine as we stood under the shade of a cypress. Neither of us believed it to be as barbaric as Aunt Marion proclaimed. Neither of us denied the fascination of seeing men fight, something that, at any other time, we loathed.

The smell of roast hogs, chickens and ducks welcomed the residents of Pacific Grove and Monterey as they arrived by scores to witness the most spectacular annual event on the peninsula.

The Chinese joss house, which stood in the field, was decorated and lit brilliantly with punks. Foods were piled about the village on wooden trays for the Chinese feast that would follow the Ring Festival ceremony. In the village they would play word games and the losers would customarily swig gin until they lay drunken in the narrow, rambling streets of the wooden village.

Davey and Diana had wandered off to say hello to friends. Phoebe leaned into me and said, "I like Chinese people so much, Angelica. Their music is my favorite." I looked down upon her flame-red crown of hair, parted precisely down the middle into two long braids. Her lower lip had a faint droop to it which made her look as if she were on a perpetual mission. She had told me that her dreams, the night before, had been bad again. She was afraid to leave my side. "I'm afraid for you Angelica," she had said on the way to the festival. She sensed me watching her and turned her eyes to mine. She once said she wished I had been her mother instead of Marion and I told her that she often felt like a daughter to me. But never more than now, I thought wistfully, with my body preparing itself for change. Would some event occur to help me decide what to do?

At that moment, with the sun running its long golden fingers through the trees and across Phoebe's brilliant hair, with the plaintive Chinese music scrawling indiscernible messages in the afternoon air, I thought that God would give me an answer, that my situation would find its own solution. Andreas would have scoffed at me, waiting for a solution from God. *The gift of life allows you to solve your own problems. That is God in action.* But Andreas was no longer mine. Andreas was lost to me in every way that mattered. Who would help me now?

A Chinese man with an American flag led the procession. The largest men were the ones chosen to fight. They positioned themselves around the pole and prepared to draw blood for the honor of capturing the traditional golden ring. Suddenly it was quiet. The audience grew somber, then a unanimous gasp rose from the observers—the fuse was ignited. In a moment, the tall pole exploded against the blue sky, spreading smoky tendrils and sparks. The firecracker atop the pole burst apart, flinging the gold ring into the mass of hefty Chinese men. They fought each other, clawing, kicking, and shoving, to claim the ring. One young man was pulled from the group and was slung to the side of the brawl. The battle raged in a swirl of blue smudges tumbling over one another, the bright red buttons winking atop their caps. At last a muscular arm emerged from the sweaty mob, clutching the prized ring. Laughter and congratulations followed. Another year, another leader.

When I saw the winner bearing his golden ring I thought of the young Chinese man with the slit throat we saw die in Chinatown, a specter of my childhood.

The crowds began to disperse. Diana and Davey Willingham came up from behind us. Diana's face was flushed, her eyes glinting. She said, "Mrs. Willingham has invited us all to her house for ice cream." She looked at Davey and smiled. She was happy to belong somewhere. Pacific Grove was growing. Davey had a promising career as an architect. He was handsome, industrious and he cared much for her. He would not betray her as Royal Shaw had. Life was magnanimous in that. It was possible to love a second time.

I answered, "Phoebe will be very happy to go. I have an appointment."

Diana looked at me perceptively, took Phoebe's hand and the three of them walked happily away. I watched them pause at the joss house on their way across the field. Diana's long white fingers gently touched a wax flower that adorned the wall, and she smiled at Davey as if he had placed it there for her.

I walked slowly on the path to Green Gates and did not encounter anyone save an occasional twittering bird and grazing doe.

I creaked open the arched green gate and crossed the brick courtyard that Knute had put in the summer before. I took the path that meandered to the left of the large house, the path bordered by clusters of freshly watered violets. "The violets are crying," we said as children.

Andreas was standing, arms folded across his chest, on the steps of the gazebo, looking directly at me as I came into the rose garden. He did not move. Not even the roses moved, or the low slung limbs of the apple trees. I crossed to him and stopped to catch my breath. The air was heavy with pollen and I felt faint. I saw him through different eyes now. Betrayal in love is the final disillusionment. Pathos and contempt were new sensations. I had never before been called upon to forgive someone. Was I capable of it?

He said, "Everything lives in the universe, Angelica, not just the moon. I wanted to tell you that ten years ago, was it ten or twelve? But what I've wanted to tell you since that day was simply that we *are* the universe, have an identical nature. We create and we destroy." He took a step toward me.

"And we have done both," I said, not moving closer to him. I looked at the hands that had been on my body, had been on Isabel's body. Did they know the difference? Had his mouth kissed hers? Perhaps it had not bothered.

He said, "We can do either again." It was an offering of sorts. He came down the steps, reached his hands out to my face and brushed the hair back from it. He liked to play with my hair when it was loose. His fingers touched my skin.

"I cannot forgive you," I said.

"You cannot let this—this mistake destroy the rest of what

we had. I love only you. It was nothing, Angelica, I swear to you—"

"No, it is everything," I replied.

He sank onto the lowest steps of the gazebo. The strain of the past weeks showed around his intense blue eyes. His mouth was drawn, his stature weakened. I thought it odd that he looked more like a victim than did I. We were both hurting. He, for what he had done. And I, for what I could not do.

He said, "I will marry her to give the child my name. The moment we are pronounced man and wife I'll leave the church, leave this town and never return. My feelings for Isabel are the same as yours, they haven't changed, Angelica. She is from the darkest side of life. She is almost missionary in her desire to drag others from the light."

"Some of us stand firm, Andreas. Some of us cannot be dragged from the light. So you see, we are different."

He stood up, lunged toward me and clutched my shoulders in his hands. "You can come with me, Angelica," he said urgently. "We'll go to England. We'll put all of this behind us, I swear to you. I'll divorce her. You and I are not subject to the conventions that others have imposed." His hands tightened on my shoulders.

"Oh, but we are. Why else would you give the child your name?"

"Because it is my child," he answered hopelessly. "In time you will forgive me. I know you."

"Not as well as you think." I paused and looked about the garden. I knew I would never see Green Gates again. He released my shoulders and leaned hard into the gazebo post. The diamond shapes in the lattice work quivered.

"Andreas," I said gently. "I cannot remember my mother or father, though sometimes I imagine I do. The only warmth I got was from you. This child that you and Isabel have—that Isabel is having—will need a father to protect her, or him, for we both know what evil Isabel and her family are capable of. Your child will need your protection and love. You needn't live with Isabel, but you will need to stay here in the Grove for the sake of a child who is to be pitied far more than you and I. You know, I've never been much of a martyr. I was well taught by you to see the self-indulgence in that. Nevertheless, it is I who will leave Pacific Grove so that you can raise your child here without having to be reminded of what you—gave up."

"You will not leave."

But his plea was useless. I would not give in. I could feel warm, salty blood oozing in my mouth where my teeth cut into my lip.

He came toward me and put his arms around me and my head fell on his shoulder. It was goodbye. "My darling, Angelica, do you see that the violets are crying?" he asked.

Chapter Thirty-Two

Theda stood before me, head lowered and hands behind her back, not in any particular deference to me but because her hands were as lumpy as cobblestones and the skin thin and red from this morning's kitchen scrubbing. They were testament to Aunt Marion's unreasonable standards of fastidiousness. Theda had a strong thick neck that bowed forward from the curve in her back. For the first time I noticed that at thirty or so years, she was old and worn from backbreaking work. It was a dear price for Aunt Marion's beloved objects of antiquity, which still looked pristine because of Theda's expert care. As a child, I had wanted to draw closer to Theda, but the wish was always precluded by Aunt and Uncle's formidable standards of decorum.

"Theda . . . Oh Theda, how can I ask you this?"

"Miss?" she answered gravely, as if her throat were parched. But it wasn't Theda's throat that had dried up. It was her life. Now I understood such things. Life could put a bow in your back and bleed dry the juices from your very soul.

"You've been with us since I came here to live."

She nodded, her head slowly bobbing.

"You gave me warm soup when I was sick. A child doesn't forget these things. It was also from you that I learned that material things aren't as precious as we make them out to be. But you have worked all these years as if you were doing penance and that is why I hate to ask another favor of you, a vital favor . . . ."

"Anything, Miss," she nodded, her lumpy hands relaxing at her sides as if my appreciation were in some way healing.

I continued. "All I can offer for this important favor is money. Though it will not be much, it will be several months' wages." There was no reaction and I understood that Theda knew by now that money would not alter the direction of her life.

"I need your help," I said.

"Anything, Miss," she smiled, showing a chipped tooth. Her head craned forward inviting me to speak. "I'm glad to help."

"I am with child."

She sucked in her breath. The cobbled hand swept up to her mouth and lay across the chipped tooth. Her eyes widened, her brow furrowed. She stood motionless.

I cleared my throat and braced myself. "It is very early in the pregnancy, thank God. Your sister, Eunice, I am told, used the services of a doctor in Chinatown, in San Francisco last year."

The hand did not move from the mouth as she gasped, "How did you know—"

"The walls are not quite so thick as my aunt and uncle imagine them to be. I have been privy to information that would have otherwise eluded me."

"Dear Lord—" she murmured.

"Theda, you must tell me."

"I couldn't, Miss, I just couldn't. The doctor's name—why, your aunt and uncle—"

"They do not know, of course, and they will never know. No one, Theda, but you and I will ever know. I promise you that and would hope that you would promise me the same."

"Oh, Miss." A tear wedged itself in the corner of her left eye.

"Theda, I have listened at keyholes all of my life because I learned that that was where the truth is hidden—on the other side of a locked door. I knew that Eunice was with child, that she went to San Francisco and that she came back having 'miscarried.' That is what I learned at the keyhole last year."

"But, Miss . . . ." Theda's hands recovered themselves and slipped behind her back.

I whispered, "It's the only way for me."

"But Mr. Sparring . . . ."

"Mr. Sparring . . . Andreas . . . ." I forced the words from my throat, "is going to marry Isabel Orwell."

She looked horrified. "No! It can't be."

"But it is."

It took her only a moment to accept the news. She was accustomed to failed dreams. I would not become like Theda. I would not lose the treasured dreams of my childhood as she had. Aren't there people whose dreams have come true? Who are they? Tears poured from my eyes.

Theda came quickly to my side and stroked my back and shoulders with her big hands. "There, there, Miss. You was in love."

"I'm still in love. I've loved him since I met him and sometimes I think Andreas and I loved each other before we were born. Isabel—what he did with Isabel—is only part of it. It's just that, he is not the man I thought he was. He was life as it appeared to be. He is a lie."

"But a mistake, Miss, a mistake."

"I must have the doctor's name and address. I've got to go and you must go with me. I have it planned, Theda," I said, my voice shaking, my fingers pulling on the loose threads of an embroidered pillow. "I'll tell Aunt Marion and Uncle Robin that I need to get away. They'll understand because they have heard the news that Isabel and Andreas are to marry. You and I will go up to the City for a few days—shopping—to the dressmaker's. You will chaperone me. I know they will allow it. We will go and see the doctor and then come home a day or two later just like your sister Eunice did. This afternoon I will send the doctor a letter arranging the appointment. You must get me the address."

Theda looked me in the eyes, which was rare. It was the first time I noticed that she had only a few lashes on each eyelid.

"Theda, I'll do anything you wish if you will help me with this. Anything. God knows you deserve it whether you help me or not."

Theda sighed and, holding me close, in her low, rough voice said, "All I ever wanted was a husband. Now it's too late. Nobody has to do nothin' for me, not that anybody ever did. I remember when my ma was pickin' through the potatoes, oh, I was just a little mite. She threw a big bruised one in the pail by the dry sink. She screwed up her face and peeked out from under that old cloth she wore on her head—it was brown— and says to me, 'That's what God shoulda done with you, Theda, when he was pickin' over this people.' Then she cackled and says, 'Throw you into the pail with the bad ones.' My ma," Theda went on without the trace of an inflection in her voice, "My ma told my pa that night that I was the best proof that even God makes mistakes. I asked my ma why she hadn't thrown me in the pail and she slapped me hard across my face and said it was the talk of the devil . . . . Miss, your baby shouldn't ought to live if you don't want it." Her voice ended on a chilling, plaintive note.

After a long pause in which not a floorboard creaked or a gull whined outside, I said, "I can't tell Andreas. He would whisk me away somewhere and we would marry and be sad and worried for the rest of our lives because you see, Isabel is also carrying his child. It's better if he doesn't know, if he never knows. And I think sometimes, maybe in years, I will forgive him and we somehow can be together again. Yes, I know we will be together again but I cannot say how."

Dr. Lum Gam lived on Grant Avenue in Chinatown. As soon as Theda supplied me the address I wrote, "I will need your assistance with a particular problem on the morning of April 17. I am quite sure that your surgical endeavor will lighten my burden. Enclosed you will find partial payment for this service." I signed it "Mary Tucker."

Trip arrangements had not been easy. Aunt Marion had twittered anxiously about women alone in the defiled city and gave detailed descriptions of the repulsive scent of the bay. Uncle Robin had pontificated on the women of good breeding who had been brutally taken advantage of and even gave a discourse on those believed to be kidnapped and sold into white slavery and shipped to foreign ports. Prattling on about the troubles of the world had always kept them from examining their own.

What finally convinced them was a lie. I announced with sang-froid that Andreas and Isabel were to be married on the nineteenth, which was why I wished to be gone that week. They believed me since they hadn't heard otherwise. When I had told them, Aunt Marion buried her face in her winged kerchief. "It's just as well," Uncle Robin announced somberly. "Your Aunt and I were just this morning discussing the possibilities of a college for you somewhere in the East or South."

They had misgivings about Theda's appropriateness as a chaperone but they could think of no one else at the time and admitted she was big and strong. They agreed that I would stay with Cousin Dixie and I accepted the arrangement, knowing Dixie Devlin would never lay eyes on me. I would simply send her a note upon my arrival that the trip had been cancelled.

And so with few words and under the fire of pathetic babblings from Phoebe, Theda and I left on the train, the morning of April 16, an hour after Andreas had called at the door to speak to me. It was urgent, he had told Phoebe, who relayed the message to me just as I was buckling the straps on my luggage.

I would not see him. His presence would weaken my resolve. Indeed, when I was with him I became him. If I were to tell him about the child it would have to be at some time in the future.

I had requested a window seat and noticed as I removed my coat for the journey that Phoebe's tears had stained its cloth buttons. I could not have known, as I huddled near the window, that Phoebe, who was crazed with worry, had gone to Andreas that afternoon and told him that Theda was accompanying me to San Francisco for reasons other than shopping. I could not have known that he would follow us north.

I saw nothing of the wild land as the train sped toward the City, but I saw my life reflecting back at me through the glass. I could also see the curve of my head and hat when the light was right. But I could not see my eyes. In many ways, I was a stranger to myself. The events of my life seemed distant, as if I no longer possessed them.

The train compartment felt constrictive, and halfway through the journey, I left the security of my window seat and stumbled to the back of the train car and stood outside in the whipping wind. The tea that Theda had ordered had not helped my stomach sickness. When I returned to my seat, she settled me in and whispered, "It will be over soon."

When we arrived in San Francisco, I was weak-kneed and nauseous. People bustled about the station as if every destination were vital. I stumbled down the steps behind my luggage and nearly lost consciousness. I could feel Theda's strong arm going around my waist. "We'll soon have you laying down," she soothed. It was a frenetic crowd. Twice we lost our porter.

"Come along now," Theda said, "We'll soon have a place to rest." And she used her elbows as weapons, slashing through the crowds to secure a carriage.

The wooden hotel was one of moderate price perched on a hill with a view of the bay. In an accented drawl of some sort, our driver assured us that it was a decent place for decent people. He helped us down and unloaded our luggage. After being paid and thanked, he spat in the street and swung his horses out from the curb with a jolt that tumbled our bags on the walk in front of the hotel.

The lobby looked respectable enough, Theda noted, though I paid no attention. The young amiable desk clerk said, "The bellboy will escort you up. Room ten," he added, smiling at me, "has a view of the bay. And just down the street, this side, you'll find an excellent tea room."

We thanked him and followed a tired little man up thinly carpeted stairs.

"Why is he looking at me that way?" I asked Theda.

"What way? The desk clerk?"

"He's looking at me strangely," I whispered. "As if he knows."

"He knows you're pretty," she whispered back. "That's what he knows."

I looked back at the lobby. The clerk winked at me.

I thought: He knows what I am going to do. They all know.

That's why the driver spat at me, that's why the desk clerk is jeering, that's why the people at the station would not let us through. They know. They all know what I am going to do.

Chapter Thirty-Three

Jade and onyx figurines crowded the waiting room. Tables and chairs carved into monstrous claws, tongues and nostrils looked poised for attack. The smell of incense, sickly sweet, was the most unnerving.

As directed, Theda and I sat quietly in our chairs awaiting word from the small woman dressed in black. She smiled at us before she disappeared behind bamboo curtains, which snapped and clicked as she passed through them into an adjoining room.

Weak shafts of light broke through a small window and formed pools upon a carpet printed with great claret-red urns. After a moment I realized the tendrils twisting out of the urns were snakes.

I shuddered and Theda grasped my hand. "It will all be over soon," she said calmly, for at least the tenth time that morning. But her face was worried as she winced at an odious fire-breathing dragon that hung on the wall over her shoulder.

I drew my handkerchief out and put it over my face. I thought I might be sick again but my stomach was painfully empty. I had not eaten for two days, rejecting the food that Theda offered me last night in our room. Whenever fear gripped me, and it came in constant waves, I thought of Theda's sister Eunice as she had been just two weeks ago in church singing "Rock of Ages" with her new husband Reginald. She was clearly pregnant. Her stomach was so large that the hymnbook lay almost flat atop it. And after church she had laughed gaily and walked languidly home with Reginald hugging her stomach as if she had never known a Dr. Lum Gam, had never required his services just a year ago, as if she had never watched a tiny cat woman being licked by strings of bamboo as she crept away from us into a secret room.

God had not struck Eunice dead. Contrarily, she had been given a new man to love, a new life to live. Dr. Lum Gam did not kill her with one of those swords on the wall and the lady behind the bamboo did not dope her with opium and toss her on a ship bound for Marrakech or Baghdad.

That's what I told myself as the minutes dragged into an hour. Acutely, we heard bustling noises from the street outside. Chinese pinged off the lips of the street vendors, reminding me only faintly of our own Chinatown in Pacific Grove, which now seemed halfway around the world. Through the small window we saw a cartload of whole skinned pigs tossed upon the street, their squiggly tails springing upon impact.

Above the clamor outside a woman's shrill cry tore through Dr. Lum Gam's waiting room. It came from behind the rattling bamboo doorway. Then soothing voices were made to quiet the woman. She sobbed.

Theda sprang from the chair. "We can't stay, Miss."

"We will." I rose up to meet her eyes, my hand grasping the

arm of the chair: a hideous head of a gaping dog. I whispered, "There are no options. My aunt and uncle would send me away, don't you see? They would have my baby taken away from me. I would not be allowed to love it anyway. Even if I dared to have it. Theda, please, you mustn't. My life has been arranged this way."

Simultaneously, we sat down, clasping each other's clammy hands. Several minutes after the sobbing ceased the cat woman clicked through the bamboo curtain. She smiled, her lips thinning into the gaunt hallows beneath her prominent cheeks. She tilted her head and stretched an arm toward the bamboo doorway.

Neither Theda nor I moved.

"Please," she said.

I was the first to rise from the chair, my hand breaking away from Theda's, which hung in mid air over her lap.

"So sorry," the lady nodded, looking down at the writhing snakes imprinted on the carpet. "Only the nice lady here," she said.

I turned to Theda, "Wait for me here, please. Don't worry, Theda."

Theda asked, "How long will it be?"

The little woman's eyes did not leave the floor. "Maybe one hour, maybe two. She rest a little. Then go home. You see. Happy again, very happy. No more problems for lady."

Theda's eyes blinked rapidly. Her crooked tooth bit into her upper lip. It was odd to see her sitting without a polish cloth in hand, without vegetables to slice laid out neatly before her. Poor Theda. Someday I would make this up to her.

The lady swept the bamboo aside and stepped through the doorway into a passage that led to another small room. A bamboo-strung exit on the opposite side matched the entrance.

"Lady take clothes off," she said.

"All of them?"

She nodded. "Then you drink this please." She handed me a glass of amber liquid.

"What is it?"

"Make you happy. Make you feel better. Is Chinese herb."

She set the glass on a table next to me and said, handing me a black silk robe, "You have this pretty robe." I took it from her. It was the same kind that often hung in the shops along the Monterey Bay in Chinatown back home.

She soundlessly backed out of the room, her head nodding as if I were royalty. I sat on the only chair in the stifling alcove and began to unbutton my coat and pull off my boots. When I had stripped to my petticoats, I drank the tea. Within minutes, I knew that I had done the right thing. My head swam in an exquisite oceanic fantasy. Naked by then, I cinched the black robe around my waist and dreamily sank into the chair. The woman crept into the room and guided me through the other door to a table softened with bedding. Like everything else in the room, it wavered before my eyes, more like a vision than anything real. I laughed at the woman, because I had always loved cats and she was a beautiful cat. I thought that Theda and I would have to bundle her up and take her back to Pacific Grove with us.

Then a man came into the room, a man with a round black cap and a black beard as long as his arms. He was the jailer and had come to set the child free. The child was not afraid. The man placed the cloth over my face and the room became black and starry like the winter nights over Lover's Point. I felt pain somewhere and I cried out but not loudly. Was it a whimper? Something was being ripped out of me. My heart? My lungs? I could not breathe. I could not cry out. I was tumbling through the silver stars that hung scattered in an abyss. Was I dying? Were the child and I leaving together? No . . . no! Because I must die with Andreas. That is what he promised me.

The stars sparked out and the darkness lay silently like the soundlessness that follows a passionate musical work. There was darkness, only darkness.

Chapter Thirty-Four

I awakened in my hotel room and recalled having been moved. I remembered Theda's arms lifting me into a rickety wagon and my being helped up creaking stairs by the room clerk with glassy eyes.

Hours must have passed as I slept.

Theda sat idly in the chair near the window, staring out into the dark city, her thick hands squeezing each other. A lamp was lit near the bedside table, making the square window of black look painted on the rosy walls. I mumbled, trying to speak, then Theda hobbled to my side.

"Miss, you're awake," she said, relieved. But her voice belied her fear. "Thank the Lord. Here," she said, placing a tray of food on the table near me. "I had the room clerk bring it up. Don't worry Miss, he thinks you've taken ill, a cough I told him. Here now, you got to eat a little and have a cup of soup. And see here, Miss, there's even the tea that I've kept warm for you with a cozy."

"It's over then, it's over?"

She nodded, woefully, and said, "Just like we said it would be. It's over."

"And gone—the child is gone."

Theda hung her head, her chin pressing to her chest. Was she praying or contemplating the turpitude of our act?

"The lady, the doctor's lady said you were to rest for three or four days. Now keep your head on the nice feather pillow. It'll be just fine, you'll see. We'll send a telegram. We need to do what the Chinese lady said." She put a cup of water to my lips. "Your skin is as white as milk. I thought—an hour ago I thought—that you was . . . ." Her voice made a purposeful drop in tone. "We must get you rested up."

I closed my eyes and slept until an elongated, golden moon appeared through the black window of the night. The lamp burned low. Theda had fallen asleep on the other bed, her hands at peace, crossed over her breast. In repose her face was washed of its pain. Sleep smoothed the full, twisted lips and the stretched cords of her neck.

I struggled to sit up. The clock on the chest of drawers read three-thirty. The cold room had chilled the food on the tray near my bed. The radiator was either off or broken.

I reached for the glass of water but my hands trembled and knocked it over. The sound awoke Theda who jumped up from bed. Recovering, she smoothed back her web-colored hair and brought a cup of cold tea to my lips. She touched my forehead. Her hand felt cold to me. "Theda, I had a dream. It wasn't the moon out there, but an eye. An enormous eye ogling us."

"Poor lamb . . . ." she said unsurely, as if groping for more words. "Poor dear lamb," she clucked, a phrase she normally reserved for the dead.

For the next hour or longer I passed in and out of consciousness, dreaming of fires, and I wondered if I were not in hell. But Andreas came in the dream and laughed at me, saying, as he has before, 'Hell is a metaphor for suffering. What kind of a beast would a father be to burn a naughty child? Angelica, we build our own heavens and hells.' As I lay in bed I thought: then this is my own hell. I painted it around myself, created it and then walked into it. But now I must create something different. I must forgive myself, that is what I must do. But the fire, I thought, waving in and out of consciousness, the heat keeps me from starting over, from creating a new moment in time.

I slipped from my dreams into a deep sleep until I heard noise, a shout, followed by a long low groan from Theda.

The bed was shaking. Or was it the room? It heaved violently. I watched helplessly as Theda was thrown against the wall, then struggled to her knees and crawled across the buckling floor as the room reeled. The windows shattered onto the floor. Theda groped across the glass trying to reach my bed. The building creaked and swayed. Ceiling plaster dusted the room. At last— it seemed like minutes though it could only have been seconds— she reached my side and lunged toward the lamp that was about to spill upon the bed.

"Get under the covers, Miss, under the covers!" she yelled. Then her voice was lost in the rumble emanating from the walls, the room, and the street outside. I prayed then, as I did in childhood, as if my life depended upon the fervor with which I summoned God's attention.

And then the room clouded over, became a murky, heavy field of nothing, dark and dusty. I smelled smoke. Something was burning, filling the room with dense brown particles. I could no longer see Theda's face, only the thick ankles and black boots that came out from under the bed where she had hidden from the ravages of the earthquake.

I dreamed again. It was Andreas. I saw him through the smoke and the flames. He threw boards against the wall. Was I dreaming of the burning fence? Or had he come into the room to save me from this hell? Pale sunlight began shining through the window casing. I could see flames behind Andreas in the hallway leading from the room. The room was stilled. Theda quickly crawled out from under the bed and without hesitation ran to the closet, seized my clothes and adroitly tore them into strips, tying them end to end. Feverishly she worked, her hair hanging over her face as her hands knotted the fabric. Outside people were screaming. Shrill, frenetic voices rose above the crackling and rumbling of the flames that had ignited our room. Andreas was there. He took Theda's makeshift rope, tested its strength by tugging on it, tossed it through the window and told her to climb down it and wait for him to lower me. Theda, silent and terrified, clambered over the sill and disappeared.

Andreas lifted me from the bed and carried me to the window. When Theda had descended the cloth streamers made from my sea green dress, he found the end and tied it around my waist. "Be a good girl, Angelica and don't move." His voice was hoarse. "We're going to lower you down."

Confused, I tried to do as he said, and hung limply over the knots at my waist. My legs felt wet and sticky, and dangled lifelessly under the ballooning nightgown like a marionette's. When I reached the bottom it was hard to breathe, then I felt Theda's comforting arms catching me. After she quickly untied me, Andreas pulled the green rope back up and used it to climb down.

The street was thronged with horrified people in sooty nightclothes watching the block of buildings burn down. Clouds of soot and ash rolled over us. Andreas carried me across the road to a little flower-filled park with neat hedges. Theda joined us and helped to lay me down on the cool green grass. Then I heard her sobbing.

"Lord, Lord, the blood," she cried. She raised her hand from my nightgown and held it up to show Andreas. Theda's beautiful, gnarly hand dripped a shining vermilion.

It was my blood.

The moment before I lost consciousness, I caught the light in Andreas' eyes sinking away, dimming greatly, I thought, as happens at sunset along Moss Beach when the sun has finished its day and looks to depart at the edge of the earth for places we've only imagined.

Chapter Thirty-Five

*W*here was I?

My vision was hazy but I realized that I must be in Cousin Dixie's house because I remembered as a child seeing those towering carved doors across the room whose knobs were beyond my reach. Like the brass ring, Cousin Dixie.

And then from faraway I heard Andreas' loud voice wrenching the truth from a penitent Theda. I loved you Theda. Oh God, no one ever told Theda that she was loved. And then I heard her wailing miserably and I wanted to stop Andreas from shouting but I couldn't move and I couldn't make any noises.

I knew I wasn't dead because there was an old doctor dressed in black rattling metal instruments in his bag. He murmured to my tiny Cousin Dixie about blood poisoning. He must have seen me before but I could remember only once his cold stethoscope against my chest and the hard probing of his hands under the blankets. Not like your hands, Andreas. And I thought it was funny and wanted to tell Andreas because there were pretty flowers all over the walls and the doctor looked like a beetle in my garden. Don't kill the beetles in the garden, Angelica!

Then there was a woman who wasn't Theda who kept turning me over and taking away my sheets because they were drenched, she said. She wasn't kind like Theda. She never touched me. Like Aunt Marion never touched me.

People kept talking about the fire. It was drawing closer. Was it about the fire my mother and father burned in? The lips that had turned to ashes. They kissed me when I was little and then they kissed Aunt Marion under a camellia bush. I think there are camellias on Dixie's walls.

And then later I smelled smoke. I woke coughing and thought I saw Andreas sitting across the room near an urn with a brilliant green plant. Was it already time for our walk to the cove? Every day we checked the baby seagull with the broken wing. We had hidden it in a safe place in the rocks and bandaged it and watered it and fed it sardines. We did everything we could to save it but it died anyway. Because it was its time to go, Andreas said. He said everything has its time.

Then Andreas was at my side. But his eyes weren't blue anymore. They were silver, like the moon. Oh, dear, he hadn't shaven. Uncle Robin won't like that.

Andreas was so very sad.

"Angelica, listen to me," he said softly. "There's been an earthquake here in the City. There's also a fire, you remember? It's now burning in our direction and so we'll have to move you. Do you understand? The buildings along this street are catching fire. Your aunt and uncle have reserved a place for us on tonight's train to Monterey. We're to leave this hour."

Then Cousin Dixie appeared, taking Andreas' place at my side. "Angelica, my dear cousin, if you need morphine for the trip the doctor will administer it." I could feel her touch my cheek and I could smell lavender. Oh, Cousin Dixie, I cherish the silver brush you sent to me one Christmas. And now it will lay alone for years on my dresser untouched but for the comforting bay wind that visits though my window.

A tender hand brushed the hair off my wet forehead. Dixie was sitting on the bed next to me. "You were such a little child when you last came to visit us and we took you to the carousel. Can you remember?" Her lip quivered.

Cousin Dixie don't be sad. Everything has its time.

She whispered, "You went round and round, ten rides at least because you couldn't catch the brass ring. We were so tired that we promised we would buy you a brass ring but you would have none of it. You said it wouldn't be the same. We told you that your arms were too short to reach it, and they were, Angel. We told you to return when you were older and catch all the brass rings your arms could hold. You rode a white unicorn with a pink flower harness and a golden saddle. Everyone asked, 'Who is the pretty thing with the exquisite black hair?'"

Then Andreas took his place again at my bedside. Our eyes locked and the truth came to us at precisely the same moment. We both knew that I was dying. And we could not speak of it.

Then the train was speeding away from the fire through the ink-black night.

The shadows swept by, the whistle wailed, and the wheels clacked over and over in a numbing recitation. Theda held my hand, rocking and humming gentle and sad songs.

Andreas put his head next to mine and stared courageously toward our destination because, as he had always reminded me, everything has its time.

I was at home and they all knew I was dying. Phoebe had seen it in her dreams. She wept endless tears over me and no amount of urging would coax her from my bedside.

The wallflowers danced up and down, up and down, pulsing in the shadows of the close room as days and nights passed. Fires burned in the hearth, the mist of Monterey Bay crouched in the corners of my room. I thought that was why I couldn't see the bureau drawer where Andreas' love letters lay in a small rosewood casket, bound in yellow ribbon. I remembered Theda singing one August when the sun failed to shine for twenty-eight days. She taught me the song her grandmother taught her.

> In a little rosewood casket,
> Sitting on a marble stand
> Is a package of love letters
> Written by a true love's hand.
> Go and bring them to me, sister
> Read them o'er to me tonight
> I have often tried but could not
> For the tears that blind my sight.
> Take his letters and his locket
> Place them gently on my heart
> But his golden ring he gave me
> From my finger never part.
> When I'm dead and in my casket
> When I gently fall asleep
> Fall asleep to wake in heaven
> *Darling sister, do not weep.*

I could feel that Andreas was always there in the room and the puffy Reverend Hawes, looking like a peaked bulldog, came also to visit me. Once they were very loud and the Reverend called Andreas a thick-headed theosophist and Andreas accepted the compliment. Phoebe had said, "Hush, the angel is sleeping . . . ."

At times I would awake. The pain welled inside of me and Andreas would slip over to my side and say wonderful things to make me happy.

Then at last he said, "Angelica, listen to me. You said once that you wanted to die on the sea. Do you remember?"

"The sea, yes, you and I . . . ."

He went on, "And we said if one of us should be near death that we would sail out to sea in a boat and keep going until we were both gone forever."

"Yes . . . ."

"I have a boat, Angelica."

"I can't breathe, Andreas. Don't let them put me in a box."

"Then tonight. I'll come for you tonight."

Phoebe's voice asked, "Do you wish it, Angelica?"

I whispered, "I'm not seeing so well, Phoebe. Put Andreas' grandfather's ring on my finger, will you? I must wear my mother's wedding dress for our marriage on the sea. Phoebe, I must wear mother's white lace dress with the fifty buttons. Maybe mother will come to our wedding on the sea, for just last night I spoke with her. She told me it was my time to come to her. It was beautiful . . . I need to go . . . . She was so beautiful, Phoebe, like Diana."

Later, when it was very quiet in the house, except for the soft patter of rain on the roof, Andreas and Phoebe dressed me in the soft white gown and Phoebe tied honeysuckle in my hair. Andreas placed the ring on my finger and hung his head for a minute as if in prayer. He carried me down the stairs and out the door and down the slope to the railroad tracks that followed the curve of the bay. The wind blew and the rain washed over my wedding dress. Phoebe stopped in a bright little puddle to say goodbye to us. As Andreas pushed the boat out from its mooring, I saw Phoebe clearly. It was as if a star as lonely as she had thought to shine upon her for my sake.

The rain grew black and cold. Our boat pitched on the inky dark sea. The sail unfurled and we moved toward open water. I lay near Andreas whose arm rested on my breast. His voice was soft and spoke of other times . . . something about the seaweed drying in the sun along Moss Beach, and the sounds of empty shells. I spoke to my mother in an empty shell, long, long ago. At last she answered me.

Andreas made me remember the time in the field when our kisses could not stop and the meadow was our bed and the sky, aching with blue, kept the secret . . . . Let Andreas and Angelica die into each other at last.

Chapter Thirty-Six

Candlesage

Morning broke. My eyes flashed open. I tried to get out of bed but my body was impossibly heavy. I was freezing. The penetrating chill swept from my feet to my brain as I made the transition from that life to this. Horrified, I tried to make sense of what had happened. Had Angelica died? Oh, God, I was cold. I felt as if a part of me had died with her. Was such a thing possible? I paused, breathing deeply, trying to clarify my thoughts. But debilitating pain went through my body, just as Angelica's afflictions had overcome her. I felt for my feet, my legs, my hands, my arms. I was alive. I was Paige Brighton. But I was foggy, disoriented. Angelica's death was so real to me that I would have expected to have awakened somewhere between lives—a bodiless apparition. And perhaps I had been—for a moment.

Lucetta had been right. I had felt trapped, unable to return. I placed a calming hand over my heart and reassured myself repetitively, reciting "It's okay, you're okay."

I surveyed the room. The strewn contents of my luggage had been moved from the foyer downstairs and were folded neatly on the dresser top. The wardrobe stood empty by the door. The shutters were open and morning hovered outside the windows, intimidated by an overcast sky. This would be a day when morning, afternoon and evening would pass without variation; the same dull grey lumbering from daybreak until dusk.

I remembered my confrontation with Neil. He had insisted that I not leave Candlesage, not to go to Andreas. He practically accused me of schizophrenia. I went upstairs, took a pill and went to sleep. And in that sleep I returned in time, and once again assumed my life as Angelica. Pacific Grove . . . the San Francisco earthquake . . . Angelica's death on the sea in her mother's wedding dress. But Andreas died with me . . . with her. The pact we had made had been fulfilled.

It was seven-thirty. I reached for the bedside clock and brought it to my ear, hoping its rhythmic ticking would lull me into a short nap.

I fell asleep and awoke at nine to the smell of coffee, I presumed from Aunt Belle's room next door. The pain in my body had subsided, my lucidity had returned and with renewed fervor I began planning my trip to Pacific Grove. Langston's letter had been clear. He wanted me. At that moment nothing else mattered.

The sound of the telephone jarred my thoughts. I ignored it but the ringing persisted. As I suspected, it was Marla.

"Yes."

"Paige, honey?"

"Marla . . . can I phone you back?"

"You're not still sleeping?" she asked.

"No. I'm reading."

291.

"Well, put your book aside. I need to talk to you, a motherly talk, and don't say no. You need one."

"Don't be ridiculous. I don't need any such thing."

"It's about yesterday," she said coyly.

"Yes?" I asked, confused.

"Neil phoned me after you'd gone to bed. You certainly went to bed early! And without him! He said you two had had a disagreement, an argument over Senator Holt. He said he'd acted like a real ass. I love it when men admit they're wrong, which, by the way, is almost always. Anyway, I couldn't imagine what Neil meant about Langston until I remembered two weeks ago at dinner, when the Senator was there. I don't think you were listening to him—you were shnockered, weren't you? But he started talking about the environment, and Monterey Cypress trees. Imagine. At the time I didn't think anything about it. But then when Neil called me last night and said that you were having some fantasy about Langston Holt, I started thinking . . . ." She waited for a comment.

"Go on," I said.

"Well?"

I said, "Marla, I can't talk about it. Really . . . ."

She continued, "But then I thought, what a coincidence. Cypress trees? I told Neil that if you said you had a good reason to visit Langston, then you had a good reason. You've always had an overactive imagination, but you're not loony tunes. That's what I told Neil. I told him to let you go up to this place—what is it—Pacific Grove—and to get his nose out of it." She took a breath. "Do they have any spas there? And then it dawned on me. You had a premonition, didn't you Paige? That man that you saw in your bedroom that morning, the 'vision,' was Langston Holt, wasn't it? You had a dream about him but you didn't know who he was. How could you? You never read anything but old books, you hardly ever even read newspapers or watch television news. It was him, wasn't it? Oh, come on, Paige. What difference does it make if I know?"

So I answered, "Yes, Marla. It was him."

"I knew it! I just knew it," she said with the smug tone of a mystery novel fan who has divined the criminal before the last chapter.

I said, "I had a dream about him. But he also had one about me."

"My God," she gasped. It was a plot twist she had not expected.

"He invited me to Pacific Grove. That is something Neil does not know. And," I added, "will not know."

"Invited you," she mumbled, digesting the information. "This is really weird, very parapsychological. And at the Daisy Cotton that morning you said you knew him from somewhere, the man who came to you in your room that morning. So you must have seen his picture somewhere, in a magazine or something. In a way, it's creepy. Really. I might just have to start believing in something besides vegetables *al dente* and stretch and tone. I mean, maybe there really is something to ghosts and ESP."

"Marla, please don't give up stretch and tone. Look, I have to go now. I'd appreciate it if you didn't tell Neil about our conversation. I know you won't. I'm mad at him, disgusted really, but there's no reason to hurt him. He shouldn't know about Langston's invitation."

"Hey," she said knowingly, "it might hurt Lang more than Neil, if Neil finds out he's invited you up to his charming little hideaway in Pacific Grove. It could cost his campaign *mucho dinero*. My God, Paige, you've made my week, I have to say. This is the best thing that's happened since Retin-A. Paige Brighton and Senator Langston Holt meet in dreams . . . deja vu, clairvoyance ... Ed Cayce ... Jeanne Dixon—remember her? Be careful the tabloids don't get hold of it. Call me in a few days, will you? I'll be on the edge of my seat with a brand-spanking new Tarot deck until I find out what's happening. Promise! Promise you'll phone me."

She made me cross my heart and hope to die prior to hanging up. Before I could pull the covers off and head for the shower, I heard Aunt Belle's 'shocking pink' morning voice outside my door. "Breakfast, sweetie!" Aunt Belle's husband had labeled her garish squeal in honor of an oft worn hot pink robe she had knitted for a silent auction. It had been returned, without comment, in a grocery bag.

"I'm not hungry," I stated dully, hoping I sounded ill.

"Of course you are!" continued the garish voice. "Oh Paige, honestly! A little tiff with Neil and look at you, holed up in there like John Wayne at the Alamo!"

I hurried out of bed and let her into my room, hoping to put a quick end to further inane comparisons. Quietly, I said, "Neil and I are not your business. Stop yelling up and down the hall. Here, give me that tray."

But it was Neil who took the tray as he appeared stealthily in the doorway. "I'll take it in for you," he remarked, swinging into the room and shutting Aunt Belle out.

After placing the tray on the table he turned to me and said coolly, "Go anywhere you want, Paige, at anytime. Yesterday I was acting out of anger and out of concern. Frankly, I don't think you're fit to travel anywhere alone."

"I'll be fine."

"Will you?" he asked, his mouth twisting, his eyes narrowing. He didn't want to let me go, but he would.

"I will be okay," I said. "I understand about yesterday. I know you're angry and concerned and I don't blame you, Neil. It has nothing to do with you, this trip I'm making. It's no reflection on you, is what I mean. You know that. And I can assure you, I'm not hearing voices." There was defiance in my explanation. I could not let him think that my softening would in anyway alter my decision. Yet I felt sorry for him, and was troubled that he thought he had failed me, that he was losing what he most wanted. I searched his face for a sign of surrender, of acquiescence. There was nothing in his demeanor to suggest that he had lost anything. His vibrant grey eyes were tied to mine. His body was relaxed, hands on hips, as they often were, suggesting self-assurance. He always looked as if he were in the process of winning me. Sometimes even I believed he would.

Two hours later I stood on the Candlesage portico waiting for my tattered baggage to be brought down and placed in the car trunk. Aunt Belle had gone into near shock when I announced to her, bags in hand, that I was leaving Candlesage for a few days. But a shopping trip to the nursery to buy fall blooming annuals (and whirligigs, which she had unanimously decided were needed in the kitchen vegetable patch to offset the statuary garden) had lightened her spirits.

The beautiful white lips of the marble woman appeared to curl into a smile. I was leaving; something she would never do. The necklace had been removed. Neil would never mention it to me because he needed to avoid the truth.

As I began to get into my car I noticed that the dent Vincent had left there last New Year's Eve had been hammered out. I walked to it and ran my fingers over the spot that had dimpled the car; my visible scar. Neil had a way of correcting unpleasantness.

"Paige." Neil was striding across the drive. "I thought you should know Vincent's out on bail."

"Thank you," I said, getting into the car. "I'll be careful." He backed away. As I drove off, I watched him in the rear view mirror growing ever smaller until he finally vanished from sight.

I stopped at the first gas station to get maps. An attendant with gold caps on his teeth told me that Pacific Grove was between Pebble Beach and Monterey on the farthest tip of the Monterey Peninsula. He said he had eaten at a restaurant in Pacific Grove two years before while attending the Monterey Jazz Festival. I put on a Bach tape and drove the smoggy arteries of Los Angeles north toward Santa Barbara.

The dark ocean lay reposefully against the hard blue of the sky. A few white clouds tumbled in slow motion. They also were traveling north. I thought how good it was to be alone, snug in one's own car, in control of the situation. There was no one to interrupt my thoughts.

It was the first time I had had a chance to weigh the events of my past life. Angelica had had an abortion. She—I—had terminated the pregnancy and in so doing was going to die. Andreas arranged our deaths on the sea. I was curious about Isabel. What had happened to her and to her child? It was a safer subject than others. I resisted the thoughts of Angelica's end, of her last days of suffering. And about Andreas' infidelity: as Angelica, I found it agonizing. As Paige, I found it largely forgivable. I confessed to myself that I was, however, too needy to be objective. I would trade all the hurt in that last life for the promise of something more in this one. I would overlook the fact that desperation paled rationality.

As I drove north, I found myself preoccupied with the traffic behind me. My eyes repeatedly darted to the rear view mirror. Was I afraid of Vincent? I had the nagging feeling I was being followed. But the freeway along the Ventura shore looked normal enough. There was an old white VW Rabbit driven by a frenetic looking blonde man with thick glasses. In the other lane there was an attractive young man with brown hair in a black Porsche with a UCLA sticker on the windshield. Beside him was a boy with huge blue eyes and a mop of golden-white hair. The child bounced a toy elephant on the dashboard and looked as though he were talking. If Shea had lived, he would have been that boy's age. He may have even looked like him.

I knew that what I did was right. Shea was suffering. He had been so white against the hospital sheets that from across the room I could see only his eyes. His hair had fallen out. We joked together that he was as bald and brilliant as the October moons he loved. They had told me that at any hour, at the very most a day or two, that he would die. There was nothing more anyone could do. All alternatives had been explored and exhausted. He was suffering so. I could not wait any longer and I could not have Shea wait. He had repeatedly said to me, "Mommy, Mommy, I want to go now. My grandma is waiting. I saw her. I want to go to the beautiful place."

I had shut off the oxygen. Shea's death had not made me uneasy until now, until I had discovered my past life as Angelica. Maybe it was not guilt I felt but sadness because I had felt very deeply at the time that I must honor the last wishes of a little boy who had no other choice but to leave me.

Neil had guessed. He knew that I let Shea die. Did Neil think that guilt over Shea's death had caused my hallucinations? Was it guilt or was it fear that kept me checking my rearview mirror? Was knowledge of Angelica's abortion magnifying my fears?

My knuckles had gone white on the steering wheel. I relaxed my grip and thought of taking a tranquilizer. Neil was right again. I was probably not emotionally strong enough to make this trip to Pacific Grove. I felt jittery. Maybe I had just forgotten how to be alone.

It was past noon. I decided to take the off ramp inland to have lunch at San Ysidro Ranch. Before I married Vincent, I had been at San Ysidro with Edmond, a long-time friend and "incurable bookworm," as Aunt Belle called him. We had spent a serene weekend with Colette and James Joyce, swimming, eating and riding.

I parked, entered the Plow and Angel restaurant and seated myself near the garden window. The room was clean and spartan in its furnishings. A woman across the room laughed at her companion's witticism, glanced in my direction, then appeared to dismiss my presence as inconsequential. I was grateful that I would never have to explain Andreas to the cunning and conventional world in which the laughing woman lived.

I was lightheaded in spite of my cup of hot coffee and omelet. The simple garden outside the window was filled with flowers. It was still except for a tall bent man with a rake who passed by the window. He looked as though he'd escaped from a Van Gogh.

Beyond the hills to the east I saw an airplane, a silver smear on a buttermilk sky. As I sat my cup down upon the saucer and returned my gaze to the sky I saw something burst among the clouds. The airplane had been blown into silver fragments. Terrified, I knocked the cup off the saucer. I stood up craning my head toward the window. A jolt of orange flame and smoke filled the sky. Turning to the dining room I said, "A plane has blown up! Look . . . my God, a plane in the sky, up there!"

The wary woman and her guests looked at me with an ennui that was unsettling. As if following a well-memorized script, they turned away.

Andreas . . . Senator Langston Holt . . . the airplane . . . .

I paid the bill and stumbled from the pristine white room.

Once inside my car I jammed the automatic lock and clutched the steering wheel, using it to pillow my head. It had been a vision. It had not been real . . . had it? For now the sky bore no evidence of a plane explosion. For a few seconds at least, I was absolutely positive that Andreas—Langston Holt—had been on that plane. Cold sweat washed over me as I struggled for composure. A few moments later I turned on a local radio station. A cheerful weather woman gave the temperature. There were no reports of a disaster.

I started the engine and knew that I was either losing my mind or that Paige Brighton was now clairvoyant. As I left San Ysidro I wondered if there were not such a thing as knowing too much. Isn't that what Lucetta had told me?

Chapter Thirty-Seven

Searching for the familiar, I read a sign that said Lighthouse Avenue. I could tell by the curve of the bay that I was near Pacific Grove. The bay's configuration was one thing that had not changed in eighty-seven years.

Lighthouse Avenue had been extended beyond the old city lines. The street was a black vein with garish signs and small shops. Where had the forests gone?

At a traffic light I rolled down my window and shouted to a man in a yellow car. "Is this the way to Pacific Grove?"

He pointed, "Up the road. Lighthouse jogs to the left. This is New Monterey."

I was overwhelmed with curiosity and a need to see the places I had only visited mentally in this life. Yet the purpose of my visit receded as I looked about me—the familiar juxtaposed to the new.

There was nothing new about New Monterey. Were it not for the incredible blue of the bay beyond the buildings on the north side of the street, it could have been any strip of the 'old hippie' Southern California ambience, replete with used bookstores, small restaurants and thrift shops.

In several blocks the disarray of stores became a collection of modest, well-kept Victorian homes and prim storefronts. I turned left and was able to connect with Lighthouse Avenue and then Forest Avenue.

A car blasted its horn at me. I pulled over and parked in front of a grocery store called Grove Market. My stomach leapt into my chest, my knees knocked together. I was home. One set of buildings in downtown Pacific Grove remained the same, I noted. I recognized many of the houses along the side streets. They were standing intact with sparkling paint and scrubbed windows and blooming window boxes.

I jumped from the car and ran around the corner into the building that was once Tuttle's Drugs. I expected to see Mr. Tuttle in his white apron and trim mustache filling jars behind his counter. But there was a young woman there instead, wearing the traditional uniform of the apathetic—jeans and a T-shirt. She looked up from her magazine. I backed out of the store with an apology and paused in the sunshine. I was home.

Impulsively I began to run down Forest Avenue toward the bay. How many times had I gone along these streets as a child, at just this pace, skipping home from school, running from Luther Orwell's assaults, or returning home from a secret meeting with Andreas? There were houses everywhere now, not just those fanning out from the downtown streets and adjacent blocks. Things had changed. I could feel the heart of Pacific Grove as I raced down Forest Avenue. I could feel the wind from the bay, smell the ocean and see, here and there, monarch butterflies fluttering jewel-like among the flowers and trees just as they had for centuries.

Time had not paled the color of the sky, nor of the sea. Beyond the noise from the cars there was a stillness that, like a cherished folk song, prevailed through time, a peace that had been handed down from the past.

The old houses had green plaques on them, names of former owners. I ran along the avenue from house to house, reading off the names of those whom I once knew . . . as Angelica. The green plaques with gold writing inscribed the dates the houses had been built.

A grey-haired man in a plaid shirt stood outside his house, watering a privet hedge. He smiled and nodded.

"Nice town," I said pausing to catch my breath. "I like your house."

"Been here before?" he asked "to Pacific Grove?"

I stammered. "Yes, yes I have. A long time ago."

"People always come back," he said.

"That's what I hear," I said, smiling as he emptied his pail of water on a bush.

"I noticed the green plaques on the houses."

He nodded. "Heritage Society. Can't tear the old ones down unless they're ready to fall. Conservation's big in this town. Preserve the past, you know."

"I'm glad of that, really happy," I said, lingering on the walk beside him. "They're all dead now . . . . I mean, are there any of them still alive, the people? Any old timers?"

"Sure," he said, shaking water from his hands, wiping them on his pant legs. "A few. See them in the newspaper once in awhile, someone's been around since the turn of the century. That sort of thing. You should try going over to the Heritage Society, the old barn up on Laurel Avenue. They'll tell you what you want to know. That is, if they're open. People in this town mostly work when they feel like it. It isn't like

Southern California. I can tell you're from Southern California."

"Sorry," I shrugged. "Thank you." The old barn on Laurel was still standing!

I walked on reading the name plaques. These had been my neighbors, my friends. I might as well have been in a graveyard. I saw their faces emerge from the plaques. Mothers, fathers, children, picnics, Sunday school, the Chautauqua, Chinatown, the schoolroom. Children who were now very, very old if alive at all. Or had they, like me, come back to live again? Had the man in the plaid shirt watering his shrubs lived before? Had I known him?

Forest Avenue ended at the bay. Past the houses one could see the ragged rocks of Lover's Point. The grey configurations were precisely as I remembered them.

I wanted to see Aunt Marion's house—my house. I was convinced as I approached the corner across from the bay that I would discover our house like something bundled up in a secret drawer and found a century later. I was willing to uncover memories once too sweet or too painful to endure.

The wind had risen slightly and the bright blue sky was edged with dark grey clouds. Even the weather was as it had been then—utterly changeable. One minute the sky was blue, the sun was warm, the next instant could very likely obliterate all color and light, leaving a dismal veil of fog or clouds over land and sea.

Across a narrow parking lot I saw a few people in the winter sunshine sitting on the rocks or hopping along the sandy shore at Municipal Beach near Lovers Point, a slender crescent of golden sand above which perched a new, modern bath house. It was a restaurant painted slate blue, like the sea. The Japanese Tea Garden was gone. A drained swimming pool and a boarded-up fast food stand indicated that summers here would bustle.

The rock walls had been a strong contrast to the fragile walls of the Japanese tea room that once sat so peacefully above the crashing ocean waves. It had been Diana's favorite place to meet for talks. Had she married Davey Willingham? Had she been happy? Had she been spared the razing of the Japanese Tea Garden? I tried to mentally reconstruct the curling roof and the bright tossing paper lanterns that I had seen for years from the window of my bedroom. If Diana had been there at my side, she would have raised a perfect white finger to point out a missing stroke of color, maybe a fluttering banner or a vase of vivid red poppies. She would have laughed musically, daintily, appreciating the memory.

Houses were now everywhere along Ocean View Boulevard. If my house still stood it would be just beyond the curve of the road.

My teeth rattled as I walked. I could hear my name being cried out on the wind over the bay. Seals and otters moved in the shadowy water that lay beyond the rocky coves, the shallow, glistening tide pools.

When I saw my house I felt like water had been thrown on my face. Architecturally it had changed little. It was now brightly painted, with white trim. The gardens were immaculate. It was far grander than I remembered it. Through the windows I could see lit paintings and crystal chandeliers. It posed at seaside like a small Victorian palace.

I felt my knees weaken, my hands grow clammy, my mouth go dry. I propped myself up against a gatepost.

Andreas, you remember, don't you? Did you take the walk through town, Langston? Did you see my house and remember?

Someone asked, "You okay, dear?"

I turned around. A large lady with a scarf knotted under her chin stared at me.

"Yes, thank you. I was just looking for Chinatown."

"For what?"

"Chinatown."

She shifted her blocky body from one foot to the other and pointed east. "Well, there's a leftover Chinese building on Cannery Row, if that's what you mean. You know, Steinbeck and Doc Rickett's friend, Wing Chong, or Wong Dung or something like that. Used to be a market and now—can't remember. Everything's changed since the aquarium."

"Aquarium? But what happened to Chinatown? It was over there. Just past the Hopkins Marine Station." We found ourselves pointing to the same spot.

She chuckled, her large breasts heaving, "Oh, *that* Chinatown! Well, let me think a minute." She rubbed her rather whiskery chin and announced, "Burned down around the turn of the century."

"No. It couldn't have. I was here until 1906."

"Beg your pardon?" she asked skeptically. "You were here, you say?"

"I mean, my grandmother said it was here in 1906."

"That's it!" She snapped her fingers. "Burned down in 1906. Arson, that's what the history books say. Said folks got tired of smelly squid fields. What some people will do!"

"The Chinese were here first! They were good people. And it wasn't so bad, the squid fields, I mean," I murmured. "An aquarium?"

"Yep, the aquarium. Since then, the whole place has turned into T-shirt row. In my book it's a shame really. The place wasn't crowded just ten years ago, but now . . . look, look at the traffic."

I cut her off, "I can't believe the people would have burned down Chinatown."

"Oh, you'd be surprised what people can do, dearie!" She

hugged her large parcel and continued on her way. "'Fore I'm dead there'll be nothing but hotels along Ocean View. Makes me sick to my stomach. Nobody cares about the old days. Money, money, money."

She waddled toward Lover's Point, her head downcast, mumbling to herself.

Across the road from my house were steps that led to a walking trail, a strip that was once the Southern Pacific Railroad track. But the track was gone, the sound of the old steam engines swallowed up by the churning of the bay and of the years that had swept by. I crossed the street and began to walk slowly, absorbing everything the seascape offered. On the left side of the broad trail, the rocky land sloped into the bay just as it had then. Dozens of squirrels appeared and disappeared in the rock crevices, many lingering for handouts. Fishing boats were coming in from the sea, cutting their way through the choppy bay water heading home to their slips at Fisherman's Wharf in Monterey. Across the bay, miles away, I could see a steam plant of some kind and thousands of miniscule squares that could only be houses. Once upon a time there had been only trees.

I sat on a bench and stared out at the bay. Memories flooded back, memories of the most tender kind. God, I was lonely, alone, solitary. I felt like I was the only piece left of a board game. Where were they all? They were not dead, I believed that much. Were they pausing on the other side awaiting rebirth? Had they reappeared here, or in China, or in Alaska? Where was Diana? Aunt Marion? Uncle Robin? Theda?

The encroaching fog crawled between me and my view of the bay. The sea's shimmering dark blue turned to flint as rolling mist flooded over it.

I pulled my sweater collar up to my chin and plunged my

hands deep into its pockets. I am not Angelica, I am Paige, I told myself.

The sound of the faraway foghorn, the whine of the gulls were so familiar to me they could have been fossilized noises.

I began to walk back to Lover's Point. The fog was denser and dusk was falling. I passed the parking lot and walked beyond the drained swimming pool and around the restrooms behind it. There was no one in sight now. It was as if the dreary weather had swept them away.

I crossed grassy lawns shaded by wind-bent cypresses so that I could get as close to the sea as possible. I climbed down a cluster of rocks that spilled into the water. I had not been here, by the bay, since my death out there, on the sea, in a small boat with Andreas.

What was the sea trying to tell me? For I was sure that my name—the name Angelica—was being whispered over the churning sea, through the shrouding mist.

"I am not Angelica, I am Paige." I whispered back. Then like an electrical charge feelings broke inside me. This was my grave.

I shouted to the bay that sucked at my feet, to the chilling fog that choked the twilight air, "I am not Angelica! I am Paige!" No one heard me. I turned away and walked back to my car.

Chapter Thirty-Eight

*G*reen Gates.

The house that had held such warmth for Angelica in her life played upon my emotions. I had driven back and forth in front of its encompassing stone walls last night but had chosen to wait until dawn to make an appearance. I had slept in my locked car at Moss Beach, just down the road from the house, after having exhausted myself with Angelica's memories. There was not a philosophical question that I did not try to answer for myself as I listened to the intrepid wintry ocean burst upon the expanse of white sand. Actually, I had slept very little. As I creaked open the arched green gate I thought of how ravaged I looked in the clothes that had doubled as my pajamas. I had made a quick stop at a café but lacked the will to try to improve my appearance. There was a time when I would have cared how I looked.

The brick paths were timeworn and the gardens overgrown. But a birdbath to the left of the front entrance bubbled with finches as they bathed noisily among the tangled branches.

I walked up the steps of the covered front porch. The arched teak door, built by old Charles Beauchamp in 1902, was intact, as was the bronze lion head doorknob, which had blackened with age. To the right of the door was the old ship's bell that, with a simple yank, had always brought Andreas, Signe or Knute to the door.

Bracing myself, I rang the bell. At the sound a lone crow flew from the roof, wheeled and came to land a few yards from the steps.

I twisted the lion head knob. The door was not locked and opened easily.

The entrance hall, which was probably twelve feet wide and thirty feet long, had not changed much except that the hardwood flooring was now terra cotta tile. Through the double glass doors at the end of the hall were the apple orchard and the tiny white guesthouse with the Dutch style clipped roof. Roses still bloomed in flowerbeds scattered throughout the brick paving which separated the guest cottage from the main house.

The hall was shadowy though the sun had now risen. A long church pew ran the length of the hall past double doors to the living room on the right. On the left a staircase rose to the rooms on the west wing of the house. I crept into the hall and stopped at Angelica's portrait which hung over the pew near the glass doors. It was being painted when she died. Andreas never much liked it. He had said it was not soft enough, that it was not yielding. As I raised my fingers to stroke her face, I heard his voice behind me.

"A hundred times. At least that many," he said. He was standing on the staircase landing with a book in one hand, a pen in the other. I was surprised by his reading glasses. He took them off and put them in his shirt pocket. "Maybe even more than a hundred. Actually I stopped counting the times I stood before that portrait wondering what the hell was wrong with me. Standing right there, where you are now. Was I insane? Mid-life crisis? Depression?" He walked down the stairs and slowly placed his book on the library table next to the stairs.

It was remarkable. Langston could easily have been the young Andreas descending the staircase with a book in hand—maybe Plato's *Meno*—as he had often done in our other life. He would be anxious to share a philosophical spark found somewhere in the book's arsenal, something he could marshal in his battle for independent thought.

I could have been the exuberant and young Angelica waiting impatiently for him in the entrance hall at Green Gates, ready to report another shocking Pagrovian offense against liberation, such as the outrageous city decree that women must wear double-crotch bathing suits at Lovers Point beach, information I could vividly recall imparting to Andreas. In this very hall I had made a thousand breathless announcements, the swimsuit requirement no more absurd than any other. And some more celebratory. I could remember standing at this place where the portrait now hung and gleefully announcing to Andreas the homecoming of the town's chief antagonist, the avant-garde Julia Platt, one of the few liberated women in our town . . . .

Our world of Pacific Grove was small and yet boundless.

Only now did I understand.

"Because," he continued, "I was in love with a girl in a portrait. Things happened in her eyes. And then I began dreaming . . . and then remembering. And the little old lady with the dyed red hair, the one who owns this house, became an unlikely savior. She knew who I was. She didn't tell me at first. I guess she thought it better if I were to discover it on my own. I dreamed of the portrait and then I began to see another face in her face, other eyes in her eyes. Your eyes, Paige, your green eyes through her dark eyes." He moved closer to me. "Your lips through hers. A different woman . . . the same love . . . compulsive love . . . blinding love . . . irrational. I called it everything but nothing explained it." He took my hand and raised it to his lips. The touch of his lips on my skin was so very familiar. He kissed it as Andreas had so many years before.

"Let's sit down." He took my hand, leading me through the passage to the living room. "I'll put on some coffee. Not very good coffee—I can never make it right." He smiled and let go of my hand.

Please touch me again, I thought, watching him disappear through the kitchen door.

Shadows lingered in the living room. The smell of wood smoke wafted in the air. Dark blue and red furnishings, rich wood tables and ceramic and brass lamps were spread comfortably in the room. The oriental carpet had not changed. The andirons were the same: enormous bronze dolphins from Sweden that Signe polished each year for Christmas. She dragged the black monsters from the hearth and out into the garden sunshine where they were transformed into golden treasures worthy, Knute had said, of Poseidon's chariot.

Andreas, what will we do?

"She's got the world's loudest coffee pot," he said, as he returned to the living room, pausing at my chair. He stared softly into my eyes, wanting to say something that he could not find the words for.

I waited, feeling the full force of those moments. The silence was a prelude to a consummation of everything we had been and now were. I wanted him to say something that would verify our relationship. I wanted him to make a promise.

But instead, he sat in the chair opposite mine, near the hearth, which had been laid for a fire, and struck a match to ignite the paper and cones beneath the wood.

"Phoebe doesn't like the big electric bills. She told me to use the fireplace when I could."

"What is she like? Is she as wonderful?"

He nodded. "She's hardly changed. It's funny, isn't it? People don't change much." He prodded the fire with the poker, then looked back at me. He put the tool aside and leaned back into his chair, hands folded over his stomach. I did as he did, leaned back and let my hands loosen their grip on the chair arms. The room was heavy with a feeling I could not identify. Was it melancholy?

He said, "The first day I saw Green Gates, or should I say the first time I returned to Green Gates, I was driving up the street from Moss Beach—they usually call it Asilomar now. I looked over at the house and drove my car into Phoebe's mailbox." He smiled. "I think I paid a little restitution in conjunction with physical damage. Phoebe drives a hard bargain. But, anyway, I saw the house and knew that I had seen it before. I thought naturally that what I had seen sometime or somewhere in my life was simply its likeness. But it grabbed me, overcame me. It was a drawing force. Like a magnet. Actually, it caused a physical sensation like illness. I sat outside staring at Phoebe's crunched mailbox and thought I had had a stroke or a heart attack or something. Then I saw the 'For Rent' sign. I had already rented a house up at Jacks Peak. I don't know why—at least I didn't then—I was compelled to get out of my car, go through the arch with the green gates and up to the front door. And then she answered the door—a very old, thin as a reed, red-haired woman with a knowing smile. The kind of smile that knows something you don't know. When she opened the door, she looked me up and down, and before I had a chance to apologize for the mailbox, she handed me the key and said, 'You'll do.'

"I took the key from her and wrote a check for the first month's rent. I wrote it automatically and hadn't the least idea why. The memory is foggy. It happened so fast. Kind of like the way you act when you're panicked. Without thought of anything but survival. I had to know what had drawn me to the place. I honestly thought I was losing my mind."

He took a deep breath and looked at me intently, as if I should know the purpose of such a look. I could feel him reaching out to me. It was the same thing Andreas had done to Angelica. He was taking me over. Strange how when with Neil I was so protective of my identity. With Andreas I eagerly gave myself away. Perhaps that is why I longed for him to say something 'important.' My fate hung on every word, on every nuance.

"The feeling did not abate once I settled into Green Gates. It got worse, intensified. I began hearing voices, children's laughter, old rhymes. Especially in the garden," he murmured looking from the fire in the hearth to my face. "The old woman, Phoebe, began watching me closely. It's funny now. We've even laughed about it. But she would watch me from behind the trees and corners. Waiting for me to discover the truth, watching out for me in case I should. She told me later that she did not realize it was me—that is, she did not realize it was Andreas until the next morning, after a dream she'd had.

"I began to ask questions. Who had originally owned the house? She told me 'Knute and Signe Sparring.' But it was when she brought out the portrait that I began to dream about a man named Andreas who once lived in Pacific Grove at Green Gates. Who was Andreas? Who was Angelica?"

I added, "And why us—Paige Brighton and Langston Holt?"

A voice behind me cracked, "Because you are blessed! That's why! You had it then and you have it now."

I turned toward the withered voice. The thin, crooked old woman with the wild look in her eyes and the hair twisted up like a bird's nest could only be Phoebe. Teary-eyed, I got up from my chair and embraced her. My young cousin, my guardian angel . . . the old woman whom I had seen that night in the apple orchard at Green Gates . . . the old woman who thought she had seen Angelica in the trees. In my arms, her body felt skeletal.

We broke our embrace to look at each other. Her hair was the color of a pumpkin and her face was snow white and crinkled. But the eyes were daring, strong and young.

Her chin quivered and her cane shook. "I always knew you'd come back," she said, almost whimpering. "The night I tied honeysuckle in your hair and accompanied you through the storm to the boat, I knew you'd come back to me some day. In those days, I thought you'd sail back. I spent years watching the bay from your bedroom window. The clouds parted the night you and Andreas left me and sailed out to sea. And a star shone down over me and I shouted back to the star, 'She'll come back to me. Angelica will come back.'"

"Yes," I nodded. "You knew things we others didn't."

She snapped, "Nonsense! You knew as much as I did but you just didn't *know* it. And you did too, Mr. Sparring-Holt."

He smiled at her, rising from his chair. "Nobody knows as much as you do. Then or now." He was teasing her and she knew it.

"Well," she nodded with spunk, "in a way it's true. Now get out of here. Angelica and I need to talk. Scoot."

"Now, come here, come. Sit, sit." She ordered. She reminded me of a little blackbird, the way she perched on the edge of a rickety Queen Anne chair, her cane directly in front of her with hand stretched out and resting on its knob. It looked liked manzanita burl.

"That's right," she said. "It is manzanita. My husband Denholm carved it for me from a stinky old branch that washed up on Moss Beach. But Denny didn't live to see me use it."

"How did you know what I was thinking?"

"Silly girl! I've always known what you're thinking. I've just gotten better at it." She leaned forward and whispered, "When I was a child I was psychic. Now I *am* a psychic. I've written three books on the subject and one of them was a bestseller. What's the matter, don't you read?"

"Actually, Phoebe, I read a great deal. But mostly fiction."

"On second thought, you don't know my pen name. It's Annabelle Seasons!"

"Yes, I have heard of you. You wrote *My Stars*. That was it, wasn't it? Phoebe—you're Annabelle Seasons?"

"I'll give you an autographed copy before you go." She nodded firmly.

"Go . . . I haven't thought that far ahead." My voice sounded forlorn. Go where?

She leaned over and squeezed my arm with incredible vigor. "This meeting is important. Very important, Angelica. Did you notice the light?"

"What light?"

"What light, you ask. Are you blind? The swirls of light between the two of you. When I came into the living room that's all I could see at first. Light is holy. Light is pure." She swept a thin, black-clad arm in the air. "Between the two of you. I must record this meeting. It is vital. Yes, I know it too—what you are thinking. That you are twin souls, he and you. It's true. It's no different now than it was eighty-seven years ago. My lord, has it really been that long? And look at you, Angel, not a wrinkle in your face!" She chuckled and then abruptly silenced herself as if laughter must be kept in its place. She peered toward me. "You must tell me what it is like to remember a past life, to meet your lover again and to recognize him. You must tell me. The world needs to know. Oh, don't worry. For God's sake, do you think I'd use your real names? Well, only if you want me to. You see, I'm wrapping up my very last book. It is essential that I know this. I've waited a lifetime . . . a lifetime."

"Everything hurts," I said. "That's what it's like. Pain."

"Why?"

"Resistance, isn't it?" I suggested. "God, I don't know why it hurts. Because I want something, I need something beyond my reach, I think. I don't know. Because I feel like someone has stolen an essential part of me. He's a part of me and I can't get it back. I want everything else to end so that he and I can begin, to start over."

"But you can't do that! No one can ever, ever start from nothing. You are a vessel into which many lifetimes of experiences are poured. If you emptied out all of those experiences you'd be nothing! Now, change your mind, that's okay. Change your mind. Chart a new course. But start over? Don't make me laugh." Then she laughed and suddenly said, "I thought you'd be more advanced, more enlightened. But God works in weird ways. You are beautiful and I am so fortunate, or blessed, I should say, that I have been given this incredible experience. Angelica! I can hear what you're thinking and I tell you now there are no clean starts! You are an accumulation. Sounds ugly but it's not. It's wonderful. You are one of the few who have remembered from one life to the other. It's the beginning. There will be more and more now because it's time. It's that simple." She paused and then said, "Why are you here?" Her eyes narrowed, her lips thinned. I could see little Phoebe peering out of her almost comical pose.

"I'm here because I want him." It was a flat statement. I started to go on but then she stopped me.

"Well, I know that much!"

"That's all I know right now."

"Well, you'll know more in a couple of days." She nodded. "I will learn from you and you from me. First answer me this: I need to know how your crossover began. How did you first learn of it? Dreams and flashbacks I'll bet. I need to know how much you remember. Is it sequential? I think Mr. Sparring-Holt remembers what you remember, that your memories are the same and yet individual. Can you recall it at will or do you dream or go into a trance? Have you worked with parapsychologists? Your passage from that life to this one and back—is it painful, fun, frightening, or what? There are a million things to learn, to record." She took a deep breath and slumped forward.

"You want to know now?"

"Yes, yes. Right now. I haven't got long to live."

"Are you joking?"

"Of course I'm not joking. You think I'd joke about a thing like that? Honestly Angelica! Sometimes you remind me of you-know-who."

"Who?"

"My mother, of course."

"Aunt Marion. Oh God . . . you can't be serious."

"I am serious. Just as serious as I am about dying."

"What's wrong?" I gently asked.

"I have cancer and I have a very short time . . . which is fine with me. This, this reunion with you and Andreas, this confirmation of everything I have believed in, is the grand finale of my life. So, yes, I would like to know now."

I told her. As she listened her agitated eagerness was replaced by an intense calm as she clung to each word I spoke. When I finished she said nothing, merely rocked her cane forward and backward as if in contemplation.

"I'll go get coffee," I said, and slipped into the kitchen, leaving her in silence. I found dark blue mugs hanging near the sink. I poured myself a cup of coffee from the grinding coffeepot on the counter. The kitchen had been replaced with smooth white cupboards and glass doors. It was blue and white and was charming with bird pictures, drying herbs and flowers and baskets brimming with fresh green apples.

I heard her shout from the living room. "Okay, now it's my turn!"

I resumed my place at her side, noting that her back had straightened and the mischief had returned to her eyes.

"I know, I know," she said, " I look like something that should be put out to scare the crows. And I do, you know. The crows are deathly frightened of me."

"I can't imagine why."

"Oh, Angelica! I wish we had more time to get to know one another. When we were young, we didn't laugh much, did we? It was mother. A tragic woman. Pitiful."

"What happened to Aunt Marion? I've wondered."

She leaned her cane against the chair and sat back sighing. "Honestly, there were many long lonely years after you died . . . terribly lonely for me. Lonely for mother and father. Father was too old to join up when he tried to in 1917. The war effort needed doctors. But he died a year later of influenza he contracted from a patient. Mother was crazy. Well, I should say she got crazier. She couldn't keep help in the house. She said no one would ever be a match for poor old Theda. Mother died two years after Papa, probably from the germs she'd feared all her life. There was never a complete diagnosis. I think she just scared herself to death. She never trusted anything. She did her darn level best to reason the 'devil' out of me. Didn't work, did it?"

I smiled. "And Theda?"

"Now there's a bright spot." She said, her lips crinkling into a smile, "What a woman. Reminded me of Gertrude Stein. Her looks, I mean. Formidable. That's what Uncle Robin always called her. Well, I found Theda working as an orderly in a hospital in San Francisco. That was after mother had died and I could afford to pursue my own ambitions. I bought her a nice house outside of the City and gave her a pension. After that, she spent her time caring for foster children. Children, she said, who weren't wanted by their mothers. Every time I mentioned your name to her, she bawled into those big gnarly hands of hers. She kept a picture of you in her room. All those foster children couldn't take your place, I guess. On her seventieth birthday, her foster children gave a grand old party for her. They invited me. It was written up in the newspaper. Picture of her and her husband."

"Husband?"

"A bicycle repairman that she married when she was fifty-four years old. That's right. Theda got herself a man! Alvin Rashkow. He taught drama school at night. A widower. Let's see now . . . who else was there?"

"Diana," I said.

"Oh yes, Diana. When Signe and Knute got older, after a quiet life at Green Gates, they sold the place to me because they said it was too much to take care of, and Diana was settled in L.A. and wouldn't be back. But you wouldn't know! Does the name Diana Phillips-Carey mean anything to you?"

"Yes . . . an actress. The stage and, oh yes, then she did silent movies. I've seen pictures of her. My God. Diana Sparring."

"That's Diana, all right. She became a stage star, then a film star when she and Davey moved to Los Angeles. He was a set builder, something in the movies, died fairly young. Her daughter is older than you, come to think of it! Diana died some years ago, a great queen. But in the early days, she would bring her kids back here, to Green Gates. And they'd play about the fountain and chatter with the squirrels just as you and Andreas had. Oh, how she missed you when you died. I don't think she was ever quite as pretty after that. Dark around the eyes. She married twice after Davey died but never buckled under with those two nasty divorces. Always level-headed. I still hear from her kids. I'll give you their address. The daughter—Julia—is very interested in reincarnation. She might understand."

"And you, Phoebe? Outside of your books?"

"I married my college philosophy professor. Actually, he was the department chair. We both liked Voltaire, both loved Emerson, Plato, Wittgenstein and Kierkegaard of course."

"Of course," I murmured, trying to recall whether it was Wittgenstein or Kierkegaard who said—

"I married young, never had kids and was in love with only one man, good old Denholm. We had a bundle of laughs. He put up with my eccentricity and we lived right here most of our married life. He knew that I talked to ghosts and watched for them in the garden. You were here a lot, Angelica. You and Andreas were here often in the garden. I watch ghosts like other folks watch birds or nude sunbathers. Do you remember coming to visit?"

I shook my head. "Nothing. Except that I came here two or three weeks ago, a visit at night. I had gone to sleep and traveled here ... actually I flew here, I dare to say, with a magnificent crow."

"Oh yes, I know. I was picking apples for the Senator's pie and he ups and goes to Laguna Beach. Midnight it was. I knew I saw you." She clutched her cane and tapped it on the floor. "Of course, Andreas didn't come back to haunt me until after World War I. You danced alone, whispering his name in and out of the apple trees until he died."

"What? What are you saying?" I stammered.

"Andreas. I knew that you would forgive him for marrying Isabel, even though I couldn't forgive him, at least not for a long time."

"Isabel? What are you saying?"

"What do you mean what am I saying?" she asked impatiently. "I'm saying, it took me a long time to forgive him for marrying Isabel. When he died a World War I hero, I finally gave in. My forgiveness of Isabel and Andreas was the real beginning of my enlightenment. I had to learn about unconditional love, about—"

"But you are wrong!" I interrupted her. "You have to be, about his death. He died with me, with Angelica. Out there, in the bay. He died the night I died." I was out of my chair, standing over her in shocked agitation.

"I thought you knew." The small pale face turned up to me, disarmed for the first time since our meeting.

"Knew what?"

"But then how could you have known? Poor dear. *You* died that night."

"With Andreas. I died with Andreas. That was our pact."

Her thin body crumpled forward but only for a moment. She looked at me, her watery blue eyes brilliant. "I thought you knew the truth and had forgiven him. Oh, dear."

"You mean, he did not die with me that night on the sea? He lived on? Tell me the truth Phoebe. I don't believe you. You've made a mistake . . . ."

"Oh, my dear Angelica." She held out her hand and took

mine. Her fingers were cold and bony but her voice was soft as she said, "You must speak to Andreas. I can tell you what happened. But only he can tell you why."

Chapter Thirty-Nine

*B*ehind the tall door at the left of the staircase landing I heard the faint tapping of a computer keyboard. Without knocking, I opened the door. He was seated at a desk facing a window. From outside scraggy brown tree limbs pressed against the borders of the glass framing an ocean view. In the distance a crow hunched on a thin cypress branch stretched parallel to the ocean. That is the sea in which Angelica drowned, I thought. Alone. He turned around and stood up.

The room relied chiefly on the desk lamp for light. Its winsome glow on that dark morning made everything else in the room look forsaken. As he moved toward me dark slashes of shadows sweeping from his brow to his strong chin made him look as if he were in the process of being carved into life.

"*Angelica*," he said in a tone that could have been inspired by Beethoven, "maybe that's what love at first sight is all about. Maybe it's the refusion of an old connection. Maybe it's an amalgamation of an immutable force. Twin souls . . . it sounds like something a teenager in love makes up." He circled me saying, "When we met on horseback near the purple hills of Candlesage you knew, didn't you, Paige? You knew that I knew that you were Angelica. But what you couldn't know is what it was like to turn my back on you, to ride away. You couldn't know what it was like to get through dinner that night with you just a few feet away. I wanted to be a Hollywood swashbuckler. Stand up, turn the table on end, put a blade through Neil's ribs, throw you over my shoulder and set sail for Tortola."

He stopped in front of me. "What could I blame the madness on? The shadowy influence of the Carmichael fortress? The vintage Cabernet? Lust? I even considered the pesticide residue in Mo's tender young hearts of celery. But then, her vegetables could only have been organically grown. I was ready to blame it on anything but the truth. That until now my life has been unclaimed, almost waiting to be lived. You were—are—the end of the search. The only dream in a long sleep." His hands moved toward my shoulders and dropped to my elbows. He drew me to him. His lips touched my throat, just barely, then touched my throat again and again, then moved to my mouth where his lips enclosed mine.

I pushed away, breaking his embrace. "You let me die alone. I didn't know. I was holding on . . . ." I gasped as if reliving the moment. "You let me die alone! Why?" My chest constricted. "Was everything a lie? You let me die in the sea and then you married her."

"Andreas married Isabel. I did not marry her. Andreas did." He turned away from me, sank into his chair and turned off his computer.

He asked, "Do you remember anything about that night?"

"Of course. It was dark, very dark and the rain was cold. I was delirious, freezing, so sick. The dress was soft and so long it covered my feet. I was wearing your grandfather's ring. We said good-bye to Phoebe and pushed off from shore. And I could smell wet honeysuckle. It was pinned in my hair. You spoke to me but the waves were huge, the sea rough. It was a terrible storm . . . I can't relive it. Not again."

"Isabel was on the boat."

"What?"

"Isabel."

Then I remembered. I had called Andreas to come to me as I hung onto the side of the boat. He had been grappling with someone. He tried to reach me.

He went on. "I don't know how she found out. Maybe someone told her I had bought a boat. Maybe she or someone she knew had been watching your house. The whole town of Pacific Grove knew that you were gravely ill. I spent every moment in your house. Undoubtedly Isabel was hoping for the worst. Anyway, she followed us down to the shore and slipped into the boat cabin ahead of us. The wind was fierce and we made little progress toward open sea. Instead of sailing until we could go no further, I knew the storm would be our end, would capsize the boat. I wasn't afraid. I was ready to die. For you. For us. I hoped it would be quick, for your sake. The waves got bigger. It was when the lanterns went out and the boat was heaving dangerously that Isabel emerged from the cabin screaming that we were all going to die. She shouted for us to turn back. She said, the baby will die. She was holding onto me, screaming as I fought both her and the storm. I let her go, shoved her away and turned toward you. But you were—you were gone. How like Angelica to slip quietly into the sea . . . . I put Isabel in the cabin and bolted it shut. I pulled down the sails—what was left of them—and waited to be pulled under. As fate would have it, we were washed into the rocks near Lover's Point just before dawn, in sight of your house, the view from your bedroom window. The candle still glowed from within the house as if you were up there waiting for my return.

"I unbolted the cabin and stumbled to the shore never looking back. Isabel could have been dead for all I cared. I went into Del Monte Forest alone and stayed for—I can't remember—two or three nights. Every night I wandered down to the shore and sat on the rocks. I called your name until my throat bled. I thought you'd come walking out of the foam in your mother's wedding dress. I thought it would be impossible for you to die without me. I was alive. Surely then, Angelica was alive. One night the surf was pounding on the shore. Like white chargers—you know how it is. I thought I saw you, your white arms spreading out above your head in a white veil of sea spray.

"A month later, under the duress of my parent's and Isabel's, I married her in a civil ceremony. I hadn't seen her since that night on the boat. And I never saw her again after the ceremony. I said good-bye to her on the steps of the courthouse in Monterey. She chased after me shouting. Her last words to me were, 'You killed Angelica.'

"I went back East, finished my law degree but never practiced. I was a living dead man so, I thought, why not become one? Whatever money mother and father sent me, I donated to charity. When the war broke out—thank God for the war—I was the first in the city to sign up. I learned that it's easy to be a hero if you don't care about living. For a year I saved other soldiers. Then one time I went into the trenches and did not come out. That was how Andreas died. A bloody corpse in a foreign land."

"And—Isabel's—your child?" I asked in a leaden voice.

"I never saw my son Daniel. My mother and father raised him, here at Green Gates, I guess. Isabel gave them custody when

I died. Phoebe said he escaped the Orwell clutches and turned out just fine. He loved me from my parents' photo albums and from my war medals. It kills me to think that I gave him up. I was grateful for Signe and Knute's intervention. They gave him what I could not. And another thing. Much to my shock, Phoebe tells me he is still alive and living in Mendocino. What I wouldn't give to see him."

He had moved to the bed and sat beside me. We watched the ocean behind the glass. A tree branch brushed the munnions as a crow strutted through the dark, damp leaves.

"About the war . . . I thought that by saving the lives of those kids, I would somehow be forgiven for all the other mistakes I made. I don't know if life works that way or not. Restitution, I mean. I just don't know."

"I don't know either," I said.

"I want you, Angelica—Paige."

"But you would have to sacrifice too much," I said. "Give up too much. Your political career."

He nodded as if tired. "That, yes. Then there's the situation with Beth, something my supporters—including Neil—are pushing me to solve. No one wants a divorced man in office. It could make a difference. We've been separated on and off for months, but you know that."

I stood up matter-of-factly and wondered what had numbed me to the fact that he was married. I hadn't the slightest idea. How could I have been so blind? Is this why Neil said I was making a fool of myself?

"No. I didn't know." I started toward the door grabbing the knob. "I need a moment to think about this."

He followed me across the room as I left it and opened the door across the hallway. "But everyone knows we're separated."

"I didn't even know you were married."

"Didn't know?" he said. "You're not serious . . . ."

"I don't watch television and I don't follow politics," I answered harshly. I opened the door to the other room as a means of escape. It was clearly the guestroom. Langston followed me and closed the door behind him.

He said, "I'm sorry. She—Beth—found someone else for awhile. I wasn't sure, am not sure. That's why I'm here without her. I asked her not to come." He paused waiting for a response. "She wants the marriage. I have my doubts."

I sat in the rocking chair by the window. In the garden below I could see the stripped rose bushes straining toward the grey sky, the guesthouse roof was so thick with pine needles that it looked thatched. The gazebo's intricate network of pristine white lattices looked fragile enough on that November morning to crumble. Like me.

He sat on the lace-covered sleigh bed and joined me in gazing out into the morning.

I said, "When I saw you that morning at dawn, in my bedroom, I thought, when I find him, and I knew I would, that would end one life and begin another. The moment I found you—that was to be the moment of my rebirth. That was when my life would begin. Stupid, isn't it? Nonsense to hope that after years of false hopes, even tragedy, that I could still dream."

"It was my dream too," he said, sighing, running his fingers though his thick, sandy-colored hair. "Do you think I'm not confused by all of this? Christ, I don't know what to do. I wanted you here with me, which is why I sent the letter. We've got to think this out. But that's where I'm having trouble. I need to think, but my feelings are driving me. I want you but I'm afraid I can't have you. But I ask myself, why not? Don't laugh, but all of my life I have had a dream of trying to make the world a better place. That's why I chose politics. Like people who go into medicine, or anything else, there are those who do it because they really care about other people and there are those who do it for the wrong reasons. I always wanted to help. I am close to being in a position to really make some positive changes. I have to. Where does my allegiance lie? With you? With a world I hope to influence? I honestly don't know. I'm being pulled in both directions. If I stop thinking rationally about the world and everything I think I should do, then *this* becomes more than a transitory meeting. It becomes about you and me and nothing else."

I reached out and touched his hand. When our fingertips met, he slipped his hand around mine and pulled it toward him. He kissed my hands and the inside of my arms to my elbow. We were then in each other's arms. We sank onto the bed. It was as if not a moment had passed since that day in the sunstruck meadow in 1906.

Chapter Forty

s he left the room, he kissed my cheek and said, "Many things are possible without you, Paige, but love isn't."

I nodded, "I know."

I heard him walk down the stairs and answer the front door. When the ship's bell had rung he had remembered an appointment with one of his aides, who now greeted him in the large entrance hall.

I got out of bed and draped the lace cover gracefully over me—like a wedding dress—and went to the window to gaze upon the brooding pines. I thought of what a tender lie we were, Langston and Paige, reaching for something galactic—which we knew was possible in the other, non-physical world, but was not attainable under the limitation of mortal longings, material conditions and human failings. Was this our lesson? Our karma, as Lucetta would say? Did we have to play out the hands we were dealt in this life in order to win in the next life? I was amused at the idea of life as a predestined crapshoot, a stacked game of chance. I could have discovered that from any shill in Nevada.

Langston had spoken of a housekeeper who had apparently moved my luggage to the upstairs landing. With it was Phoebe's book, *My Stars*. I retrieved them and slipped back into the room. The adjoining bathroom had a claw foot tub and jars of bubble bath. After bathing I read her fascinating book for awhile and decided to go for a walk, dressing for the cold day in jeans, turtleneck sweater and lined suede jacket. Langston and I had decided to meet again that evening. He wanted to walk on Moss Beach. He had enthusiastically planned the next two days. We would visit all the places that were meaningful to Andreas and Angelica, starting tonight at Moss Beach.

I reached for an antique silver brush on the dressing table with which to comb my hair—and nearly dropped it. I recognized it as Angelica's precious, well-loved gift from her Cousin Dixie Devlin. As I caressed the handle, a chill went up my spine and my heart skipped a beat. It was not easy separating lives.

"It's still there," Langston's aide, Paul Perry, said from the hall below. "The car with the guy in it just across the street. He's got dark hair. Big guy. Know him? I'd say he's a little too preoccupied with this house."

"Here," Langston said. "Take these. I haven't time to worry about strange men in strange cars. Will you phone Beth for me? Tell her that the kids should wait until Thanksgiving to come over. I'll be tied up until then. I'd call them myself tomorrow, but I know that they're waiting to hear. Tell her that if they come on Thanksgiving eve they'll only have to miss one day of class. That should appease her unyielding sense of responsibility."

They said goodbye to each other. The door closed. Langston returned to his computer and I waited until then to leave my room, cognizant for the first time of myself as an interloper. Until then I had not wanted to think of our relationship in terms of anything that was not eternal, omniscient. But Langston had a wife named Beth. I imagined her Hapsburg jaw, blunt haircut, Ralph Lauren long skirt and sweater with a patch of lace showing somewhere, saying something like "Lang dear, lower your voice!" Then there were the children ... what children? Two girls? Three boys? Two boys and three girls? Three years old? Eighteen years old? He would have his own parents, a pale-skinned woman who would cry when he announced his divorce, his withdrawal from the nomination race. "Good God, Langston, don't you see what you are doing? All this for—who is she anyway?" And his tall, attentive father who would, upon the news, simply fold into a leather chair, speechless.

Now I hurried downstairs to clear these thoughts with a brisk beach walk. But when I reached the entrance hall, there was Phoebe, leaning on her burl cane, looking directly into my eyes, reading what was behind them.

"I need to talk to you," she said, marshaling me through the living room and into the formal dining room beyond it.

She pushed me down into one of the carved leather chairs. "You must be strong, Angelica."

How much stronger would I have to be, I wondered. "I'm not sure if I can be."

The room was dark except for the white walls and the two glass doors that showed a cool blue from the patio beyond them. I looked at her curiously, waiting.

"I've got some horrible little powdered sugar donuts, if you want some," she said, sitting next to me, spreading her hands flat against the top of the table before she lifted them and placed them on top of mine. Her hands were crinkled, thin, and brown. Still though, something in the fingers, perhaps the shape of the nail, belonged to little freckled Phoebe. They made me smile.

"Angelica, now be still. For God's sake, your brain is skittering around the surface like one of those long-legged water bugs!"

"I'm afraid of what you're going to say to me. You told me that I would have to be strong. I can't imagine . . . ." I did not want any more cautionary advice. I'd had enough from Lucetta.

"You don't want a donut or tea or something? I've got Tang."

"No, thank you."

"Now listen, don't move your hands. Just be calm. This is good news . . . in a way . . . ."

"Yes?"

She whispered solemnly, every trace of frivolity gone from her voice, "You are going to have a baby."

I pulled my hands from beneath hers. We stared at each other. The milky blue in her eyes became crystalline. How did I know she was speaking the truth? Because my period had been due a week ago. I had thought it was my nerves.

"You know a tall man with silvery brown hair. A tall, nice man. I like him. Noel? Nate? Something like that."

I nodded, "Neil."

"That's right, Neil." She took my hands back into hers. "Yes. Yes. It is Neil's child. And this birth is very important to you. Oh, all births are important." Her eyes twinkled in the same way they had when she was young.

I asked, "How do you mean?"

Her face broke into a brilliant smile. "This child you carry is your son . . . the only son you have ever borne. This is your child coming to you again. This is true, Angelica. This I know."

"*Shea* . . . Do you mean *Shea*? Don't play with me, Phoebe . . . ." I choked.

Taking my hands back into hers she said, "Angel, Angel, when have I ever lied to you? This child, this spirit you call Shea, he has chosen you again. It's the truth."

For the first time I was aware of a clock ticking. "Shea . . . ." I breathed into the still dark room. But I wanted both . . . I wanted Andreas—Langston—and I wanted Shea. Was it possible?

"No!" she snapped. As if calming herself, she took a long, deep breath and shoved back a strand of red hair that had fallen from the disheveled, lopsided bun sliding from her head. "You can't have them both. The choice is obvious. I think you need one of those disgusting little donuts and a cup of tea. I'll get it." She rose from her chair. "It won't happen—between Andreas and you—not this time."

"But it can," I said, following her into the kitchen. "It could if I wanted it to."

"Of course! If you wanted it to but . . . ." She shrugged her thin shoulders ominously, as she turned on the stove and opened the cellophane which housed the pitiful, small donuts. She smiled. "They must be okay. There's nothing moving on them."

"What I mean is . . . . You know, I can win when I want to. But so much of the time in my life winning hasn't been very important to me. You know, having it all. I haven't required it. But this . . . I know I could have them both. I know I could." My voice had become frantic.

"You don't really have to eat these. I'd hate for you to remember me best for my revolting, tacky little donuts, which, by the way I gobble like mad. But no, Angelica, you will not have Andreas this time. To tell you the truth, I thought you would. When he came here, when I saw you at midnight in the apple orchard, I thought the two of you were very close . . . very close. I thought the reunion would last the rest of your lives this time. You must accept this situation gracefully."

I took the donut piece and the paper towel. "Then why was I able to recall everything about my other life? What was the point?"

She glared at me, "How am I supposed to know? I don't

write the scripts, I only analyze them. Even God needs a drama critic and this is a drama after all. Life is a drama. It is a gift. You must study the reason why you were chosen to know. Profit by knowledge. These are good, aren't they? If you don't want any more I think I'll eat the whole package."

"Be my guest," I said sipping at what tasted like licorice tea.

She licked a finger, leaned toward me and asked, "Who's Vincent?"

"How did you know about him?" I asked.

"Stop asking the obvious, Angelica. I keep calling you Angelica because I don't remember your other name. I asked about Vincent because I sense his presence. You're thinking about him?"

"The man I'm divorcing," I said. "He's my ex-husband."

"But who was he then, back then, in Pacific Grove?"

"What?"

"Come on, let's go back into the dining room. Are you still hungry? I've got some leftover noodles Romanoff, boxed of course."

I followed her back into the dining room. "Why did you ask me that? I haven't given any thought to it."

She asked, resuming her seat at the dining room table, "Who was Vincent?"

"I don't know."

"Don't you Angelica? This Vincent . . . he is still very angry, very angry." She was worried now. Deep wrinkles moved across her forehead. "He's a bad man. Eh! I don't like him at all. He's a bad one, but why? Because when we go from one life to another we take who we are with us. What's in our brains, what's in our hearts. We've got a lot of baggage and it's never left behind. Only our bodies are left behind. You came into this world sad and lonely. Look at your life. You are mostly afraid. And why? To die as you did for the reasons you did. Vincent came into this life angry. He chose an angry life complete with angry parents and angry experiences. He needs to learn forgiveness and acceptance. It's very simple. But he hasn't learned, has he? Who the hell knows when he will! It is you he needs to forgive. Just as you need to forgive him for what he's done to you in this life together."

"I've done everything I could," I stated flatly, throwing down another gulp of lukewarm licorice tea.

"Yes, yes. It's time for you to go on. But Vincent has learned very little. He is still angry with you, though his soul purposely chose the situation in your last life."

I asked, "What situation?"

"Think." She sipped her tea. "Delightful taste, isn't it?"

"I did something wrong, then?"

"*Nothing's really wrong because there's a lesson in everything.* He *chose* the lesson in your last life together. It's what he needed to experience. He's rather a dark soul, but still, you must forgive each other. You don't know what it is?" She paused for a moment. "I shouldn't have eaten those donuts. He was the child you were carrying *then*. The one you aborted in Chinatown. In your last life, Vincent was the child of Angelica and Andreas."

I was stunned and did not fully understand. "This child now . . . ."

"No, no, my dear. The child you are carrying now, Shea, has *nothing whatsoever* to do with the child Vincent was back then. That is, they are two separate spirits. But Vincent, you have stayed with him to console him for an interrupted last life. Haven't you always gone beyond the call to understand him, to nurture him, to win him over to the side of 'right,' as it were? He doesn't understand that it was as much his own choice as yours, to end his life in that particular incarnation. You've done your work. He hasn't responded. You can't do it for him, make him a good old soul. He has been evil—or as we like to say—ignorant—in many lives. It's good you've left him. But he's dangerous. I'm afraid. I'm advising you to telephone him, to talk to him, try to settle it between you. I don't like what I see . . . . Maybe he can't be reasoned with."

"What do you see?"

She shook a finger at me, a finger still dusted with sugar. "No, events could change. Will you telephone him? Will you tell him you forgive him and will you ask for his forgiveness? It's just about all you can do. Except don't feel guilty about *anything*."

I nodded. "I will phone."

"Now wait a minute. Your heart has to be in it or it doesn't count!"

"I'll try. In time."

"No. Now. You've got to do it very soon. Promise me, Angelica. It may or may not help but it's for your own good."

"I promise. I will."

She sighed, relieved, but clutched her side. "Damn! I can't believe anything could taste so good going down and hurt so much when it gets there! Come on, let's go back into the kitchen. I have something more to tell you."

She rattled on about inconsequential things. Copper pans in need of polishing. The brick work in disrepair. There was a small leak in the roof.

"I wanted to tell you about Isabel. She remarried after Andreas died in the war, giving custody of their son Daniel to Knute and Signe when she got hitched again. She married a little man with absolutely no hair on his head. And believe me he didn't look like Yul Brynner. His name was Helmut. And he should have been wearing one. His teeth were so badly stained from tobacco that Isabel would never let him smile. He finally left her. The first time I saw him smile was when she died years later. She ran out of money during the depression and was prosecuted for shoplifting. She died as poor as a church mouse in some rest home somewhere, not a friend in the world. She forgot about Helmut and toward the end raved about how her husband Andreas had left her for a woman named Angelica. In a way it was true."

"So, then, has she made restitution for what she did?"

"I doubt it. What she did will take several lifetimes to work out. So selfish. So devious. She's back here working on it. Right now."

"Who is she?"

"Oh, no. That would be telling. I've got to lie down now. It hurts. So what? It's always hurting, something is. But I must tell you this, Angelica. After this child, you will have another—a daughter. Diana is returning as your child."

Stunned by this, I helped her out of her chair. "Can we talk later about this? Tomorrow?"

"You won't be here tomorrow. Where's my cane? Oh, there. This is, I believe, the last time I will see you."

She leaned into me, placing a cold white hand against my cheek. "You are still so beautiful. God, how I've missed you." She put her arm around me. It was light enough to be hollow. Little Phoebe whose freckles had fallen into a sea of facial lines smiled with tears in her eyes. "The next time around, Angelica, I hope I'm as pretty as you are and you're as clever as I am. I'm ready for a change. And God knows you could use some gumption."

"But what about tonight? Can I see you tonight? This news . . . ." I asked, tears coming to my eyes.

Her head fell on my shoulder. Tenderly she said to me, "No, not until next time. You were so kind to me, Angel."

We cried together. I said, "And you to me, Phoebe."

Chapter Forty-One

*D*usk.

I left a note on Langston's desk asking him to meet me at Moss beach when he arrived.

I walked down the curving street past the dunes to the beach, and now it lay before me, a broad crescent of rich sand upon which rushing waves broke low and softly. The wave foam was pink, a lighter shade than the color of the sky. The color of Langston's lips, maybe, or the color in the palm of his hands. His hands and his mouth that moved over me like the surf on the shore.

There were a million metaphors between myself and the horizon. Perhaps the poetry left by dreamers over time returned to others in the churning mist. Maybe that is what makes the sea inspirational, why those who are lost go there to find what they need. Maybe that's why I was there early. To find myself again. I was going to have a baby. I would either have to give up Andreas or default on my life. In a way, the same was true for him.

So there was tonight. A perfect closing under the moon, an ebbing tide (the perfect metaphor), a light wind and the brilliant yellow flash of the lighthouse on the bluffs to the north.

Don't be bitter, Paige, I said to myself. Everything has its time.

There were two people on the beach. Their coats were so thick they looked inflated. Each of them had a dog. The dogs chased each other through piles of seaweed. The owners stood apart, watching their animals. Then the dogs moved up over the soft dunes to the road. The owners turned and followed. Everyone was going home.

The bottom of the sun touched the line of the sea and the sea engulfed it. The sun, now half gone, had mutated. More brilliant. Redder. The color of sex and war.

The moon, glowing and white, looking like a milk mustache . . . there's a moon over your lip, Shea—here, let me help you wipe it off . . . made a splash in the sky. Everything on the beach looked better for it: the pink-tinted foam bursting from the waves as they crashed to shore, and the wet, shimmering, moonlit sand as the waves retreated back into the sea.

Was I too old to have a baby at my age? The moon was kind and glancing down at my hands I thought they looked young. When I looked up, he was walking toward me on the beach, into the coming night.

"Am I late?" he called happily.

"No," I managed.

"What a night. No fog for the moment."

"For a moment," I said. I knew his thoughts. He thought this was like a night long ago. There were so many to remember.

His heavy grey jacket was unzipped. I studied the plaid on his shirt. It was better than biting my lip or saying something stupid. Red and blue lines crossing green strands over his chest.

And then I thought, oddly, of Neil's statuary garden and I gasped. He did not hear me.

"You are beautiful," he said. He took my hand and I leaned close to him so that we could kiss. His face was rough. He had not shaved. I rubbed my cheek hard against his beard because I wanted my skin to burn. I wanted to feel where he had been tomorrow when I was gone.

He breathed into my ear, lips lingering, "*Angelica*," just as I knew he would . . . the last syllable of my name merged into the cool ocean mist just as the sun dropped from sight.

"I have something to tell you," he announced quietly. "I've thought about it and I've decided I agree with you. We should be together. A divorce won't be easy, but I just don't see how we can go our separate ways. I mean, if going on alone was the right thing to do, then what would be the purpose of this mystifying reunion? I think you said this yourself, in the garden at Candlesage."

The familiar and graceful way we hugged was amazing to me, as though we had never been separated by another time and life. As our hands intertwined we began to walk toward the shoreline whose glassy surface had been quieted by the setting sun. The last gull of the day swam across the sky.

"My kids are coming for Thanksgiving. So I'll have to wait until after the holidays to tell Beth that I've finally opted for divorce. Funny, there was a time when she wanted one herself. She's assumed politics would keep me put. She'll be shocked. You know, Paige, once I made the decision to step out of the race, to divorce, suddenly neither was important anymore. The notion that I have a mission to somehow help save humanity is really self-serving."

"Maybe not," I said. "There *are* higher purposes."

"After I decided to end my political career I realized that.

The world doesn't want out of the mess it's in. We have all the answers to monetary, environmental and international crisis but most of us are either too afraid or too greedy to do anything about them, to give anything up. Why try to save someone who would rather die? World starvation could end next year. Why doesn't it? Not enough people want it. The environment is languishing. Educated people know it. Why don't they do something about it? Really do something?"

"I've asked myself that a thousand times."

His put his arm around my shoulders and looked at me. "And have you found the answers? It's so irrational it defies understanding. So why should I beat my head against a brick wall? Maybe I've lost my savior fantasy. If I have, life will be easier. Look, look out there, there's an otter."

"Yes, he's got a shell on his stomach. I think he's cracking it open to eat, and he's floating on his back near a kelp bed. I can't see more. It's nearly dark." I thought, that little spark of life on the cold November sea is doing what he must to stay alive. "There's always a struggle," I added, loving Langston's enthusiasm as he spoke his heart.

"When I look out at the otter I can't help but wonder how many oil slicks, viruses, plastic containers and fishing nets it will have to evade in order to live. I'm hopeless. It's crazy, isn't it? Why have I given up? Some of it is futility, yes. And some of it is this—this new understanding. People pass from the earth but they don't die. And if humanity doesn't survive, the earth will, in time, regenerate itself, I suppose."

"Or not," I added sadly.

He laughed softly and held me tighter. "I sound like I'm campaigning and I'm making you sad. I've said enough. Now stop walking, Paige, for just a moment. I want to look into your eyes before it gets dark. Because I said to myself on the way over

342.

here, Langston, you only think her eyes are that green. It's because you love her. They are probably moss green, or toad green but not emerald green. But they are. They are greener than anything I've ever seen and I wonder how on earth any man has ever stayed out of them. God knows I haven't."

As the mist rolled in we walked north on the beach until we reached the first rocky cove. While we walked, we talked, grateful not just that we had found each other but that we knew—as few did—the great mystery: there is no death.

We went on about our past life together, we exchanged stories like old people testing their memories. We found a niche in the rocks in a nearby cove, and sheltered from the light fog, argued about who broke Signe's big yellow cookie platter. You did, I told Andreas, remembering the precise afternoon in the gazebo. It was hot and a monarch butterfly lit on the edge. Oh, no, no, he said. That was a different plate. He said the yellow platter broke the day of my tenth birthday party when a fat boy with mud brown hair tried to play catch with it after all the cookies were gone. No, no. Yes, yes.

We remembered Chinatown, the shipwrecks along the coast, just out there. We remembered the Chautauqua, the stern constable, the fence that kept out the undesirables. We remembered Diana, our friends and families. And there were people we helped each other remember—the tall, scandalous Mrs. Edeene who lived on the knoll south of downtown and refused to bake for her family who were forced to beg for cookies.

We wondered where the dead people were now in this life. We wondered if we knew them. I said nothing of Vincent.

And then Andreas said, "I'll bet you don't remember the first time we met."

"No," I shook my head. "I was too young."

He touched my hand softly. "You were two years old, just

past two, I think. Robin and Marion brought you over to Green Gates to meet us. You wore a pink and white striped dress with a white apron. I walked over to you to say hello. You bent over and picked a tall snapdragon from Signe's garden and hit me across the face with it."

"I didn't!"

"Then I kissed you. Our first. Much to the surprise of my parents." His mouth found my cheek. "Like this, this is how I kissed you." His lips were soft, his voice lost in the surf sounds. He whispered, "Not like this." His mouth covered mine. Then he said, "Nor like this." His mouth opened, his arms opened. We sank back into the cold sand.

As we strolled back to Green Gates he said funny things and I tried to laugh. I thought only of Shea. Had our lovemaking on the beach injured him? I wasn't bleeding, was I?

He said, "When I die, I'll remember tonight. I will make it my last thought."

"I thought we had died, for a moment. For a moment, I wished we had," I said.

"Why do you say that?" he asked. "There's nothing ahead of us that we can't deal with."

"I wish it were true," I said putting my arm through his. "There's too much working against us." I did not let my steps falter as we approached the stone arch at Green Gates. I told myself not to smile, not to cry.

"What?" He stopped and faced me. "What is it Paige?"

"I'm pregnant. With Neil's child."

Chapter Forty-Two

What was the last thing I said to him that morning under the stone arch at Green Gates? "I am a fool to think that my life is anything but a soliloquy. I lived it without the people I needed the most and without a stage, or an audience." And at that moment of parting, not even celestial applause, an acknowledgement that I was finally doing the right thing, would have made my life seem worthwhile.

Andreas did not say goodbye. But he had asked me to reconsider. I could not. Then he told me that our walk towards eternity was the only thing he was sure of.

I was glad that it was raining as I drove away. The water on my car windows prevented my seeing him standing in front of Green Gates, and looking as he did that first morning he appeared in my bedroom at dawn, as though his very life depended upon mine, and then vanishing from my sight like something I had merely dreamed into being.

I had not tried to see Phoebe the morning I left. Her comment the day before, about our never seeing each other again, had also been a directive. Our time with each other in this life had passed, our purposes met.

I steadied myself as I drove up the winding road . . . home. Home to Candlesage.

Neil would be expecting me, was probably marking time like a husband who leaves the light on, who listens for his wife's familiar footfalls in the hall. He had revealed his own premonitions more than once, that ultimately we would be together. Somewhere within all of us there's the knowledge of our destiny. Perhaps he was more intuitive than I'd ever imagined.

But I couldn't discount the fact that I too was a victor in this story of our lives. Andreas—Langston—would not tamper with his destiny. I would marry a man, the father of my child, who would give Shea everything that Vincent could not. I was being given a second chance in the same lifetime. When Shea was sick, those fervent prayers to any God, to life, to the universe, to the powers that be to let him live, had, in a manner, been answered. I was grateful that I knew through experience what others too often don't: there are pauses in our relationships but there are absolutely no ends.

Neil hugged me in the foyer. I was surprised to find it comforting. I walked zombie-like to my room with Hitchins bouncing the bags behind me, and Aunt Belle "yoo-hooing" from behind her cigarette smoke and the spinning whirligigs in the garden.

After a bath, I lay in the room and relived every detail of the past two days. I committed it to memory . . . *don't forget the look in his eyes when we said goodbye.*

Neil allowed me a day to myself, before we finally spoke at breakfast the following day. He was attentive but not obtrusive. He showed his affection in simple ways: a rose from the garden, a smile from across the room. From somewhere within me I found a peace that I had never before known.

Breakfast had been set on the terrace overlooking the statuary garden. We dined alone under a warm sun.

When we finally spoke of important issues, he said, "Vincent didn't show up at a settlement conference yesterday. His lawyer hasn't heard from him in days. A court date has been set for next month." He smiled and sipped his coffee. We were like married people. There was comfort in it.

I said, "I'll be glad to get it over with."

"We'll schedule an appointment with your lawyer for next week if you're up to it." Kindly, he touched my hand as I reached for a fork. I smiled at him and meant it for the first time in weeks. "I need to talk to you, Neil."

After breakfast we walked in the garden along a flagstone path bordered by towering red oaks. I was glad not to see the statuary.

"I'm happy you're back," he said plucking at an oak branch, shrugging his shoulders as if he were helpless to feel anything else.

"I'm back for several important reasons, Neil. But there's an especially important one. I'm pregnant."

Simultaneously we stopped.

"We can get married as soon as you like. It's very early in the pregnancy. I'm barely two weeks late but I know. If you are in no hurry, that's fine. Fortunately, a child doesn't need a last name to be born."

We began walking again at precisely the same instant, our footfalls in perfect unison. How odd, I thought.

He smiled briefly, "You know how I feel about this. But what about you?"

"Well, I've been given another chance, haven't I?" I was glad his voice was strong, assured.

I continued, "My love for you has never made me want to promise things. But I can promise you now that I care very much about you, that I feel good with you. I'm no longer angry. I understand about your concern. That's what I'm happiest about. I had recently thought of you as—as an enemy, Neil. I no longer feel that way. I think of us as dear friends, like we always were. And I was thinking this morning that we should talk about Simone, when you feel like it. I think it would be good for both of us. I do love you, Neil."

Neil was a modern man. He never asked about Langston Holt, my trip to Pacific Grove or my 'delusions' about anyone named Andreas. When I invited Lucetta over one afternoon that week, he actually looked happy. He told me that Mo had taken the news well. "She wants to move to Newport," he said. "She's wanted to for some time."

When he told me, I hoped Mo's and my restricted relationship would normalize. Neil's mother would believe anything he told her. I could hear him blaming the shock of my divorce for my unprovoked hearthside attack and mental collapse. Perhaps he would someday believe it himself.

I was not surprised when, three days later, Langston's aide Paul Perry phoned with a message. "Senator Holt has asked me to phone you and tell you that 'little Phoebe has gone.' She has dedicated her book to you, Mrs. Brighton. Senator Holt would also like you to know that you have inherited Green Gates."

In the days before Thanksgiving Aunt Belle read wedding books and dog-eared pages of baby name journals. She began gathering yarns suggested in a book called *Knits for Gnomes*. Neil spoke daily to my lawyer or his, while Mo made estimations of the best place for a nursery. I tried not to think of Langston. It would not have worked. It was not our time. We would have hurt too many people.

The logic, however repetitious—never quite overcame my sense of loss.

When I thought of Phoebe, and I often did, the air around me warmed. She had been absolute about my not having a life with Langston.

On Thanksgiving I knew why.

Mo had friends in for drinks and dinner in the afternoon. Leave it to Mo to have live turkeys roaming the gardens. Everywhere at Candlesage sprays of orange and golden flowers exploded from tabletops, walls and doorside baskets. Aunt Belle had bustled in with gifts of knitted orange turkey wattles too small or big for anyone to wear, thankfully.

Guests drank their golden wine. Smells of roast turkey and dressing bonded the guests: "The turkey smells wonderful." "I'm famished." "Can you believe it's the holidays already?" "Save the wishbone for me."

But I was uneasy that afternoon. I blamed my shortness of breath and nerves on my pregnancy. Just as I was about to excuse myself for a stroll in the garden, Hitchins rushed into the room. His pace was uncharacteristic, his face ashen. Urgently, he tapped Neil on the shoulder, whispering in his ear. Then, as if it were contagious, the color in Neil's face drained. He put his wine glass down and rushed from the room, saying to me, "Stay here."

Someone from the kitchen wailed mournfully. It was Aunt Belle. Mo ran toward the kitchen ready to chastise someone. Several guests followed.

And then I knew. My tea glass slipped from my hand and splintered on the floor. I pushed past the guests and shoved open the kitchen door. Everyone in the room was staring at a wall-mounted television set. A newswoman was saying, ". . . when asked if she knew the identity of the man who allegedly carried the bomb onto Senator Holt's flight, the Senator's wife had no comment. A spokesman for the family said that Senator Langston Holt was flying home to have Thanksgiving dinner with his family. The man who allegedly carried the bomb onto the airplane has been identified as Vincent Brighton, a Newport Beach accountant, who also died. It is believed that all passengers on board perished in the flight. An investigation is under way."

The stranger in the car outside of Green Gates that morning . . . Vincent had followed me to Green Gates . . . perhaps had even been on the beach with us that night . . . had plotted Langston's death in a jealous rage.

Andreas. Everything has its time.

Epilogue

Candlesage
Three-and-a-half years later

E veryone applauded as Carson blew out the three candles on his birthday cake. The little candles' blue trails drifted intact before vanishing against the hot August sky.

"Smile for daddy," Neil coaxed, creeping with a camcorder around the enormous chocolate cake. But our son Carson plucked the candles from the cake and sucked the frosting off the bottoms. His silver paper hat tilted on his forehead.

"Here, give me that thing," Lucetta said to Neil, who relented. "Now listen, my little man," she said to Carson, "I want you to smile and smile big. You look like a unicorn. How many teeth do you have? What? I only see two. Whoops, three, six, eight. That's it."

"Belle, Belle dear!" Hitchins grunted as he nudged Aunt Belle from her matching wicker rocker. "Wake-up. You're snoring again." Everyone present noted silently that his catnap hadn't exactly been noise-free.

"So what," she answered petulantly, still a little drugged from the champagne. "It isn't my party. I can snore if I want to. Carsie doesn't care, do you, Carsie?"

Carson's third birthday was an event to which Hitchins had been invited as Belle's guest. As her fiancé, new rules had been established. He would not retire from service, but now had the status of family member. Aunt Belle had written Miss Manners and was impatiently awaiting a reply. It had also placed Mo in a quandary, for recently he was seated at the table when she came for dinner with her new restaurateur friend Mark and she asked Hitchins to go to the cellar for more wine. He was half out of his chair before Neil cleared his throat and Belle strong-armed him back to her side.

Hitchins had welcomed the addition of Vincent's dog Sumo to the growing family at Candlesage and had personally adopted him. In the three years since Vincent's death, Chester and Sumo had made their peace. Belle said the newfound friendship was thanks entirely to the matching wardrobe she had knit for them, although Hitchins always claimed Sumo's sweaters made him look "rather gender uncertain."

Across the lawns, Marla and Eugene were arriving late. Between them they dragged a five-foot stuffed elephant in a top hat. Marla shouted, "It's from my Save the Elephants campaign! Now don't worry anyone. You'll find a place for him. Happy birthday, Carson sweetie. Oh, you cute, adorable little angel. Look at him, Eugene. Look." After kissing Carson and pinching his chocolate-covered cheeks she turned to me. "You know, Paige, not even my shrink knows why Eugene and I didn't have kids."

"Oh, he knows," Eugene quipped. "But we won't get any answers from that guy until he bankrupts us."

Carson dropped his cake fork and after allowing me to wipe his hands and face, fled gleefully to the five-foot elephant.

Marla hugged me and patted my stomach. "You don't even look pregnant, for God's sake. Are you sure you're three months along? Whenever I see you I feel like I should have a measuring tape and a scale in my old Versace." She turned to Neil and said, "Are you sure about the due date?"

He replied lightly, "Lucetta predicted the exact day and time of Carson's birth and even put it in a sealed envelope. This time she was more forthcoming." He looked toward Lucetta who was filming the party. There was a wry note to his voice. "She hasn't been wrong about anything yet."

In the first year of our marriage, Neil had been cautious and at times obstinate about Lucetta's 'recalcitrant' philosophy. What changed his mind was a lucid dream of Lucetta's in which Simone Marchand appeared.

Lucetta was able to recount every detail of Simone's last session with Neil, even the silver anklet that had fallen off midway through the visit—every detail necessary to convince Neil. It would seem that Lucetta had indeed met with Simone and needed to deliver a message to him. The dead woman's message to Neil had been simple: she was entirely responsible for her death and Neil needed to absolve himself. That it was she who needed to be forgiven by him for her lies and for the part she played in his car accident. She had then thanked him for all he had done for her.

Nothing in Neil's textbooks could explain the phenomenon. And so he became a believer, much to his intellectual chagrin.

Marla turned to me, "Paige, be careful about all this pregnancy business. You are past *forty*." She stuck her finger in the cake, drew it out and licked the frosting from it. "Who did this cake? It's divine. Give me the name of the shop. I've got a Labor Day party–oops, pun!—and I swear I'll never use that other shop again. You know the one. The man who never plucks his nose hairs. Now Paige, have you picked out a name for the baby?"

"Diana," I answered, accepting a glass of lemonade from Neil who leaned over to kiss my cheek.

"After anyone I know?" she smiled.

"A woman I used to know," I said. Lucetta put down the camera and winked at me.

Marla sighed, "Well, thank God you're not using that other name. What was it? You know, Eugene, the one that reminded you of caterpillars."

"Phoebe?" I asked. "Oh, but she was more like a butterfly . . . ."

"That was it. Phoebe." Marla applied herself to cutting a wide piece of cake.

The afternoon sun slipped behind a cloud and a slight wind fluttered the edges of the umbrellas. The lawns, Neil said, were as green as my eyes, and to me the sky was ghostly blue.

In the towering red oak a crow appeared. Carson pointed at it and smiled at me. "Mommy, look, the birthday bird."

Neil explained to Eugene, "Every year on Carson's birthday that bird shows up." He smiled and whispered, "Probably belongs to Lucetta."

I looked at my watch. It was four-thirty. Only seven and a half-hours to go. Midnight, my time. Andreas did not have a time. There was no time on the other side.

It would be our fourth reunion. It was the night Carson was born that Andreas came to me and we were reunited out there—somewhere between here and the Truth, that is how I explained it to Lucetta. Somewhere between here and the Truth in an indescribable swirl of light and shadow we met. It was the first time I had seen him since Langston died in the plane crash eight months earlier. He came the night I myself had almost died, the night Shea returned to me through Carson's difficult birth. The doctors thought they saved me—but it was Andreas. He had come to me while I lay unconscious. He had told me that it was not time for me to leave, that he would wait for me. I made him promise that if I lived, he would come to me again. Our communication was wordless. He agreed to return to Green Gates each year the night of Carson's birthday. He had last year and the year after, and he would this anniversary night.

Seven hours. Five hours. Two hours. One.

After Neil and Carson had fallen asleep, I closed my eyes and drifted quietly away. Once again I found myself over the misty garden at Green Gates. And then I was swept up in a sea of stars, a radiant ocean of magic and light that passed through me and swirled among trees and flowers, whirling amidst animals of the night who were great, reverent glowing beasts. Everything in the garden became illumined from within, was made of pure light. Iridescent. Transcendent. Weightless.

But there was something blissfully deeper, something fearless, guiltless and not of the world because it was without conflict or competition or blame. I understood this, for every imprint of the world I held within me vanished as I descended slowly into the garden behind the green gates. And this is the way it had been and always would be with Angelica and Andreas . . . as we dance in this garden, in the timeless moments between our lives. And it is what all people yearn for because somewhere within them they remember their own dances in the shadows and the light.

And then, as if born of this illumination, Andreas stood before me, his arms open. I approached him, moving slowly.

As we joined each other for the dance he whispered softly, "Everything on the other side has its time. But here in this garden, Angelica, we have eternity."

A special thanks to: Blake for resurrecting the manuscript; my mother The Reverend Martha Ann Stewart who lived and taught the life unconventional; Ray Bradbury of Mars and Los Angeles for conjuring up my first agent; and Nada Doyle because a promise is a promise.